MEN WHO ARE HOT TO TROT

Whet your appetite, arouse your senses, and savor the unusual with this first-rate collection of sexually charged gay fiction, including:

Critic's Choice . . . A young porn writer picks up an older man, then finds he's a literary critic. Soon they learn the sword is mightier than the pen . . .

For the Asking . . . Everyone gossips about Travis and his boyfriend, but this is the true story. It starts at The Pub on a crowded night. But no sooner do the two men meet than everyone wants a piece of the action.

Hands On . . . In-depth, hands-on games are for the crowd at the Pit—and Tommy is going to prove that even a boy toy can hold his own.

BMW Boys . . . The guy drives a BMW, so why not let him in to use the phone? So what if he and his pals seem very, *very* straight? And who says three's a crowd?

edited by Austin Foxxe

MANHANDLED

Gripping Tales of Gay Erotic Fiction

An AOL Time Warner Company

This book is a work of fiction. Names, characters, places, and incidents are the product of the authors' imagination or are used fictitiously. Any resemblance to actual events, locales, or persons, living or dead, is coincidental.

Warner Books, Inc., 1271 Avenue of the Americas, New York, NY 10020
Visit our Web site at www.twbookmark.com

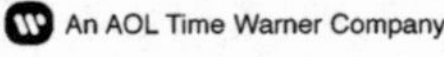

Printed in the United States of America

First Printing: June 2003
10 9 8 7 6 5 4 3 2 1

ISBN: 0-446-679992
LCCN: 2003101814

Book design and text composition by Ralph Fowler
Cover design by Janet Perr
Cover photo by David Vance

Contents

Acknowledgments

I'd like to thank all the authors who contributed to this collection—those who have worked with me for years and those with whom I've just become acquainted. To the "old guys," thanks for hanging in there with me; from here on out, things can only get better. And to the "new guys" who worked with me for the first time, hopefully this won't be the last. And to John and Megan, who I'm sure lost some hair and probably gained a few gray ones working with me, thanks for all your help and support. I promise I'll be *so-o-o* much better next time! Again, thank you all. Without you this book would not have been possible.

My very best,
Austin

MANHANDLED

BMW Boys

Douglas

I live in New York City, on a quiet block near Central Park. I run there a lot, and the one thing that keeps me going is all the hot guys who run past me. Sometimes I'm so worked up by the end of a run that I go right home and jerk off.

One Sunday afternoon, I'd just finished up a long, sweaty run. I was headed home when I noticed a couple of guys looking under the hood of a black BMW parked in front of my building. They were both kind of cute, and there were two others sitting in the car. I slowed down a bit so I could check them out, and my heart almost stopped when one of them looked up at me and spoke.

"Hey—you live around here?" He had a bit of a blue-collar, New Jersey accent and dark, Italian looks. I realized right away that he was straight. Oh well.

"Uh, yeah . . . ," I answered.

"D'you think we could use your phone? We're havin' some car trouble."

I hesitated for a moment. Should I let a complete stranger into my home? But he seemed honest enough—and owned a BMW, for God's sake—so what was he going to steal?

"Sure. I live right here." I turned toward my building. As I was unlocking the door, I realized—to my surprise—that all four guys were coming in. They were all dressed pretty hetero-casual: baggy jeans, T-shirts, flannels, baseball caps. Very Abercrombie & Fitch. They weren't model-handsome, but they were all cute in that average-Joe kind of way.

The first guy introduced himself as Tony, as typical as that seemed. He had a nice-sized build, dark hair, and sparkling green eyes. The other three looked around my apartment while Tony used the phone.

"Shit!" he said after he hung up. "They won't be here for a fuckin' hour!" he said. At just that moment, he noticed the porno tapes I kept behind a chair that happened to be near where the phone was sitting. He picked one up and looked at the pictures on the box. "Oh, shit! You gay, man?"

I was a little worried about the tone of his voice, but answered weakly, "Yeah . . ."

He hesitated a moment, then looked around and said, "Well . . . I think we might have a very interesting way to spend the next hour. . . ." He grabbed the bulge in his pants. "Think you could do something about this?"

I was completely shocked. His friends seemed a little shocked too—but he was obviously the leader of this crowd.

He asked me where the bedroom was and went in. I followed. He was standing near the bed, his face so tough, yet so innocent. I walked toward him slowly, and tried to kiss him. "Hey!" he said, pulling away. "I ain't gay! I just like getting my dick sucked. You *do* like to suck dick, don't you?"

I got his meaning, and didn't care if he was straight. I put my hand on his chest and worked his soft nipples through his T-shirt. I slipped off the unbuttoned flannel and then his T-shirt. He had a beautiful, soft-yet-sculpted Italian football-player build, with a smooth, olive complexion. His pecs were round and soft. Dark bushes of hair peeked out from under each of his arms, one of which had a tattoo. He was hot.

I lowered my mouth to his nipples and worked them with my tongue, biting a bit into his soft flesh. In response they stood at attention, and his body was so warm to the touch. I kissed my way down to his jeans, slowly unzipped them and pulled them down along with his red Jockey shorts. His cock was magnificent—still soft but huge and thick, bursting out of an extra-thick mound of dark hair. I gripped it with one hand and put my other on his soft ass. I held his dick up and worked his tight balls with my tongue. They had a wonderfully musky scent.

"C'mon!" Tony urged with a moan. "Suck my dick, man! Take it!" He put his hands on my head, and I obeyed. His dick was beginning to get firm. I sucked the head, moving it around in my mouth. I worked more and more of the shaft into my mouth as it got ever firmer, ever bigger. Seven inches, eight inches. By the time it was hard he must have had nine or ten of the most solid, fat inches of man meat I'd ever seen.

I began to work it harder and faster with my mouth and hand. "Oh, fuck yeah!" he moaned, rubbing one of his nipples. I wanted it all. I reached my hands around and grabbed his ass, and in one swift motion I darted my mouth over Tony's entire stiff, hot cock. I could feel his enormous, engorged head filling my throat. His body twitched with surprise and delight as he firmly grabbed my head and held it against his groin. "Oh, yeah! Oh fuck, man, yeah! Take it! Take it all!"

I deep-throated him several times. He met me each time with his soft body, his hot, saliva-covered balls hitting my chin and my nose buried in his full, moist, musky mound of hair. "Aw, fuck, yeah! You really love that cock, don't you, man? You guys really know how to suck a fucking cock!"

I continued to slurp Tony's throbbing piece of Italian meat. I couldn't get enough. One of his friends had come into the room and was watching the action, his own bulge growing noticeably bigger. The other two, a bit more shy, were watching from the door. I had visions of group action, but knew that that fantasy was just too good to ever come true. My jaw was beginning to get stiff and my throat was sore, but I didn't care. I wanted more of this man.

The friend walked over to us, and stood behind me stroking the bulge in his jeans. He took one of my hands in his, and guided it over the bulge, grinding himself against my palm so I could feel his stiff member through his jeans. It didn't feel big, but it sure felt hard.

He let it out. It was small, but thick and veiny. I stroked him with my hand while I continued to suck Tony. Then Tony pushed my head off his dick and gave me my orders: "Hey—give Vince some of that!" I couldn't believe his name was Vince, because he looked like a Vince I knew in college—dark, awkward, and small with no build, but somehow attractive.

I twisted around and took Vince's cock in my mouth. After Tony, Vince's small member was refreshingly easy to take. And it had a cleaner, sweeter taste. I took turns sucking the two of them. I'd hoped they'd turn some attention toward each other too, but they kept their distance from one another.

Tony grabbed my head and rammed all ten of his inches down my throat once again. "Aw, fuck—I'm gonna cum!" He held my face in his hairy mound. "I'm gonna cum! You wanna swallow my fucking cum?!" His cock throbbed in my mouth and I moaned as I felt his hot man juices pulsating down my throat. His engorged head shot his cum so far down my throat I couldn't even taste it, but I felt its warmth flowing down my pipes. Vince was jerking himself into a frenzy.

"Aw, fuck, me too!" Vince pulled my head toward him to give me a taste of his cum, but it was too late. He shot a huge load onto my face, neck, and chest. He spread it on my chin with his still-pulsating member. "Oh, yeah . . . oh, YEAH! You like the taste of that, don't you, faggot?" Normally that name would have offended me, but for some reason I now found it strangely exciting.

The two other friends had entered the room. One was adjusting his bulge. The other, the only blond one, had taken off his shirt and pulled his baggy jeans to his ankles. He had a skinny but unbelievably rock-hard and ripped build, and exceptionally large nipples. There was a tattoo on one of his arms and he wore a thick, silver chain. He was working one of his nipples with one hand and his cock with the other. "Hey, Mikey," Tony said to him, "why don't you let the cocksucker do that for you!"

I was exhausted—but the idea of three cocks in one day was too much to refuse. I'd never even been with two guys before, much less three. He stepped out of his jeans and approached me, his lean, sinewy body flexing with each step, his long slender cock bouncing and beckoning for attention. He got onto the bed and sat on his knees. I got on the bed on all fours, my own cock throbbing in my shorts, and began to work Mikey's slim cock. It was warm and delicious. I licked his balls to give my jaw a rest, and it turned out that was exactly what he liked. "Suck it, man! Fuck, yeah . . . eat my fucking nuts!" He had the heaviest Jersey accent, and for some reason that made me even hornier. He threw his head back in ecstasy as I ran my tongue over and under his tight sac. "Oh, fuck, yeah!" he said. "He really does love to suck fucking cock, man!"

"Tell me about it," Tony responded. "I'm ready for another round!" I felt Tony climb on the bed behind me. He wrapped his hands around my waist to undo my shorts. Realizing they were elastic, he pulled them down to my knees with a hard tug. They caught my raging hard-on, and with Mikey's cock in my mouth I squealed in pain. "You ain't felt nothing yet, boy!" he said. "Wait'll I get my cock in this little pussy!" He pulled the shorts all the way off, as well as my shoes and socks. All I had on was my T-shirt, which Mikey grabbed hold of and used to pull me onto his cock. Seeing that Tony was stripping me naked, he pulled it over my head and I slipped it off.

"You want it, boy?" Tony said. "Huh?" I could only moan my assent with Mikey's cock in my mouth. "What?" he said. "I can't hear you!"

"Yeah!" I said, letting Mikey's wet dick fall out of my mouth. "Fuck my ass!"

"Yeah?"

"Fuck me, please!" I begged. I couldn't wait. "Fuck me hard! I want your cock inside me!"

"You want this cock?"

"Oh, yeah!"

"You want me to fuck your ass?!"

"Please!" Mikey impatiently grabbed my head with one hand and pointed his cock back into my mouth with the other. Tony slapped my ass a few times and rubbed it. It stung. I felt his hot cock rubbing in my crack, and wanted him inside me so bad.

"Please . . . ," I said, "there's condoms in the night table." Tony pulled one out and started to slip it over his cock. Noticing the lube in my night table too, he slathered some on his cock and on my asshole. "Fuck me!" I begged impatiently.

"You ready? You wanna be my little whore?"

"Please!"

I felt his head pressed on my butthole. He held it there for a few seconds, and then—without warning—he entered me all at once. I don't think he'd ever fucked an ass before.

I screamed in pain; his dick was so fucking huge. But as he slowly slid in and out, working deeper and deeper into my ass, pain gave way to sweet delight.

"Oh, fuck, yeah!" Tony yelled. "Oh, man! This ass is tight like a sweet little pussy! Oh, yeah! Fuck!" He seemed to be in some disbelief about how good my tight, velvety ass felt as it embraced his swelling dick. I couldn't believe it, either—I'd always fantasized about being with two guys at once, and that dream was finally coming true. One cock ramming in my ass and another in my face—it was outrageous! Two hard bodies banging into me at either end: Tony's huge cock tearing my ass apart, Mikey's slim member working its way down my throat. Vince was watching and stroking his meat back to full glory.

"Oh, yeah! I'm gonna cum!" Mikey said as he pulled out of my mouth. His dick jerked and he shot a full load of hot jism on my face. A lot of it hit my forehead and ran down my nose. I tasted it with my tongue as it dripped off.

Vince was ready for more, so he got in front of me and I sucked his cock again. It was easy to take his small dick in my mouth. He wrapped his hands around my head and fucked my face; each time he slammed his body into me, Mikey's fresh cum made wet, sticky strings between my face and Vince's soft stomach.

"Fuck! Eat my cock! Take it all! Aw, fuck, yeah!" Hearing this shy-looking, awkward boy order me around was really a charge, and I could still taste his previous orgasm on his iron-hard shaft.

Meanwhile, Tony was really working my ass. "Oh, yeah, bitch! Take my fucking cock! Take it! Take it in that cunt!" He slammed my ass with all the force of his body, faster and faster. He really couldn't seem to get enough. If this was the first time he'd fucked an ass, I'm sure it wouldn't be the last. He loved it, rattling my entire body. "Ah, fuck! I'm gonna cum!" He pulled his cock out, pulled off the condom, and stroked his cock furiously. He shot another nice load on my back, and some of it even shot all the way up into my hair.

Before I knew what was happening, I felt a cock inside me again. But it wasn't Tony—it was the fourth guy! In my abandon, I'd forgotten all about him. He was big, probably 6-foot-4, with dark hair on his head and his well-defined chest. His cock was even bigger than Tony's.

"Give it to him!" Tony ordered. "Fuck him hard! Yeah, this pussy-boy likes to get fucked!" His cock was so huge, I really didn't think the initial pain would subside. And it didn't—but the pleasure was just as great. I never felt so entirely filled by another man; I thought his dick would come out my mouth and meet Vince's.

"Hey, Joe," Mikey said to him after a minute. "Let me try a piece of that ass!" Joe pulled out, and Mikey slid in. Mikey fucked me harder and faster than any of the others had.

"Take it!" he said. "Take it, you little fucker—take my cock in your ass! Take it in your little pussy, fucker! Tighter! Tighter! C'mon! Tighten that cunt, boy! Tighten it! Take my dick! Tighten that ass!"

He fucked me so hard that I slowly slipped down onto my stomach, his slender cock still reaming my ass. I almost thought I wouldn't be able to stand it, but soon Joe pushed him aside and gave me his cock again. I still couldn't believe how huge he was. He straddled my ass and slipped it in. "Oh, fuck! Oh, God, yeah! Take my fat cock!"

I was still sucking Vince, who wanted to try my ass, too. Soon he went behind me and pushed Joe aside.

"I want to see your face when I'm fucking you," he said. "Turn over!" I turned over and put my legs in the air. He entered me. His small dick was refreshing after Joe's had almost torn me apart. "Mmm, yeah!" he said. "Tell me you like it!"

"Oh, yeah!" I moaned, my eyes closed.

"Look at me!" he said. "Tell me you like my cock!"

"Oh, yeah! Feels good . . . Pump it in me!"

"I said open your eyes, boy—I want you to see me fucking you!" So I did. His face scrunched up with each bang into my rattled body. Joe came over behind my head and bent his cock into my mouth. I now realized he was uncut, so I gave special attention to his fleshy head. Soon Mikey took another turn, fucking me hard once again.

"Ohhhh!" he yelled. "Yeah! Fuck yeah! Take my cock! Tighten your hole, boy!" My entire bottom felt like it must have been black and blue. "Oh, fuck yeah! Take my fucking cock!"

All four of them kept taking turns fucking me at both ends; I can't remember how many times. Eventually I came without even touching my cock. My jism shot onto Mikey's chest, who was fucking my face at the time. He seemed a little upset. "What the fuck—?!" he yelled. "Don't fucking blow your cum on me! Clean it off!" He got on all fours over my face so I could drink my jism off of him. "Eat your cum! Eat it!"

Joe then straddled my chest, his knees in my armpits, and shoved his dick into my mouth. He held it steady with one hand and pulled my head over his huge dick with the other. Mikey was reaming me again. "Make me cum! Tighten that ass!"

"Oh, fuck! I'm gonna cum!" Joe pulled out of my mouth and drizzled a huge load on my mouth and chin. When he climbed off, I realized that Vince and Tony were jerking off next to me. I grabbed Tony's cock to help him. He came for a third time, all over my chest. This boy couldn't get enough! I milked every last drop out of his man meat. Soon Vince moaned. "Oh, yeah! Oh, yeah! I'm cuming again! Taste it!" His load ended up on my hairy chest too, and I ran my hand through it and licked the mixture off my hand as Mikey plugged away.

"Aw, yeah!" Mikey yelled. "I'm gonna cum! I'm gonna cum in your ass! You like that, boy? Huh?" I was almost comatose, and could only moan in assent. "What? You want my cum in you, you little fucker? You want me to fill your hole? You want my cum in your ass? Aw fuck, yeah! Here it comes! Take it! Take it!!" He slammed into me harder than ever, and I swear I could feel his hot load splash inside the condom he had worked so far up my asshole. "Aw, yeah! Fuck! Mmm, yeah!"

He pulled out. My ass was in shambles. Mikey straddled my neck, pulled off the condom, and made me suck the cum off his cock. "Taste my cock again. Lick it clean." I licked those juices off, and finally passed out from exhaustion.

I woke up about two hours later. The boys were gone,

and so was the car. My entire bed was stained with cum; my entire body was sticky and caked with dry man juice. My throat was so sore I could barely talk, my ass so numb I could barely walk.

In other words, I was in ecstasy.

Bunkhouse Bruisers

Hank Arnold

Rowdy charged out from under his showerhead and slammed my sorry ass against the wall of the washhouse, shoving his grinning kisser close to mine. His hot breath all but steamed the water off my cheeks.

"I caught'cha checking out my backside this time, you little horndog," the naked cowhand whooped. "Admit it! You're hot for my tail."

"I'm not," I grunted, frowning, trying to squirm out of his clutches. Having big, muscular Rowdy grappling me was firing off sensors in my gonads that were gonna have my dick announcing to the whole damn bunkhouse just how queer I was if I didn't get away from him.

He held me against the wall at arm's length. "Nuthin' wrong with appreciating a man's finer *ass*-ets," he chuckled. Rowdy fancied himself a smart man. He was always showing off by announcing how he was working on the *Denver Post* crossword puzzle.

Far as I was concerned, smart *ass* was more like it. *Oh, shit, thinking about Rowdy's ass* . . . there went my dick. And he was holding my arms, so there was no way I could cover my stiffer.

He leaned into me again. "You are such a pretty little cowpoke." His whisper tickled my ear; his stubble scraped my chin. "All smooth and hairless like you been scraped clean. I wouldn't mind licking off them fine, soft hairs, if you want." He pushed himself out to look at me. "And here I'm such a big ol' older, hairy piece of meat." He looked down. He focused on my dick. His jaw dropped. "Talk about a big ol' piece of meat. . . ."

Oh, man, I got as red as some of them peppers Cook serves us, "to keep your nelly-ass balls from dryin' up."

"Hank, son," Rowdy wheedled, "where you been hiding that howitzer?" He tucked his head and winked at me. "Is that mine? Looks like my sweet butt brought out the best you got to offer. Why don't we figure something extra special to do with it."

I really started struggling to try and break away, but that dick of mine had a fucking mind of its own. It wouldn't go down. There was no way I could allow Rowdy to show me off to the rest of the boys. Everybody on that damn ranch was straight. If they found out I wasn't, my life would be hell, if not worse.

He was stronger'n me and had a really good grip. No matter how I twisted and strained, he hung on—and I had even been a second-string wrestler in high school.

The only thing left to do was to knee him. I didn't

want to think about what damage I might do, but I was desperate.

I shot my knee out. "Haw!" Rowdy jumped back, grabbed me under my raised leg, and yanked up, dropping me like a sack of feed onto the shower room floor. His big body came crashing down on top of me.

The water from the showers, still running full blast, hit me full in the face before it splintered off the muscles of Rowdy's broad back as he jumped onto me, straddling my midsection and pinning me down.

In one quick move he reached back and caught my legs under the knees with his arms and yanked them up around his sides. My body slid underneath him. My hard dick bumped off his tailbone and up his backside.

He rose up on his knees and hopped his butt up onto my chest. I punched at him best as I could, but I could hardly see from the water in my eyes. Suddenly I felt my hands locked tight inside his big fingers. I was trussed up like a calf about to get branded. Except I'd never seen a cowhand sitting on a calf's chest, with a big dick waving in the calf's face. And that sure was what was waving in front of mine: a thick, meaty pole, curving down from its heavy weight and dripping with greasy precum. It was filling and straightening up faster'n I could get the water shook off my face.

By the time I could see clear, that wet, brown fencepost, with its blood-filled maroon knob, was pointing straight at me. It was the finest example of rock-hard manhood I had ever laid eyes on. And it was only inches from my lips. All I had to do was lean forward and pop it into my mouth.

While I was shooting my head forward, I might have reasoned—in the hope that I wasn't about to get my skull beat in—that even a straight guy might like a good blow job from a queer, but, truth is, I wasn't thinking about anything except getting that western sausage lodged somewhere down my gut in the vicinity of my belly button.

Rowdy was pure prime. I had admired his dick—along with his butt, and the low-hanging set of furry ovals that dangled underneath his dick—many a time in the showers.

His body went tense, and I heard the air suck into his chest as my jaw stretched wide and my lips locked over the veiny pole. He had a fine, manly stalk. I paused long enough to let my tongue circle the fat bulbous head, dipping and curving over the round prow and the splayed flange. Digging my teeth gently into the gristle of his throbbing shaft, I felt the thick, bulging veins pump against the inside of my cheeks.

Rowdy's thighs, clinched around my chest, began to relax. I shoved my head farther down his pole, sucking and slurping as I went.

He let his arms drop, freeing my legs. Lowering my feet to the slippery floor, I set my heels against the rubber matting and pushed. Underneath him, my body slid forward, my shoulders went up the wall, and my head tilted in. I munched in about half of his honker.

A low rumble started in Rowdy's chest; air whistled through his pursed lips. One hand curved around my head to help take the strain off my neck as I sucked, and the other hand slid around his back to grab hold of my dick.

"Mmmmm." He pumped his butt back and forth,

pushing his meat all the way into my mouth and pulling it out, 'cept for the big, juicy head. On the backstroke, I scooped precum out of his piss slit onto my tongue and laved the grease down as much of the shaft as I could wrap my trapped mouth-snake around before he drilled forward again.

I dove deep into his pubes, sinking my nose into his soapy bush. His dick pushed into my mouth, past my tongue, and down into the depths of my clutching throat, giving my gag muscles a run for their money and his monster meat a real workout.

"Hol-lee . . . Son, you are a wonder," I heard him mutter. "That is a wonderful mouth."

It's a damn wonder of a mouthful, I thought, savoring the tasty beef and grinding my chin against his heavy hangers. He milked my dick with his fist the same way I milked his dong with my jaw. And soon enough we were getting rewarded for our efforts.

I went first, powering out a load that almost backflushed into my trussed-up nuts, since Rowdy had such a tight grip on my rod. But once he figured I was cuming he loosened his fingers and I spewed a fine fountain of cum, wetting his back, which was already being needlesprayed by the shower.

My body jerked and I powered out another healthy burst of cream, and another, and finally a couple of shots that we only later learned had roped all the way up into his thick dark hair.

A chuckle bounced up from his flat abs and, after determining I had finished shooting my wad, he let go of my meat and swung his arm around to join his other one in cupping my head. Firmly fucking my face, he brought himself nearer and nearer to the big roundup.

His body went stiff as he lifted his butt off my chest to shift his hips forward. My face mashed into his belly and his massive member seemed to grow thicker and longer as his nuts tightened against my lower lip.

Suddenly, his body jerked and thrashed around. Inside my mouth, his dick swelled and started propelling load after load of cum down my gut. The sweet stink of his seed mingled with the clean scent of the deodorant soap and the smell of the musty, water-soaked walls of the shower shed.

I reached up and plowed my fingers through the wet coating of thick hair that covered Rowdy's front—and back—and thighs and butt. The mat was thick enough to grab hold of. My hands ran across his stubby nipples, and that was what I hung on to as my throat gobbled down his erupting dick milk. I pinched and squeezed them, which only seemed to prolong his being able to squirt jizz down my gullet. Finally, 'bout the time I thought I was gonna pinch his tits off, he finished emptying his nuts with a big, contented sigh.

I needed some air, but Rowdy's arm-sized pole was taking its own sweet time shrinking back to normal size, and I sure as hell couldn't stretch my jaw any wider to breathe around it. Reluctantly, I pulled my mouth off of him.

Sweet oxygen, moisture-laden and thick but fresh and clean to my parched lungs, flooded in. I felt a huge emptiness in my mouth and throat, and once I had sucked in more air, I started to gobble down Rowdy's dick again. He pushed my head back with the butt of his hands, though, then caught me under the chin and tilted my head up, grinning down at me.

"You're the first who's been able to take it all, honey mouth. I reckon that's gonna make you and me special partners."

"Fine with me." I returned his grin, licking my lips and craning my neck toward his semihard again. He still held me back. He frowned.

"That might be a problem."

"Like what?"

"Like me!" It was the angry voice of the other young cowhand, Jake—who was a couple of years older'n me—standing in the doorway of the shower room in his boots and underdrawers.

I had thought Rowdy and me might not be the last ones out of the shower shed, but thinking about Rowdy's butt had clouded my head.

Jake was good-looking and hot, but a stubborn and hardheaded cowpoke. We'd tried to be civil, 'cause I thought he was straight like everybody else, but somehow it just hadn't clicked. Now I knew why: we were two horny, closeted ranch queers after the same piece of ass.

"Damn you, Rowdy, I knew you wouldn't be able to keep your hands off fresh meat." Jake stomped into the room, his boots sending up mean sprays of water from the rough concrete floor, which was beginning to steam from the cool evening air settling in.

"Now, Jakey baby, you know sometimes Daddy just—"

"Daddy's just gonna get his ass whupped, is what,"

Jake hollered, storming over as he shoved down his Jockeys and pulled out his dick. He jerked Rowdy's head back and jammed his meat down Rowdy's throat. "That'll shut you up, you two-timin' bitch," he snarled, throwing his leg over Rowdy's shoulder to hold him down.

Now it's true that Jake was in damn good shape—sure as hell tougher'n me—but I know full well Rowdy could've pitched him off; Rowdy was one powerful mess of muscles. Instead, Rowdy just happily guzzled that kid's dick and started munching away like it was his evening meal.

Jake leaned down and shoved his face next to mine. His smooth cheeks smelled piney-fresh. He must've hung back to shave while all the other cowhands had hurried on to supper.

"Is his dick up your ass?" he demanded.

"What?"

"Is my man's penis stuck up your rectum, shithead?! I can't tell from here, and I'm not about to move away to take a look."

Rowdy closed his eyes and sucked away at Jake's dick like a hungry calf at his mama's udder. *Udderly* contented. I snickered.

"What the fuck are you laughing at, shitface? If I had another dick I'd shove it down *your* throat." His good-looking face got red, even as the water was starting to cool off.

"If you had another dick, I sure wouldn't mind sucking it," I said. "From what I just saw, that was one fine-looking example of young cowpoke's poker." Rowdy's eyes flew open.

Jake got flustered for a second, but then started yelling

again, ignoring my offer. "He *has* got his dick up your butt." He turned toward Rowdy's contented face. "I never could get you to fuck me and now you're fucking *him.*" He turned on me again. "Fuck you and that stump of yours," he yelled, waving at where Rowdy was sitting on me. "I told him I bet you had a honker that would gut a bronc."

Rowdy just continued sucking like mad. That kid must have had a dick of iron. I sure would have already blown my wad.

Jake wasn't exactly making a lot of sense—I mean, Rowdy was sitting on me, not the other way round—but I did like the sound of what I was hearing. With my butt still trapped, my "stump"—which by now was repumped and rarin' to go again—started scraping its way up Rowdy's hairy crack, nudging against his tailbone.

"Damn, this man gives great head," Jake announced. Rowdy's mouth was working wonders. Jake swung his other leg around so he could fuck Rowdy's face full on. Jake's big chest was heaving, and he was calming down. "Did he blow you?"

I shook my head, noting that Jake had a fine, smooth ass, not inches from my face. It was a beautiful hairless contrast to his fuck buddy's dark, older set of saddle-polished butterballs.

Rowdy jerked his head toward me, answering Jake's question.

"You sucked him off?" Jake snarled derisively at me.

Rowdy took a breather, and gulped some air. "Hank took it all," he purred smugly. "I told you sooner or later I'd find somebody who could, tight lips." He went back to sucking on the kid's meat tube.

Jake was obviously torn between wanting to instantly end my tenure at the ranch and wanting to congratulate me. Not being too swift a stud, and having pretty much run out of invectives, he just gawked while his big juicy lips hung open.

I had a vision of what pleasure those juicy lips could bring to my restiffened stump.

"I could fuck you if you want," I said to his butt. "I bet that fine bottom would suck up this pore li'l pisser of mine in a flash."

Rowdy frowned and sucked harder than ever. Distracted as Jake was by Rowdy's expert blow job, he knew revenge when it was presented to him.

His eyes narrowed. "Yeah. I'd like that."

Rowdy started to protest, but Jake's tight grip nailed the older cowhand's head to his crotch. I slithered out from under Rowdy, shot over to the wall where my clothes were hanging, grabbed a rubber out of my jeans, and was wrapped and ready before Jake had a second thought.

"Now, go easy," he instructed me while smirking down at Rowdy, as I hunkered up behind him. "I've been wanting it, but I've never—Aaaggh!! Shit! Fuck! Damn fire!"

I reached around and grabbed his tits while I worked my dick all the way up his rectum.

"Aaaggh!!" He hollered like hell—but he took it.

I leaned my head on the cowhand's sweat-covered shoulder and gnawed at his earlobe while peeking over and down at Rowdy, who looked up and smiled at me as best he could while running his mouth up and down Jake's dick. From where I stood, the kid's meat looked like it had growed two or three inches when I punched my fence post up his ass.

"Aw! Fuck, man! Shit!!" Jake's head whipped back and forth as I whipped my dick in and out of his butthole, and as Rowdy whipped his mouth up and down Jake's not inconsiderable length and width. But his hollering was getting less intense, turning more into moans and groans.

We were three fine figures of western manhood, I mused while concentrating on blasting a hole through Jake's tight butt . . . and we deserved to feel each other's potential to the fullest.

"OK," Jake said, hyping himself. "OK, I can take it." He puffed a little, relaxing his ass as I plowed in and out. "Yeah. Fucking, yeah . . . yeah *yeah.*" Jake seemed to have decided he liked what was happening to his middle. He swung an arm around to slap my ass—*hard*—as I crammed his hole.

He used Rowdy's thick hair to hang on to and pound the guy's head into his crotch. Rowdy didn't seem to mind at all.

While I fucked the tar out of his butt, my hands got busy grinding Jake's tender nips into hard little dicks, and from what I could tell, down at his crotch Rowdy was busy masticating Jake's pole into hog slop.

I had to admit, Jake was one fine receptacle. He stood between us, the water cascading over his fat-free, trim bod, his head thrown back, a contented groan rumbling up from his heaving chest as we worked him over.

I blew first—again, dammit—ramming a load up Jake's ass that surprised me, considering I had already spewed a cup of cream over Rowdy's back. I gushed a condom full enough for some of my syrup to squeeze out the back end and drain down onto the inside of Jake's muscular thighs.

Staying implanted up his butt with my body snuggled against his back, I nuzzled my head into the crook of Jake's neck while my fingers went from torturing to nurturing his tits. His hand that had been whacking my ass went to cupping my balls.

My shooting my wad up his hole seemed to be the trigger to keep Jake going. He kicked up fucking Rowdy's face a notch or two. Rowdy's big brown eyes drifted closed and he took it like a hungry cowboy at the end of the trail desperately devouring Cook's grub.

Then the hungry cowboy came. All I heard was muffled grunts, but I felt his jism streaking hot and heavy over my ass to drizzle down my legs as I straddled him to fuck Jake.

Finally, it was Jake's turn. He began to snicker, then his pumping body slowed down, then it froze and stiffened in place, then he groaned and began to gasp. If I wouldn't have knowed better, I would have figured it for some kind of seizure, but whatever it was, it sure gave him pleasure and it went on and on and on, with Rowdy guzzling Jake's cum like there was nothing better to nourish him this side of the Mississippi, and damn if I didn't get a little envious.

Jake's orgasm was so intense his gripping asshole even squeezed a couple more globs out of my dick.

Finally, having blown our wads, we got out of that damned shower shed, which had cooled off to where I was about to freeze my balls off. In the barn, in the hayloft, the both of them heated me up right nicely, though.

I had it in my head I wanted to be butt-plugged by Jake's huge member. So the guys did what they could to help me achieve my goal and still be able to sit in a saddle. I had a handful of condoms that they dressed over a variety of smooth-handled farm implements with which they proceeded to puncture my anus.

When we got to something his size, Jake replaced the rake handle up my rectum with his own mighty meat and fucked the living daylights out of my ass, while Rowdy sucked my nuts up through my dick and down his throat, just like he had done to Jake.

Then, having me spread open, Rowdy mounted me while Jake and I sixty-nined.

Way fucking awesome.

It took them about half an hour to nut me. Then Jake wanted to work on learning to take Rowdy all the way down his throat, so we had a few practice sessions, and Rowdy obliged by blowing a few more loads down our young gullets. And that's how we ended our first time together. The next time, I got to fuck Rowdy's beautiful ass—the thing that had gotten it all started in the first place.

Jeb, our foreman, says I've gotten a lot easier to deal with. I was too uptight when I first came on board, he told me, but I seem a lot more mellow now. He reckons it's because I found a couple of buddies in Rowdy and Jake.

He's right.

By the Balls

T. Hitman

Disgusted, pitcher Mike Mitchell slammed his glove on the dugout bench. He knew every camera in the ballpark was likely on him, but he no longer cared. He was so pissed following the worst of a string of bad outings, he almost couldn't hear the boos from the home-team fans anymore.

Almost.

He thought about tipping the sports drink cooler, or taking a few golf swings at a batting helmet with the nearest piece of lumber—hell, even punching out the guy he blamed most for the shitty performance, the team's catcher. Instead, he grabbed his jacket and started toward the dugout stairs, pushing his way through a sea of sweaty uniforms. It wasn't until he recognized the number 18 on the back of one of the shirts that he lost it. The short brown hair, arms of concrete, and dirt-stained, sweat-soaked pinstripes belonged to his battery mate, catcher Jorge Cordero.

The other man stood with one leg arched up on the stairs and was fastening the last of his protective gear, his shin and knee guards. A jolt of rage as sudden and red-hot as what he'd felt on the mound when Coach Riggs took him out of the game exploded inside Mike. He aimed an elbow at Cordero's back and gave a forceful shove on his way past while growling a swear under his breath.

"Dumb fuck!" he huffed.

He didn't make it two more steps before Cordero grabbed hold of his pinstripes. Angry Spanish erupted in his ears. Mitchell pulled free of the hand on his sleeve and heard his uniform tear. The catcher was on him in a flash, and a brief struggle ensued, with punches and insults flying. Their teammates eventually pulled the two men apart.

"Get the fuck out of here!" center fielder Steve Spencer huffed in Mitchell's direction.

Mitchell sucked in a deep breath of the dugout's hot, sour air and aimed a look first at Spencer and then at his restrained catcher before trudging down the stairs. He knew the fight would replay on sports TV for days, nationally as well as locally, that he'd be branded baseball's current overpaid and underachieving villain, burned in effigy by fans, talk radio, and his own teammates.

He cut through the tunnel, past security, and into the clubhouse, where signs posted at his insistence warned, *No Media!* If he hurried, he could be out of the locker room before the last out and avoid having to deal with the rest of the team.

Mitchell quickly unbuttoned his perspiration-drenched

baseball shirt and yanked it off his back along with the sleeveless black T underneath. He kicked off his cleats, peeled down his uniform pants and smelly white stirrup socks, then his jockstrap and cup, leaving everything in a nasty pile on the floor. He grabbed a towel, shampoo, and soap and stepped into his slides. A minute later, he stuck his head under the water in the shower, knowing full well how screwed his life was going to be after today.

Fuck 'em all, he thought as he washed away the grime of his bad performance. *I'm Mike Mitchell, one of the aces on this team, and I make more money in one day than most men do in ten years. Nobody fucks with me!*

He ran the bar of soap over his nuts and found them heavy and swollen. He tugged and scratched at the loose sac, proud of their size.

That's right, fuckers. I'm the one with the balls and the contract—and you better not forget it!

He dried off and wrapped the towel around his waist before crossing back into the locker room. By this point, the rest of the team had begun to shuffle in from the dugout, and he could tell by their scowls that the news wasn't good. He tried to ignore their stares on the way to his locker, but there was no getting past the sudden rumble of Coach Riggs's voice once he got there.

"Mitchell!" bellowed Riggs across the now-filled locker room. He turned to see the team's top guy standing at the door to his office, red-faced and ready to explode. "Get your ass in here!"

Mitchell shook his head. "I'm getting dressed." He turned back in the direction of his open locker. The clubhouse suddenly fell deathly silent.

"You don't hotfoot it in here this fuckin' second, Mitchell, I'm gonna drag you in here by your nuts. *Now!*" Coach Riggs shouted before slamming the office door.

In his three months with the team, Mitchell had never seen the coach so pissed, not even when arguing over shitty umpiring got him ejected or cost the team a game. He knew Coach Riggs meant business.

Taking a heavy swallow and cinching the towel tighter around his waist, Mitchell headed toward Coach Riggs's office. He figured he was about to be ripped a new asshole for his behavior both on and off the field that afternoon, but it didn't matter. He had agents and a contract and the union to protect him. He could be the biggest dick in all of pro sports and nobody could touch him, no matter what he did or who he did it to. What did he have to worry about from the coach—or from the whole fuckin' team for that matter? Still, he was happy that the drawn blinds in the coach's office would prevent the rest of the guys from seeing his humiliation.

He entered the office and closed the door behind him. "Yeah?" he said flatly.

Coach Riggs stood at the open drawer of his old, paper-stuffed filing cabinet. "You're looking real pretty and clean now, considering how ugly you were out there an hour ago," he said sarcastically. He pulled out a document and then slammed the drawer shut, loudly and with enough power to make the toned biceps of the thirty-eight-year-old's former pitching arm flex. He slammed the document down on his desk, which Mitchell noticed was curiously void of any other objects, even the blotter that was usually there. "Know what this is?"

Mitchell glanced at the papers. "A contract."

"It's *your* contract," Coach Riggs said.

"No shit," answered Mitchell. "I figured that."

Coach Riggs rounded the desk and got right in his face. "Don't get cocky with me, 'cause I don't have to put up with your shit. And I won't."

"Because you've got the owner behind you, that it, Coach?" Mitchell defied.

"Even better than that, tough guy. I got your contract to back me up. You fuck with the fans, that's your own choice and problem. They've got long memories, and you'll pay for it every time you enter a ballpark for the rest of your career," countered Coach Riggs. "You don't want the media at your locker, that's fine with me, too. The reporters already hate you. Gives them something to write about. But you start taking cheap shots at your battery mate, I got every right to bust your ass."

Mitchell folded his arms, which pumped up impressively. "Cordero made bad calls."

"And you've made bad pitches. A lot of them. You've dropped the last four games you've started. And you don't have one friend on this team."

Mitchell laughed. "I don't need their friendship."

"Like it or not, this is a team," Coach Riggs growled menacingly. "And you're going to start acting like a team player." He aimed the rough thumb of his former pitching hand at a paragraph of the contract's minutiae. "You signed this, knowing your contract calls for good sportsmanship. I got a case against you that will cost you plenty of cash if you don't turn your season around—right now—

by marching out there and apologizing to your teammates for being such a fuckin' asshole."

"Apologize?" Mitchell said calmly. "How's this for an apology, Riggs. *Go fuck yourself.*"

Mitchell shot his middle finger at Riggs before reaching for the door. He fully intended to leave the office and finish dressing. But waiting just outside and blocking his escape stood a trio of imposing bodies: twenty-six-year-old Spencer, who'd turned his ball cap backward to expose his blond crew cut; the team's lanky rookie shortstop, Derek Peters; and his catcher, Jorge Cordero.

"What the fuck?" asked Mitchell.

"You're the one that's fucked, dude," he heard Coach Riggs chuckle over his shoulder. Then Riggs growled, *"Do it!"*

Cordero and Spencer rushed him, pushing him back into the office and forcing him against the desk with incredible strength.

"Get the fuck off me!" Mitchell howled, but the two men ignored his demand. He watched the fresh-faced rookie close and lock the door. Peters then grabbed hold of his legs, and the three men hauled him onto the desk, pinning him down at several points, by the arms and shoulders and both ankles. With the guys at such close range, Mitchell's next angry breath filled with the raw, manly stink emanating from their bodies.

"I told you that one way or another, you weren't leaving this office till you adjusted your attitude," said Coach Riggs. Struggling on the desk, Mitchell could only look on as Coach Riggs moved in close to tower over him.

"We've had enough of your shit, fucker. It's time for you to learn some respect!"

To his shock, Mitchell felt a hand take hold of the meaty bulge of his crotch and squeeze it suggestively.

"Hold the fucker down," Spencer shouted at his ear. The hand was his, and his comment was directed to Peters, who had him by the ankles. The square-jawed center fielder grabbed Mitchell's towel and ripped it open, exposing his freshly showered cock and balls. Mitchell put all his strength into fighting against his teammates, but to no avail. He'd believed his humiliation would end after he faced down Coach Riggs in his office, but the truth was, it had only begun!

What was about to happen still hadn't sunk in. The sound of a zipper opening near his face and the fumble of Cordero's fingers between his naked legs soon woke him up to the reality of his situation. The fuckers were going to do him! Worse, he remembered the blank top of Riggs's desk, and now knew they'd planned this. Mitchell turned his head to face the coach, only to have Riggs's half-hard, hairy cock slap his face. The musty smell of man sweat filled his nose, and a trickle of gummy salt stained his lips. He coughed and sputtered. Riggs gripped his cock by the root and batted Mitchell's cheek, an action that pushed the coach's tool to its full stiffness. Mitchell howled out his disgust as Coach Riggs wiped his hard cock and meaty nuts all over his face.

"Yeah, Coach," Spencer urged. "Show him we ain't gonna put up with his crap no more!" Right after he said this, Spencer planted a knee on his shoulder to pin him and covered part of Mitchell's body with his own, an action that put the other man at face level with his cock. To Mitchell's shock, he felt a warm set of lips envelop the head of his limp dick. Spencer gave his cock several hard sucks, enough to make it start swelling.

Mitchell turned away from the coach's boner and screamed out a loud, desperate *"Help! Somebody fuckin' help me!"*

Spencer spit out his dick. "Shut up!" he ordered. But Mitchell didn't. He heard a shuffle and tipped his head back to see Spencer kick off one of his size-12 cleats and yank down the stirrup sock. Spencer balled up the smelly sweat sock and jammed it into Mitchell's mouth in mid-shout. The musty, foul taste of foot-soaked cotton ignited on the pitcher's tongue.

Cordero exclaimed a loud, cocky "Woo-hoo!"

Mitchell focused on the Latino catcher's rugged, clean-shaven face, close-cut dark hair, and mean good looks. Farther down between his big, bare feet hovered Derek Peters. The rookie, five years his junior, was no less in control than Spencer or Cordero. With his buzzed hair, lanky frame of ropy muscles, and a boyish smile that was now feral and lusty, Mitchell never would have figured Peters would have conspired to humiliate him. It was all so hard to believe!

But the young rookie was playing with his feet and his solid, hairy legs while holding him immobile, breaking every rule of conduct and maleness in a pro baseball team's locker room. And then there was Spencer, the no-bullshit, tough-as-nails team captain. In his short time with the team, Mitchell had heard dozens of stories of Spencer's reputation as a pussy hound. The supposed legend was now sucking on his prick! Spencer's manly stink from nine innings of hard-played baseball filled Mitchell's nostrils, along with the nasty taste of his big jock feet.

Another hand fondled his pride and joy. Mitchell struggled to see it was the rookie, and that—even worse—somehow, in his rage, he'd started to throw wood. The big piece of baseball player dick hanging over his nuts was responding to Peters's strokes.

"That's right, dude," Spencer growled to the rookie. "Have some fun with the fucker's dick."

Mitchell shifted and jerked, trying to escape Cordero's weight. He did his best to expel the ripe stirrup sock lodged in his mouth, but was unsuccessful.

"You mind holding him, Coach?" Spencer asked.

Riggs grabbed Mitchell's arm and pinned it beneath him. "Not at all, Spence."

Mitchell again panicked. Thus freed from restraining him, the center fielder tugged off his shirt and T-shirt, kicked off his remaining baseball cleat, and hauled off the sock. His uniform pants went next. The male stink in the air seemed to double. Spencer now stood only in his jock and cup over a pair of onionskin compression shorts.

Mitchell had seen the other man naked in the showers a hundred times. He knew Spencer was a mass of solid, blond-haired muscle, from his strong guns to his ripped chest and abs down to his legs. He remembered what was hidden in Spencer's cup: a fat, long cock and two egg-shaped low-hangers covered in dirty blond fur.

But he'd never seen Spencer hard. That all changed when the team's captain peeled off his wet, rank jock and shorts to stand naked and stiff mere inches away from Mitchell's sock-filled face. Spencer leaned in. The warm, sweaty underside of his cock glided over Mitchell's cheek. Spencer fished the stirrup sock out of Mitchell's mouth, replacing it with the head of his dick.

"Don't even think of biting me, fucker," he threatened. "I swear I'll rip your fuckin' nuts off."

Reluctantly, Mitchell took the other man's helmet between his lips. He'd sucked dick before—in college, not that he would have admitted it to anybody—and he'd tasted his own precum enough times to understand it wasn't entirely disgusting, so he knew what to expect from Spencer's invasion. The center fielder leaned over him, shoving the head and a good five inches to the back of his throat. He also delivered good on his warning by taking hold of Mitchell's balls. Spencer gave his sac a rough tweak. Mitchell sucked harder and deeper. The other jock's musty-smelling bush scraped his chin while his sweaty balls draped his nose, filling his lungs with their fumes.

One of his attackers—the rookie, he figured—forced his legs apart and arched them up. Mitchell thought about kicking as hard as he could, but with a mouth on his dick and a chokehold on his nuts, he reluctantly decided against it and tensed in anticipation.

With a deep sigh, Cordero urged, "Yeah, eat that pussy."

Mitchell moaned around the cock in his mouth when first a tongue and then a finger invaded his most private place, his asshole. A rush of heat surged through his guts as the finger pushed deeper, forcing its way in all the way. It probed his hole, and eventually located his prostate. Mitchell seized in place and nearly blew his wad into the mouth humming on his tool.

Spencer rolled off him and yanked out suddenly, leaving the gamy taste of nut-juice on his lips. Before he could protest, Jorge Cordero replaced the bone in Mitchell's mouth with his fat, uncut piece of meat. The bitter heaviness of foreskin trapped and sweating in a cup lit his taste buds, and the smell of the other jock's ripe nuts filled his nose.

"Suck it," Cordero demanded, his voice breathless and tinged with a Spanish accent. "Suck my dick, asshole!"

Mitchell worked on the catcher's Latino meat as the finger up his ass pulled out. A warm breath teased his hole, along with a tongue, wet and hungry. A shuffle sounded as Peters climbed onto the desk and on top of him.

And then the unthinkable happened.

He'd been so focused on the cocks in his face, he hadn't realized the young shortstop wasn't only interested in fingering or rimming his shitter. The rookie's face swam over his, handsome and intense as the head of his dick pushed against Mitchell's hole.

"No!" Mitchell tried to argue. But opening his mouth allowed the catcher to stuff more of his manhood down his throat. Cordero's crisp, dark carpet of hair brushed Mitchell's chin, while his cum-packed nuts dragged across his nostrils. Mitchell clenched his asshole in an attempt to expel the rookie, but Peters's long, skinny dick penetrated him anyway. The entire world temporarily turned red before Mitchell's watery eyes.

"Fuck the bitch," Coach Riggs growled, shooting Mitchell a mean look. "How's it feel getting bred by a rookie, tough guy?"

Drops of fresh sweat from Peters's handsome face rained down on Mitchell's. Drunk on the taste of Cordero's funky, uncut cock, he trembled each time the rookie thrust in and the head of his cock nudged his prostate, teasing him with pleasure. Mitchell got so focused on that nagging itch deep inside, he didn't resist when Coach Riggs let up on him. Something hot sprayed the side of his face. Mitchell tipped his eyes to the right to see Riggs pounding his meat. Another shot of jock cum hit his cheek.

"Fuck, here it comes!" the coach moaned.

Riggs moved in closer and pressed his shooting hose against Cordero's shaft, forcing a second dick between Mitchell's stuffed lips. A blast of Coach Riggs's sperm doused his tongue.

"Drink *that,* you overpaid fuck," Riggs huffed between gasps for breath. He finished unloading, pulled out, and shook his dick clean on Mitchell's face.

The coach's orgasm seemed to push Derek Peters over the edge. Mitchell heard the rookie grunt, and as his fuck-thrusts intensified, the cock lodged up his ass felt as though it had doubled in size. The shortstop closed his eyes and bit down, growling out a sigh through clenched teeth.

"Fuck, yeah!" Peters spat.

A blast of wetness flooded Mitchell's asshole, powerful enough to force him to the edge of shooting. Peters briefly slumped on top of him, pinning his dick against the tails of his pinstriped uniform shirt, before jumping off him and leaving his can filled with young jock cum.

Cordero blew next. Giving no warning except for a deep baritone grunt, he stepped back so that only the crimped lower ridge of his uncut cockhead was balanced on Mitchell's tongue and squirted several shots of bitter cock snot across the pitcher's taste buds.

"Ay, papi!" Cordero grunted. He savagely pinched Mitchell's nostrils shut. "Swallow it!"

Mitchell gulped down the catcher's load. Cordero released him, stepped away, and deposited the last of his spunk on Mitchell's face beside the dregs of their coach's cum. That left only Spencer, who took hold of Mitchell's straining hard-on and squeezed it by the root, tight enough to keep him from shooting.

"Finish him off, Spence," urged Cordero, who stood still stiff with his pants around his ankles.

Spencer nodded. "I really want to nut in his mouth, but the rookie's already lubed up that asshole of his for me."

Mitchell stared at Spencer's cock, which was easily twice as thick as Derek Peters's, and panicked. Using the temporary lull caused by three of his attackers having shot their wads, he jumped off the desk and tried to escape. He got only a step toward the door before the three spent jocks rolled him back onto his stomach atop the desk.

Spencer grabbed a handful of Mitchell's butt. "I've been watching this butt of yours from center field all season," he chuckled. He slid a finger between the cheeks, found Mitchell's hole, and wiggled it into the wetness of the shortstop's load. "I'm gonna finally get a piece of it."

"Yeah, fuckers, well enjoy it while you can," Mitchell grunted defiantly, even though Spencer's probing was intensifying the pleasurable itch inside him. " 'Cause once

I walk out of here, everyone's gonna know what you did to me!"

Spencer lined his cock up with Mitchell's cum-slickened asshole. "Nobody's gonna listen to any shit from you," he said. " 'Specially after that stunt you pulled out there today."

"Yeah, and nobody believes this shit goes on in baseball," added Cordero. He swung his cock like a bat at Mitchell's face.

Spencer pushed his dick into the pitcher's hole. Mitchell seized in place and howled. He willed his chute to open as best he could to accommodate Spencer's invasion, and held on to the side of the desk as the catcher stuffed him to capacity. Spencer reached between his legs and grabbed hold of Mitchell's boner, stroking it as he rode him on the edge of the coach's desk.

"That's right, asshole," said Riggs. He gripped Mitchell's face by the chin and held it while Spencer plowed him. "You seem not to have grasped the reason behind this little attitude readjustment session. From now on, you're gonna be kind and courteous to your fellow teammates, you shithead." Spencer slammed in hard in rhythm to the coach's words. "You're gonna go out there and win on the days that you start, and you're gonna give no less than a hundred percent—in the clubhouse as well as on the mound!"

Spencer grunted out a feral "Fuck!" His stroke-hold on Mitchell's cock sped up.

"And you're gonna wear those pinstripes with pride, 'cause if you don't start acting like one of the team, there's twenty-five other guys out there in that locker room who're gonna have a go at your ass and mouth just like we did. And that ain't counting the trainer, bench coach, and the rest of my staff," Riggs threatened. "You got that clear, dick-breath?"

Mitchell nodded and groaned, his expression a mix of pain and pleasure. They'd broken him. They'd won. But it was a small price to pay for the incredible feel of Spencer's cock squirting up his ass, and the center fielder's hand around his shaft, which at long last jacked him into shooting.

Before he'd finished cumming fully, Spencer wiped a hand across Mitchell's face, forcing him to taste himself. Huffing a swear under his breath, Spencer dismounted, leaving Mitchell soaked in cum, sweat, and the stink of baseball and man-sex. Saying little more, the three players picked up their uniforms and headed out, leaving him once again alone with Coach Riggs.

"Get the fuck out of here," Riggs said, dismissing him with a mean look and a wave of his hand.

Mitchell eased off the desk and stood. He reached for his towel and mopped his face. "The rest of the team's gonna know," he said. "I swear to you, they'll know what you did to me today!"

Coach Riggs pulled out his desk chair and kicked his stirruped feet onto it, crossing them casually, unimpressed with the threat. "They already do, fucker."

Mitchell turned around to see that the others hadn't shut the door, and that beyond the open frame a dozen men from the team stood just outside the office looking pissed off, arms folded, most in a state of undress.

"Don't forget, shithead, I expect you to win the next time I hand you the ball—or I'll be handing you *two.*"

All that week and for several after, the local and national media vilified Mike Mitchell. Though he didn't win every game he started over the rest of the season, he only lost a few, and not for lack of effort. He knew if he didn't do his best, his teammates would have him by the balls.

Cherry Pops

Dan Kelly

I hadn't been single in years, and didn't want to be, but my friends kept insisting that I enjoy it while it lasted. They were under the impression that someone who had been off the market for as long as I had basically regained his "fresh meat" status. They were also sure I would be snatched up by a wonderful guy before long.

So I let them play dress-up with me . . . and before you know it, we're in a leather bar, and I'm wearing jeans, a leather vest, and a dog collar.

I'm just hanging out at the bar, talking to one of my buddies, and this huge arm comes down, banging an empty beer bottle onto the counter. My vision is blocked by a wall of muscle, bear fuzz, and tattoo. My eyes are practically poked out by these two raging hard nipples, perfectly framed by a chain-link harness.

My perspective shifts—actually, it crawls its way up

the towering figure in front of me while I feel a bunch of my chest hairs being sharply tugged at just hard enough to be uncomfortable, but not hard enough for me to burst out with "What the fuck do you think you're doing?"

And the man looking down at me with demanding eyes says, "Who knew under all those conservative clothes there was this nice mat of fur?"

"Oh . . . hi." I smile back at the disarming raised lip that's both sweet and severe—a smile I look forward to seeing whenever I need some contracting work done around the house. "I didn't know this was your scene."

I could've guessed, though. My handyman reeked of testosterone every time he came over. It smelled doubly delicious on hot summer days when not even the air-conditioning could prevent his strenuous tasks from leaving his tattered T-shirt with large wet pit stains and treasure-trail streaks down the midriff.

"Yeah? Well I knew damn well that behind your goodie-goodie little happy homemaker exterior, you were this wild animal," he said with a smirk. If I wasn't half-naked already, I would've felt so with the way he was gazing down at me.

"Uh . . . actually, I'm just playing around. Came here with my friends."

"And this is OK with the husband?" He pressed really close to me and my mouth went dry.

"Um . . . we're not together anymore," I replied flatly.

The bartender came over and asked us if we needed anything, just as my handyman was saying something, which I was almost sure was "Can't say that I'm sorry."

"What?" I asked after he had dismissed the bartender.

“Follow me,” he said, and began to walk off.

“Wait a minute,” I called. “Where are you going?” Two hundred-plus pounds of mass turned around and responded with a look. His eyes weren’t being so specific now. They were teasing me, not telling me what they expected to be seeing in front of them in the near future. “I’ ve . . . my friends. I’ve gotta tell my friends.”

His dark brows came together in a V of unspoken impatience. I thought it in my best interest not to keep him waiting.

As he sauntered out, I followed him . . . Well, actually, I followed the thick patch of hair right above the seat of his jeans. Each tendril was perfectly placed, forming a weave that resembled an arrow pointing the way down to the large globes beneath. I couldn’t focus long enough to contemplate what I might be getting myself into.

Out on the sidewalk, I called, “Where are we going?”

“Come on,” he said, not looking back. He used a set of keys to open a door between the bar and the next storefront.

I followed him in and up the steps. “You live right above the bar?”

“It’s not as quaint as your perfect little white picket fence, but it’s home,” he said as we entered the apartment.

And it *was* home. Nothing freaky. A small living space with a sofa bed and a kitchen area only feet away. Neat, clean, and cozy. Nothing to make me feel threatened, only typical living necessities—remote control, coasters, *TV Guide*, some nudie mags, and a box of condoms on the coffee table—to make me feel at ease.

"Nice place," I said as he threw his keys on the kitchen counter.

I didn't get to look around much. He was hovering over me, inches away, practically suffocating me with his chest once again. I tried to back up a little, but the now-closed door got in my way. His arms were around me, his large hands on the back of my head and easily directing my mouth to one of his huge nipples—but he didn't force my mouth onto it. He just left it there, touching, poking at my lips.

All sense of reason left me. I didn't bother to argue with him. I took in his swelling knob and sucked it, felt each and every hair that swept across my tongue. I savored the softness of his nipple in my mouth and drew it in deeper until my lips struck hard pec, then I sank my teeth into that. He breathed out a bit and stroked the back of my head with one hand. The other grabbed my vest and pulled it off in one swift tug. It dropped to the floor as I switched to the other nipple.

I wrapped my arms around him and pulled him in, but his arms blocked the meeting of our torsos as *my* nipples began being circled. I felt my knees weaken as they responded, came alive, became buttons for him to play with . . . his fingers squeezing . . . and tugging. My upper body instinctively tried to pull away. Part of me wanted to scream, but my groin began to rotate of its own accord. I sank my teeth harder into his pec and felt his nipple morph into something new as it was suckled beyond its expectations. My nipples knew what it was going through. Through the excruciating discomfort, they were able to detect an incredible sensation that struck my every nerve—positively. Part of me wanted to tell him to stop, afraid he was going to mangle my nipples permanently, but another part of me insisted they could take it.

Just when I thought that my brain was going to fry trying to decide what it was enjoying from the tit torture—the pleasure or the pain—he separated from me, still holding me by the back of my head. And then I was being smothered by an armpit. I could smell his fresh musk, the release of sweat, in each strand of hair. He obviously hadn't used deodorant before coming down to the bar—it was pure, natural, unscathed man-pit. I lapped up that delicious man flavor, munched on the muscles surrounding his deep pit, ran the surface of my tongue along the smooth, taut skin that stretched across his cavern.

"You little fucking whore. You made me wait so long for this. All those times you'd sit all innocently talking to me when I was on a coffee or lunch break. I wanted to rip you apart right there, and you fuckin' knew it. Look what you do to me."

He gripped my hair like a handle and pointed my head down to his crotch. Exploding like a starburst around the head of his bulge was a dark, wet stain of precum. He brought my head down to it; I felt so degraded being led around like an animal. I placed my mouth over the spot on his jeans and slurped on it. The moist coarseness of the material and the hot object beneath it made me literally foam at the mouth.

He threw back his head for a minute as my lips ravished his cockhead. That was about the only sign that I was actually doing something right. He was so calm and collected, as compared with me—a quivering mess. The controlled, rhythmic, quiet inhalation and exhalation of air from his nose and mouth was incredibly erotic to me, though. He pulled me back up to my feet and slammed his mouth onto mine. His tongue crawled along the roof of my mouth as his shadowy whiskers stabbed at the area surrounding my lips. I was sure I was going to pass out from the realization of a long-dormant fantasy.

Then I was led—still by the hair—over to the coffee table.

"Get down. All fours. And I want your head under the table."

I did as I was told—and physically made to do. Then he was on the other side of the table in front of me, crouching by one of my hands, which I was using to hold myself up. He took my wrist, placed it against the table leg, and whipped a leather string out from under the sofa bed. He wound it around my wrist.

"I'm not really comfortable with this," I croaked as I landed on my elbow, a bit of panic setting in. I reached with my free hand to untie the cord.

He grabbed me under the chin and placed a shockingly passionate kiss there, and when he pulled away, I almost detected in his threatening eyes that familiar, friendly handyman's gleam that I knew so well. Then he grabbed my free hand and pulled it to the other table leg. I couldn't fight him if I tried . . . and I did try, slightly, for the fun of it.

"Don't worry. I need you around. You pay me some

big bucks. You'll leave here in one piece and able to walk. Sitting might be a problem, though." He raised the corner of his lip again.

"What are you going to do to me? I don't do stuff like this." I realized there was still a bit of fear in the pit of my stomach, but it was an exhilarating concern that seemed to speed up my heartbeat and pump the blood to my dick in double time. I was throbbing painfully down there, and felt my own puddle of precum becoming a small reservoir.

Then he was coming at me with a blindfold. I tried to duck my head out of the way, but I was no match for him.

"No! I don't like this!" I stammered as my chest pounded and the world went black. "Let me go."

"Shhhhh," he said, and then there was a kiss again, more unexpected because I couldn't see it coming.

"Take it off or I'll scream," I said, thinking that I sounded so "faggy," and also that it might have been a bad thing to say, because now he might gag me as well.

"No one's gonna hear you. The music downstairs is too loud," he said, his taunting tone not even attempting to put me at ease. "Besides, you should save your voice for all the begging and pleading you're gonna need to do."

"Come on, man, just let me go." I tried to sound calm. "We can have a good time. I wanna see you 'cause you're so delicious to look at."

"I think you've seen enough of me. You think I didn't notice all the times you watched my every move when I was putting up shelves or moving furniture around for you? You acting like you're the supervisor, like you're the boss of me."

"No . . . I never meant it that way—," I began, but

then there was a loud crack as something came down on the right cheek of my raised ass.

"Ow! Fuck! What are you doing?" I cried.

I was answered with an equally stinging whack on my left cheek.

"Did I say you could talk?" he growled.

"I just—," I began, and then caught on quick and let out only a wince when contact was made again on an already hot piece of flesh.

"That's right. It's time for some payback. We need to teach you a little lesson. You wanna play the little tease?"

There was a tugging at the waist of my jeans, a bit of a struggle, and then a clean tearing sound. I felt the tightness of my jeans give, and suddenly my left leg was completely exposed. More tugging and tearing, and my right leg was free. Then with one yank, the material that had hidden my jewels was gone. I didn't want to contemplate what sharp object he had used to rip the tough denim material to shreds that way.

I was well aware of how much I was blushing. I had gone commando due to the bad influence of my friends . . . and now I was paying with embarrassment. I felt cool air creep over my cock and balls as they dangled between my legs, felt it seep into the heated crack of my ass as my back arched and my hole peeked out for a look. I heard a "whoosh" of air come from my captor's mouth, and then his knees kicked my feet farther apart as he dropped down between them.

His hands began kneading the meaty mounds at the top of my ass. Soon, he was putting a firm pressure on them, grinding into the flesh with his knuckles. I wheezed as my ass began wiggling of its own accord . . . "squirming" might be a better way to describe its behavior. It was humiliating to be at his whim—and so enjoying it. My body was relinquishing control to him.

"Uuuuhhhhh!" I gasped as his fingertips brushed lightly down my ass crack, drawing two straight lines on either side of my slit. The tickling of the hairs and sensitive flesh surrounding it caused it to sink inward. I so wanted him to make another pass.

"Beautiful fuckin' hole," he grunted, but his fingers were now dancing over my scrotum, not pausing or hesitating, moving right on to my dangling balls and then slipping down the shaft of my heavy, hanging cock. One finger found the head, circled it, and captured the precum that was streaming from it. He slobbered the juice all over my shaft and slowly stroked it.

I tensed, afraid I was going to shoot my wad prematurely. I was so on the verge I couldn't stand it.

But he seemed to catch on. His hand left my cock and returned to my balls. He laced his fingers into the forest of hair covering them, and tugged. There were a thousand little intense stabs as each follicle was challenged at its root. They held on strong and resisted the strain, carrying my balls back with them. Then they were released and my balls swung like a pendulum between my legs as his fingers nipped at the hair on my perineum and back up my ass valley, which had been so recently treated with delicacy. My slit seemed as appreciative of the rough play as it had been of the tenderness.

Then everything stopped.

I waited. I became incredibly aware of my own body . . .

totally naked, completely exposed. Scrunched under this coffee table, the edge of which was resting on my lower back. My ass sticking way up in the air, with no form of protection. Waiting for who knew what. Waiting. It seemed like an eternity. How much time had passed? Ten minutes? Twenty? Forty? An hour? Had he forgotten about me? Fallen asleep? Gone back downstairs? No, I would've heard him leave. Was he just standing there looking at my ass, balls, and cock, all completely accessible for him to objectify? Why did I just wait and not say anything? I was almost ready to call to him to ask what was going on.

That's when a large object jammed against my ass slot. Although my asshole was thrilled at the touch, I feared what it might be—it felt rather large. And dry. I prayed he wasn't going to stick some obscene inanimate object up inside me without any sort of lube.

The object ran its way up and down my crack, and then found my balls. They were pushed gently from side to side. Then they came to rest on something. It felt like he had put a book under them. Or a plate. He was about to have my balls on a platter. The adrenaline seemed to be swimming inside them. They were swollen with anticipation. But within a second, they felt like one of those balls that's tied by a rubber band to a small wooden paddle: they were being lightly bounced along this flat surface. I was extremely concerned for their well-being. Any harder of a tap, and they'd be screaming in agony. Right now, they were just being harassed enough to be curious as to their fate.

There was an ever-so-soft pat on my ass cheek. Then

my other ass cheek. Then both at once. Then the pattern was repeated. And once more, only with a little more pressure. And again. More pressure. And then steadily, in a distinct rhythm, like a metronome keeping time on a piano. With each contact, there was more strength put behind the swing, so slight an increase that it would have been unrealistic to suddenly yell "Ow!" So I took it . . . and liked it. Heat rushed to the domes of my ass, and I could feel them turning red.

Steady and continuous: thwack, thwack, thwack, thwack, thwack, thwack, thwack, thwack, thwack, thwack, thwack, thwack. The sound bounced off the walls.

My buns couldn't take the assault. Too much stimulation. Overload. Some of the excitement had to be rechanneled. My left leg began shaking uncontrollably as the intensity grew. The entire coffee table was vibrating along with it. My ass was on fire; my throat was letting out a long, continuous "Uuuuuuuuuuhhhhhhhhhhhhhh."

Suddenly, nothing. Silence. I hitchily inhaled some air. My head was spinning. The darkness behind my lids was filled with colored spots of light.

THWACK!!!

The room echoed at the sound, precum poured from my piss hole, my ass must have gotten far redder, and I did scream . . .

. . . and then I heard it. A quiet, short giggle, almost boyish. He was enjoying this, enjoying making me melt . . . enjoying bringing me a sick sort of joy—making me give in to something I had so long denied.

THWACK! THWACK! THWACK! THWACK!

The friction was like lava between the surface of the paddle and my ass. My bark was more controlled this time. Now, the pounding was more evenly spaced and less frequent, but HARD. At the tops of my cheeks. Near the bottom. Dead center. Left cheek. Right cheek. My entire bottom was scorched. Behind the blackness of my blindfold, I envisioned the paddle gripped firmly in his huge hands, swatting my ass with the strength of his bulging arms, perhaps a bit of sweat dripping down his stony features as he inflicted the punishment. All the times I had smiled so coyly at him, egging him on, testing to see if he would want me if he could have me. I deserved this. I was a cock tease.

"I deserve it!" I yapped, appalled at my admission. "Teach me a lesson!"

"That's right, my little bitch whore. This'll keep you in line."

That was the last thing he said. He administered my punishment until I was sure my butt was about to begin bruising. I wondered what it looked like right now. I was guaranteed to have nasty welts tomorrow. I couldn't believe I was allowing myself to be treated this way . . . as if I had a choice in the matter. OK. I could've stopped it sooner. But I didn't know it was going to come to this . . . really.

The paddling stopped, at last. I needed relief. It burned. Burned so bad. It was beyond me how someone could enjoy making another person feel such pain . . . and how he could do it so well.

I became restless. I unconsciously tugged at my bonds.

I needed to squelch the fire on my ass. Then I heard the sound of a refrigerator door opening behind me. What was he doing?

My nerves jumped, my balls shrank, my nipples sharpened into points, and a shiver ran through every fiber of my body at the freezing-cold temperature of whatever touched my ass next. The contact was soft, but the shock to my system was unbearable. This subzero object was run smoothly over my flaming bottom, and I could almost hear the steam sizzling off the surface as ice met fire. There was a confusing combination of relief and discomfort from the cold, which caused a burning of its own due to its temperature. My cheeks were quickly going numb. Then my balls . . . They were hard as stone as the icy object covered every inch of them.

And then he did it. He brought the object between my cheeks. He used one hand to part my cheeks and the cold traveled the outer rim of my fuck chute. My asshole became a funnel, sucking away from the arctic object. I squealed.

"That's right. This hot hole is begging for it. Look at that baby pucker. Beautiful hungry fucking hole."

I got an idea of what was about to happen to me, but it wasn't going to be as soon as I expected. Over the table, he grabbed my hair and pulled my head back.

"Suck on this," he commanded, and my mouth opened to a chilly cherry-flavored phallus. I sucked greedily. Popsicle. "That's right. Make that baby all nice and wet for me."

The pop was pulled from my mouth, leaving a coating of sweet spittle on my lips, and danced across my ass and balls once more. Then it made my fuck hole pulse again. He was toying with me. I needed to feel it so bad.

Finally, he pushed forward. My asshole fought to fend off the icicle that invaded it. The sensation assaulting the nerve endings in my fuck hole sent chills through my body.

"Aaahhhhh!!!" was all I could manage.

Then it was in me, opening me up, numbing my tunnel while simultaneously making it come alive. It didn't waste any time. It punctured my sphincter and worked its way savagely up my works. Yet, at the same time, I felt my intruder shrinking inside me as my hole melted it rapidly.

"That's right, eat it all up," the handyman coaxed. One big arm encircled my entire ass, fingers wedged between my cheeks to keep them apart, while the other hand rapidly drilled away at me. "We got a whole box here for this hungry pink hole."

I wondered how many Popsicles came in a box as the nearly diminished ice dildo was removed and another full-sizer was jammed up my ass. My thermal fuck cavern immediately went to work on it. I was groaning, crying out, and shaking all over now as my body became one giant erogenous zone. By the fourth chilly treat, I began to settle in and enjoy the ride. Receiving each new Popsicle was like experiencing the sensation for the first time. My inner walls were stunned with each gnawing invasion.

As Popsicle number five was being consumed, I realized I wasn't even there anymore. It was just my handyman and his pretty pink pucker, as he was now calling it. His fuckin' hungry pretty pink pucker. In my temporary blindness, I was completely removed from my body, shut off from the world. Willing to give him time alone with my ass. In between Popsicles, he'd smother the cheeks in kisses, lick and suck sticky sweet cherry juice off my balls and butt, dig his face into the crack and lap the red goo from hole and hair.

By Popsicle number six, handyman's face practically got stuck in between the cheeks as he drowned in cherry juice, which created a temporary glue between his sharp whiskers and pretty pink pucker's surrounding coat of fur.

Finally, he hit the bottom of the box. Eight Popsicles had been consumed. The hole was a dripping mess, yet totally unsatisfied. Ass flesh was still hot. Cock and balls swollen. Rectum wanting to expel the buildup like nobody's business. The pucker was sure it was not going to be able to hold back the torrent of liquid that wanted to gush forth, but the handyman stopped it up quick. And his rod was bigger than any Popsicle the pucker had yet encountered.

Then, I was back. I cried out in rhythm to the pounding I was getting. Cherry juice spilled freely from my aching fuck slit as the handyman's cock dipped repeatedly into the pool my pucker had become. The built-up pressure in my fuck cavern was steadily relieved as he screwed the juice out of me. Juice that refused to be forced farther into me and leaked out from all sides of his jackhammering cock. My pucker was slobbering all over itself. The handyman was hell-bent on torturing my swollen ass. He would tickle it ever so gently with his fingers as he rammed deep inside me, and then follow that with unmerciful open-handed slaps. My fist wanted so badly to grab my cock and beat the jizz out of it.

The coffee table I was tied to and stuck under seemed ready to collapse as it was shaken by the handyman's weight. It creaked and groaned as loudly as I did as he came down on it with his stomach, pumping into my upraised ass. His bulging thighs ricocheted repeatedly off my butt, driving me into the ground while a mess of gooey liquid attempted to paste our flesh together.

And then the handyman vacated me, ripped off my blindfold, and was standing in front of me. He yanked off his condom and tossed it across the room, then leaned over and undid one of my wrists. Without hesitation, my hand went for my cock. I began tugging furiously on it while the handyman did the same to his cock . . . which was poised before my upraised face. I did my best to lap at his dick and balls as he reached over the table and dug two, three, and then, unbelievably, four fingers of his other hand up my ass. His fists seemed unable to distinguish which was doing what job, so both worked briskly. He slapped away at his cock while nearly his entire hand gave my asshole—and particularly my prostate—an agonizingly deep tissue massage.

I thought I was going to bust a gut as I came. His cock was smacking me inadvertently across the face as I let loose with a stream that had my asshole clamping down on his fingers. I thought this finally reminded him that this was a *person's* asshole he was tearing away at, because his hand stopped, but actually he had merely gotten distracted.

My eye got the first gusher. Then his hot cum streaked across my face, covering my lips, clogging one of my nostrils. He screamed out a bunch of expletives in sync with his expulsion.

When at last we both finished, each of us panting, me with my throat sore and hoarse from so much guttural expression, he dropped onto his back on the sofa bed and blindly reached for my other bound wrist and undid it. I crawled out stiffly from under the table and used a nearby leftover from my jeans to swipe most of the cum from my eyes, nose, mouth, and cheeks.

I dropped face-first onto his chest, completely spent, and breathed in his now-pungent sweat. His chest heaved up and down and carried me with it. At last, I found the energy to look up at him. He looked down wordlessly at me.

"You're a fucking bastard!" I griped.

And there was that charming, slight smile at the corner of his mouth. "You ain't felt nothing yet."

He brought his face toward mine and began sucking some remnants of cum and cherry juice off my bottom lip and chin.

Critic's Choice

Karl Taggart

I didn't tell him I was a writer until after I'd fucked him and even then wasn't totally honest about it. He was a well-known literary critic; I was a pornographer. Match made in hell.

At first I didn't realize who he was. He'd turned from the bar to survey the room and caught my eye. Slim, elegant, dressed in dark slacks and white turtleneck jersey. Graying hair, high forehead, cerebral look. He was incredibly handsome. He had an aristocratic face, the kind you'd expect to see in some English country manor or maybe the House of Lords: high cheekbones, sharp chin, everything sculpted, perfect, but still the hint of softness that age brings. Not always unwelcome, I'd found, especially in guys like this. I knew instantly what he wanted and moved in. He bought me a drink and got his hand onto my crotch, groping until I was hard, tracing the length of my cock, rubbing it along my thigh.

We took a cab to his condo in that burgeoning area of San Francisco called South Beach. It was there that I found out who he was. *Holy shit*, I thought. He'd said he was Jason but a glance at his bookshelf told me he was Jason Falk. Recognition hit full force. My cock went limp—along with the rest of me.

He offered a drink and I took it, downed it quickly while he undid my jeans, got his mouth on me. As he licked and pulled, I savored the feel but found there was something between us—that reputation of his: literary predator. He had destroyed more than one up-and-coming writer.

I'd had no idea he was gay. I knew him only by his penetrating essays and scathing reviews, watching as he deconstructed everyone and everything he encountered. Sexual orientation, even now, seemed a minor point, but here he was sucking dick like the rest of us. Suddenly human.

Who he was soon mattered little. When he had me hard, he rose and stripped. He had to be a good forty-five, but it was a well-maintained middle age. Only the slightest thickening at the waist, a smattering of gray in his pubes. His chest was smooth, nipples dark. Not a particularly muscular build, but trim. His foreskin was ample, cockhead concealed, his balls riding low in the sac. The sight of him made my cock twitch.

"Fuck me," he said when he stood naked. No kissing, no prelims, just an overpowering need. He led me to his bedroom, pointed to a bowl of condoms and a jar of lube, then crawled onto the bed, got on all fours, stuck his rump up at me. He reached back and pulled open his cheeks. His hole pulsed at me.

His hips were narrow, the kind I liked; his crack nearly hairless. I stripped, then ran a gob of grease into him and he moaned, squirmed, started riding my fingers. When I pulled out he began chanting "Fuck me," and I did it, shoved my prick into him and just kept going, thrusting full out from the very first. He started a kind of keening sound and I could tell he was absolutely gone, that life for him was a dick up the ass, fuck literature.

I made things last. Every time I felt the rise, I eased up, which caused him to squirm and moan and beg. It was apparent that he liked to be ridden hard. When I'd pick up the pace he'd squeeze his muscle with approval, let out a groan.

Twice I added lube, enjoying the sight of his gaping hole. He got a hand on his dick now and then but didn't do any stroking. Everything was about me doing him, him taking all I could give and still wanting more. When I finally let go, I made it known, pounding him until his butt cheeks were red and liquefied lube ran down onto his balls. I let out a verbal stream as well, him still doing his fuck-me chant, me doing a fuck-you back at him, louder with each squirt until I could have been screaming, who the hell knew at that point.

When I pulled out, he rolled onto his back and pulled his legs high, the ultimate presentation: stiff cock dripping precum, asshole dripping as well. He was breathing hard and I knew he was ready for the grand finale. I shoved two fingers into him and with my other hand grabbed his dick and started pumping and it was at this point that I again thought about who he was. The world saw him as inviolate, the almighty critic, judge, jury, and executioner, but I knew the reality. He let out a cry as he came, eyes closed, head pushed back into the pillow. His cock—substantial, uncut—shot big gobs of jizz up onto his chest as his entire body shuddered through the climax. Afterward he lay inert, silent. I simply watched.

"Karl, wasn't it?" he said finally, eyes still closed.

"Yes."

"What do you do for a living, Karl?"

"Why do you ask?"

"I like to know something about the men who fuck me."

"I'm a writer."

The pause was significant, and I wondered if he thought I'd orchestrated this to get into his good graces, manuscript concealed somewhere in the heap of clothes on the floor.

"Indeed," he said. "What do you write?"

I've never been ashamed of what I do, am quite proud actually, but at that moment, with that man, it wasn't the disclosure I wanted to make. "Novels, short stories."

"And are you published?"

"Yes. The stories, not the novels."

"Any I might have seen?"

"I doubt it. Small magazines."

"But you persevere."

"Yes, I persevere."

"Good."

Suddenly I couldn't resist telling him, "I didn't know who you were at first."

"And you do now?"

"I caught a look at your books when we came in."

"Ah, the essays, yes. Bit of a giveaway. Not a problem, is it, fucking the critic? Every writer's dream, I'd imagine."

He rolled over onto his side, propped up on one elbow, and studied me, hand tracing my nipples, stomach, then getting down to my cock. "Magnificent," he said as he petted it.

When I began to harden, he crawled down and got me into his mouth again, sucking fiercely, as if we'd just begun. He got a hand onto my balls and worked everything until his face was flushed and sweat beaded across his forehead. He pulled back and said, "I need so much more. Can you stay?" He licked the tip of my dick for emphasis.

"Sure," I told him, and I pushed him down onto my cock, made him take it until I was ready, then got him onto his back, got his legs up, and made him wait while I pulled on another rubber, lubed my dick. The sight of him like that intoxicated me and I knew I'd stay as long as he wanted, maybe longer. The best thing about a writer's life is there are no hours. The only thing I get up for is a good lay.

"Fuck me," Jason murmured, more to himself, I thought, than to me. I'd enjoyed a few pig bottoms, but this guy's energy was a different kind of relentless. I got the idea this was all part of who he was, that maybe after destroying people on paper he needed to do penance in bed—get reamed over and over after he'd undoubtedly spent the day doing the equivalent to someone's life work. I found myself aroused by the opportunity to issue punishment. After all, how many writers get to fuck a critic? I let my dick hover at his hole, poking around like some anteater looking for a meal. "Fuck me," Jason said, louder this time. He held on to his cock, which remained soft, and kept his legs high. I could tell he loved the position—abject, submissive; stark contrast to the man on paper. Literary top, sexual bottom. I smiled as this ran through my mind and, in acknowledgment, pushed my cock into him.

We kept it up for hours, drinking and fucking until dawn came, then falling into a heavy sleep. When I awoke I had no idea the time and was alone in the bed. I got up, washed my face, wrapped a towel around my waist, and went to find Jason.

He was at his desk, clad in a green silk robe. He typed steadily, even when I came up behind him. "Have a good sleep?" he asked, fingers still hitting the keys. I knew how that was, how you can get words lined up in your head and carry on a conversation while still typing, nothing able to derail you.

"What are you writing?" I asked.

"A review of the new Fleming book. I started it yesterday, then went out instead and met you. I must get back to it."

"Is the book any good?" I'd read all of Tony Fleming's novels, thought them wonderful, looked forward to the new one.

Jason sighed, stopped typing, and sat back. "He's done better."

"You liked his other work?"

"Not particularly, but at least it was coherent. This new one is an exhibitionistic jumble, the kind of peacock display that gives literature a bad name."

I put my hands on his shoulders, dug my fingers in. He squirmed with discomfort. "You must let me finish," he said, and put his hands back on the keyboard. I let him type a couple lines, but the thought of what he was doing stirred me. My cock was filling, and as he pounded the keys I slid my hands down inside his robe and pulled it open.

"Karl."

"That's enough criticism for a while."

"But I have to—"

I pulled the chair from under him, which sent him to the floor. There I held him down, stripped away the robe, rolled him onto his stomach, and stuck a finger up his ass. "You don't have to do a goddamned thing," I growled. As I lubed him with spit, I thought about fucking him until he expired, obliterating that anger he vented on us, venom fueled by his own inadequacy, because critics were usually failed writers who'd turned.

"Karl, please," he said, as if there were a struggle taking place when in reality he lay waiting, pucker twitching in anticipation of his punishment. I pulled open his cheeks, stared at the eager hole, and he said it again, "Please," but this time the plea was there, he wanted his penance. He had to be taken.

"You want me to fuck you," I said, and he uttered a long, high-pitched moan, then turned around and stuck his ass up at me. When I made no move, he pulled apart his cheeks, worked his muscle so his hole opened and closed like a fish mouth. Still I waited, and he worked his own finger over to his rim, played around, then went in. "You need a dick up there, don't you, Jason. You need fucking in the worst way."

"Please," he rasped as he fingered himself.

"What do you want?" I teased, sitting back on my haunches. "You have to tell me."

"Stick your cock in me. Fuck me."

"How much fucking do you need, Jason?"

"Lots," he said with a whimper. "I need cock; I have to have it. There is never enough."

I lubed my swollen meat and got up behind him, prodded his hole, and he cried out, "Christ almighty, do it!"

I hesitated, savoring the final moment, the ultimate control, then shoved my prick into him in one stroke. In response he let out a yell that sounded like a mix of pain and pleasure, just what he wanted. As I thrust steadily into his eager rectum, I thought how we were perfect for each other, he doing his penance with his ass, me exacting revenge with my cock. We may have been on opposite sides of the literary equation, but in bed we were the ideal couple. He the insatiable critic, me the inexhaustible writer—the ideal critic's choice.

For the Asking

David Wayne

People are always asking me how I met Travis, and I always tell them that we met here at The Pub, which is true enough. If they want more details . . . well, I generally make 'em up fresh every time. That's why there are so many conflicting stories about Travis and me. I always loved a mystery. I've discovered that I love *being* a mystery even more.

But you say that Jamie told you to ask me. Well, that's something else entirely. That means I'm going to tell you the true story of Travis and me and the night we met, and I swear, Scout's Honor, that it's the real true story.

And maybe, by the time I'm done, you'll understand why I'm telling it to you.

I first met Travis right here, on the very spot where you and I are standing now. It was a Thursday night—The Pub is always cruisiest on Thursdays for God-knows-what reason. The place was packed from bar to back room with men, but Travis caught my attention the instant he pushed through the door. He just didn't fit in. Hell, he didn't even make the effort to fit in. If anything, Travis's appearance was a concerted effort to hide just how handsome he was. In a room full of stretch Lycra, he was dressed in a pair of work-stained Levi's and a worn leather jacket. Beneath the stubble on his face, though, his jaw was hard and square; his T-shirt, timeworn and damp with sweat, clung to a torso that was finely muscled. I remember all of these details in retrospect, but at the time, they were eclipsed by one thing: his eyes. Piercing, playful, and squinted just slightly, Travis's eyes surveyed the room; I was acutely embarrassed when his gaze locked onto mine as if he had sensed my stare. I became even more embarrassed when he began to wade toward me. He walked through the crowd like he was haunting the place. People shivered and stepped away as he passed, but no one turned to see what had disturbed them.

At last he reached me. His eyes scanned me up and down, then he turned and pressed his firm belly against the bar railing.

Jamie was the bartender that night, like he is every Thursday night. I knew Jamie in the usual ways that gay guys get to know each other. He was the ex of an ex, for one thing. Furthermore, I'd sucked him off once in the sauna of one of the local bathhouses. I was pretty sure, though, that Jamie didn't remember that little incident.

The point is that the bar was a din of chattering voices and drumbeats, and Jamie was having trouble keeping up with the orders. He appraised Travis's threadbare appearance and filed him in the "light tipper" category before turning his attention to the other clamoring customers.

I found myself shouting, "Jamie, two beers."

Jamie looked at me, looked at Travis, then raised a disapproving eyebrow; but he dropped a pair of wet, brown bottles in front of us and scooped up the bills I'd laid out.

"One of these for me?" Travis gave me a half smile.

"If you want," I answered.

Travis stared at me for an uncomfortably long time.

"Yeah, I want." He took a swig from the beer I'd bought. I watched his Adam's apple bob as he swallowed, and I felt something kindle in my groin. Those flames were fanned when Travis shrugged out of his jacket, revealing a broad chest and beautifully muscled arms.

"My name's Jack," I said, sticking out a hand in greeting.

Travis took it, his hand warm and firm in my grasp.

"I'm Travis. It's a pleasure." He released my hand, letting his fingertips graze my palm. He looked me in the eye as he did this, his eyes kindling with thinly veiled amusement.

I was at a loss. I hate that awkward moment when you meet someone in a bar and it's not clear whether or not you're going to fuck, so you have to find something to talk about.

"So, what do you do?" I hazarded lamely.

"What do you mean?"

"You know, your job."

He snorted into his beer. "Am I going to have to fill out a credit report, too?" His lips curled in a smile, signaling that he was enjoying my disorientation.

"Just curious I guess," I finally managed.

He was silent for a moment as he stared out into the crowd. "I hate pissing contests. No offense, but you don't care about my work. Fact is . . ." He turned to look at my face. "Fact is, I'd be disappointed if that was all you wanted."

His left hand slid down his side, his thumb catching in the belt loop, leaving his fingers curled next to the none-too-subtle bulge in his jeans. He watched me staring at his crotch, and then I felt his eyes slide down my body, giving me a similar appraisal. He gave a friendly laugh.

"Look," he said, "I know what you want. You know what you want. Why don't you just ask?"

His face was blank, his expression very matter-of-fact. I felt my stomach churn. I felt something twitch a bit farther south, too. He stretched casually, his T-shirt slithering up his torso to reveal his abdomen and the recess of his navel.

Maybe you'll find it difficult to believe how hard it was to say what I wanted. In my mind, I could see him naked. I could hear the rumble of his throat as passion lowered his voice to a growl. I could smell the musk of him. I could taste the sweat of him. The desire burgeoned within me, but the words couldn't get past the watchdog of my tongue.

He downed the last swallow of his beer and waggled the empty bottle. "Thanks for the beer."

He started to slip on his jacket, and I knew with

absolute certainty that he would leave—and that he wasn't going to make this any easier.

"Last chance," he said. "Just ask. What do you really want to do?"

"I . . . I want to sleep with you."

He smiled, a look of victory in his eyes.

"Well, I'm hoping that 'sleep' is a euphemism . . . but close enough. Come on." He took my hand and guided me through the dancing throng. As we stepped through the door, his hand slipped from my grip and moved to the small of my back, shepherding me through the densely packed vehicles—a Gordian knot of steel and fiberglass that wouldn't be untangled until closing time.

"There's no way you're going to get your car out of here," I said uselessly.

He gave me a wolfish grin. "Who says I have a car?"

And with that, he pulled me into the darkness of the alley behind the club. Moonlight spilled into the narrow space between the buildings like a waterfall into a grotto. The light glinted off the cases of empty bottles, and I could smell the stink of stale beer. As we slipped into the shadows, my hands trailed along the wall, and it pulsed beneath my fingers to the occult rhythm of the drum and bass seeping through the mortar.

The alley dead-ended, and we found ourselves in the darkened alcove of a disused back door. Travis leaned against the wall and pulled me into his grip. In the darkness, our lips met. Travis's arms encircled me, and I succumbed to his embrace as our tongues danced. The kiss seemed eternal, but eventually—painfully—it came to an end. I opened my eyes to meet Travis's stare.

"There's one condition," he said.

"A condition for what?"

"Sleeping with me."

I was no longer thinking about sleep, but I played along. "What's the condition?"

"You can sleep with me tonight, but first you have to fuck me as hard as you can."

"What, right here?" I said incredulously.

"Why wait?"

His hands were already pulling at my belt. It cinched tighter about my waist, then went loose. As his hands unfastened the top button of my jeans, he leaned into me, pushing me against the wall. One hand crept into my jeans and tugged playfully at the hair growing from my groin.

"No underwear?" he teased. "Naughty, naughty boy."

I heard my zipper descend as his hand slipped deeper into my pants. Like a curious dog, my cock rose up to sniff the stranger's hand. He grasped it firmly, noting its heft, then pulled it out through the open V of my fly. He squeezed and I swelled in his palm. With my stiffening cock as a leash, he pulled me toward him. Our lips met and his free hand grasped the back of my head, pulling our faces tighter. Our kiss was frenzied, and all the while he jerked roughly at my exposed prick until it stood out from my body like an embedded knife. I clutched his hips and thrust my groin against his, feeling something stiffen in reply within the denim enclosure of his jeans. I sucked his tongue into my mouth, chewing on it and bathing it with my saliva. Without breaking the coupling of our lips, I slid my hands around his waist to the top button of his jeans. He wasn't wearing a belt, and his fly seemed to burst open of its own accord. I pushed his jeans down his flanks, and was amused to hear the clatter of change as his pants pooled around his ankles. My fingers traced across his abdomen, dipping downward to find the root of his cock. I pushed at the base and found it as stiff and firm as my own. Our fingers brushed as we brought our cocks together within the confines of our two palms.

I broke our kiss, moving along his jawline to the tender flesh beneath and behind his ears. I bit gently and he moaned, crushing against me. He spread his legs, and I nudged my cock between his thighs. I drove forward, my prick forging through the forest of coarse hair behind his balls. The sensation of his rough hair against my cock's tender head was excruciating and exhilarating. The fingers of both my hands worked their way into his crack, and my right index finger found what I was searching for. His hole gaped open, and, slick with just the sweat of our bodies, the tip of my finger slipped inside him. He gasped, and I pushed deeper in reply. I strained forward with my hips, hoping to let my cock join my fingertip in the warmth of his asshole, but my dick's reach stopped agonizingly short. Travis's knees buckled slightly, but even that wasn't enough. There was a whisper in my ear, and it took a moment's concentration to recognize it as Travis's guttural chant of "Fuck me, fuck me, fuck me. . . ."

I pushed him away with my free hand, keeping my finger tucked into the opening of his chute. Wordlessly, I pushed on his shoulder, signaling him to turn around. He pivoted on his heel, but the tangle of his pants snared him. He tripped forward, catching himself with his hands on the wall opposite me, and let out a startled yelp. I drove my finger deeper inside him, and he yelped again, his muscles tightening. I pulled back slightly and he relaxed, then eased himself down onto my finger. I hunched my hips forward and let my cock burrow between his cheeks to crowd my busy finger. He sensed the pressure and pushed backward against me. I thrust my hips, nosing my dick in deeper and deeper into his crack. I was leaking lube, and with a few strokes he was wet.

He turned his face, and in the moonlight he was unmasked. The guarded irony had slipped away, and all that remained was desire. I didn't have to ask if he was ready. Pulling my finger out, I positioned the head of my prick at his opening. I thrust forward, and his knees buckled as I stabbed into him. There was a moment of eerie calm as we adjusted to each other's bodies. We were frozen at the brink of ecstasy. And then, clutching one another, we fell into it.

I won't say that that first time with Travis was indescribable—just that description doesn't do it justice. I'm sure you know what it's like to fuck a man, and I'm sure you know that even though the mechanics are roughly the same every time, every time it's different.

God was this different.

I didn't fuck Travis so much as ride him. He moved as if electrified. I grasped his writhing hips and plunged into him again and again, slamming against him as if he stood between me and ecstasy; my cock was a battering ram and his body the unyielding door. The alcove was cramped and the sounds we made were echoed and amplified. My ears were filled with the moist slapping of our bodies and the guttural sounds that had supplanted language. I felt something exploding behind my balls, and I pressed my face into his back, wishing that I'd gotten his jacket and shirt off so that I could taste his flesh. All sensation was eclipsed as I felt myself ejaculating inside him. I accented each spurt with a savage twist of my hips, and found that I was still thrusting long after I was spent, as if I'd forgotten how to do anything but fuck. At last my body stilled, and I slipped out of him, my cock deliciously raw. As I took in gulps of air, my spent passion turned to tenderness. My hands circled his waist and I kissed his neck.

"I kept my end of the deal," I whispered.

"Mm-hmm . . ." was his only reply.

I backed away, breathless, and leaned against the opposite wall of the doorway. Travis was still spread-eagle against the wall, his back heaving. In the monochrome moonlight, posed against the decaying brickwork, he looked for all the world like a Bill Costa photograph.

As I reached to pull up my trousers, he turned toward me. The first thing that caught the moonlight was the rigid shaft of his cock, so engorged it actually jerked with each beat of his heart. The second thing that caught the light was his face . . . and that wicked, wicked smile.

Travis is fast; everybody knows that. You can tell by his feline, feral bearing. But unless you've actually seen him move, you just can't appreciate it.

He was on me before I could let out even a squeak of surprise, and we fell in a tumble into the open air of the alley. I tried to say something—*anything,* but his lips silenced mine. His body was heavy on top of me, and I could feel the heat and insistent pressure of his cock between our bodies. At first all I could think was, *This jacket is CALFSKIN*—and then I just didn't care anymore.

My eyes closed, and I just let go.

Just as suddenly as he had leaped on me, he was gone. I opened my eyes in bewilderment, lifting myself onto my elbows. Something yanked my pants down around my ankles, then pushed my knees up to my chest. Instantly Travis was on top of me again, backlit by the moonlight, which was dim compared with the demonic light flashing in his eyes. I kicked feebly, my legs trapped by both his weight and the tangle of my pants. Something poked at the opening to my ass. I thought it was a finger until the sheer girth of it became apparent. I panicked, tightening against it. Travis's face dropped down to mine, and something in his kiss said, "Trust me."

Again, I let go.

Travis's hands were braced on my shoulders as his cock slowly worked its way into me. I was hungry to have him inside me. I writhed to accommodate him, but pinned as I was there was nothing I could do to speed the process. His cock crept into me with the stealth of an assassin and I was powerless beneath its advance. At last I gave up movement and lay still. It seemed like an eternity, but at last I felt the solid brace of his pelvis against my backside and knew that he had reached his limit. I felt his cock flex inside me, and I reveled in the fullness of it.

Just as slowly as it had entered, Travis's cock began to retreat, leaving a void as it withdrew. I would have begged him to fill me, but I'd forgotten language as such. I simply moaned in distress. When he actually popped out of me, I gave a cry. Travis laughed low in his throat, then kissed me. His tongue drove itself into my mouth, and just as suddenly, his cock drove itself back into my body. Soon he had worked out a rhythm, his tongue and cock collaborating to fuck me at both ends. I felt an uncomfortable pinch in my groin and realized that my stiffening prick was trapped pointing downward. I reached between us and pulled it free. Still wet with semen, it slipped easily between our bodies. I managed to get in a few strokes before Travis raised my arms over my head.

I think Travis could have continued until dawn at that excruciating pace, but as if cued from some external source, he began to increase the tempo of his thrusts. Unable to move my limbs, I focused my movements on my tongue and lips. I was intoxicated by the slide of his tongue in my mouth as it mirrored the slide of his cock in my ass. With each thrust, the rough texture of his belly sent a thrill through my cock. Travis broke the kiss, gasping for breath, but the intensity of his thrusting into my body didn't abate. My mouth uncovered, I began to cry, to howl. Travis was almost silent, but I could feel the rumble of a barely audible growl in his chest.

I looked up, and the stars were eyes, looking down on us, and I knew that Travis and I, at that moment, were the center of the universe—that everything was watching us. The epiphany pushed me over the edge and the orgasm hit me like a tidal wave. Travis cried out, and he thrust deeper than he'd been before. I felt my bowels fill with the warmth and wetness of him. He hovered above me, trembling, and didn't move or speak until his softening cock was expelled from my body.

I opened my eyes to look at him, and found myself

frozen in fear instead. Above us, there were no stars—only eyes and leering faces. Five, ten, fifteen men encircled us. Travis sensed my tension and looked around. He said nothing, simply extracted himself from my embrace and stood up. He offered me his hand, still keeping a wary eye on the onlookers. I accepted his help and pulled myself to my feet, feeling foolish with my pants around my ankles, and thinking that I didn't want to die like that.

One of the faces stepped forward, and there was a familiarity to him that I didn't immediately recognize. He looked different in the night air, away from the strobe lights and smoke machines. It wasn't until he spoke that I recognized him.

"Um . . . ," he said. "Can I be next?"

My God, I thought. *It's Jamie.*

So that's how I met Travis, and that's how our little organization got started. Weekly meetings are held every Thursday behind The Pub. No trouble with the cops because we've got two cops in the club. No trouble with the bar because . . . well, because we've got Jamie.

Jamie liked you enough to tell you to talk to me. I can see Jamie made a good choice, and I can see by the look in your eye what your answer is going to be, but I have to ask you the question anyway, because it's club rules. Yeah, I can tell what you want just by looking at you, but it doesn't mean anything if you don't say it yourself.

So here's your chance. Just ask. What do you really want to do?

Getting It Write

Dale Chase and Austin Foxxe

The last thing I do Friday night at the magazine is send Darren Davis a copy of the latest issue, which features one of his stories. As I write his address on the label—22 Alvarado Street—I realize I've memorized it, and feel a twinge of pleasure. I like Darren a lot—even though we've never met. Our relationship is conducted purely via e-mail: him the writer, myself the editor. We've known each other for over a year, and in that time a kind of friendship has grown along with our working relationship. There are lots of writers in our stable, but none portray man sex quite like Darren. Nor do they give it that touch of romance that, for me, brings it full circle. He's got a distinctive style, with highly charged scenes full of raw emotion. I always look forward to his stories, always read them first. Now, I glance at the address and wonder what he looks like, what he's up to at the moment.

It's late when I leave the office. The parking garage is nearly empty and, as I head toward my car, movement in the shadows catches my eye. I detour from my path and slow my pace, cautiously approaching a blow job in progress. A dark-haired guy in jeans is on his knees, head bobbing at the crotch of a blond who watches his partner intently. My own dick stirs at the sight, but then, I'm already primed from reading several of Darren's latest stories. What Darren started, I suddenly long to finish, and I move in and let myself be seen. The blond looks at me and, when I put a hand to my package, he nods. My approach remains cautious, but it's more to avoid startling the guy with the dick in his mouth than any real apprehension. I pull my cock out when I reach them and the blond takes hold and starts stroking it while I lean in and kiss him.

We keep at it for a few minutes, a hot little threesome. Then the guy in jeans rises and I'm handed off to him. His grasp is firm, his hand callused. My meat is dripping now and when he slides his other hand down onto my ass, I let out a welcoming moan. He prods a bit, then goes down to his knees where my dick waits. He takes it into his mouth and begins to suck, and I am conscious of little more than my overwhelming need. He works me steadily, and when I withdraw and begin to shoot my load I see stars—literally—as I feel a sudden impact and sharp pain at the back of my head. My final seconds of consciousness are spent holding my dick, as if doing so might somehow keep me upright.

I awaken to daylight and concrete against my cheek. I'm cold, and a throbbing pain radiates from the back of my head. The light that works its way into my eyes is painful. I close them and think of where I am, but have no idea beyond on a cold floor.

When I sit up my head reels and I think I might vomit. My pants are unzipped, but otherwise I seem intact. I stand slowly, shakily, and have to steady myself against a wall. It's when I've finally gained a bit of balance that I realize I have no idea where I am. A few cars are parked nearby. Is one mine? I check my pockets for keys and find none. No wallet, either. Just me. What on earth has happened?

I find the stairs and end up on Hollywood Boulevard, but know this only from the sign at the corner. Nothing is familiar. As I watch the light change, I search for where it is that I belong and discover that I don't know. Threads of panic begin to tighten around me, even as I tell myself to stay calm, that it will all come back. I reach up to the sore spot on my head and feel a crusty lump. Have I fallen and hit my head, momentarily jarring my memory?

I sit on a bus bench and try to recollect my life, but all I find is an empty slate. The more I try to remember, the less there seems to be, as if my efforts are pushing things away. And then I get to the most basic question of all, the one we never ask: Who am I? It has to be there. You don't lose your name. I look down at my palms as if the lines might give me a clue. Nothing. Pure panic sets in then, a chilling wave that makes my stomach churn. I am truly adrift. There are signs everywhere, plenty of places to go, but none hold reason for me.

I draw my legs up and circle my arms around them, closing into what I have of myself—a body, nothing more. I'm real, I tell myself. I'm here. Misplaced for the moment, but someone nevertheless.

I have no idea how long I sit there. Buses come and go, people sit next to me, then depart. When I look at my wrist to check the time, I take comfort because the gesture is automatic, something of the life that has escaped me. The pale stripe of skin at the wrist makes me realize my watch has been taken, and to finally confront the fact that I've been mugged. Hit on the head, everything stolen, left in a parking garage. There was undoubtedly a car with my name on it, and I watch traffic for a bit as if I might see myself drive by, but nothing triggers a memory.

The sun is high overhead when I make myself get up and start walking. But to where? I concentrate on that, on finding where I belong. As blocks pass, a number comes to mind: 22. I look at a building address: 5460. My number is too small, but still, it has to mean something. I cling to it, repeat it over and over as I wander into a gas station. In the office I note a wall map of Hollywood. An X marks "You are here." I look at crisscrossing streets, but their numbers elude me. I go to the bathroom, pee, then look into the mirror. It's frightening to confront yourself for the first time, to see yourself as new when you know you're not. It's beyond comprehension. I look away, panic seizing me, then force myself to go back and search the face: young, dark hair, brown eyes, nice-looking. Maybe 22 is my age.

I finally have to look away, because the mirror can't give me what I want. I go back outside and sit on a curb, reciting my number like a mantra. And then, as if I've finally gotten past the overture, the rest of it comes to me: Alvarado. Alvarado Street. I spring to my feet and hurry inside to the map, so anxious that the clerk has to help me. "There it is," he says after a search. "About a mile away."

"Which direction?"

He points me out the door and up the street. "Turn right, then go up six or seven blocks."

"Thanks. You've just saved a life."

He gives me a skeptical look, and I run out to the sidewalk, rushing along until the throb in my head asserts itself and makes me dizzy. I slow to a walk and finally reach 22 Alvarado Street.

I linger out front, because the place brings me nothing. Since I've recalled the address, I expect a kind of homecoming, that relief when you return to your own place after a long trip. Instead, I feel like a foreigner.

It's a small wood-frame bungalow on a tiny lot, white with dark green trim. The neighborhood is old, though well kept. There's no car in the driveway. Of course not— it's back in the parking garage where all this started. I go up to the door and try it, knowing it will be locked because people are careful about such things. I go along the porch and try a window and, as I tug at it, the front door opens.

"Hey!" a male voice says. "What are you doing?"

I freeze, lost again. I stand with my mouth open, unable to speak because I have no idea what to say. My heart starts pounding, my head reeling, and I have to steady myself against the house. The guy comes over. "You all right?"

"Not really," I say as my legs start to buckle. He grabs me, keeps me from falling, and helps me inside, where he eases me down onto a sofa.

This is a mistake. Act first, think about it later: It's my greatest failing, and now look where it's gotten me. This guy looks so out of it. "How about some water," I say as he slumps on the sofa. He nods, and I know something is going on in him, but I'm not sure I want to know what. I'm not into the drug scene, though he appears to be. He damn well better not OD on me.

He drinks half the water, then looks up at me, and I think he might cry. "What's wrong with you?" I ask.

He shakes his head and answers: "You won't believe me."

"Try."

"I got mugged in a parking garage and I can't remember anything." He rubs the back of his head.

"Let me take a look," I say, and he bends forward, lets me examine him.

"Here," he says, and I see the patch of dried blood, the crusty gash.

"We should get you to an emergency room," I tell him. "If you can't remember anything, you've probably got a concussion."

"OK, but can I rest here a little bit? I think the worst is past, I just can't remember."

"Anything?"

He shakes his head, then stops and looks at me. "Nothing except this address."

I pause. This is getting eerie. I've lived here six years and know he's never been a guest. I clearly recall even the most casual pickups.

"You know this address?"

"I thought since I remembered it that I lived here."

Now it's not only eerie, it's sad. I'm starting to feel for the guy, not to mention noting how cute he is. Younger than me, late twenties maybe, my type: small and slim. "Hate to tell you this, but you don't."

"I kinda figured that when it didn't look familiar. I thought it would all come back—you know, that seeing something familiar would trigger everything. But it's like this wall has gone up and I'm feeling my way along, looking for the door, only all I get is more wall."

"Why don't you lie down," I say. "Rest a bit. It's all right."

I get a wet cloth and clean the blood off his head, then apply an antiseptic. When he's cleaned up, I fight an urge to take him into my arms and comfort him. I'm such a sucker for underdogs.

He stretches out on the sofa and I sit across from him. I think of stories about this kind of thing and how contrived they are. Such a convenient gimmick, except now it's real—not only that, it's stumbled into my living room.

"You can't recall anything?" I ask again.

He shakes his head and utters a small cry. I tell him I'm sorry, that I didn't mean to press. "It must feel awful."

He offers a sharp laugh and I let it alone, try another tack. "I'm Bill Larsen," I tell him. "I live here alone and work for an insurance company downtown. Any of that ring a bell?"

"No."

"Odd that you know this address but don't know me. There must be some connection."

"If there is, I don't remember what it is."

"OK, how about we just start from scratch, like two guys who just met. You hungry?"

"Not really."

"Well, I'm gonna fix us something anyway."

I'm scrambling eggs when he joins me in the kitchen, refills his water glass, and slides onto a stool at the counter. My cat, Mickey, is underfoot and hops up into his lap. "If he bothers you, just push him off," I say, but the two become instant friends. I like that.

"How about we give you a temporary name," I suggest. "Just until we figure out who you are."

He's rubbing Mickey's neck. "Sure. Why not? Gotta start somewhere."

"OK." I take a long look at him and run down a mental list of names, settling on one I think fits him. "How about Alex?"

He says it a couple times. "Yeah, I guess."

"Fine." I set a plate of eggs in front of him. "Let's eat, Alex."

We don't say a whole lot during our meal. I mean, how do you talk to an amnesiac? I know I should get him to a hospital, but my mother hen side has kicked in and besides, there's something about him I really like—a kind of sweetness I haven't encountered in a while. When he finally starts eating, he does so with a smile, and I feel a little rush, as if I'm claiming him in some way. I remind myself he's a lost soul, not some stray dog I can rescue, but that thought makes him even more appealing.

After breakfast he asks if he can shower. "I woke up on a concrete floor and I feel really grungy."

"No problem."

As I step into the shower, I experience an awful moment as I realize I could be stepping into my own shower and not know the difference. Under the warm spray, I try to calm myself. I push away the uncertainty and concentrate on Bill, who has taken me in without question. Not many people would do that. I have no idea who I am, but being with Bill is somehow very comforting. The way he talks seems vaguely familiar, as if we've spoken many times before, but that can't be. Maybe it's just wishful thinking. He's attractive, after all, and self-assured, yet so warm and open. As I soap myself I think I'd like to get to know him a lot better—once I figure out who the hell I am.

While he showers, I sit and think of how real life is too absurd for fiction. Nobody would believe this if I wrote it. My editor would laugh at such an idea, yet here it is, the honest-to-goodness truth. When I hear the water stop I remain seated. Alex comes out wearing just a towel. His dark hair is wet and curly. His chest is smooth, with subtle definition. He stands in the doorway and says he feels better, but he looks like he's about to cry. I go to him, wrap my arms around him, and tell him he's not alone.

“We’ll figure it out,” I say. “Until then you can stay here with me.”

“But you don’t know anything about me.”

“Well, you don’t either, so that makes us even. Besides, I like what I see.” I look into his brown eyes, so trusting, so vulnerable, and I can’t hold myself in check. I lean in and kiss him and it’s like everything in me turns loose, all that emotion I usually spend on the page suddenly boils over. He responds without hesitation and I lead him to the bedroom.

He drops the towel and I get a look at all of him as his cock starts to fill. I reach down and take it in hand, and he moans and squirms as I pull. I get my lips on his again, get my tongue into his mouth. Seconds later I’m out of my clothes and easing him back onto the bed. “My mystery man,” I tell him between kisses. “My Alex from nowhere.”

I don’t think the mystery part has any influence on what happens next, because we are soon beyond any kind of who’s who. I’ve got my face in his crotch, sucking dick, and he’s doing the reverse, feeding on mine like a starving animal. We lie this way for some time, gorging ourselves on each other, and then he surfaces, climbs up onto me. His cock is against mine, he’s gently humping, and he tells me, with the sweetest smile, “Right now I don’t care who the hell I am. This just feels like home.”

“I know what you mean.” I give him a long kiss, then roll him over onto his back, pull up his legs, and slide a finger into him. He clamps his muscle and I know I’m gonna solve him, that I’m going to get inside him literally and figuratively. I pull on a condom, get myself lubed, then push into him. All the while my eyes are on his because the connection is more than just cock and ass. When I start to pump, he smiles, then laughs. Tears are on his cheeks now and I think maybe he's seeing how crazy it all is but that, like me, he knows it's right, that we've been thrown together in the craziest way and it may be the best thing ever.

I lean down and kiss him while I thrust steadily into his tight little hole. He's got a hand on his cock, working it slowly, and we set up a rhythm that lasts and lasts. I want to cum in the worst way but hold off, slowing up every time I feel the rise because I don't know what will happen next. He's got a life somewhere, maybe a partner who's frantically searching for him. The idea makes me want to devour him, take all there is and then some.

He lets out a sudden groan and starts squirting big gobs of cum up onto his stomach, and I pound harder at the sight, letting go finally, unleashing a monumental climax. I cut loose verbally as well, telling him how good it is, what a great ass he's got. Finally, I wind down, empty physically and emotionally. I slide out of him, toss the rubber, take him into my arms. He nuzzles against me and tells me, "I didn't think I could. Not knowing . . . just so lost." He laughs. "And now . . ."

"Amazing," I say, and we share a warm laugh, then drift off to sleep. It feels like hours have passed when he nudges me awake. He's got a copy of *Men* magazine in his hand, one of the ones I write for. "I think I found something," he says. "I'm not sure, but . . ." He opens it to the masthead, to the names of the publisher and editor, contributing writers, illustrators. "Alan Frazier," he says, pointing to the name. "I know . . . I mean, I think . . ." He's shaking. I take the magazine from him, look at the names: Alan Frazier, Editor in Chief, and there below it, among the contributing writers, Darren Davis, my pen name. And then I see it all.

"Omigod," I say, and I start to laugh. "That's it! You've solved it!"

"I'm Alan, aren't I? The garage . . . it's at the magazine. Hollywood Boulevard. I don't live on Alvarado, I live on . . . on . . . Halston. It's coming back, all of it . . . only . . ."

"Alvarado Street."

"Yeah, I don't get the connection."

I point to the list of writers. "Darren Davis," I tell him. "I've been writing for you for a year and a half. We e-mail all the time."

He looks down, shakes his head, and I know he's retrieving information from that badly shaken memory. I take his hand, hold on, give him time. When he looks back up at me he asks, "What's the last thing we said in our e-mail?"

"You were talking about having to cut one of my stories and I was arguing about it. 'Big Job' was the title."

I see it hit home. He lights up with recollection. "Yes!" He grabs my arm, laughs. "You wanted me to cut the second scene instead of the last."

"And you said you'd think about it. That was late yesterday."

He slides back up against me, lets me get an arm around him. "This is so bizarre," he says. "You couldn't write this story."

"Why do you think you remembered my address?"

He ponders this a bit, then says, "I know. I can see it now, the last thing I did before leaving the office. I was sending you a copy of the latest issue and, as I wrote your address on the label, I realized I had it memorized. And I wondered what you were like, what you were doing at that moment."

"So, what do you think?" I ask. "Is this fate or what?"

He crawls on top of me, gives me a long kiss. "It's meant to be, that's what it is." I slide a hand down to his ass, give it a squeeze. Maybe there's a story here after all.

Hunger Takes Over

Thom Wolf

My eyes met his as soon as I opened the door. He stood out in the crowd.

A dozen or so expectant faces turned toward me. For two seconds I had their undivided attention. I was not who they expected me to be and the moment of adulation was over. They weren't interested in me, but they were not going to move aside to let me past. I had to force my way through the crush of closely huddled shoulders. A couple of ladies in their sixties thrust souvenir programs beneath my nose.

"Would you sign these for us?"

They didn't really know who I was. I obliged them with a hasty scrawl across my photograph at the back of the program.

"Is she coming out yet?" one of the two women asked.

"I have no idea."

They both smiled and thanked me before shoving

their way back into the crowd to await the arrival of their favorite diva.

Although he stood in their ranks, he was not part of the crowd. I could see that he did not share their hunger for a rapid scribble and a sincere word from an aging star. He stepped toward me as I tried to leave.

"Could I have your autograph?" he asked. His voice was deep, older than I would have expected.

I smiled. "You can, but it won't be worth anything."

He did not smile. "That depends on what you measure as worth."

"I'm not a star in this show. I dance in the chorus."

"I know." He was standing close; I could feel the warmth of his body. "You also understudy the leading man."

"In four months he hasn't missed a single performance."

"I live in hope."

I opened his program and began to write.

"What's your name?"

"Jimmy."

As I wrote he stepped even nearer. His thigh brushed against mine. The pressure was light but deliberate. I could smell his scent; the fragrance of his body aroused me: sweat, cologne, and the sweet aroma of laundry softener. His chest was leaning against my arm as I wrote; I could faintly feel the masculine beat of his heart.

I gave him back his pen and program. We looked at each other and did not move. He was tall, an inch or two bigger than myself, and his body was lean. It was a warm night and there was no need for a jacket. He wore a clingy red T-shirt and an old pair of faded jeans. I could see the hard points of his nipples. His eyes were dark liquid pools that could easily discern my desire.

We understood one another.

We walked up the road together. The streets were quiet. We didn't have much to say. I slid my arm around his waist and drew him to me as we walked. The ass of his jeans was faded and worn. I could feel the heat of his buttocks through the thin fiber. He was not wearing underwear. Neither was I.

The night was young yet. We went to a nightclub. It was packed. We fought our way through the crowds and began to dance. We were crushed close together. We inhaled from a bottle of poppers and submitted to the heat. My blood pounded in my ears. The crotch of Jimmy's jeans was as worn as the ass, and I could feel every curve and contour of his cock through the faded denim. He rubbed up against me, grinding his hard dick against my own.

We could not talk above the music. We communicated through touch. We bumped and ground our two bodies, driven together by the frantic beats. Someone behind me tried to grab my ass but I ignored him. My clothes were clinging to my body like a damp rag.

Jimmy moved closer. His mouth was open as he pressed his lips to mine. He slipped his tongue into my mouth and we shared saliva. His arms were around my shoulders. I unbuttoned the fly of his jeans and slipped my hands down the back. I cupped his ass; I dug in and lifted and crushed the hard flesh. He moved his hips in short circles between my cock and my hands. The front of his jeans was damp with precum.

I worked a finger into the crack of his ass and stuck it

up his hole. There was no resistance to my intrusion. He kissed me with increased fervor, slipping his tongue into the recesses of my mouth. He dug his fingers into my hair, holding my face close.

I could smell the sex that was brewing between us. Very soon I would be replacing the fingers up his ass with my aching cock.

Jimmy's jeans were hanging down the back of his thighs and his ass was exposed for anyone to see. I shoved my hand deep and lifted his body toward me. I pressed my lips to his ear. I kissed the generous lobe before sucking it into my mouth. He squirmed. I shoved my tongue into his ear and he let out a gasp that could be heard well above the music.

"Let's find a corner," I said.

I hitched the seat of his jeans back up over his bare ass. He did not fasten the buttons but let them hang loose. As we shoved through the crowd, hands reached out toward us. Someone grabbed my tit, someone else found the throbbing bulge in my crotch. I shook them both aside.

We found a couch in a corner of the club. Jimmy lay down on the black upholstery. He lifted his ass and shrugged his jeans down his thighs. I lifted one leg at a time and removed his shoes and jeans. I knelt on the floor between his thighs.

His cock was lying hard against his stomach. He had leaked a damp pool of precum onto his T-shirt. I started with his balls and a soft trail of kisses. His scrotum tightened and rolled lazily beneath my lips. His flesh was smooth, natural rather than shaven. The skin of his balls was two shades darker than the rest of his body. I licked up the seam of his sac, the heavy nuts hanging down on either side of my tongue.

His body moved beneath me, and when the tip of my tongue slid up from his balls to the root of his cock, the throbbing organ jerked at my moist touch. I looked up to his face and my eyes met his penetrating gaze.

"Do it," he mouthed.

I opened my mouth and closed my lips over his fleshy knob. His cock was swollen to the rigidity of a rock; there was not a centimeter of give in the tight skin. A beautiful clear pearl leaked from the tip of his purple jewel and mixed with my saliva. He lifted his ass from the couch and slipped his dick farther into my mouth. I've never been much good at deep throat, but I gave his cock my best effort. Saliva oozed from the vacuum of my lips and dripped down the shaft of his organ. I held his balls in my palm; they were loose and wet.

A crowd had begun to form around us. No one spoke, they just watched. It was my second captive audience that night.

The taste of salt was now strong on my tongue. He was leaking precum furiously. I sucked and licked and swallowed. My fingers were wet; I stuck a couple in his asshole. That did it for him. The cock tensed between my lips and his most precious secretion flowed into me. His spunk was hot and strong; I allowed it to ooze slowly to the back of my throat before swallowing. His asshole tightened around my fingers.

He remained hard. I removed my fingers from his ass and quickly took off my pants. I took a rubber out of my back pocket and then tossed my pants into an untidy heap on the floor beside me.

Jimmy rolled over on the sofa. He got up on his knees and rested his arms over the back. I looked at his perfect ass. His buttocks were firm and round, the texture of his flesh creamy and smooth. As he leaned forward, the crack parted and I saw the small dusty brown hole. It was a flawless ass.

I had trouble getting the rubber down over my cock. My head was swollen like a huge bloated apricot and my fingers were inefficient with haste. At last I fitted it securely. I tore open a sample of K-Y lubricant and smeared the jelly over myself. My cock trembled and pulsated at the slick caress of my fingers.

I planted a hand on the cheek of Jimmy's ass and spread him wide. He pressed back toward me, and his asshole bulged like a hungry mouth. I spread the jelly over his hole and shoved a couple of fingers up inside him. He was hot and sticky; the strong muscle gripped my fingers. I pushed slowly in and out, fucking him with my hand. He grunted and moaned and pushed his ass back at me every time I withdrew.

I removed my fingers and stood up. I held my cock poised over his prone figure. I put it inside him. We sighed together and I slipped into place. I felt the tight, powerful passage of his ass along every trembling inch of my cock. Someone behind me cheered. I started to fuck. His ass was relaxed and I could slide back and forth without fearing I would hurt him. I held him by the waist, holding his perfect ass still while I controlled every movement. I was wholly aware of each sensation, my balls pressed against his underside as I buried myself in him.

The crowd around us was moving in closer. Someone came up behind me and put his arms around my chest. He unbuttoned my shirt and tossed it onto the floor beside my jeans.

"It's spoiling my view of your ass," the man said as he stepped back.

I had a good range of motion. My cock slipped out of Jimmy's asshole until only the bulbous head remained inside him, then I shoved in until I felt his buttocks press hard against my pelvis. We fucked hard, incited by the driving rhythm of the music and its erratic beat.

I shoved Jimmy's T-shirt up to his shoulders, exposing the graceful curve of his spine. I slid a hand beneath him and located an engorged nipple. I twisted the large nub between thumb and forefinger as Jimmy jerked his ass rapidly in reaction to my ministrations. He arched his back and thrust his hips onto me with increased vigor.

The sensations in my cock were exquisite. Every morsel of flesh throbbed as I sheathed myself on his ass. My hips were jerking frantically. My eyes were beginning to sting with the sweat of my exertion. A man stepped forward out of the crowd. He held an open bottle of poppers beneath my nose. I inhaled. In one rapid instant my pleasure was increased a hundredfold. My head and cock felt fit to burst. The man offered the bottle to Jimmy and I fucked him even harder as he inhaled the potent fumes.

My stomach muscles clenched in excitement and I came in spasms. My knees began to buckle beneath me as my entire body went into rapture. I filled him with the aching length of my cock and allowed the hot milk to flow. A deep cry of satisfaction tore from my throat. I ejaculated one long, intense spurt after another. I leaned on Jimmy for support as my seed and my orgasm ebbed from me to him.

I removed my cock and sat down naked on the couch beside him. The leather stuck to my clammy ass. It felt good. I saw the faces of those who had gathered to watch. There were about thirty people standing there, and at least half of them were holding their cocks in their hands. My chest rose and fell as I took deep rapid breaths.

I removed the rubber from my cock. Cum dribbled from the sheath and spilled over the head of my dick. Although it had already begun to lose its color, the temperature of my cum remained hot.

A man stepped forward from the crowd. He was blond and broad-shouldered, about twenty-seven or twenty-eight. He got down on his knees in front of me and began to lick up the spunk from my cock. I remained hard.

Others began to move in fast. A young guy, dark, in his early twenties, already had a condom in place. His jeans were open; his hard cock and balls were framed by the parted flaps of denim. He stepped up behind Jimmy and slipped it to him, taking my place in his ass.

The blond was devouring every drop of dying sperm; he held my pink shaft at the root and licked me clean. He opened his mouth wide over my head and sucked up the last pearls of cum lingering in my slit. My desire had not been satiated by the orgasm. The blond kept me turned on; I was horny and wanted more. I eased his head up from my cock.

"Take my ass," I told him.

He smiled, a hot smile, a voluptuous smile. I raised my knees up to my chest and lifted my splayed ass to the edge of the sofa. Now everybody could see what I had. My body held no more secrets from these strangers. Several men stepped closer. A couple made contact with my eyes, but most kept their gaze focused on my asshole. They stroked their hard cocks at different rates. As I watched one of the guys let loose his load; it spurted from his circumcised cockhead in long thin ropes. When he was done he shook his organ, displacing a lingering glob of cum from the head. It fell to the floor. He did not put his dick away when he was done, he just left it there, hanging loose as he began to soften. He continued to watch me.

The blond pressed his mouth to my musky asshole. He gently kissed the smooth pucker. I felt his tongue slip inside me; my ass opened to take him. The sensation was wet and languid, tickling my sensitive flesh. I pulled my knees up higher and thrust more of my ass into his face. He held my hips and brought my ass to his mouth, eating me like a fruit.

Through half-lidded eyes I gazed at Jimmy. He was on his hands and knees just off to the side of me. His face was glazed with a veil of perspiration. His lips were parted, and he let out a series of gentle sighs. The dark boy was plowing hard into his ass; he was keen and enthusiastic. He came within a few minutes. Another man, this one older, was ready to take his place. As the boy removed his cock from Jimmy's ass the man stuck his own, larger organ inside.

The blond had finished eating my ass. He stood up

and unfastened his shirt and trousers. He had a long pink cock that he covered in a clear-skinned condom. He smiled as he wedged the tip of his dick into my muscle. I opened my arms and he lay down on top of me. He had a fine dusting of dark blond hair across his chest. His nipples were hard and raw; they rubbed deliciously against my own as he began to pump into me.

I tightened my ass around his long, pulsating shaft, massaging and gripping him. I wrapped my arms around his back and held him tight, excited by the manly smell of him. He held me by the waist and lifted my ass up to his dick; I humped his cock hard and fast.

I felt his knees go limp for a second and his body trembled as he came. His cock jerked with the unburdening of his load. He climbed off me and another man took his place. One after another they came. The faces became indistinct. I swung my body around so that my face lay under Jimmy's groin. As another man began to mount my ass I took Jimmy's cock in my mouth and sucked him.

From my position beneath him I had a magnificent view of his splayed ass and the huge dick that was hammering into him. A massive pair of low-hanging balls slapped against his underside. Jimmy's cock tasted stronger than before; it wept a continuous flow of precum as he took a pounding from behind. I withdrew him from my mouth as I felt his organ tense. He sprayed my face and hair with a gargantuan load of strong-smelling cum. I licked a gob from my top lip.

Strong hands took hold of my body and lifted me out from under Jimmy. The man who held me was enormous. He had already stripped naked and was sporting the biggest erection I had ever seen. He sat me up on the edge of the couch and began to kiss the cum from my face. He worked his tongue in long, lazy circles around my eyes and nose, devouring every last glob of Jimmy's seed. I could smell the beer and cum on his breath. I ran my hands through his thick black hair.

I touched his body—he had huge hard tits, dusted in a coarse layer of dark hair. His low-hung pecs were the size of dinner plates and his nipples were at least two inches in diameter. I rolled the two hard studs between my thumb and forefingers, pulling and teasing. I longed to have them in my mouth, to swirl my tongue around their throbbing points and hear him gasp.

When my face was clean of cum, he lifted me up and turned me around so that I was facedown on the hot leather surface of the couch; I inhaled sweat and sex. He shoved his fingers up my ass; I was loose and relaxed. His fingers were almost as big as some of the cocks that I had taken that night, but when he stuck his dick into me I immediately knew the difference. My loose, fuck-worn ass expanded farther to accommodate the Goliath.

I was grateful to the kid who held a bottle of poppers beneath my nose; I inhaled the fumes and suddenly my ass had no problem in taking the monster cock. He leaned all the way up into my bowel; I experienced the pleasure and pain of a virgin asshole staked for the very first time. The hands around my waist were like shovels, and they held me rooted to his shaft.

He pulled his cock back. He pushed it forward.

I raised my head and looked toward Jimmy. The men had finished fucking him. His face was scarlet and his whole body dripped with hard-earned sweat. He crawled across the couch and knelt before me. He smiled and kissed me softly on the lips. I opened my mouth and the kiss deepened. He tasted of salt, sweat, and cum.

My legs where shaking. The giant was pounding my ass with the kind of force reserved for complete strangers. I pushed onto him, wanting all of him. Fucking him, fucking me. I gripped his cock, refusing to surrender him. Without touching my dick I felt the beginning of an orgasm. I held it back but the effort was more than I was fit to sustain. If the man had not been holding tight on to my ass I would have fallen over flat on my face.

I shot onto the black leather in long, white, ropy spurts; I seemed to spout a gallon of my globby seed. I collapsed forward into Jimmy's arms, my heart thundering in my chest. I felt the man pull his cock out of my ass. He took off his condom and blew his cum all over my back, managing to squirt it everywhere from my ass to my hair. I could feel the warmth raining down on me. He wiped his dick off on my bare ass.

About an hour later, I went with Jimmy to a cafe. It was quiet, and we took a table in the window. Our clothes hung like damp rags on our tired bodies. The waitress came over and we ordered coffee. We faced each other across the table.

Jimmy rested his hand on my knee and smiled. His face was as red as my burning asshole felt.

"So what happens next?" he asked softly.

I shrugged. "I'm tired. I have a show tomorrow. I need some rest. Do you want to come home with me?"

He squeezed my knee beneath the table. "Sure."

Sliding Home

Mac O'Neill

"Hey, man, you want a beer?" Greg West asked, glancing vaguely toward the living room where Pete Palmer was sitting.

"Sure." Pete nervously rubbed the palm of his right hand with the thumb of his left hand. He was sweating profusely, although Greg had the windows open and the ceiling fan was rotating above him with a dull, incessant whir, like a misplaced propeller blade.

Greg had already stripped off his sweaty jeans and sneakers, and was naked except for a worn, institutional-white jockstrap. He groped distractedly at the white meshed fabric at his crotch and then, bending slightly at the waist, peered into the white light of the refrigerator. A moment later, Pete heard the unmistakable fizz-pop of cold aluminum beer cans being snapped open, one after the other.

"Thanks," Pete said when Greg handed him the cold beer. His piercing blue eyes darted apprehensively over the rough mounds of Greg's tremendous physique, taking in as much of his friend's muscular flesh as he possibly could without appearing to be too interested. He took a deep, cold chug of beer and wiped his mouth with the back of his hand. Furtively, his eyes followed the shifting, marblelike cheeks of Greg's white ass protruding provocatively over the rear elastic of the jockstrap. For a moment, his eyes lingered on the definable, unmistakable knoblike curvature of cockhead compressed against the teeming cotton pouch between the hairy flesh of Greg's enormous thighs and the flesh of one partially exposed testicle. Throwing his head back, he took a long quaff of beer and closed his eyes, as though suddenly overcome by a migraine.

The first time it happened, Pete felt as if he had physically left his body and was merely watching, off to the side, like some impassive, mysterious observer. Then, he couldn't even admit to himself that his mind could entertain such wanton, unnameable desires. Yet, there it was, vandalizing his mind; festering beneath the surface, like a bad wound, aching and throbbing, refusing to heal. He seemed in a state of perpetual arousal. His balls ached, but even worse, his heart appeared to beat only when Greg was around. Then it happened, as though he had willed it upon himself; the Rubicon was crossed.

They were driving back from a softball game in Orlando one evening when Greg pulled down a dark country road to find a place to piss. The night was hot and muggy—a typical Florida evening, when the humidity was so sticky and palpable that breathing was like trying to inhale damp cotton candy.

Greg found a long gravel road leading along the Gulf of Mexico and pulled the pickup alongside a towering growth of sea grape. Pete got out and walked around to the driver's side of the pickup. He stretched exuberantly, looking absently toward a small cay in the Gulf. Greg followed him and casually unbuttoned his jeans. His groin was covered in obscene tufts of wild dark hair, like animal fur. Pete took a hearty chug from the bottle of beer in his hand, which was now lukewarm, and stared at the dense overgrowth spilling out of Greg's open fly. The light from a pale full moon splashed across the calm, glassy Gulf.

Reaching into the fly of his jeans, Greg did a kind of semisquat and pulled out his penis. It was fleshy, heavily veined, and massively wrinkled, with a good four inches of puckered cowl hanging past the helmet-shaped cockhead. Easing the foreskin back with his thumb as he had done a thousand times before, Greg let loose a long, steady stream of warm piss. Pete glanced obliquely, if only momentarily, at the translucent yellow stream; it sounded amatory, like summer rain splattering against hot pavement.

Greg watched passively as Pete watched him relieve himself. Then, with a slight, almost imperceptible movement, the stream of warm piss showering from his cock splashed against the sand at Pete's shoes. *"Hey!"* Pete protested, jumping backward. His eyes shifted toward Greg's, which were impenetrable in the dark night.

Pete knew he should have objected, but every ounce of logic and reason had deserted him months ago. He wanted this man more than he had ever wanted a piece of pussy. He wanted his hairiness, the bold, blatant masculinity that reached out and took whatever it wanted without question. He closed his eyes, surrendering his virility to one more masculine than himself.

"Sorry, man," Greg half-grinned. With his cock still dangling out of the fly of his jeans, Greg grabbed the sweaty T-shirt he was wearing and pulled it up over his head, throwing it into the back of the pickup. His chest was sculpted, massive, matted with tufts of dark hair; as he turned slightly sideways, the bulging flesh of his immense pectorals protruded above his hard, flat belly like a set of masculine teats. Testosterone and sweat seemed to ooze from every pore of his half-naked body and mingle with the salty night air, like the scent of some overpowering feral aroma. He didn't utter a syllable, and seemed acutely aware of precisely what he wanted and that Pete would give it to him. He gripped his cock.

The fleshy appendage filled his fist. He shook his dick to arousal until it grew in girth and length. Before Pete realized what was happening he could feel his fingertips stroking the dense cloud of wiry, black pubic hair that stretched above Greg's sweaty crotch in a dark, wide triangle to the perimeter of his upper thighs. He buried his face in the dense fur and inhaled the pungent, musky scent of sex and male sweat.

Expressionless, yet with a tacit air of arrogance about him that absorbed and aroused Pete, Greg stared at his friend down on his knees before him in the sand. He lifted the swollen meat of his cock to Pete's mouth, then leaned back against the hood of the pickup. Pete would do the rest, and Greg would watch and savor the moist warm touch of his friend's mouth milking his sex.

Pete pulled the soft fleshy meat from his mouth and admired it for a moment before nibbling and toying with the extended, velvet-textured foreskin. He pulled back the soft jagged cowl and took the expansive smooth knob of Greg's cockhead, which seemed too meaty and voluminous for him to properly service, into his mouth. He sucked hard, awkwardly at first, feeling the peach-shaped knob dilate and press against the back of his throat. He pulled it from his mouth and licked the underskin of the enlarged shaft.

Quietly, Greg reached down, grabbed the shaft of his meaty cock in his fist, and inserted it in Pete's mouth; he felt his nuts hitch and graze Pete's chin. He moaned so deep and low in his throat that the sound, both sensuous and solicitous, aroused Pete's nipples.

Pete felt his own cock rise again in his jeans, hard and hot against the moist flesh of his inner thigh. He liked being controlled and subservient to the ex-Marine, and when he felt Greg's massive hands firmly clutch his head, he moaned spontaneously, his cum squirting uncontrollably inside his jeans along the hard flesh of his upper thigh.

Greg reached down and cupped Pete's chin in his broad, rough hand. His cock, corpulent and ridged obscenely with thick, extended veins, pulsated with sexual ardor. He pumped Pete's moist mouth with his own distinctive rhythm: fast and hard, then slow and easy, feeling his supple, enlarged cockhead sliding easily down Pete's throat, as if the two were intentionally made to fit each other.

Pete reached up and squeezed the muscular shelf of Greg's protruding chest, kneading the round flesh in his hands, feeling the dense hair and thick, gumdrop-size nipples rub against the flesh of his palms. He curled one of his hands into a tight fist and brought it down hard against Greg's pecs. *"Oh, yeah,"* he thought he heard Greg moan. He pounded the protruding flesh of chest muscle again, hard, then again, almost instinctively, as though something dark and nebulous was commanding him to.

Greg moaned again, clasping Pete's head firmly in his hands, the long stray hairs sprouting from his nuts flush against Pete's chin, like a beard. He drove the meat of his shaft deeper into Pete's throat, causing Pete to gag and gasp for breath. Then, without preamble, a profuse ejaculate of warm semen gushed from the meaty center of his cockhead, in quick, furious squirts. Pete swallowed hard, but the cum kept flowing, filling his mouth until it dribbled down his chin, dripping to his chest like salty raindrops.

Greg stood gasping for a few minutes and then, slowly recapturing his breath, patted Pete impassively on the cheek, as though he were petting a favorite dog. He rubbed his hand across his belly and stretched his massive arms into the air. Speechless, Pete watched as Greg nonchalantly stuffed his cock back into his jeans and climbed back into the cab of the pickup, as though nothing as intimate as man-to-man cocksucking had taken place. Nor did he or Greg ever speak of it.

Now, here he was again, uncertain if anything was going to happen; fooling himself into thinking that he didn't care. He had come to the gradual realization that with Greg, man-to-man sex happened spontaneously; no gushing or wooing or prolonged foreplay, just fortuitous and circuitous events that led to the eventual satisfaction of Greg's sexual appetence. He had become a willing pawn and an ardent player in his own search for sexual fulfillment. He now lusted after Greg West in the same manner he had first lusted after Julie Palmer. But this was different, more hard-edged and desperate, unquestionably masculine.

Greg turned to Pete, his fingertips deep in the dense hair at the center of his chest; he scratched his left nipple abstractedly. "Hey, buddy, I'm going to jump into the shower. How about you?"

Pete nodded casually, camouflaging his vehement lust for another masculine male. "Sounds good," he replied, agonizing briefly over the slight, almost perceptible tremor in his voice.

In the bathroom, Pete stripped off his clothes and watched Greg's naked body out of the corner of his eye, struggling to keep his semierect cock from becoming fully erect. When the water was just the right temperature, Greg glanced over his shoulder, his eyes gravitating briefly to the dark triangle of pubic hair above the pendulous prominence of Pete's exposed dick; he smiled condescendingly, scratched the full sac of his drooping nuts, and climbed into the shower, arrogant and positive that Pete would follow.

"Hey, get my back for me, man," Greg said nonchalantly, handing Pete a bar of soap. Then, with that same unnerving, patronizing smirk, he added: "And keep your cock away from my ass, understand?"

For a brief millisecond the expression on Pete's face resembled that of a panicked animal's, trapped in the ominous sight of a hunter's loaded gun. He hated himself for the boyish, love-struck way he sought the approval of such a glaringly masculine man.

After Pete had soaped Greg's muscular V-shaped back, Greg rinsed off and grabbed the soap from his hand. "Turn around and I'll do you."

Pete swallowed hard and leaned into the shower, bracing his extended arms and hands against the tiled shower wall, his back to Greg. He closed his eyes and felt his dick stiffen. He winced as Greg's soapy hands roamed freely over the corded muscle of his exposed back; water collected in his pubic hair and dripped from the smooth curve of his cockhead to his toes.

Then, abruptly, Pete gasped; Greg's hand had moved from his back to the white, marblelike cheeks of his ass. He closed his eyes and swallowed hard as Greg's hand moved between his thighs, under his dangling cock and balls. A sudsy hand slipped between his cheeks and, with a slight pressure, rubbed slowly, provocatively, against his sphincter.

Under the splashing water Pete could hear Greg's

breathing growing heavier, like his own, fraught with tension and undeclared desire. His cock grew so hard that it hurt. From behind, Greg soaped up his cock and probed Pete's ass with a soapy finger, first one, then another, stretching and lubricating the tight sphincter muscle until it accepted a third finger. *"You're pretty tight,"* Greg said in a deep, feverish tone, more to himself than to the man he was about to fuck.

Pete gasped aloud and arched his back. He wanted it; wanted whatever Greg was about to give him. He was so flushed and unnerved, burning with such an intense prurient desire, that he didn't hear himself moan, or realize that he had pushed the cheeks of his white ass back against Greg's body.

Greg gripped Pete's shoulder firmly with one hand and poised his swollen cockhead at Pete's puckered sphincter. *"Oh, yeah,"* he moaned, and thrust his hips forward; Pete's virgin ass was tight, like a fist, gripping his cock.

Pete groaned and gasped for breath, air coming in short bursts to his lungs. He flinched hard at the sudden intrusion of being penetrated by his leatherneck friend. His ass had swallowed Greg's cock whole; the pain was excruciatingly intense, but he didn't cry out, just accepted it as Greg began to thrust roughly into him. After a few minutes the pain gave way to pleasure such as he had never before experienced. He forced his ass back, into the moist, wiry nest of Greg's pubic hair, taking as much of Greg into him as he could. He could feel Greg's muscular body press against his bare, wet back, and Greg's hot, steamy breath against his ear.

Greg brought his hand down hard across Pete's wet

ass, leaving a bright red impression. He thrust his cock forward with the full force of his body weight and watched the distended, heavily veined shaft of his dick disappear into the tight grip of Pete's moist insides. He bludgeoned him hard, ramming his dick so fiercely against him that the thick vein in Pete's neck stood out as he bucked and groaned. He wanted to ride Pete, give him a good, long Marine fucking like he had never had before, but the tightness of Pete's ass muscles condensed around his swollen cockhead with such a smooth sucking sensation that he could barely control his climax. He slammed his naked body into Pete's backside with ferocious abandon, plowing him again and again, straining to get every inch of his hard cock inside him.

Pete reached behind himself and clasped a hand around the back of Greg's thick neck, bucking and gasping each time Greg's cock slammed into the firm white cheeks of his aching ass. Finally, when Pete was unable to take another inch, Greg withdrew his cock.

Without preamble he stepped out of the shower, grabbed a towel, and began drying off, leaving Pete embarrassingly erect and unsatisfied. He threw Pete a towel and told him to finish him off in the bedroom.

Pete watched in awe as Greg's naked body turned and left the bathroom. There was something stimulating about watching this man's exposed body: the curves of hard muscle, the elongated tube of flesh bouncing lightly beneath the dark bush of pubic hair. He studied him so intently that it was as if he had never seen a man walk upright before.

"I want to watch you finish me off," Greg said in that

casual manner he had as Pete entered the bedroom. He was sitting on the edge of the bed, his hand buried in the pubic hair at his groin, his cock dangling provocatively over his suspended balls.

Pete lowered his naked body between Greg's thighs. He could feel the heat of Greg's intense stare upon him, watching, waiting. He closed his fist around Greg's pendulous cock and felt its girth. Greg reached down and brushed his fingers lightly against the stubble of Pete's cheek. Then he grabbed Pete's head and pulled him in close, whispering: "You want it, don't you, buddy? I mean, this is what you want. You've wanted it all along?"

Pete nodded, aroused by the tacit understanding that had developed between them. He knew what he was doing now. He took Greg's engorged cockhead into his mouth and, from a kneeling position, looked directly into Greg's eyes. Greg winced from the pleasure; his eyes locked on Pete's. He reached down and brushed a finger against one of Pete's nipples, then leaned in close to his ear. "You're *my* cocksucker, huh?"

Pete nodded, steadily milking Greg's cock. He worked his mouth down to the wild pubic hair around Greg's dick, feeling it brush against his nostrils. He cupped Greg's dangling nuts in his palm and squeezed until Greg winced and moaned, from deep in his throat, *"Oh, baby,"* so intimately that a shiver ran up Pete's spine.

Pete slid his hand up and over Greg's swollen cockhead, milking the Marine's engorged sex until he felt Greg's muscles tense and the familiar, pleasing sensation of warm semen filling his mouth. He swallowed hard, sucking every last pearl of cum from his partner's cock. Greg writhed and moaned at the intensity of his ejaculation, at the violent sensitivity centered in the tender flesh of his swollen cockhead.

Pete stood, his cock hard and distended, oozing with precum. He stepped forward into Greg's chest and guided his cock to Greg's mouth for the first time. Clasping Greg's head in his hands, he pumped his cock down Greg's throat. Greg clutched the cheeks of Pete's firm white ass in his palms and squeezed hard, forcing Pete's substantial cock deep into his mouth. Pete was so aroused, it took him all of a minute to cum, and he suddenly found his voice. "Swallow it, Greg," he muttered, his eyes fluttering, then clamping shut as he felt the rise of cum surge from his cock into Greg's masculine mouth. Greg reached up and clutched at Pete's supple brown nipples, pinching and twisting them hard between his fingers.

Pete withdrew his cock and slapped it across Greg's face. He leaned down and lightly punched the hairy ripples of Greg's stomach muscles. "Love pats," he would come to call them.

Night Moths in Acapulco

Cuauhtémoc Q. Kish

The ceiling fan buzzed frantically above the bed, pushing the stale smells of the room's previous occupants down on my pink, slightly burnt flesh, assaulting my remaining sensitivities. I was uncomfortable. It was sticky-humid, and my pants felt like they were glued to the hairy, sweaty crack of my perfect white ass. Practically suffocating inside my pink-stuccoed motel room, I sought relief. I felt the need to escape into the night's tropical breeze.

I made a beeline for the strip—a row of tightly clustered restaurants, shops, and discos that, when open, bow down and cater obsequiously and exclusively to the moneyed tourist. Neon attracted me tonight like a bored moth drawn to the promise of an evangelical, pure white light.

Brightly lit signs beckoned me, their intensity juxtaposed against the dark, black-opal night sky. The constant pounding of the ocean's waters proved a stark contrast to the dead quiet of the stores, already locked up tight for the night. I slowly moved along the boulevard in a methodical, forced attempt to tire out this body that was still *up.* It was almost four in the morning, and few people were about—just a few holdouts from the late-night discos, most stumbling unevenly in an effort to rediscover their prepaid lodgings.

Up-tempo tangos were dancing inside my head when this intoxicating, sensual head-beat was suddenly interrupted. I had just passed a vintage pizza joint on the strip—old, seedy, established. My eyes focused on a shadowy, gray figure dancing in the window. Or was it just my imagination? Quite possibly it might have been simply the mix of man-made neon and natural darkness that had created this vision in my mind.

But the figure in the window continued to play a game of shadowboxing with me as I slowed my pace; it wouldn't be dismissed. I turned and noticed the billowing, off-white clouds of the early early-morning intimating an arabesque movement toward their half-moon dancing partner in the sky.

Ignore the shadows, a voice inside me said. I walked on, but was involuntarily pulled back to the dancing shadows in the window. The pair of summer blue-cotton pants I was wearing tightened without any apparent reason. My excitement grew as though sexual conquest was imminent.

The fluttering inside my groin intensified as I approached the entrance: CLOSED—WILL REOPEN AT 11, the sign read.

I peered inside the restaurant, the smell of Italian cookery still wafting from within. My bloodshot eyes focused on a human form within the restaurant, his hands flapping like a pair of moths on fire. His hands continued their circular movement behind the glass-walled entrance, and I acknowledged and finally accepted their blatant invitation.

My approach was cautious. Aside from the fluttering of fingers, I could distinguish little, except a vague form of anatomy. The door to the entrance was slightly ajar, and I followed the inviting fingers that held the door open from within.

As I walked toward the entrance I noticed a pair of eyes, and froze in mid-step. I was immediately mesmerized by the almond-colored visual confrontation in the dark. I paused, then walked through the entrance into the restaurant.

The lock on the door clicked shut. I looked back just as his meaty hand grabbed my own and urgently pulled me closer, taking me farther inside. As I allowed myself to be led past dark booths padded with red leather, I discovered the brown face that housed the almond eyes, still partly hidden in the shadows of the restaurant.

"What do you want?" I whispered, my desire making itself known.

"Come this way," urged the voice, as white teeth beamed through the darkness.

My gaze was lost, not so much in his smile of ocean pearls, nor on his butterfly hands, but on a pale, off-white stick he clung to; its purpose I had yet to discover.

As clouds continued their arabesques in the skies above and then gave way to gentle moonlight, I was able to admire my new companion's distinguished, bronzed chest.

My hand moved forward to touch his sculpted, earth-brown body, encircling his pecs and alighting upon his firm, aroused, quarter-size nipples. I became aware of our breathing—communal, though individually patterned and separately identifiable.

My body was aroused, but I remained relaxed and calm. My eyes had begun to grow accustomed to the semi-darkness. I noticed red-checkered tablecloths stacked unceremoniously and condiments gathered and placed on a metal tray table.

As if in a trance I continued to follow this moving bronze form, marching forward in a relaxed, tropical beat, the off-white stick marking time as we continued our dance in the dark.

Without turning around he reached back and lightly grazed my body—not to arouse, but to stop further progress into the room. He placed one of the checkered tablecloths on the floor. Removing his pants, he lay down upon the tablecloth, then slid my pants down and pulled me on top of him with a hungry urgency.

It was then that I noticed his legs: thin, almost nonexistent. They didn't belong to the sculpted torso that my hands had traveled over only a few moments ago. I was transfixed, unable to move, a weighty block of cement.

The butterfly hand that met mine was now tense, and I felt its urgency.

"No, I can't."

I wanted to escape; I felt betrayed. But those almond eyes delivered a message without words, unspoken words that commanded my body to move forward upon his, aroused once again. He guided my throbbing member between his legs, just below his scrotum. His heavily veined and muscular hands pressed upon my back and drew me forward; I melted into him as our colors collided and I felt his ball sac cradle my blood-engorged shaft. I found his thick, cinnamon lips, moist, energetic. I slipped my tongue into his mouth as he slipped his into mine and we both explored the caverns within.

I licked a path down his cheek and pulled at his earlobe in a playful manner, blowing hotly into his ear. I continued with a darting tongue lash that aroused him to extend his body upward, pushing my cock into a deeper spot near his anus. At the same time I felt his throbbing member press into my abs and gently pulsate while I completed my exploration above the equator.

I broke loose from the hold he had on my cock, and we quickly changed positions, then both inhaled sweat and sex while sixty-nining one another. We rocked back and forth, pummeling hungry mouths, as we both grew in size.

I began fondling his sphincter and rammed three fingers up his tight hole. He screamed with delight, panting, and I felt his muscle tighten around those fingers like a clamp.

I repositioned myself, kneeling between his splintered legs, pushing the head of my dick into his opening, my purple bulb asking for entrance. He handed me a rubber and a bottle of olive oil. I massaged his butt cheeks and manhole with 100 percent virgin oil while he sheathed my cock and guided it into his lubed entrance.

I cupped his balls with one hand and ran my fingers up and down his eight-inch shaft with the other. He pulled on my buttocks with his butterfly fingers, pulled hard with an intense urgency and bucked up toward my engorged monster.

Entering him, I began an urgent thrust, fucking him as if it were our last night on earth, and this our last taste of lust. His cock swelled in my hand as I pounded his ass. His excitement furthered my own, and I knew our fevered union could not stand this pace for long. We were two night moths being drawn inevitably toward an orgasmic flame. And then suddenly we were engulfed. Our bodies quaking, he shrieked out an orgasm, tightening his butt and accelerating my climax, causing me to fire off a thick, hot, white load.

I slowly pulled away from his body. Nothing was said. I knelt, then rose from my kneeling position as he reached for his cane and inched himself up slowly, trembling ever so slightly.

He escorted me to the entrance, the cane once again marking our departure.

"Promise you'll return."

"Tomorrow," I heard myself whisper.

I drifted out the door as if in a trance. I focused on the cracks in the cement pathway and edged myself forward; then I stopped suddenly and looked back.

I saw the butterfly fingers moving in the storefront window. It began to sprinkle, and I welcomed the coolness of the rain. I looked up at the streetlight and saw moths fluttering and whirring above.

Night moths in Acapulco. A delicious sight, I thought, as I retasted the night.

The Act

Dale Chase

I didn't get the part. Never mind how long I'd known the director or how many times he'd fucked me in the past, he gave the role to someone else, and I had to wonder if Derek Fall was really a better actor or just a better fuck. Watching him prowl the stage only complicated things. Every time I looked at him a battle started inside me: jealous fury squared off against overwhelming desire.

The part was the best thing to come along in years, and every young actor in San Francisco auditioned. Six of us were called back to the ancient Lindsay Theatre for a second reading, and it was then that I knew I was in trouble. Not only did Fall's reading match my own, but I got hard watching him. Winning a lesser part was little consolation, and I found rehearsals of the four-man, two-act play more difficult than anticipated, because in addition to mastering my supporting role I had to balance envy and lust, which caused me more than once to forget my lines and endure an embarrassing silence that Fall seemed to relish. At those moments I could feel his smirk, even though his gorgeous James Dean face never betrayed a thing.

After a week's rehearsal I was clearly undone, and writer-director Abel Groff, gay theater patriarch, called me on it. "If you're in some kind of snit at not playing the lead, please get over it because you are not doing justice to the part you've been given, not at all. Don't you see, Brian is trapped by his feelings, he's tangled without hope, he's suffering! All I'm getting from you is distraction."

I couldn't respond.

"All right," Abel sighed, "just work on it, will you? You're a fine actor, Carl, and you'll do a wonderful job if you'll let yourself get into the role." He studied me then as only a man whose dick had been up my ass could do. "You probably just need a good fuck," he added, glancing at his watch. "I'd do you myself if I didn't have an appointment." And then he was gone.

I remained in the cramped communal dressing room long after the theater was dark. Fall's image clung to me. He'd made a production of changing from jeans to tight black slacks, enjoying, I was certain, my unease around his exposed cock. He'd revealed it slowly, his sizable shaft lingering in the mirror, and I'd feasted on the sight of it, long, thick, and half hard. My asshole had clenched involuntarily, my own dick stirring.

Anyone else I would have already approached, but Fall had a way of daring me to make a move while threatening me if I did, all of it accomplished in a charged and brutal silence. I hated the way he hoarded his words, saving everything for the stage, and the way he toyed with me like I was some defenseless prey.

His looks, of course, drove me wild. Never mind how cold the blue eyes, they bore into me like a rigid cock. His blond hair and exquisitely cut features—he truly was James Dean incarnate—seemed almost crafted, and yet his presence was truly animal, so base and raw that I was continually unsettled. Abel was right—I did need a good fuck. And I knew from whom.

Things were no less difficult onstage. Every time I was put up against Fall it was *my* erection prodding, never mind that of Brian, my poor tormented character. I passed that first week in bittersweet misery, and Fall knew it and played me accordingly. We existed in a state of near perpetual arousal, and at night I devoured anonymous cocks to exhaustion. By the next day's rehearsal, however, I would be desperate all over again.

And then, after Abel's admonishment, when I decided to forgo everything for a quiet night, an unattended asshole and lone jerk-off, the dressing-room door opened and I looked up into the mirror and saw Derek Fall in all his glory.

He approached me as if it were scripted, and while I hated his arrogance, I stood for him, pulled down my jeans, and presented the ass he had owned from day one. "Pussy boy," he growled as he shoved his cock into me. He said it again as he began a vicious stroke, and I responded as I knew he wanted me to. "*Your* pussy boy," I said, riding his dick and crazy with heat because I knew how the scene would play because it *was* a scene, Abel Groff's scene, although onstage the sex was simulated, clothed in shadow. Now it was alive, and as Derek Fall rammed his sizable dick up my ass, I knew we were playing our respective parts, but, of course didn't care. I had what I wanted, I was getting my fuck, and as I writhed on that magnificent tool all that mattered was that cock up this ass, never mind if the ass was Brian's or mine.

Fall didn't utter a word during the entire act, and outside of the rhythmic slap of flesh the room remained silent. I longed to cry out but didn't, taking his hose to the root and still wanting more. I couldn't get enough of him now that he was inside me; it felt like a cobra was sliding up into my bowels and my asshole pulsed in exquisite delight as it swallowed what seemed a mile of cock. Other than hands on my hips and dick up my ass, Fall gave me nothing, and once he'd pumped his cream into me in a massive gusher, he simply withdrew. His exit was as abrupt as his entrance, and I was still bent over the dressing table as I heard the door close.

He didn't seem to care that I too had delivered a massive load, the milky puddle validation that we had indeed shared the act. My hand was still on my cock, as if it needed consolation, and my asshole throbbed in recollection. I stood up slowly and stared at the door, knowing it was Fall who had fucked me but having the eerie feeling the encounter had been with his character, that Jake Cavett's prick had been the one up my ass.

"No, no!" Abel Groff screamed the next morning during rehearsal. "I told you how to play it. Can't you follow simple directions?" He was onstage in seconds, shoving me aside to show me Brian's move toward Jake. When he turned to me after the demonstration I offered nothing, and this enraged him further.

"Well?" he shouted.

"Yes," I managed, glancing at Fall, who leaned against the sofa back, erection prominent inside his jeans. Approaching him was agony, my own need overwhelming poor Brian's. I didn't care about scenes or characters or any of it anymore. I just wanted to pull out Fall's dick and climb on.

I managed to get through rehearsal but suffered a near collapse at day's end and again remained behind in the dressing room. I half expected Fall to come in for a repeat—he knew it'd be a given—but heard instead fading chatter and the clicks and groans of a theater shutting down for the night. For a while I considered quitting the play—an eager understudy could step in—but knew I'd go on, unable to resist Fall's promise. Exhausted, I finally forced myself out the door.

A single light illuminated the stage, and I paused in its meager stripe to remind myself I was an actor in a play and would be performing before hundreds of people. It was, after all, an act; I should simply get on with it. I had gathered a bit of calm when I heard footsteps in the wings. Derek Fall stepped from the shadows and strode toward me, and I thought of Brian, who lusted after Jake so pathetically—and yet I dropped my pants and waited.

Fall freed his cock, and as I stared at the magnificent pole I wondered if it ever went soft. The head was blue-purple and swollen with need, precum oozing in stringy gobs. He backed me to the sofa and I eased down and raised my legs, offering him the only thing he wanted. I watched his face darken as he slid his piston up my alley, and when he began pumping it was with a jackhammer fury that sent shock waves of pleasure through me. As he fucked me I wanted more than anything to pull away his clothes and confront the animal who took me with such authority. I wanted everything of his—lips, tongue, nipples, balls—but for now took what was offered, the pile-driving cock that tore into my ass.

My dick stood tall, and I wrapped a hand around it and jerked madly as Fall's prick drove deep into my rectum. He never let up, hammering my ass with his fat bone, searing my chute until my gut began to churn. I searched his face for some kind of reaction, some bit of pleasure, but he remained expressionless even as he slammed into me, balls banging my ass. I could tell his load was rising only by his urgency, frantic now, cock wild and untamed, insatiable and pumping furiously. My own prick was on fire and ready to let go but still I kept watching his face. I wanted to see him at that most vulnerable moment. I wanted something of his besides another pint of cream, a grimace or groan or squeal; I wanted a man instead of an animal.

When Fall finally came it was another gusher, as if he hadn't gotten off in weeks, but still he didn't react up top. I'd never seen a dick so disconnected, all that fury trapped inside his meat as if it had a life of its own. My own cream spurted in reply, arcing up onto my shirt in answer to his long climax. Never before had so much juice sprayed out of my cock, but even after I was empty my balls felt heavy, ready for another go. Only then did I begin to realize the enormity of my need for Derek Fall.

As before, once he'd gotten his fuck he abandoned me. I kept my legs up long after I heard the outer door slam, its echo like a cell door closing. My flaming hole faced empty seats but I saw instead an imaginary audience who, I decided, were entitled to a better finale. I squeezed and stroked my softening prick, cum gathered at the slit; I cupped my balls and pulled at my bag; I slid a finger into my dripping pucker and played in the fresh cum; I let the audience linger where Jake Cavett had been.

"Oh, Christ," Abel Groff said when I ran into him that night at a club we both frequented. "He's fucking you, isn't he."

I nodded.

Abel sighed, shook his head, then reconsidered. "Maybe it's not a bad idea. Maybe . . . Tell me, has he used any of Jake's lines?"

"No," I lied.

"But you're his Brian."

Was I? Brian was ineffectual, weak, so incredibly needy. Anyone could fuck Brian. "I don't think so," I told Abel. "It feels very . . . me."

Abel eyed me. "You're a good little pussy," he mused, "and maybe for the good of the play, if Jake is fucking Brian, then we've got a bit of reality, don't we? What more could a director ask?"

Abel refused to fuck me that night, even when I presented myself to him in the men's room at 2 A.M. He was at the urinal, dick in hand, and I went limp when he turned me down. "For the good of the play," he said, adding quickly, "I know, I know, it's unheard of, Abel Groff begging off, but I want it pure, don't you see? Jake and Brian and nothing else. You've got his cum up your ass, and that's purity." He zipped up and patted my shoulder. "Go home," he said softly. "Let Brian sleep."

It was an awful night, passed in dreams as frustrating for their lack of clarity as for their paltry payoff. At one point I lay in the dark clutching my dick, trying to figure out if it had been Brian or me, deciding finally it didn't make any difference.

Fall and I had a culmination scene late in the second act that was to be the focus of the following morning's rehearsal. So far we'd skated through it; Abel concentrating on earlier bits, leading us up to it much as Jake led Brian. The scene wasn't the play's climax, however—sex in that context would have been cliché even for Abel Groff. No, the climax was Jake's suicide just before the curtain fell.

Now Fall and I were alone onstage. The rest of the cast had been called for afternoon and we had just a few crew members. The old Lindsay had never seemed more cavernous. Even though it was just a rehearsal, I'd dabbed makeup over dark circles that shadowed my eyes. My entrance was calculated and determined; I wasn't Brian and I wanted them to know it. I was Carl, and it was all an act.

Partway through Abel's instruction I tuned him out because he didn't matter anymore. Derek Fall—Jake Cavett?—was in charge, and he and I knew it; possibly even Abel knew it, although no director is ever going to admit a loss of control. My dick began to fill in anticipation of Fall's body against mine, and I glanced down to see the all-too-familiar bulge at his crotch.

The scene was Jake's ultimate acquiescence to Brian's advances, which had for most of the play been limited to mutual hand jobs and cocksucking—all shadowed, all simulated. Now Brian was to be granted his wish. Jake would, with all the rage pooled inside his balls, fuck him full on. This required the usual bit of nudity, and Abel reminded us yet again what we didn't need to hear but what he obviously enjoyed saying: "Remember, you can get it out, you just can't put it in."

Part of Abel's success had been controversy over the "getting it out" that was such an integral part of his plays. Audiences could always count on at least one or two cocks making an appearance, and this had brought on attempts to shut down every one of his productions, but San Francisco's liberal majority had prevailed and exposed cocks had been allowed to stay. The new play, however, went a step further, and word was already out that an erection would be visible in the second act. Talk was heavy; Derek Fall's prick was going to be famous.

Abel insisted we take it all the way during rehearsal, which meant Fall had to produce a stiff prick. All I had to do was bare my ass, but the foreplay, that long arduous scene in which Brian pleads for his sexual life, was so emotionally demanding that by the time Cavett presented his cock I was as battered as Brian.

The entire second act takes place in Jake Cavett' s bedroom, much of it his raging soliloquy on love and loss. Bottle and glass stand empty on the dresser, bedclothes are tangled, and Jake retreats to an overstuffed chair and opens his jeans. He has a hand down inside working his cock, eyes closed as if this is his only solace. At this point I make my entrance.

It didn't matter that Fall had fucked me. I was Brian now and Jake Cavett was going to do it because we were onstage and had an audience, however limited. There was something extra required in slipping inside someone else for a sexual act, in playing a part, but this time I knew it was different, and as much as I tried to be Brian, to assume his need instead of my own, I played the scene for myself. When it came time for Jake to push Brian over the arm of a chair and enter him, to present the much-anticipated and highly visible erection for all to see and for me to receive, I felt myself open to him, asshole begging as he slid his rigid prick between my legs in a masterful simulation.

The fuck was real, never mind theater. As we writhed for Abel and the few others present, I squeezed my thighs together and took him, his massive dick working me with a steady thrust. His meat skated my balls as it plowed blindly forward and I wanted more than anything to grab my dick and jerk off but, of course, that wasn't in the script. I had to take him without any visible response other than gratitude, and take him I did, thighs slippery with his precum, asshole pulsing with the mere proximity of that swollen sausage.

Jake cries out "Pussy boy" as he gives it to Brian. He has succumbed at last to love and its attendant pain; he rails against it all, professes love and hate as one, swears, then comes. Abel and the others could not see his cream spurting between my legs, or my own seconds later. I had not touched myself. Derek Fall's heat and the raw pleasure of his skin against mine had been enough to send me over.

Cavett's disintegration begins at this point. His dick is still up Brian's ass when he starts to come apart and lashes out in his own brand of cruel self-preservation, closing with, "You're just a fuck, Brian. A good one, but that's all you'll ever be."

"Wonderful!" Abel Groff shouted. "Let's stop there."

Fall's dick was softening, and I let it slide from between my legs. My heart was pounding and I heard an awful rush in my ears. I managed to pull up my jeans and gather enough strength to face our director, but when Abel saw me he knew I was in trouble. "Let's take a break, shall we?" he said. "Ten minutes."

We both watched Fall hurry away, then Abel put his hand on my shoulder. "It's fabulous, you know. The energy between you is absolutely electric; it plays all the way to the balcony. Opening night there won't be a limp dick in the house. The theater will reek of cum."

"Abel . . ."

"I know, but it's what we want, Carl. Anguish, pain, passion, two men unable to connect except with cock and ass."

"It's exhausting," I said.

"I would imagine. We'll work on the dialogue next." He looked into my eyes. "And remember who you are. He's rejecting Brian, not Carl."

We picked up exactly where we'd left off, Brian enduring Jake's wrath because he'd stirred him above the belt as well as below. The scene is devastating for Brian, ending in shouts, broken glass, and slammed doors. We ran through it so many times I began to lose myself, and Abel called it a day when I finally broke into tears.

Derek Fall didn't fuck me again until opening night. As the play was fine-tuned I gradually came unglued, managing to keep Brian alive while Carl went under. I continually sought out fresh cock but found myself accepting only James Dean types, surly blonds who invariably disappointed, never mind how big a sausage they crammed up my ass or how beautiful its owner. I finally had to admit I was hopeless about Fall, and worse, that it was probably a one-way street.

The dressing room was frantic opening night, with too many well-wishers and hangers-on. Fall had kept his distance but managed to stand half naked long enough to catch me looking at his prick. Once he'd accomplished that, he gave it a long artful stroke, put on his costume—torn jeans and T-shirt—and left.

It was a packed house, but where I usually enjoyed exhilaration I now felt anxiety. My hands shook, I snapped at assistants, and I pushed one fellow actor so far he stormed out after a single departing comment: "Get fucked, Brian."

I was alone in the dressing room when Abel came in. Seeing my distress, he said, "You'll do fine. Let Brian have his night, OK?" He kissed my cheek and left, not waiting for comment.

"Five minutes," someone called outside the door.

When I walked onstage I had no idea who I was. Brian and Carl had finally become one, and I felt hundreds of eyes watching this hybrid creature who played the part for real, who said the lines and hit the marks and lived the agony Abel Groff had scripted. By the end of act one I had nothing left. I ran outside and stood in the alley taking deep breaths, trying to regain some bit of balance for what lay ahead. I halfway wanted Abel to come out and console me, but he didn't. I think he knew we were beyond that.

When act two began I watched Jake Cavett's raging soliloquy from the wings, fighting what I knew was fast becoming a truth. Tears were in my eyes when I made my entrance.

Brian's move toward Jake was calculated, almost coy, but as his failure became apparent, as Jake sat unblinking, hand inside his jeans, Brian grew desperate and began to plead, offering unconditional love in addition to his body. When Fall stood and pushed me toward the chair I dropped my pants, baring the ass I so wanted him to have. He came up behind me, erection brushing my crack, and then instead of sliding between my legs he pushed into my asshole in one long glorious stroke.

I didn't care that there was an audience. I wriggled back onto his cock and clenched my muscle, because I wanted him to know I was there—Carl, not Brian—and he responded with a full-on fuck, one I'm sure Abel thought the ultimate mastery of sexual simulation. And never mind that Fall had gone in before. This was a whole new game, and as I felt that long prick shoving in and out of my channel I hoped desperately that what had happened to me was happening to Fall as well, that Jake had been pushed aside and now, onstage, before hundreds of eager faces—and who knows how many stiff pricks—he might at last be himself.

Thanks to creative lighting and carefully planned angles, the audience could not see what was happening to me. Confident they were watching a simulation, they enjoyed an innocent thrill while I received the prick of a lifetime. Their presence made the entire act so incredibly public that my swollen cock began to throb and I unloaded into the chair as Jake raged behind me, driving his dick into me with renewed fury. I took it all, letting his angry words flow past as that snake of his plowed my chute, and when he came I squeezed for all I was worth, sucking dick with my ass to quench an unbearable thirst.

The rest of the scene—Jake's retreat, denial, shouts, the hurled bottle—was just that, a scene. I let Brian endure it and at the appointed moment made my exit. Standing in the wings, I had only a minute's respite before the finale began: Jake's suicide. I forced myself to watch him down the pills and liquor; I felt an awful dread even as his cum dripped from my ass.

The lights dimmed as Jake fell to the bed, then everything went dark, and when the lights slowly came back up to an eerie shadow they found me onstage. I felt for a pulse and let out a cry; I had no trouble with the requisite tears.

Jake Cavett was on his side, curled slightly, eyes closed. I climbed in beside him and took him into my arms, kissed his cheek, and placed my hand over his crotch to knead the lifeless prick. Not a single sound, barely my own breathing, then a slow fade to darkness. When the curtain fell it took the audience a moment to react. Stunned silence, then applause.

I was grateful Fall didn't leap from my arms. He lay

still and let me prod his dick until others rushed onstage to pull us up, hug us, congratulate us. I didn't want to let go, but rose to take my bows with the rest of the cast, then just the two of us side by side, and finally Fall alone, to thunderous applause. From the wings, I joined in.

Abel had arranged a party at a friend's penthouse, and after an hour of backstage crowds and champagne I was finally alone. Before leaving Abel made me promise I'd be along soon. "You're sure you're all right?"

"Fine," I told him. When he raised a brow I added, "OK, not so fine, but I survived."

"You were wonderful, Carl." He patted my shoulder and left.

I needed to change but managed only to take off my makeup. Time was what I wanted now, room to absorb what had happened, to sort out performance from . . . performance. I wandered out onstage in a confused sort of elation, reminding myself that the man had fucked me in front of five hundred people. I flopped onto the bed and burrowed into the covers. Fall's scent was there, and I closed my eyes and inhaled deeply.

"Carl."

He'd crept in like a cat and stood leaning against the headboard, beautiful in the half light. I rolled onto my back and opened my arms. When he slid on top of me I felt no bulge at his crotch and none of that awful tension he usually carried. He seemed to have uncoiled, as if the play had solved him, and yet I still wasn't sure just who I had here.

There was no urgency now. Fall simply hung on for a few minutes, burying his face in my neck while I ran my hands up under his shirt and kneaded his back. He was lean and smooth, taut as an animal, and I explored every inch of him, gradually working down into his jeans. I squeezed his ass and he groaned softly, then pulled back and began to strip. I lay paralyzed at the sight of him: skin tawny gold; cock quiet, flaccid, yet still so formidable, something that belonged on a lion, not a man. His chest was hairless, well defined, the nipples ripe; his stomach had a strip of hair that splayed out into a golden bush engulfing the cock I coveted. Just looking at the whole of him sent me into a frenzy, and I reached out and took his sizable prick into my mouth.

He eased back onto the bed and lay beside me as I swallowed all I could of him, tongue inching down his shaft, squeezing and sucking until he began to fill. As he stiffened I licked him to the root, then pulled back and fixed on his knob until I could feel him oozing juice, at which point I raised up off him to finger his dripping slit and stroke his magnificent meat. And I realized only then what he was giving me, that this was the first time he hadn't arrived fully primed.

When he began to pull at my crotch I stopped working his cock long enough to shed my clothes, then slid back down to him, but in reverse, my dick in his face, his in mine. We took each other then and lay sucking pricks onstage, bare as newborns and playing to that imaginary audience.

I wanted it to last forever, my hand cradling his heavy balls as I sucked his fat knob and licked that long sweet shaft. Everything was in slow motion now, the feast of a lifetime, and as much as I wanted to shoot my wad I wanted more to keep eating, to suck my way to infinity or die trying.

Fall's prick finally began to grow hot inside my mouth, jamming into my throat with a thrust that told me an eruption was imminent. My own load was churning as well and I began to push into him, to fuck that beautiful mouth I had never so much as kissed. Fall was moaning and slurping, lapping at me as I jammed into him while taking his massive meat deep inside my throat, sucking it until it began to squirt. Seconds later my own explosion hit and we lay feeding off each other, hands squeezing ass as we swallowed gobs of cream in the ultimate exchange.

Even after we were spent we didn't let go. I buried my face in his balls, inhaling his musky scent, while he ran his fingers through my dark bush. He was so incredibly gentle I had to remind myself it really was Derek Fall's dick in my face. And then he slid a finger into my crack, and farther, into my pucker, probing lightly, as if he hadn't been there before, then pulling out to gather spit and sliding back in. I knew then, as he finger-fucked me, that we would go on to Abel's party and that later, behind a locked bathroom door or on a remote terrace corner, he would fuck me. Derek Fall would fuck me.

Wrong Number

Bob Vickery

At a quarter after four, Nick tells me to carry a load of two-by-fours up the ladder to the journeyman carpenters on the third level. I stare at him. "Can't it wait till tomorrow, Nick?" I ask. "It's almost quitting time."

Nick's mouth curls into a lazy grin. I know I'm not going to like his answer. "Sure, Rossi," he says, his voice low and easy. "I'll tell the new apprentice, the one who's going to replace your ass if you don't do what I tell you, to do it first thing tomorrow morning." He raises his eyebrows. "Is that what you want?"

"No," I say quietly.

"Good," Nick says. "Then I suggest you get your ass in gear." I stare at his back as he walks away, my eyes shooting daggers at him. But that doesn't stop me from checking out the easy strut of his body, the butch little pivot of his ass as he makes his way to the foreman's trailer.

I don't get home until after six. The muscles in my upper torso ache, my shirt is plastered to my back, and my pits are ripe and smelly. I pull a beer out of the fridge, pop it open, and fall back onto the couch. The beer pours down my throat like the jizz of God, and I close my eyes and savor the sensation. When I open them again, I glance to the side table where the phone and answering machine sit. The message light is blinking, and I push the "play" button.

"Surprise, surprise, Tony. This is Mike." The voice is loud and pissed. "Surprise" is right—my name's Angelo. "I bet you didn't think I'd find you, but I got your number from Carol." *Carol who?* I think. *I don't know any Carol.* Angry laugh. "You know she can't keep a secret. Anyway, you had your little fun and games, now you better get your ass back here *tonight*!" There's a bang as Mike slams down the receiver. *What was that all about?* I wonder. I don't know who the fuck Tony is, or Mike either for that matter, or how this Carol wound up giving him my number. As I eat my dinner and watch the evening news, I find my mind wandering back to the message, wondering about the little drama behind it. Maybe Tony owes Mike money. Maybe Tony's been fucking around with Mike's girlfriend. Hell, maybe Mike and Tony are lovers, and Tony's tomcatting with someone else. I guess I'll never find out.

The next day when I come home from work, the message light is blinking again on my answering machine. I push the "play" button. "Tony, Tony," Mike says, his voice low and anguished. "Don't do this to me, baby. You're ripping my heart out." His voice breaks on the last word.

There's a long silence. "I'm sorry we fought, man," he says. I have to strain to hear him. "Come home, baby." He hangs up.

I sit down and stare at the machine. This is getting pretty heavy. For the rest of the evening I keep thinking about Mike and Tony, about what the story might be with them. Since dumb-fuck Mike didn't leave a number, there's no way I can call him and straighten him out. There's something about his voice that snags my interest, a roughness to it. I'm not good with accents, but I'm guessing blue-collar Jersey. I try to picture what he looks like. I see tattoos, a stubbled chin, a torn T-shirt with a pack of Marlboros rolled up in the sleeve. This gets mixed up with images of the guys at the construction site: Danny with his sleepy, half-lidded eyes, Carlos with his muscle-packed torso, even that sonuvabitch Nick with his lopsided smile and easy strut. My dick stirs and pushes up against my Jockeys. Even when I go to bed and drift off to sleep, I find myself wondering about Mike and Tony.

I wake up to the phone ringing like there's hell to pay. The clock on the bedside table says a little after two. I fumble for the receiver, finally find it, and put it to my ear. "Hello?" I mumble.

"Tony?" a voice on the other end asks.

Shit! I think. "Tony's not here."

"Oh, yeah? And who the fuck are you?" Mike's words are slurred. He sounds drunk.

"I'm nobody," I say. "Stop calling here. You got the wrong number."

"Don't give me that shit! Get Tony on the line or I'll rip your fucking lungs out!"

I laugh. "You don't even know where I live. Good fuckin' luck!"

A pause. "You fucking Tony?" Mike asks. "You swinging on his dick? Because, if you are, you're dogmeat, fucker! Do you hear me? DOGMEAT! Just say your fuckin' prayers if you're fucking my Tony."

"Look," I say. "Will you listen to me? There's no Tony here. You got the wrong number."

"JUST SAY YOUR PRAYERS, DOGMEAT!" Mike shouts into the phone. Then he slams down the receiver.

Christ! I think. I hang up the phone and pull the covers back over me. But as I lie in bed, I find myself thinking about Mike. He sounds like an asshole, major bad news. *Oh, yeah?* I think. *Then why's my dick hard right now thinking about him?* After a couple of minutes I wrap my hand around it and start stroking, conjuring up Mike's voice again, his rough, raspy baritone. The fantasies blend to the guys at the construction site. I finally shoot my load with the image of Nick cramming his dick down my throat, growling obscenities while Carlos fucks my ass. I don't bother to wipe my jizz off and drift off into sleep with it crusting on my belly.

Two days go by without any messages from Mike. Maybe Tony finally came back home, or maybe Mike gave him up for a lost cause. I tell myself I'm relieved it's all over, but I can't explain away the little throb of disappointment I feel. On the third night, though, there's another message from Mike.

"Hello, Tony, it's me," the voice says. Instead of the usual drama, Mike's voice is subdued, almost calm. I hear voices and glasses clinking in the background. "I know you're sitting there, listening to this message. Will you please pick up the phone?" Long pause. Mike sighs. "OK, have it your way. I'm over at the Cinch Bar, on Polk Street. I just want to talk with you, face-to-face. I'll behave myself, I promise." Another pause. "Tony, you motherfucker!" Mike snarls. "You owe me this. You've fuckin' lived with me for two years, you can at least give me a half hour of conversation before you kiss me off. I'll be here till ten." Mike slams down the phone. I glance at my watch. It's eight-thirty. *Well,* I think, *I can either blow this off or do something about it.* It's not much of a struggle to make up my mind. I want to see if Mike lives up to the fantasies I've been weaving around him.

I walk into the Cinch with Bonnie Raitt singing "Let's Give Them Something to Talk About" on the jukebox. The place is packed. *It's going to be tough picking Mike out in this crowd,* I think. I slowly swing my head, searching for men sitting alone and looking desperate—which turns out to be about half the bar.

I see him hunched over a well drink at the bar, eyes glued to the door. They shoot over toward me, do a quick scan, and then flick away. The guy is a couple of years older than me, mid-twenties maybe, clean-cut, short red hair, and a tight, muscular torso straining against a polo shirt one size too small. He doesn't look desperate, just grim, his mouth pulled down in a slight scowl, his eyes hard and dull.

I walk over to him. "Excuse me," I say. "Are you Mike?"

The eyes shoot at me, pinning me down like an insect on a specimen tray. "Yeah," he says. "What of it?" There's a pause. His gaze flicks up and down my body. "Did Tony send you?" His voice is taking on an edge. I see that it wouldn't take much to push him into full rage.

"No," I say. "I came here to tell you there's been a big mistake." His eyes are pale blue, as best as I can guess from the light of the bar. With his square jaw and the spray of freckles across his face, he looks like the original all-American boy. That is, the all-American boy bent on murder. The fucker is very sexy. I feel my dick stir and push up against my 501s.

"There's been a mistake all right. You made it, fucking my Tony." Mike's tone is level and cool, his eyes hard.

"Jesus." I laugh angrily. "You're a real piece of work. I can see why Tony left you." Mike's jaw is clenched so hard I half expect him to start spitting out broken teeth. A vein pulses in his forehead. "Will you calm down?" I say. "I just want to tell you that Tony's not—"

"What did Tony say about me?" Mike demands. He slides off his stool and faces me, fists clenched. I can feel the heat from his body, smell the fresh sweat. My dick is fully hard now. I find myself wondering what it'd be like having sex with this punk, how it would feel wrestling naked in bed with him, his muscular, tight body pressed against mine.

"If you're thinking about slugging me," I say, "you'd better think again." I glare back at him, staring him down.

After a moment, Mike relaxes. He climbs back on the stool and regards me coldly. "What's your name?" he asks.

"Angelo," I say.

Mike shakes his head. "Fucking Italians. All they do is

cause me grief." His eyes sweep up and down my body. "So Tony's hanging out with his own kind now, huh? He doesn't like Irish boys anymore?"

I don't say anything. It would be so simple for me to set Mike straight, to tell the dumb, sexy fuck that he's been dialing the wrong number. All I have to do is open my mouth. But something inside me suddenly wants to play this out, keep the conversation going. "Is Tony *your* type?" I ask.

Mike glares at me. "What the fuck kind of question is that?" His voice is low and raw. He takes a steady pull from his beer, and shoots me a hard look. I meet his gaze, and after a few beats Mike's shoulders drop and he gives a short, bitter laugh. "Yeah," he says. "In spades. That was always the problem. Tony can pull the most outrageous shit with me, and the sonuvabitch knows he'll always get away with it." He gives a long sigh and stares out the window, as if he expects Tony to walk by. I seize the opportunity to take a longer look at the bulge pushing against the frayed denim of his jeans. When I raise my eyes, Mike is looking me in the face.

"Yeah," he says. "It *is* a lot bigger than Tony's." He flashes a nasty smile. "Tony's a little deficient in that department, in spite of all his other plus points." His smile widens; his eyes gleam maliciously. "But then you must already know that, don't you?" I don't say anything. Mike takes another sip from his beer. "Does Tony know you've got a roving eye?" he asks, his tone conversational.

"Jesus," I say. "You're making a hell of a big deal over a little glance."

Mike gives a hard laugh. "Yeah, well we both know

where those 'little glances' lead to, don't we? Tony's big on 'little glances' too." He regards me shrewdly. "You'll find that out soon enough, if you haven't already." Some rap song starts playing on the jukebox, its volume deafening. Mike grimaces. "Look," he says, "it's too damn noisy here. How about continuing this conversation somewhere else?"

I give a short laugh. "What's there to talk about?"

Mike shrugs. "Oh, I dunno. I still got a few things to get off my chest." I'm uneasy about his sudden calmness. He nods toward the door beyond the pool tables. "Maybe we could step out into the back alley for a while."

I shake my head. "No thanks. The last time we talked, you said you were going to rip my lungs out. I like it better with people around."

Mike raises his eyebrows. "Don't tell me you're *afraid* of me!?!" He laughs. There's nothing mocking in the laughter; he seems genuinely amused. I don't say anything. His eyes sweep down my body and back up to my face. "A big guy like you, with all those muscles . . . Hell, you could mop up the street with me." He slides off his stool and stands in front of me, arms outstretched and hands open. "Look, Angelo, no concealed weapons." I still don't say anything. "Come on," he says. "I'm sick of shoutin' over the fuckin' jukebox. Let's step outside." He walks toward the rear door of the bar without looking back. After a few seconds, I reluctantly follow him outside.

The alley behind the bar faces a crumbling brick wall, lined with garbage cans. There's a streetlight at the far end dimly illuminating the place. Music and conversation pour out from the bar. "So what do you want to talk about?" I ask.

Mike doesn't say anything. He reaches down and gives my crotch a squeeze and then backs up against the brick wall. He calmly unbuckles his belt, unzips, and tugs his jeans down. He's not wearing any underwear, and his half-hard dick flops against his thigh.

"Are you crazy?!?" I say. But my eyes are riveted on his dick. It's a beauty, all right, thick and long, the head flared, veins snaking up the shaft. My own dick starts pushing against my zipper, hollering to be let out.

Mike leans against the wall and starts beating off, his strokes slow and sensuous. His mouth is curled up into a small smile. "I just figured you'd want a break from Tony's stubby little dick," he says. "Maybe swing on something with some *meat* on it." He works his T-shirt up and tweaks his nipple. His torso is beautifully muscled, cut to perfection.

Well, before my brain even has a chance to think about it, I'm on my knees, slobbering over Mike's dick, working my lips up and down that beautiful thick shaft. Mike grabs my head with both hands and starts pumping his hips, thrusting his dick deep down my throat. I reach up and grab his ass, squeezing tight. The flesh feels smooth and hard under my fingertips. I drag my tongue down his dick and burrow my face into his balls, breathing in their ripe, musky smell. I open my mouth and suck them in, rolling the scrotal flesh around with my tongue. I yank down the zipper of my fly, pull out my own hard dick, and start stroking.

Mike slaps his dick across my face with a loud *thwack.* "Yeah," he growls. "That's good, baby. Juice those balls up nice."

I look up at him. Mike's face is hard, his eyes skewering me. They gleam with malice. He pulls his balls out of my mouth and stuffs his dick back down my throat. He proceeds to fuck my mouth in long, savage strokes, slamming his dick in like he's trying to drill a hole through the back of my head. *That's OK, Mike,* I think. *I can get into playing rough.* I take his hard thrusts eagerly, twisting my head from side to side as my tongue wraps around the thick shaft. I work a finger up Mike's asshole, knuckle by knuckle, and then start sliding it in and out. Mike groans. I wiggle it again as he plunges down my throat, and Mike groans again, louder. His balls are pulled up tight and his dick is solid rebar. He whips it out of my mouth. "Get up!" he says. "I want to fuck your ass."

"I don't have a condom on me," I say.

Mike's eyes burn. "Yeah, well, I do." He bends down and pulls one out of his back pocket.

I stay on my knees, my gaze locked with his. Finally, I nod my head. "All right," I say. I climb to my feet as Mike rolls the condom down the length of his dick. He spits in his hand, sliding it up and down the shaft, and then wraps his arms around me from behind, pulling my body tight against his. I can feel the muscles of his torso press against my back, his dick thrusting up against me, probing into my ass crack. He shoves me toward the garbage cans, using the weight of his body to push me over them.

I break out of his hug and turn to face him. "Yeah, you can fuck me," I say. "But you're going to do it the way *I* like it. Face-to-face, me watching you as you shove your dick up my ass."

Mike gives me a grin that doesn't quite make it to his eyes. "Sure, Angelo. Anything you say." He lifts me on top of the garbage cans and hoists my legs over his shoulders. I hold on to his waist as he pokes his dick against my asshole and then slowly, inch by inch, slides it in. Mike's face is right above mine, his teeth bared in a fierce grin, his eyes burning holes in mine. "How do you like that, baby?" he growls. "I bet that fills you in a way Tony never could."

I slide my hands up his torso, tugging on the hard flesh, feeling its smoothness, flicking his nipples with my thumbs. "Yeah," I say. "But can you fuck as good as Tony?"

Mike thrusts deep into my ass and I cry out. "Well, we'll just have to see, won't we?" he says. He starts pumping his hips, his thrusts fast and vicious, his grip on me as hard as iron. I reach up and pull his face against mine, biting his lips. Mike shoves his tongue deep down my throat as he skewers my ass. He grinds his hips against me, rotating them, driving his dick even deeper inside, churning my ass with it. I squeeze my ass muscles tight and push up against him. Mike's eyes widen in surprise, and he gasps with the sudden rush of pleasure he feels. "Sweet Jesus, but you're a hot piece of tail," he says. He spits in his hand and starts jacking me off, timing his strokes with each thrust of his hips.

The metal handles of the garbage can lids dig into my back, and the smell of ripe garbage fills my nose. I can hear Bruce Springsteen singing "Pink Cadillac" inside the bar, and the murmur of voices just a few feet away through the door. Mike starts fucking in time to the beat of the song. I reach up and twist his nipples hard, and he groans again. The air in the alley is close and stifling; sweat beads Mike's forehead and splashes onto my face. Mike varies the way he plows my ass: a series of long, easy strokes punctuated by a savage burst of piston thrusts. He pulls out and slams me with a particular viciousness. I lose my balance, and the garbage cans tip over. We crash down amid a heap of spilled garbage: coffee grounds, banana peels, bottles and cans. I roll over on top of Mike and pin his shoulders down as he continues to slam his dick up my ass. I reach back and cradle his balls in my hand. They're pulled up tight and swollen, ready to pump out their load of jizz. I press my finger hard between them, and that's all it takes to push Mike over the edge. He cries out as his body trembles under me, and I feel his cock throb as it squirts its hot load into the condom up my ass. I ride out his orgasm, the bucking of his muscular body under me, garbage scattering everywhere. It takes just a few quick strokes of my hand to trigger my own orgasm. I groan as my jizz squirts out, splattering against Mike's face, dripping down his cheek in thick, sluggish drops. When the last of the spasms passes through me, I collapse on top of Mike.

We lie there in silence, the music from the bar's jukebox filtering out into the stale, reeking air in the alley. Mike is the first to move. He wipes his arm across his face, climbs to his feet, and pulls his pants up. They're stained with garbage, dark spots splattered against the denim. He brushes them off in a futile effort to clean them, and then straightens up and looks down at me.

I struggle to get up, but Mike plants his foot on my chest and pushes me back down. "Of course you realize," he says calmly, "that as soon as you leave, I'm going to call Tony and tell him I just fucked his new boyfriend in the alley. You're going to have some explaining to do when you get home."

I push Mike's foot off me and clamber to my feet. "I don't know Tony," I say. "I never met him in my life."

Mike looks at me with narrowed eyes. "What the fuck are you talking about?"

"Just what I said," I say, brushing bits of eggshells off my shirt. "This Carol friend of yours gave you the wrong number. Your friend never stayed at my place. That's why I came out here. So I could tell you, since you were too fuckin' stupid to leave a number for me to call you."

Mike gives me a long, long look. I return his gaze calmly. "Is this a joke?" he finally asks.

I shrug. "I'm afraid not."

There's another long silence. Mike suddenly laughs. "You know, I think you're telling the truth." He pulls his shirt down and runs his fingers through his hair. His eyes scan my face again. "You sonuvabitch, you *are* telling the truth!" He shakes his head. "I guess the laugh's on me." He flashes me a broad grin and holds out his hand to me. "You must think I'm one big dope. You want to shake hands and be friends?"

I smile back. "Sure." I take his hand. Mike tightens his grip and pulls me toward him. His other hand arcs through the air and smashes into my jaw. I fall, crashing among the overturned garbage cans. Mike looks down at me. "You still laughing, Angelo?" he asks. He spins on his heel and walks back into the bar. After a couple of minutes, I pick myself up and follow after him. Mike is gone. I go to the john and splash water on my face. My jaw is beginning to swell, but it doesn't seem to be broken. It's going to hurt for the next couple of days, though.

When I walk back into my apartment, the message light is on. I push the "play" button. "That was a funny trick you pulled on me, Angelo," Mike says. "You shouldn't hold that punch against me. You had it coming." Pause. "I've been thinking about our little good time in the alley. You got the right name, Angelo. You fuck like an angel. If you want, next time I'll plow you on an honest-to-God bed. I'll call you in a couple of days."

I take a couple of aspirin and go to bed, nursing my sore jaw. I lie there, wondering what I'm going to say to Mike when he finally gets around to calling again.

Down in the Bayou

Jay Starre

I was deep in the heart of bayou country, the Louisiana summer somnolent between tropical storms and hurricanes. From the suburban sprawl of southern California, I had fled my parents to visit family friends before I was to enter college. I don't know exactly what I expected to find, but beneath the Spanish moss and soft breezes, I did find something—something I cannot ever forget.

Jacques was a year older than I. His father was a descendent of French pirates, and his mother was my own less interesting mother's best friend. He was boisterous and big: big hands, big gestures, big heart. I had a summer job on a fishing boat with Jacques and his pals, and I reveled in the fresh air, the freedom from my parents, and the bayou itself.

It was Jacques who offered me my first taste of beer. That same night I upchucked that first beer—along with several others, stumbling back to the cabin I shared with Jacques while berating myself for my folly. I came weaving in the front door and collapsed on the couch in the front room. There was music playing in the bedroom, some wild fiddle stuff they liked down in Louisiana. My head hurt and my throat was dry. I rose and attempted to make my way to my bed. At the door of our shared room, I froze. There on the bed was a heaving back and butt, naked, and another naked body beneath it. In my blurred state of mind I stood there like an idiot while the bare ass moved up and down, slamming the body beneath it into the bed with frantic thrusts.

That big ass belonged to Jacques. I focused on it: the soft coating of blond hair that covered it was dripping with sweat, each powerful butt muscle tensed and straining as his hips rose and fell and rose again. I was mesmerized by the vision until the sane part of me realized Jacques was obviously fucking some chick and I should not be standing there gaping at him like a moron. But the sight of that ass rising, thrusting, and gyrating was impossible to turn away from.

Then a face looked up at me. Big blue eyes, sweaty forehead, parted lips, the flush of sexual excitement all too easy to read. This was the face not of some chick, but of a fellow fisherman named Guy who was getting pounded furiously by that hefty pair of hard buttocks. As soon as I realized he saw me, I fled.

I stumbled back to the couch and passed out. When I awoke it was very early. Birds in the trees were just beginning to stir, and a cool breeze wafted in from the open screen door. Jacques was right there offering me breakfast—and I was looking at him in a different light. From that time on our relationship was subtly altered.

I was a competitive swimmer in high school, and had won several championships. Jacques said he loved to watch me swim, so we went often. I loved it too. The water was sparkling clear in the spots he managed to find, and he assured me the "gators" were nowhere nearby. When I would strip down to my tight spandex competition trunks, Jacques would look me over with a grin and offer a loud whistle before he would slap my back with a staggering wallop. "What a bod, Stanley! Lean and lanky like a fine thoroughbred horse!"

If Jacques enjoyed watching me swim, I enjoyed watching him undress. He liked to sprawl out on his bed all but naked, only a pair of loose boxers hiding his private parts. His big chest was hairy like his ass, light blond swirls of hair covering it, with two nipples poking out. His biceps were big like his hands. His stomach was not exactly rippling with muscle, but was smooth and flat with a trail of that same light hair that ran down right through his navel and disappeared into his shorts. His thighs were tree trunks, and graced with that same swirling fur. I didn't get to see him completely nude too often, although he came out of the shower and sauntered into our room now and then, his thick dick flopping above a pair of substantial nuts.

I was a cherry, a virgin, totally. I had been so busy with swimming for the past five years, competitions and all, I had not spent much time dating or even having friends. Now I was obsessed with Jacques and his big hands, big dick, and big butt.

I caught Jacques with Guy a second time. It was a warm evening when I had gone into town to fetch some supplies in Jacques' souped-up convertible. When I returned unexpectedly for my forgotten wallet, I halted at the screen door and peered inside before entering—I'm not sure why, intuition perhaps.

Jacques was sprawled on the couch with his legs spread, Guy kneeling between them. His giant hands were twisted in Guy's short dark hair, pulling his head up and down over the stiff dick rising up from Jacques's naked crotch. I stared at that dick. I had never seen it hard; it was fat and glistening with spit. It stood tall, hard, and powerful, as if it was meant to be that way, forever stiff. Guy's lips gaped wide as they swallowed the big shaft, and he snuffled loudly, the ever-present buzz of insects behind me only scant competition for his slobbering moans.

I stared through the mesh of the screen, my eyes wide and my mouth agape. I realized my cock was rising too; perhaps it was attempting to compete with Jacques's big one. I could not turn away as I watched the two of them move in a moaning dance. Together they wrapped Jacques's giant boner in a condom, which did nothing to disguise the swollen girth of it. A moment later, Guy was kneeling in front of the couch and Jacques was behind him, plowing furiously, pumping his dick into Guy's parted crack, the shaft disappearing between his pale ass cheeks.

I fled. After that I constantly imagined the two of them together.

A month later, Guy quit his job and left, which I admit did not bother me. One day I went off swimming alone, which Jacques had warned me not to do, what with the alligators and all. It was a quiet Sunday evening, and the sun was just setting when I rose from the water and stood on the shore, dripping wet.

"I told you not to swim alone," a voice from the trees startled me. I recognized it as Jacques's deep boom. "I wouldn't want to see no gator biting off that stiff dick you got waving there."

I stared into the shadows, clutching a towel in front of my skimpy trunks. I had been thinking of Jacques and Guy together, and my cock had grown hard during my final laps. He had seen it poking out from my spandex trunks. How humiliating!

Jacques was sitting beneath a weeping willow, its huge branches tangled with their baggage of moss, waving in the evening breeze. He was gazing at me, a strange expression on his face, his back against the rough bole of the tree. One of his arms was draped over a raised knee, the other was behind his back, the biceps bulging. My dick was harder than ever, and I realized I was shaking.

He was quiet for a few moments, staring up at me, a half smile on his face. He finally spoke. "I know you've seen Guy and me together, doing it. Fucking."

It was eerily quiet, except for the ever-present buzz of mosquitoes. Then a big hand reached out and touched my leg, just above the knee. It was like a jolt of lightning hitting me. The sensation of his callused fingers on my bare flesh raced right up my thigh and into my aching crotch. I jerked.

His hand was slow and gentle as he began to stroke my thigh lightly while staring up at me. His smile broadened then; his fingers had risen to the lower band of my trunks.

There was no question where they were headed. Yet still I could not move. He spoke again, this time in a whisper. "Come on. Come on."

I sank down over him, a moan rising up from deep in my chest. His hands went round my waist and pulled my crotch to his face. His mouth opened, the gaping lips connecting with the head of my hard cock through the spandex of my swim trunks. That was only briefly, before his hands ripped at my trunks, pulling them down and exposing my crotch—my bouncing balls and ramrod-stiff dick. He engulfed it with his mouth, wet heat, sucking lips, and a twirling tongue all at once scorching my poor meat.

"Oh man, oh God, yes, oh man, oh man," I heard myself groaning. I was in shock. Then I felt big hands grasping my ass, a cheek clenched in each callused paw. I was pulled into the vortex of the mouth eating me alive by those hard palms on my ass. And the hands were not idle. Jacques used them to squeeze and press my butt cheeks, eagerly kneading them to match the fervor of his cocksucking. He pulled the cheeks apart and buried his fingers in the crack, sought out my asshole and began an insistent assault on it. I did not know I had a butthole before that moment, but he made me all too aware of it then. His fingers dug at it, tickled it, made it open up for him.

"What are you doing to me?" I actually shouted when a finger slid into my quivering ass ring. The ache in my butthole was profound, but it was also as if I was suddenly discovering an itch I wanted scratched as he began to rub and poke inside me.

His mouth slipped off my cock. He looked up at me,

his eyes swimming with lust, his lips wet and soft. "I want to fuck you. Can you take it?" he asked, just like that.

"Fuck me, go ahead!" I grunted, writhing around the finger buried halfway up my asshole, shoving my spit-slick cock against his cheeks and chin. I was insane with lust, the pent-up desire inside me a dam breached, with me caught in the flood.

He laughed, rising up to embrace me. He was a huge guy. Even though I was only an inch shy of his 6-2 in height, he was so broad I felt half his size.

His finger had not left my butthole, and he lifted me slightly off the ground by the ass. I felt engulfed by his hairy flesh, like I had when his mouth had captured my dick. He was kissing me all of a sudden—something I had not expected. I was appalled for a moment: the tongue he slid inside my mouth had been all over my dick a moment before, and his mouth tasted like crotch—at least I imagined it did. But then his finger rammed deeper into my tight fuck channel, and I groaned and sucked his tongue just as deeply, now eager to taste my own cock juices on his lips. I was suddenly a total slut at his beck and call. I wanted him to fuck me. I wanted him to replace that probing finger with his huge, hard boner. Whether I could take it or not, we would see. I had to try, though. He must have been thinking the same thing.

He maneuvered me; I obliged. I was bent over, leaning against the willow tree, my trunks torn down and over my feet one at a time. I was pliant and willing as he ran his rough hands all over my back and chest and crotch. I leaned into the tree and moaned as he stroked my dick with one hard hand and played in my butt crack with the other. He leaned into me, his muscles hard, the soft down of his blond fur tickling me.

"You're so soft, so smooth and hairless. God, you feel so fucking good!" he muttered in my ear, leaning over my back as he continued to play with my ass and dick. Then he moved; he was behind me on his knees. He pulled the cheeks of my ass apart and buried his face in my crack. He was suddenly licking my butthole.

I shook all over; I moaned; I pressed my butt back against him. The swirling tongue lapping at my hole was maddening. His hard hands had my cheeks pried wide apart, my butthole open for his enthusiastic licking. Fingers groped at the rim of my hole, prying that open as well. His tongue went right inside me, where his finger had been before. I grunted like a beast, shook violently, and realized I was shooting, my dick abruptly spurting without me so much as touching it.

Jacques ignored it, or did not even realize it was happening. But I could not ignore it myself, the ecstasy was so profound; my cock lurched spasmodically while my asshole was being invaded deeper and deeper by Jacques's tongue. Then he added a finger, which slid in easily with the copious lubrication from his tongue and mouth.

That was too much. I collapsed on my hands and knees, my head swimming, my dick drooling all over the grass beneath us. Jacques followed, his hands clutching my upraised ass, his tongue digging into it. I had my face in my arms, moaning nonstop.

He came up for air, but only for a moment. His hips shoved up against mine; he was kneeling behind me. He splayed my own thighs farther apart with his hairy trunks and lifted my ass with his hands. I felt his cock against my butt cheeks, then against my butthole. I was going to get fucked! I felt his hands moving back there, and through the fog of my orgasm I realized he was wrapping his cock in a condom. I was thankful he had one. Obviously he'd been planning this.

I was still shaking in the final throes of my orgasm, and my body was limp all over. That must have been why his dick slid inside me without a hitch. There was an incredible feeling of being stuffed, of being opened up and filled and overfilled. My mouth dropped open, I moaned and spread my knees. Jacques had each of my ass cheeks in one of his big hands, and he held them wide as he began to feed me his giant meat.

"I'm inside you. My cock is sliding up your tight butt. Goddamn, it's hot as hell and sucking me up so smoothly!" Jacques groaned. That was so hot. He was fucking my ass and he was loving it!

But that was just the beginning. He must have had only the head inside, because I began to feel more and more of him entering me. I gasped and wriggled my butt and slobbered on my arms as I heard my own voice begging for more. And more he gave me, so much more I was astounded by how much dick I could take inside me.

He slowly invaded me with that giant rod, beginning to thrust just a bit, then withdrawing, then thrusting a bit deeper. I jerked with each penetration, my asshole straining to accommodate the girth, my guts feeling each prod against some inner pleasure station that made me want to open up wider and take more. Every time he poked a little deeper, that sensation inside made my dripping dick harder. By the time he hit bottom, with his hairy balls nestled up against my sweaty crack, my dick had swollen stiff all over again.

I knelt there and accepted it. My ass rim was pulsing around his cock with a sensation so exciting it vied with the throbbing ache of his dickhead prodding my prostate. When he began to stroke me with it, I was babbling with insanity.

"Fuck me! Fuck me! Stick your dick up my butthole!" I chanted over and over. He held my butt and did just that. His big hands began to caress my back, then reached under me to pinch my nipples, giving me an electrifying sensation. His hands moved lower and clamped onto my dick and balls. He held them while his cock fucked my asshole. He had me buried in his bulk, his sweat soaking me, his dick reaming me with increasingly forceful thrusts.

I opened my eyes and realized it was growing dark. The cloying scent of the woods, the buzz of the insects, the rough bole of the tree, and the gentle caress of the bayou breeze melted into my consciousness as Jacques whispered in my ear.

"I wanted your ass so long. I wanted this, yeah, my big dick inside your tight hole. Goddamn, you feel so perfect, so good."

I answered him with equal fervor, mumbling into the grass how much I wanted him, needed him. "Fuck me, fuck me," I turned my face toward him and said.

He rose up, releasing me with his groping hands. He howled, then pounded twice all the way up my battered butthole, then pulled out. "I'm cuming! I'm cuming all over your white ass!" he screamed, his voice echoing in the woods.

I felt him splatter my upturned butt with cream. The thought of his jizz all over my ass, of his cock spurting in orgasm was enough to precipitate another ejaculation of my own. I squirmed beneath him as I shot a second load on the grass.

Then he was lifting me, turning me, embracing me. It was over.

But it wasn't. For the remainder of the summer my ass got reamed. Jacques's big dick filled me up with cream time after time under the willows in the bayou heat. I will never forget that summer down in the bayou. Neither will my ass.

Hostage

Barry Alexander

Bound and gagged, Adair lay on the stone floor. He could wriggle a little, flex the muscles in his shoulders and thighs, but his arms were numb and his whole body ached. The soldiers had simply opened the door and flung him into the king's chamber.

A window slit let in a narrow band of light that moved across the floor as the hours passed. The sounds and smells of supper drifted under the heavy oak door. Adair's stomach complained of hunger—he had not eaten since breakfast—but no one came. Shadows crept across the room as the light faded. Though it was early summer, cold seeped out of the ancient stones, chilling his flesh. He heard the evening song of a thrush, high and sweet and infinitely sad to one who knew he might never again hear the morning larks.

It was hard to die for something you hadn't done. He

had known the risk when his father, Tarkun, Duke of Corydon, had chosen him to be a hostage as a token of peace in exchange for the cousin of Dakin Kenet Tejar, High Lord and King of Massalas. When you are twenty-two and have just come to full manhood, death is something you don't think about, but he should have. His father had a great love of conquest and little use for a fourth son, particularly one who did not share his joy of slaughter. Adair was a skilled warrior, but he took no pride in that, and he was sick after every battle.

Adair had never expected to become friends with the king. Only ten years older than him, the Lord King of Massalas was the most beautiful man Adair had ever seen. Not overly tall, Dakin had a warrior's body. Massive arms and shoulders tapered to a hard stomach and muscled thighs. He kept his thick brown hair cropped short for battle. His thoughtful gray eyes had studied the slender young hostage kneeling at his feet. Homesick and terrified, Adair had vowed, on pain of his soul, never to raise arms against this man who had been his father's enemy. Somehow, even then he had known that this was a man he could trust. Then Dakin had smiled at him, and he'd blushed and stammered and felt what he had never felt for all the girls he had tumbled in the fields.

Treated as an honored guest, Adair had enjoyed the privileges and honor due a prince—and more attention than he had ever had from his father. Dakin had taken his word, and given him the freedom of his household and his friendship. There had never been anything else between them, but sometimes Adair had been surprised by a look on Dakin's face that had made him wonder.

Now, there would be no more such generosity. Adair's father had attacked the western villages, then tortured and murdered his hostage, the king's own cousin, at the victory celebration. Adair had just returned from a morning's hawking when Dakin's personal guard tore him off his horse and dragged him into the castle. They had not hesitated to tell him exactly what his father had done to the king's cousin. When Adair vomited his guts out, they laughed and left him lying in his own mess. The treaty was broken. Adair's life was forfeit to the king's pleasure.

After a long time, Adair heard footsteps in the hall. The door opened, then slammed shut, and the heavy bar thunked into place. Adair shivered; the waiting was over. The sharp click of boots stopped just in front of him. His eyes traveled up the muscled thighs and bulging crotch, tightly outlined by sleek riding leathers, to the sternly handsome face. Adair's eyes lit up in automatic welcome. The king was alone. For a moment, he dared to hope.

Then he was more afraid than ever. He had never seen Dakin so icily angry. It was not to be a public execution, but a private, more personal revenge. Adair had hoped it would be quick; he was not brave. He tried to keep from trembling. His eyes cold with hate and contempt, Dakin looked down at Adair, then raised one polished boot and kicked him onto his back.

"Corydon bastard! Do you know what they did to my cousin before they killed him? They beat him bloody and gave him to the garrison to enjoy. By the time they finished raping him, there wasn't much left to kill. But your father's torturers are skilled; they kept him alive two more days."

His lips twisted in a vicious smile that tore Adair's heart. "Have you wondered what I am going to do to you?" he asked softly. A shudder ran through Adair's body. "Yes, I can see that you have."

Kneeling beside the sprawled figure, Dakin wrapped his fist in the ropes around Adair's chest and jerked him to his knees. With his other hand, he drew an eight-inch dagger from his belt. Adair stared helplessly at the gleaming weapon inches from his face. He closed his eyes tightly. Dakin laughed.

"It won't be that quick." With a sudden movement, he cut the gag away. "The guards needn't have bothered with this. I shall enjoy hearing your screams."

Adair worked his dry mouth, trying to bring some of the moisture back. He looked up at Dakin helplessly. He understood his anger. Dakin was doing no more than his right. Hostages paid for their lord's misdeeds with their bodies. Though his eyes glittered with tears, he managed not to let them fall. His father owed Dakin a blood debt, and he was the payment. He could expect no mercy.

"Have you nothing to say?" Dakin asked harshly.

"I am sorry about your cousin, Dakin."

Dakin's fist smashed into his mouth. "You have no right to use that name, Corydon slime!"

"My liege." The fist struck again, knocking his head back onto the hard stone.

"Nor that. I claim no such subject. God! I took you into my household, trusted you, and this is how I'm repaid! Do you wish to beg?"

Blood dripped from the corner of Adair's mouth. He shook his head. "Would it do me any good, Lord King?"

"No more than it did my cousin. Your father will regret his treachery."

"He will not care," Adair said softly. "He never did."

Dakin slid his dagger under the ropes around Adair's chest, sawing through the tough fibers until they split. Adair fell backward, groaning at the sudden return of circulation to his numbed arms. Dakin cut through the rest of his bonds, then stepped back. "Stand up," he commanded.

Adair struggled to stand, almost falling as he tried to remain upright on feet that hurt as if pierced by hundreds of glass shards. He staggered, then caught himself, spreading his legs wide for balance. He rubbed his wrists and cautiously flexed his back and shoulder muscles. Even if his limbs functioned, he knew, he didn't have a chance. Not against Dakin. Dakin was the best fighter Adair had ever seen.

Dakin stared at him with an intensity of expression that Adair didn't understand. He wanted to look away but couldn't. Dakin was so close that Adair could see each hair of the fine stubble that darkened his face and smell the wine on his breath. Slowly, Dakin raised the dagger and slid it under the thongs that laced Adair's tunic. One by one, the blade severed the thin leather strips, allowing the fabric panels to fall open, baring the smooth muscles of Adair's chest. Dakin set the sharp steel point at the base of Adair's throat, pushing inward. Adair stopped breathing, waiting for the sudden prick and the cold fire of steel driven into his flesh.

The pressure eased and the blade moved on, gliding slowly down his sweat-slick body. "Don't move," Dakin said. The knife slid inside Adair's breeches, and with a loud rip sliced the front of them open. The evening air was cool as it touched Adair's exposed, shriveled genitals. Dakin lifted them up on the cold, flat surface of his dagger. "Not much to look at," he said scornfully. Abruptly, he let them plop back into place and sheathed his weapon. Adair drew a long shuddering breath.

Grabbing the loose edges of Adair's tunic, Dakin ripped it open. "I gave you this," he said as he tore off the hunting finery. "And these." His powerful hands rent the already torn breeches. He jerked off the tatters of fabric, and Adair stood naked before him, wearing only his riding boots and a medallion around his neck. Dakin held the emblem of his protection in his fist. "You will not need this anymore." With one yank, he snapped the thin gold chain and threw it on the floor. Gooseflesh rose on Adair's skin. He had never felt so naked and defenseless in his life. Dakin's medallion had given him the freedom and protection of the king's favor. He had known that was already gone, but even the guards had feared to remove what the king had set in place with his own hands.

Dakin took off his belt, running the leather between his broad hands. "The dungeon master will do a more thorough job later, but I want to take you while you are still conscious enough to appreciate the privilege. I am going to enjoy this. I thought about having you in my bed before. If you hadn't been a hostage, you would have been there that first night."

He stepped closer, his leather-clad leg brushing the inside of Adair's naked thigh. He caught the boy's jaw in his hand, his thumb caressing the full lips. Adair closed his eyes to shut out the face that was so close to his. He trembled helplessly, but not in fear. For so long, he had ached for this touch. As Dakin's thigh rubbed against him, his cock started to fill. His lips parted and his tongue touched the tip of Dakin's thumb.

"You are beautiful," Dakin said softly, almost regretfully. Then his voice and his hand hardened. "A pity that will soon change. Move!"

Adair jumped at the sudden yell. Dakin shoved him toward the bed. Using the discarded ropes, he bound him upright between the bedposts, arms high and legs spread wide. For a moment Adair panicked, struggling against his bonds and trying to free himself. Dakin watched the lean body writhing in terror, muscles standing up in corded ridges as he fought with all his strength.

"So your family is cowardly as well as treacherous. I should have known."

Abruptly, Adair ceased struggling, the scornful voice jerking him back to reality. He had known there was no chance from the beginning. At least he could try to die well. "Just do it," he said.

The first slash of the belt startled a moan out of him, but he refused to scream. He bit his lips until more blood dripped down his chin. His back and buttocks were on fire with pain. The beating went on and on. He had no idea that his body could hurt so much. He could hear Dakin's heavy breathing between his own gasps and moans, and smell the rankness of his own sweat.

The pain blended into a hot glow, enveloping Adair's body. To his intense shame, he felt his cock swell; the hardened rod slapped against his belly with every blow. He was glad that Dakin could not see the front of his body.

The belt carved a pattern of pain across Adair's body. Lines of fire laced across his body in an intricate pattern woven by Dakin's rage. At first, Adair tensed his body, trying to brace himself, but the belt always struck in a different place. His muscles clenched and spasmed. As the belt thudded and slashed across his naked flesh, his mind was a red haze of pain. Too exhausted to fight it anymore, his body hung motionless, except when shaken by the impact of the blows.

At last the belt stopped, and he listened to the harsh sound of Dakin's breathing. The belt hit the floor, and he heard the rustle of clothing. Even though he was expecting it, the first touch made him jump. Dakin wrapped his arms around Adair's body and held him still. "You can't get away," he growled.

Even past the fire devouring him, Adair felt the heat of Dakin's body. The blunt knob of his cock prodded his balls. Dakin held his hips firmly in place while the full length of his hard cock slid between Adair's cheeks. Rocking back and forth, Dakin let him feel the width and heat of his massive organ. Dakin's hands moved across his back and ass, even the lightest of touches making him quiver and moan in pain. He felt the cockhead prodding the tight opening. With a quick thrust of his hips, Dakin seated the crown of his manly scepter just inside Adair's anus. Adair groaned at the invasion. He had never been used this way. For a moment, the pain made him forget the agony of his back.

Dakin laughed. "Tight, just the way I like it. But it won't be after I get through with it."

Adair tried to get his mind away from what was happening to his body; he tried to imagine himself being somewhere else, som*eone* else. He couldn't do it. The reality was too painful and too intimate to escape.

With a sudden lunge, Dakin speared into him, sinking his entire cock deep inside Adair's bowels. Adair screamed.

"I knew you would do that. I wanted to hear you scream as my cousin must have screamed."

Dakin jerked his cock completely out and slammed it back in, over and over, until Adair's screams faded to whimpers. He was fucked brutally, the hard cock driven into his ass with no lubrication but his own sweat and Dakin's precum.

This was not the man he had known, the man he had started to love for his courage and his generosity. Dakin was a ravaging animal, taking his revenge against an enemy for hurting one of his own. Dakin rammed into him, hammering his loins against Adair, striving not for pleasure but for punishment.

With a final lunge, he came. His arms wrapped tightly around Adair; his hairy chest and belly pressed against the boy's back as shudders of pleasure convulsed his body. For several minutes, Dakin didn't move, resting close and warm against Adair's pain-wracked body. His gasps ruffled Adair's hair, his breath hot against Adair's ear and neck as the final spasms rippled through his body.

Adair broke then. Sobs tore his chest and tears streamed down his face. In spite of the pain, he welcomed even this contact with Dakin's body. Bending his head, Adair touched his lips to the powerful arm circling his shoulder—intending to show forgiveness, acceptance? He didn't know; he just knew he didn't want it to end like this.

Dakin pulled back as if struck, jerking his cock painfully from Adair's sore anus. Adair felt empty and cold. He hung his head, not trying anymore to silence his tears. Dakin cut his bonds. He slumped to the floor, waiting in despair for further humiliation, or to be handed over to the guards' pleasure. Dakin dressed quietly. Adair felt him bend over him for a minute, but Dakin said nothing and didn't touch him. Then, to Adair's surprise, Dakin walked away and shut the door behind him.

Suddenly, Adair was angry—to be used like that, then left without a word while Dakin walked calmly away as if nothing had happened. He hadn't even bothered to retie him. Obviously, he thought Adair was no threat. Just like his father, Dakin thought that since Adair didn't like killing he was weak.

Adair forced his body to move, struggling to his feet in spite of the pain. He looked around the chamber and found the dagger where Dakin had discarded it. Such casual contempt made him even angrier. With a grim sense of satisfaction, he concealed the weapon under the bed, close to where he had fallen. With all the guards around the castle, he knew there was no possibility of escape, but at least he would have a chance for his own revenge before they killed him. He waited, facedown on the fur-piled bed, enjoying the luxury of stretching his unfettered limbs.

He was half asleep when the sound of boots on the stone-flagged hallway woke him. Night had fallen while he rested. When the door grated open, Adair lay spread across the floor exactly as he had fallen when Dakin cut him down. Shadows flickered, then steadied as Dakin set a torch in the wall sconce. Leather creaked as Dakin walked past him without comment. From the corner of his eye, he saw Dakin set a box on the floor beside him. *So,* Adair thought coldly, *he went to get more things to play with before he hands me over to his men.*

Dakin's boot brushed against Adair's bare thigh. To his anger and his shame, Adair's body trembled and his cock hardened. He did not want to feel this way about this man who had so abused him, beating his back raw, then raping him. But even while Dakin had driven it up his quivering ass, he had wanted that massive cock. He had wanted it and dreamed about it for so long—but not like that. Well, he'd had it, and now Dakin was going to pay for it.

When Dakin moved past, he tackled him around the legs, bringing his body to the floor. Anger and surprise gave him a momentary advantage. Before Dakin could react, Adair had straddled his body and pinned his arms above his head. The wind knocked out of him by the abrupt contact with the stone floor, Dakin twisted fiercely but did not cry out.

Adair looked down at the face of the man he had loved, the man who had brutally taken what he would have joyfully given. And he knew he couldn't do it. He couldn't even hate him. Despite his anger and his hurt, he still wanted this man. And he had given his word to obey and protect him. He'd thought he had nothing left to lose when he'd planned his revenge. He still had his sense of honor, though, and he would not lose that by hurting the man he had sworn to obey.

Anger still burned in him. He looked for some sign of fear, but Dakin's face was a mask of control. He would not hurt him, but he would show him a little of what it felt like. He covered Dakin's mouth with his, biting his lips, forcing them apart and thrusting his tongue deep inside. He ground his aching cock against the answering bulge in Dakin's groin. Adair came up for air. He looked down at Dakin's heaving chest, his lips bruised and swollen from the ferocity of Adair's kiss. And he knew he couldn't do even this to him. He pulled the knife from under the bed. Dakin's eyes widened. Now that he saw that first touch of fear, he knew that wasn't what he wanted. "No," Adair said as he bent forward and gently kissed him, his mouth lingering on the warm lips that trembled under his. He leaned his cheek against Dakin's for a moment and sighed. "Damn you," he whispered as he slammed the hilt of the knife into Dakin's palm.

He rolled off Dakin's body. "I will not break my oath to you." He gestured to the box. "My body is yours; do what you will with it," he said bitterly.

Dakin rose slowly to his feet. Head bowed, in the posture of one receiving judgment from his king, Adair knelt. It didn't matter what Dakin did to him. He couldn't hurt any more than he already did. His face was quiet, without fear, without tears, without expectation.

He didn't look as Dakin opened the box and moved about the room. Then he felt a hand on his shoulder.

“Look at me,” Dakin said quietly, all the anger gone from his voice.

Slowly, Adair raised his head. Dakin pressed a cup of wine into his hands and looked at him with troubled eyes. Beside him the box lay open, filled with clean clothes, bandages, and numbwort salve for his back.

Suddenly, Adair’s hands shook so violently he almost spilled the wine. Dakin dropped to one knee beside him and held the cup to his lips. The warm liquid slid down his throat and steadied him, as did the arm around his shoulder.

“I’m sorry,” Dakin said. “I didn’t want it to be like that either. A madness took me when I heard about my cousin. I made him go. He was afraid and I promised him he would be all right. He was very young. I wanted to get back at your father, to make someone pay. I’m sorry it was you.”

Adair looked at him, not believing what he saw in Dakin’s eyes—deep shame, regret, and unspoken longing. Dakin held out the medallion he had torn from Adair’s neck. “I’ll get you a new chain. After you’ve healed, you’ll find a horse and travel gear in the stable. Go home to your father. I want no more revenge.”

“He doesn’t want me. Let me stay. Please.” For a moment he was afraid that Dakin wasn’t going to answer.

“How can you want to after what I did?”

Adair caught his hand and raised it to his lips. “I only know I can’t leave you.”

Hesitantly, Dakin leaned closer and gently brushed his lips against Adair’s. Adair leaned into the kiss and parted his lips. Dakin drew him closer, holding him lightly to keep from hurting him. But Adair threw himself into his arms, heedless of pain as he clung desperately to him.

Dakin eased out of Adair's grip and led him over to the bed. "Let me take care of you." Adair lay facedown on the bed while Dakin eased the salve over his sore back and buttocks. He moaned as the pain eased and the burning cooled. His body still ached, but the pain was bearable—anything was bearable as long as Dakin was touching him. The king's hands soothed and caressed him, Dakin's lips touching his shoulders and back as his hands moved down. Dakin slid down between his legs and gently parted his fiery buttocks. Adair gasped at the first touch of his warm tongue traveling down the sweaty crevice. Dakin's lips touched Adair's outraged orifice. Adair trembled in pleasure, sliding his legs farther apart. He sighed as he felt the tip of Dakin's tongue probe the tight ring, then slide deep inside. He could feel the ridge of Dakin's nose between his cheeks as he kissed and licked the opening he had so brutally used. He started to fuck him with his tongue, but Adair pulled away. The feeling was incredible, but this wasn't what he wanted.

"Please," he said. "I want you inside me. I want it the way it should have been."

He could see the desire in Dakin's eyes, but the king shook his head. "It's too soon. I don't want to hurt you again. Besides, I want to hold you, kiss you, not just use you. Your back is too sore to take you that way."

"I don't want to wait. I need you now."

Dakin gave in to Adair's desire, and his own. He sat in his chair while Adair knelt over him and slowly lowered himself onto Dakin's hard, red cock. It was painful at first, but his body soon opened itself in welcome. Dakin kissed him, licking the sweat from his shoulders. Adair's mouth glided over Dakin's neck and nuzzled through his damp chest hairs to find the pebble-hard nipples.

Adair clung to Dakin, raining kisses on his face and hair. He rode in slow gentle rhythms, savoring the warmth and fullness inside him. Dakin's cock was not an invader now, but a part of him. He quivered as Dakin's hands caressed his sides, then slid over his hips and boldly took command of Adair's jutting cock. Dakin's hands were powerful, holding his cock firmly and sliding the skin up and down. His broad thumb moved over the cockhead, greased with the stream of lubricant that flowed from Adair's inflamed rod. Adair moved his hips faster, slamming himself on Dakin's shaft. Dakin's fingers teased his slit, and he felt the juice boil up out of his balls and burst free, lashing Dakin's chest with glistening white ropes. He rammed himself down one final time. His head arched back as his body jerked and shuddered, totally out of control. Quickly, Dakin delivered a series of hard thrusts with his hips and bathed Adair's bowels with royal seed.

Adair collapsed against Dakin, gasping and panting against his heaving chest. They clung together, exhausted but content. "Don't let me go," Adair whispered. "I want to sleep with you inside me and wake up in your arms. Then I'll know it's real, that I didn't dream this."

Dakin's softening cock started to harden at Adair's words. He rocked it deeper inside. His muscles corded as he stood up, still holding Adair in his powerful arms. He walked to the bed and sat down, easing them both onto their sides. He held the boy in his arms, feasting on his mouth. Adair sighed, his body surrounded by and filled with Dakin's strength.

"Don't worry," Dakin whispered into Adair's ear just before he buried his tongue in it. "I'm never letting you go."

Grudge Match

Greg Herren

The kid wants a rematch."

"Of course he does," I said carefully into the phone. I glanced around my office. Everyone was working. They all knew I was gay, but they didn't know I had been a gay wrestling video star under the name Ross Matthews. During the three years I had done videos, I had made about fifteen tapes and was one of the company's biggest sellers. "I'll get back to you, OK?"

I hung up the phone and looked out my window. Gino Matarese wanted a rematch. My win over him had been my last taped match. A week after I'd beaten him, I'd been playing tennis when my foot turned and I blew out my knee. Instinctively, I reached down and touched my right knee. That was two years ago. My knee was fine now, after lots of rehab and physical therapy, but my doctor had advised me against ever wrestling again. Forced retirement. It sucked.

I thought about Gino Matarese, and felt my cock stir in my pants. Damn, he'd been a hot one. Lean, defined, sculpted muscle, a pretty face, and an ass to die for. After I'd beaten him I'd dragged him back to the locker area and fucked his pretty brains out. It had been doubly ironic that he turned out to be my last match, since it had been one of the hottest wrestling experiences of my career. I'd followed his career since my injury. He'd taken my place as the number one star. His tapes sold well, and he had been on a winning streak for two years. I was the only person to beat him.

Of course he wanted a rematch.

And fuck if I didn't want to wrestle him again.

I *needed* to wrestle again.

Watching the tapes and beating off wasn't the same as wrestling. I missed the body contact, the sweat, the feel of trapping another man in a hold he couldn't get out of, both of our bodies straining and struggling, muscle against muscle, seeing who was the better man.

My cock was rock-hard.

I got up and went into the bathroom, carefully locking the door behind me. I undid my pants and let them fall to the floor, slipping my right hand inside my underwear and stroking my cock. I pulled it out as I remembered Gino Matarese, in his purple square cut that outlined his perfect ass, the bulge in front from his erection. I remembered my legs around his head, squeezing. I remembered him on his hands and knees, that beautiful bare ass turned up to me, as I slipped my cock inside him and began to ride him hard.

I gasped as I came into the toilet paper I had spread

out on the floor, my body shuddering a bit as I squeezed the last drops out of my cock.

Knee or no knee, I was going to fight him again.

The day of the match finally arrived. I stood in the locker room, wearing only a black jock. Gino had requested we wrestle in jocks only, and barefoot. This wasn't unusual; the company made lots of jockstrap wrestling videos. What was unusual was that Gino had never done one, and that we were wrestling in the ring. Jockstrap videos were usually made in the mat room, which had walls that were painted black and wall-to-wall mats. I'd done a couple jockstrap videos early in my video career. I preferred Speedos in the ring myself, but hey, since I'd won the first match, I was cool with letting Gino pick the setup for the rematch.

Doing the rematch itself was unusual; the company didn't see much point in filming rematches, which made sense, since the tapes would compete with each other for sales. Apparently, though, my match with Gino had sold so many copies (and was still selling) they figured it was worthwhile to tape the rematch. Usually, if you wanted a rematch with someone you wrestled on tape, you arranged it yourself and it was private.

I stood in front of the mirror and flexed. I'd shaved my torso so the tanned muscles gleamed in the overhead light. When I'd first wrestled Gino I weighed 175 pounds—all lean defined muscle on my 6-2 frame. I now weighed 195 pounds, having added twenty pounds of muscle. My body fat was still the same. My muscles were thicker, heavier, stronger. I tested my knee. It felt fine.

Gino Matarese was going down.

I walked out of the locker room and down the hall to the ring room. When I entered, I was stunned to see Bob Foster himself loading a tape into the video recorder. Bob Foster was a reasonably attractive guy in his late forties and a hell of a wrestler. He'd started the company fifteen years earlier with a stock of blank videotapes and a camcorder. He'd starred in a lot of the early tapes, took out classified ads in gay porn magazines and gone from there. He rarely handled the camera himself anymore. He primarily scoped out talent these days, finding hot guys who were interested in wrestling, inviting them for a workout, teaching them moves, and getting them ready for the camera. Bob had found me at my gym. He was shirtless now, revealing his lean torso, wearing only a pair of navy blue cotton sweatpants.

"You taping this?" I asked.

He grinned at me. He had a lopsided smile. "Are you kidding me? Ross Matthews returns to the ring for a rematch with my hottest star? In jocks? I wouldn't trust anyone else with this one." He winked. "Besides, I wanted to see this match in person." He turned the camera on. "Go back out and come in again."

I obliged, and he held the camera on me as I walked in and over to the ring and climbed through the ropes. He taped me as I stretched, psyching myself up for what was to come. A lot of wrestling is mental preparation and focus. The mind and the body have to become as one. To me, the mind-body connection that's necessary to be a good wrestler is a spiritual thing. You have to be completely focused. You can't believe there's any chance you could lose. You can't be distracted by thoughts like "You haven't wrestled in two years" and "This kid hasn't lost since I beat him" and "Bob fucking Foster is taping this himself, and he hasn't personally shot a video in years."

Stay focused, Ross.

I stretched as Bob filmed me. I knew he zoomed in on my bare ass whenever he could, just as he always zoomed in on bulges. People have always told me my best feature was my ass. In the days when I went to bars and circuit parties, it always got touched and grabbed.

The door on the other side of the room opened and Bob swung the camera around. Gino walked through. I glanced over at him. He stood in the door and flexed his biceps, bringing his arms down together in front so that every muscle in his upper body flexed, showing the striations of the muscle. He had gotten bigger since I'd last seen him. He stood there posing for the camera for a few more moments, then stalked over and jumped up to the ring apron. Then he jumped over the top rope, springing as he landed, his fists clenched. He walked over to where I was stretching my shoulders out.

"You're the one who's gonna get fucked this time, old man," he sneered at me.

I turned and faced him. "Once a bottom, always a bottom, boy."

He shoved me into the ropes, which propelled me back toward him. I saw him cock his fist for a shot at my abs, so I planted my feet and kicked him square in the six-pack. He doubled over. I turned, grabbed his head, slipped my shoulder underneath it, and dropped to my knees, driving his head into my shoulder with a good deal of force. He bounced off my shoulder and fell, landing on his back. I stood up and walked over to him. He was groaning and holding his head. I planted my right foot square in his abs and stomped. Once. Twice. Three times. He rolled over onto his side in a fetal position. I grabbed him by the hair, pulled him up to a sitting position, then put my legs on either side of his head and fell back to the mat. I squeezed his head as hard as I could, and he let out a scream that made my cock stir. I reached down and grabbed his arms by the wrists, pulling them up and inward. He was immobilized. If the pressure on his head didn't get him, the pressure on his shoulders would. I cranked the arms harder and squeezed.

He screamed again.

"Come on, punk," I taunted him. "Give it up. You know you want to. You know you want my cock up your ass again."

"No fucking way! FUCK YOU!"

His words trailed off into a scream as I tightened my legs again and yanked his arms farther up.

"Come on, boy."

"FUCK YOU! FUCK YOU!"

"OK, then." I squeezed again.

"OK, OK, I give! I give! I give!"

"What did you say? I didn't hear you."

"I give! I give! Come on, man, I give! I give!"

"That's what I thought." I let go of him and got to my feet. He lay there on the mat, groaning and holding his head. I walked back over to the corner and stood there, leaning back into the ropes, watching him. After a few minutes, he got to his knees, shaking his head. He moved his shoulders a bit, trying to loosen them up.

"Take your time, boy," I said. "I got all day to kick your ass."

"Fuck you," he said. He got to his feet. Sweat glistened on his smooth pecs. He walked back to the opposite corner, still shaking his head. He turned his back to me and leaned into the corner, his head down. He appeared to have the body language of someone doubting himself, doubting whether he could win the next two falls and thus the match. I smiled to myself. *Bring it on, boy.*

He turned to face me again. "I'm ready."

We circled each other in the center of the ring, feinting at each other, looking for an opening. Sweat was rolling down from his black curly hair. His brown eyes looked determined. This fall wasn't going to be easy, I realized.

His left leg shot out and kicked me, square in the right knee. A bolt of pain shot through it, and my leg buckled.

Fuck, I thought, and in that instant he was on me. He grabbed my head and pulled me down into a headlock, his muscles tightening around my head, but all I could feel was the pain from my knee. My bad knee. It still wasn't steady, and as he dragged me around the ring by my head it buckled from time to time.

He flipped me over onto my back, still holding my head. I hit the mat with a thud. My knee was throbbing. He let go of my head, only to slam it into the mat. My ears starting ringing. I tried to get up, but somehow he had grabbed my right leg and bent it around his. Pain shot up my leg as he twisted. I let out a howl.

"How do you like that, old man?" he panted with a grin on his face. He twisted my leg again.

Motherfucker. I was breathing hard, trying to focus my eyes. It hurt, oh God how it hurt. I raised my left leg and kicked at him, landing my foot square into his abs. He dropped my right leg and fell back. I rolled over and got on my hands and knees. My knee fucking hurt, my God, the little bastard—

He kicked me in the side.

Air exploded out of me as I rolled from the momentum of the kick. He kicked me again, and I kept rolling, trying to get away. My shoulders hit the bottom rope. Just as I reached up for it he kicked me again. The rope slipped out of my sweating hands and I fell off the ring apron and dropped heavily to the mats outside.

My head was spinning. I grabbed my knee just as I heard him drop down to the mats outside the ring. He reached down and grabbed my head and pulled me to my feet. He slugged me in the gut, driving me back into the side of the ring. My ass hit it and I fell back into the ropes, grabbing them for balance. My knee was buckling; it couldn't hold me.

He kicked me in the knee again.

This time I dropped to the mats, and he scooped me up and slammed me down on my back. Before I could get my bearings he had me up again, this time setting me back down on the ring apron. He grabbed my right leg and dragged me to the corner of the ring, pulled my leg out, and slammed my knee into the ring post.

I screamed.

I could hear him laughing and the ropes squeaking as he used them to pull himself back into the ring. He grabbed my arm and dragged me under the ropes, then planted his feet above and below the shoulder and dropped back to the mat.

My shoulder exploded in pain.

Focus, I told myself. *Every hold has a counter. Forget the pain—*

OUCH! Fuck!

—forget the pain; don't forget: concentrate, focus—

Sweat dripped into my eyes.

He let me go.

I rolled over onto my stomach, holding my shoulder. It was throbbing. My knee was throbbing. *Goddammit.* I got to my knees. The ropes squeaked. He was standing in the corner opposite from me. He was grinning. I shook my head.

Focus.

I got to my feet, and my knee buckled slightly. I looked over at him. His eyes narrowed and he came toward me. I backed up a little, my leg buckling again. *OK, watch for an opening, careful of the knee—*

He leaped up into the air and kicked me in the chest with both feet.

I fell backward, tucking my head so that the force of the fall was absorbed by my back. Still, I hit the mat with a bone-jarring thud. Before I could move he had ahold of both my legs. He held them up, standing in between them, and then stomped his right foot hard into my abs. I barely had time to flex them to withstand the stomp, and then he stomped again, twice, three, four times. My ab muscles were screaming, and then he hooked his arms around my knees and lifted me up onto my shoulder blades.

A fucking Boston crab.

I tried to fight it off, but he just grunted and strained until finally I started to turn. He rolled me over onto my stomach, holding my legs, and then sat back, arching my back much farther than it was ever intended to bend.

I screamed.

"What do you say?" he panted, leaning back even farther.

"I give! I give!" I shouted.

He let go, dropping my legs.

I lay there on the mat, unable to move. My abs ached. My knee was throbbing. My lower back hurt. I gasped for air.

He stood over me, flexing his biceps.

"You want some more of this?" he screamed at me. "Huh? Huh?"

The little fuck. His package was just above my face. His cock was hard, straining against the cotton.

I drove my fist up into it.

Gino screamed and fell to the mat, doubled over, both hands on his balls.

I willed myself to get up, to ignore the pain. I limped over to him. I used my right leg to kick him in the abs. He rolled over onto his stomach, that beautiful white hard ass coming up in the air, framed by the straps of his black jock. I reached down and grabbed the top strap, the thicker one running across his lower back. I grabbed it and yanked. There was a brief tearing sound, and then the jockstrap came free in my hand. I sat down on his back. He was still moaning, and I pulled the jock tight around his neck, pulling back.

He gagged and choked.

"Come on, boy," I muttered. "How do you like this?"

His hands came up, trying to pull the jock away from his neck. His face was reddening as he gasped for air. I smiled. *You want free, boy? OK.* I let go, and he gasped for air. I grabbed his curly hair and drove his forehead down into the mat. Again. And again. And again, until I lost count.

I got off his back. He was moaning. I grabbed him by the hair and dragged him to his feet, pushing him back into a corner. He sagged against it, arms draped over each side of the ropes. I stood there for a moment, then started punching him in the abs, those beautifully defined abs. Right, left, right, left, the air exploding out of him with each punch, his body sagging more and more with each shot. I climbed through the ropes and dropped down to the mats outside, still favoring my aching right leg. His muscled arms were just hanging there. I grabbed them both, cradling them inside my left arm as I tied his wrists together behind the ring post with the jock. I glanced over at Bob. His hard-on was tenting out his sweatpants. I faced him and flexed for him, then climbed back into the ring.

Gino's big heavy cock was stiffening as he tried to move his arms.

I slapped his face, his head jerking back. "You like this, don't you, boy? You like being worked over."

He muttered, "Fuck you."

I grabbed his cock with my left hand. It became completely hard as I squeezed it. "You can't hide it, boy. You want to get beaten up, and then you want to get fucked."

"FUCK YOU!"

I slipped my jock off. My own cock was rock-hard now. I shoved my jock in his face. "Smell that, boy? That's what a real man's balls smell like." I rubbed it over his face, then stepped back.

What to do with him now? I wondered. His body was slick with sweat, and still sagging somewhat. I climbed up onto the second rope, and started slapping his face with my cock. "You wanna suck it, don't you?" I taunted him.

"Fuck you!"

I climbed back down, and then through the ropes again. I untied the jock, and he slid to the mat, clutching his abs. I climbed back into the ring and grabbed his legs, dragging him to the center of the ring. Turnabout, I decided, was fair play. I lifted him up onto his shoulder blades and turned him over, sitting on his back. He screamed, "I give! I give! I give!"

"What did you say?"

"I GIVE, SIR! I GIVE, SIR!"

I let him go and walked over to the ring corner where I'd tied him, pulling on my dick. His ass was up, even sexier and hotter than it had been two years earlier. Bob handed me a bottle of lube and a condom. He was sweating. He nodded at Gino. "Go fuck him now."

I slid the condom over my cock and lubed it up. I was still limping a little; there was a dull ache in my knee.

He had done that.

I knelt down between his legs. "Arch your back, boy."

He didn't move.

I smacked his ass, leaving a handprint on its hard whiteness. "I said arch your fucking back!"

He whimpered and complied. I pulled his legs farther apart, staring into his musky-smelling hole. I slid a finger into it. He whimpered again, his ass rising higher into the air. He wanted it, all right. I smiled. I moved the finger around, loosening the hole up, slipping in a second finger. I moved my hips forward, but a bolt of pain shot up from my knee.

There was no way I could fuck him on my knees.

"Get up, boy." He looked over his shoulder at me. "I said get up!"

He slowly got to his feet. His eyes were downcast. I lay down on my back, holding on to my cock. "I want you to ride my cock, boy. Get over here."

He straddled me, reaching behind himself and grabbing my cock, guiding the tip into his hole. He shuddered a little when it entered him, his breath coming fast, his eyes closing. He slowly slid his ass down my shaft until he reached the bottom, a half-smile starting to form on his face. "You have a nice cock, sir," he whispered.

Sweat was rolling down his chest, streaking down his abs. His curls were damp. "Ride it, boy. Ride it nice and slow."

He started moving up, his abs flexing as he did, then slowly coming back down. I reached up and grabbed both of his nipples, pinching them. He moaned again. I heard the ring ropes squeak as Bob climbed through with the camera, squatting down above my head. I ignored him as Gino—my boy, my conquest, my prize—rode my cock.

"Flex them arms for me, boy," I said. He smiled at me, his eyes half-closed, and obliged. "Kiss those biceps, boy." He pursed his thick beautiful lips and turned his head, kissing one mound of muscle and then the other. "Now flex your pecs." He brought his arms down, and the striations in his chest muscles popped out. I punched one, then the other. His eyes closed.

"Yes, sir. Anything you want, sir."

"Stroke your dick, boy. I wanna see you cum."

He picked up the bottle of lube and squirted some on his thick shaft, never losing a beat as he rode my cock. He started stroking it, slowly at first, and then faster. His ass began riding me faster, and I could feel my own climax coming.

"Come on, boy, shoot your load!" I panted.

His entire body shuddered and he yelped as ropes of cum started flying out of the slit in his cock, landing on my abs, my chest, my face, my hair. He kept riding my cock as his body convulsed, and I let out a shout as my entire body went rigid with my own orgasm. We both remained there, my cock in his ass, as both our bodies convulsed and shuddered.

Then, he smiled down at me. "Thank you, sir," he said quietly. He reached down and rubbed his cum into my skin. "I've been waiting for that for two years." He slid my cock out of his ass, then got on all fours and kissed me, deeply and passionately.

I ran my hands through his damp hair. "You're a good boy, Gino."

He cuddled up against me, throwing his right leg over my abs.

"And that's a wrap," Bob said, putting the camcorder down.

I smiled at Gino. "You wanna grab a beer or something?"

He smiled at me. "Yes, sir."

"Come on, then." I got up and helped him to his feet. I touched his rock-hard pecs again. "Such a pretty boy."

And we headed for the shower.

Hands On

Barry Alexander

Tommy checked before he settled into the deep, leather seat of the silver Cutlass. It wasn't there. He sighed with relief. Morgan didn't always take it. Sometimes, they just went out for drinks. Sometimes, he took Tommy to the Pit and put him through hell.

The dome light illuminated Morgan's harshly chiseled features and seal-brown hair. Tommy had lived with him for several months, but he never tired of looking at his master's well-defined body and handsome face. Morgan was tall and deceptively slim; Tommy knew well just how strong that taut, muscled body was.

Morgan was silent as they drove through the dark streets. Though it was early for the leather crowd, several vehicles lined the street outside the Pit. As Morgan stepped out, a hustler emerged from a boarded-up doorway in the dark block of buildings. He flashed his smile and his ass hopefully, but Morgan dismissed him with an arrogant glance. He turned back to Tommy. "Get out." He walked to the rear of the car and opened the trunk. "Take it," he ordered.

Tommy cringed as he pulled out a large black tackle box; Morgan didn't fish. The new toy box was larger and heavier than the old one. Tommy thought of all the things it could hold and started to sweat. He'd seen the ads. His stomach clenched as he remembered some of the more vicious items.

Every eye in the bar ogled Tommy. Morgan had dressed him for show. Shiny, red spandex bike shorts hugged his ass like a lover, revealing every curve and indentation of his perfect bubble butt. A white tank top clung to his prominent nipples and accentuated the golden hue of his skin. Dark blond hair, green eyes, and a puppy-dog expression gave him a vulnerability that even sharply planed pecs and large biceps couldn't belie.

Morgan was in a good mood. He bought Tommy a couple of beers while the tops gathered. Tommy stood on display, legs spread wide, facing the bar. Fingers slipped between his cheeks, prodding his hole. You could tell a lot by the way a man used his hands. They moved over Tommy's body, clutching, grasping, greedy or tentative, harsh or gentle. It was going to be very important to know these hands. Every top would have his chance at Tommy's ass. Morgan believed that since a dog knew the hand that fed it, a slave should certainly know the hand of his master. If Tommy guessed wrong, the top got to whip his ass. Make him cum and they could fuck him or get blown. Tommy got five lashes at home for responding to someone else. So far, Tommy had never guessed wrong. He knew Morgan would have a much harsher penalty for that mistake.

Tommy couldn't help comparing Morgan with the other tops. Some of the men were so heavily into leather they creaked when they walked. Before Morgan, that was what Tommy had looked for, before he knew that it wasn't just the leather—it was the man.

Tonight, his master wore 501s and a black T-shirt. Only his thick belt and logger boots were leather. He didn't have to impress anyone. One hard look from his granite eyes could bring any bottom to his knees and worry the hell out of most tops.

Morgan finished his drink. "Showtime, boy." The men grinned, licking their lips as they followed Morgan into the bowels of the Pit. A man in a Nazi-style uniform swaggered up. Morgan blocked his passage with a muscular arm across the entrance. "Private performance," he said firmly. The man topped Morgan's 6-foot-1 height and outweighed him by fifty pounds. He objected loudly and profanely. Morgan didn't say a word. He just looked at him with those glacier-gray eyes. "Aw, shit," the man said, and backed away. "Your party, man."

A stage extended along the room's back wall, complete with spotlights, a table, and a sawhorse. Morgan positioned the table so everyone had a good view. "Get up there, boy. Strip."

The men whistled and stomped as Tommy peeled off his shorts, exposing the high, round cheeks of his ass. His seven-inch cock bobbed between his legs. His face was as red as the shorts he folded. Morgan grabbed a handful of tit and snapped clamps in place. He caught Tommy's cock in his warm fist. It swelled, filling his hand. He slapped the bright ruby head of the circumcised organ. Tommy shuddered in pleasure and pain. His cock snapped back and nudged his belly.

"Assume the position."

Tommy hissed as his clamped tits touched the table. He spread his legs, leaving his ass high in the air and his cock and balls swinging under the table. Morgan darkened the room and spotlighted Tommy's ass. A swirl of dark gold hair outlined the deep cleft and spread across the curve of his snowy cheeks. Sweat gleamed on his taut muscles and on the tight pink pucker exposed to everyone's view.

Morgan ignored the chains dangling from the table corners. He didn't believe in restraints except for training. The master's wish was the only control a well-trained slave needed. He pulled Tommy's head up to buckle a leather hood in place. The scent of leather was so pervasive, Tommy knew he wouldn't be able to detect individual scents. Morgan was making the game harder.

"You know the rules. No fists, no marks, and nothing goes in this ass that doesn't come out of the box. But I don't think you're going to feel deprived."

He must have displayed something that met with approval; the tops roared in appreciation. Tommy quivered with dread, but his cock hardened. He trusted Morgan that nothing would go too far, but the thought of blind submission terrified him.

"Tommy's been doing such a good job, I'm raising the stakes. If he mistakes you for me, you not only get to whip his ass—you get to take him home for the night." Raucous cheers greeted his remarks. "Don't forget: make him cum and you get to fuck this nice ass." Morgan's hand cracked on Tommy's butt.

Oh, please no! No damage and safe sex only, Morgan said, but Tommy would probably be bound and helpless. The tops couldn't expect him to lie there and take it like he did for Morgan.

"Choose your weapons."

Order of play and toy selection was determined by number. Tommy never knew which toy Morgan would use or when. He hated the uncertainty, the sense of total vulnerability. But as much as he hated the game, Tommy was proud of his uncanny ability to identify his master by touch. With the hood in place, he couldn't rely on sound or scent. Everything depended on touch.

Large hands yanked Tommy's cheeks apart. A massive dildo speared into him, forcing a groan at the sudden assault. He arched his back as it drove up his chute in one long thrust. Before he could adjust to the painful intrusion, the top jerked it out and spiked him again. He ground his bulging hard-on between Tommy's cheeks, grunting his pleasure. Tommy's body tried to expel the dildo, but each brutal thrust drove it back in.

The man fell across Tommy's back, crushing his clamped tits against the table. He screamed. The man never slowed. His crude humping drove the boy back and forth, torturing his tits with each movement and slamming his cock against the table edge. The man froze; Tommy felt the shudders rippling through him as the man came. His gasps reverberated through Tommy's back. Even without the threat of punishment, Tommy felt disloyal responding to anyone else. He tried to fight his arousal, but a cock has no ethics. Suddenly, the man sank his teeth into his neck, biting and worrying the skin like a wild beast as the final spasms shook him. Tommy moaned in frustrated lust when the man ripped the dildo out of his ass.

As brutal as the possession had been, it had excited the boy. The man had asked no permission, nor given a single touch in warning or introduction. He'd moved in and taken what he wanted, just as Morgan would have. A little longer and the man would have earned his reward. He reached between Tommy's legs to check.

Yes! Touch me again. Please! But the contact was too brief to produce more than a sticky streamer of precum. Tommy's thoughts were as ragged as his breathing. The top was definitely a possibility, but the weight was wrong, wasn't it?

He was still gasping when powerful thighs straddled his head. Leather-clad fingers swirled across his sweat-slick shoulders, tingled over the ridges of his spine, and spiraled over his cheeks. The lean body spread over him, driving the steel rings and studs of the man's harness into his flesh. Tommy wriggled in heated desire as the coarse stubble of the man's chin left whisker burns on his ass. He gasped at the sudden delight of a warm, wet tongue caressing him. No top had ever done that!

Like a moist, pink blossom, the tight bud of his anus dilated under a gust of warm breath. The hot tongue left wet snail trails across Tommy's ass. His hungry chute ached to be filled. At the first touch of the toy, he pushed outward, opening himself. His lips swallowed a large ball. More steady pressure, then another larger ball opened him farther, and still another. The man worked the triple plug expertly, slow-fucking Tommy to an unbearable peak. He couldn't hold back, and he no longer wanted to. Spasms shook his body as he shot blast after blast of steaming cum over the man's hand.

The man swung off and forced Tommy's head up. Something wet brushed his lips. He clamped his teeth together, but the man forced his jaw open. He recognized the taste of his own cum on a latex-sheathed dick. He cleaned it happily. He'd worry about his punishment later. After that release, the top deserved his best. He swirled his tongue over the broad head, pushing the latex into the piss slit with delicate dabs of his tongue.

The man wasn't interested in finesse. Clamping his hands to Tommy's head, he impaled his throat and ground his pubic hair against his lips. Tommy flailed, trying desperately to breathe. Bile filed his throat, slicking the passage for the man viciously humping his face. With a howl of ecstasy, the man shot, holding himself deep inside and pumping his fluids into the condom.

The cock pulled out. Tommy coughed and gasped, slumped across the table in exhaustion. *Use your head. Would Morgan trick you by borrowing gloves and a harness? By being extra gentle or extra rough? Think logically, damn it.* Suddenly, he thought of something he had never considered. Did Morgan want him to win? Were the higher stakes intended to increase interest or to make him so nervous that he would fail? What did Morgan get out of it? Did he want to show how much Tommy was under his control and remind him that the only limits to their games were Morgan's?

Or was it something else? Was Morgan so confident of their bond that he never considered the possibility of failure? Tommy found the questions disturbing. Even more troubling was his inability to answer them. He wasn't sure he wanted to. The bond existed. It worked; he didn't need to pry into its roots.

The tops didn't give him much time to think. They kept at him, poking him, prodding him, filling him with every kind of toy imaginable: vibrators, anal beads, electric butt plugs, and things he couldn't identify. He was a hole for their pleasure, an object to be used as they chose. He tried to identify the hands, to separate the maybe's from the no's, but all he could think of was what was going to come next. He was exhausted, his body sore and his anus raw from the pounding it was receiving.

The hair prickled on his neck as his body sensed the next man approach. One hand cupped his ass and slid up his spine. His body quivered helplessly in instant response. He forgot his plans to wait, to use reason and eliminate the impossible. He forgot everything but the warm hand on his skin. One touch and he knew. Without doubt. Without question. His body knew.

"Morgan," he whispered.

The sharp crack on his ass made him jump. "Right on target," growled the rich, deep voice. Tommy's breath heaved out in a great sigh. Morgan slapped him again. "It's not over yet."

Again and again, Morgan took him to the peak, but

refused to let him cum, torturing his body with pleasure and pain until Tommy was a quivering, shuddering mass of nerve endings. His hands teased and promised and tormented, controlling the boy with every touch. Tommy cried and begged Morgan to let him cum. At the first touch, he'd known Morgan's toy was bigger than anything he had yet taken, but he willed his body open, pushing against it, inviting the pain.

"More, boy," Morgan said. "Open wider."

Tommy's body went rigid with pain; muscles strained and corded. Sweat poured from his pits as a huge ball was slowly forced into his anus. Morgan's hand stroked his back as he continued to push. Tommy had never been opened so far. He tried to focus on his master's touch, not on the boulder up his ass. The ball passed its greatest width. His anal lips closed, locking on a thick handle.

Tommy was exhausted, but Morgan's touch told him it wasn't over. He wouldn't have thought it possible to stay hard with that mass plugging him, but Morgan made it happen. His right hand played across Tommy's body as he slid the giant ball dildo out again. Tommy's sphincter fluttered, gulping at the emptiness. Morgan teased and tormented him, and suddenly he wanted it, wanted that intense fullness inside. He opened his legs wider, pushing against the spike. Morgan gave it to him, filling every inch of him with an ecstatic mix of pain and pleasure. He cried and shook as his cock exploded, spraying long streamers of cum in every direction. He collapsed against the table, sobbing helplessly. Morgan withdrew the dildo gently. His hand touched the back of Tommy's head briefly, then he was gone.

Tommy lay like the dead when the last man came up. His body was beyond response, despite the man's rough treatment. A beeper sounded, and Tommy tensed. He knew Morgan was expecting an important call and would have to leave to take it. But there was no reason to worry. It was almost over.

Tommy's anus was stretched so far, he couldn't tell what the man was using. Then he felt several sharp jabs, and he knew.

A large, ungreased, untrimmed fist was trying to gain entrance. Tommy panicked; he knew what fingernails could do to his guts. He scrambled off the table. A hand grabbed him. Tommy struck wildly, feeling intense satisfaction when his fist connected.

"Catch the bastard!" Men were yelling and grabbing.

Tommy fought blindly, trying to keep his back to the corner. Someone seized his arm, but he wrenched free. The men were unable to keep a grip on his sweat-slick body. His wild blows seldom landed, but his terror and his long arms kept the men at a distance.

"Tommy!" Morgan bellowed.

The boy froze, dropping his fists and falling to his knees. He felt the vibration of booted steps approaching, and shivered.

"What the hell is this?" Morgan's voice was low and icy as he tore off the hood. "I leave you alone for a minute, and this is how you show obedience?" He turned his back on Tommy. "What happened?" he asked the others.

"We tried to hold him," said a top in a studded leather harness, "but he kept swinging. He's got a good punch."

Ruefully, he rubbed his bearded chin. "I thought you had him trained."

Tommy glanced down at the knuckles he hadn't noticed he'd split. The panic was fading, but the fear was growing. Morgan hadn't been really angry with him for a long time, but Tommy hadn't forgotten it.

Head bowed, Tommy stared at his master's boots. Morgan twisted his fingers in Tommy's hair and jerked his head up. "You've disappointed me, boy," he said quietly. "I expected better of you."

Abruptly, he released his grip, planted his boot on Tommy's shoulder, and shoved. The boy sprawled backward. He lay still, fighting tears and the urge to whimper. The words hurt more than the rough treatment. He'd let his master down. The man was Morgan's friend, maybe even had his consent. It could have just been a test—if so, he'd failed, miserably.

He dragged himself to his knees, but Morgan's boot knocked him flat again. The heavy tread ground into his skin, crushing his clamped nipple. Agony shot through his chest. Instinctively, he sought to remove the source of pain. His fingers touched the polished leather, and reason returned. He raised his arms over his head and parted his legs. Muscles corded in his neck and arms as he fought the desire to struggle. For a moment, Morgan looked down at the boy splayed at his feet, totally exposed and unresisting. Blood flowed from the lip Tommy had bitten to keep from screaming. At last, Morgan released the pressure. Tommy struggled to his knees, facing his master.

"Well? What do you have to say for yourself?"

Tommy hung his head in shame. What could he say? Morgan hated excuses. "Nothing, sir. I'm sorry."

"You know what comes next, boy." Morgan's voice was low and quiet. He didn't need to shout to make Tommy tremble.

"Yes, sir." Tommy tried to keep his voice steady. He spread himself across the table, grabbing the legs and opening his thighs as wide as he could. "Sir, tie me down. Please, sir. I don't think I can hold still."

"Yes you can, boy. And you will. For me."

The tears started again. "Yes, sir," he whispered.

Roughly, Morgan brushed his knuckles across Tommy's cheek. He trembled at the unexpected caress. His breath eased out in a soft sigh. He heard Morgan unbuckle his belt and drag it free. He couldn't stop his ass from quivering. He tensed for the first blow.

Morgan's shadow towered over him. His arm lifted; the belt dangled in a heavy loop from his fist. Tommy shut his eyes. He didn't need to watch. He was not going to move. He was not going to scream. He was going to take it. However bad it got, he was not going to shame his master again.

The swoop of leather cut the air, then fire danced across his ass. Morgan struck swiftly, giving Tommy no chance to adjust to the pain, beating him harder than he ever had. Tommy bit back his screams, but he couldn't stop the moans that tore through his chest. His hands whitened on the table legs as he struggled to stay in place. Heat burned through him. Each strip cut across a previous one and reawakened the torment. His erect cock scraped across the table with each movement of his tortured ass. His anus puckered open in frustrated longing.

The blows stopped. Morgan eased his cheeks apart. Long, warm fingers moved across his anus, slowly opening him. His muscles tried to clamp on the fingers, but they slipped away and left him empty and aching with need. The belt hit the floor, and he heard Morgan's boots walk away.

Please, no. Don't leave me! Tommy wanted to run after Morgan, to clasp his knees and beg forgiveness. *Maybe he went to get something else,* he suddenly thought. *Make him come back. Please. No matter what he brings with him.*

"What the fuck is this?" Morgan shouted.

Tommy jumped, twisting his neck to see behind him.

"Looks like blood," a man said indifferently.

"What the hell did you try to do to my boy?" Morgan didn't wait for his answer. "Tommy, get over here."

Tommy raised his aching body from the table, wincing with pain but trying to hurry. Morgan's fist clenched the man's shirt. "What did he do, boy?"

"He tried to fist me."

Morgan grabbed the man's wrist and held it up for everyone to see the ragged, dirty nails.

"So maybe I scratched him a little. What of it? He's just a goddamned slave. He doesn't have the right to say no."

"He's *my* slave," Morgan said coldly. "And he *does* have the right. He's a slave only because he chooses to say yes." Morgan drove his fist into the man's gut. "Nobody breaks my rules."

He slung the man over the table, securing him with restraints he hadn't used on Tommy. He jerked the man's pants down, then ripped off his shirt.

"You can't do this," the man hollered.

"Anyone want to stop me?" Morgan scanned the room.

"The bastard's got it coming. He could have ripped the kid wide open with those nails," someone shouted out. One top slid the bolt on the door. Another shoved a gag in the man's mouth.

"Your choice, Tommy. He owes you." Morgan glanced at the flabby ass. "It's not very appealing, but it's yours if you want it."

Tommy shuddered at the thought of touching that big white quivering butt—even for revenge. He picked up the belt.

"Go ahead," Morgan said. "He deserves it."

Tommy shook his head and held out the belt. "You were just getting warmed up, sir. I'd like to see you work."

Morgan smiled as he took the belt. "My pleasure."

Over and over, the belt slashed down. The man's screams were muffled, but audible. The table rocked as he threw his body from side to side. Morgan never missed. The man was powerless, spread open and shackled securely. Morgan felt no need for restraint. He was angry. For the first time, he lost control, striking with all his strength. From neck to ankles, he marked the man with bloody welts. His eyes blazed with rage and lust.

Tommy began to be afraid. It was too much; not even this man deserved so much punishment. Suddenly Tommy did something he had never done before: He said no. He caught Morgan's upraised arm. "Morgan, no. Enough."

For a second, Tommy thought Morgan would strike him. He let go of the arm and gently laid his hand on Morgan's face. "Please," he said softly. "Take me home, sir."

Morgan blinked, and then his eyes were his own again. He looked at the man he had abused and turned pale. "Let him loose," he told the other tops. "Take him to the hospital if he wants."

"Bastard!" the man whimpered when they removed the gag.

"Press charges if you like. But don't ever come here again."

Morgan sat staring at his hands as if he couldn't believe what they had done. The tops got the man dressed and led him away.

"He's going to be damned sore, but it's not as bad as it looks," said a man in heavy leather. "Don't worry. He doesn't need a doctor, and I don't think he'll want to tell anyone. Hell, the guy even had a boner. Maybe he's really a bottom. You might have done him a favor," the man said with a grin.

Morgan nodded his thanks. The tops left while Tommy finished dressing. He knelt at Morgan's side and laid his head in his lap, pressing his lips against the soft bulge in his jeans. He took a deep breath; the sharp scent of Morgan's sweat and crotch funk filled his nostrils. Morgan dropped a hand to Tommy's head and gently stroked it.

"I could have really hurt him. A top who loses control is dangerous. What if it had been you?" His hand was faintly shaking.

"No," Tommy said firmly. He knelt up, reading the worry on Morgan's face. He caught his hand and kissed it.

"You've never lost control with me. Anything you need to do to me, I can take. You know that, sir. Maybe it's why you can stop."

"You're not afraid of me?"

Tommy smiled. "Afraid, yes, but I won't stop trusting you." Suddenly shy, he blushed. "You haven't claimed your prize yet, sir."

Morgan's hand slid down and gently cupped Tommy's ass. "Boy, I don't think this ass could take any more tonight."

"Yes it could, sir, if you wanted it to."

Morgan smiled down at Tommy's earnest face. "Later. What I want to know is why you didn't tell me."

Tommy shrugged. "I thought maybe it was a test, that he had permission."

"Never!" Morgan said fiercely. "I don't want you ripped. I love this ass." He pulled Tommy into his arms. "And I love the man it's attached to." He bent his head and covered Tommy's mouth with his.

Tommy forgot the pain and the fear; he forgot everything but Morgan's lips on his and the feel of his powerful hands touching him, holding him, taking control.

"Let's go home, boy."

"Yes, sir!"

I'll Do Anything

Troy M. Grant

I wanted Justin so bad I was willing to do anything to get him. There were a lot of hot, eighteen-year-old seniors at my high school, but there was something about Justin that absolutely drove me out of my mind with lust. Maybe it was his body. . . . Justin was a wrestler and had a smooth, firm torso just rippling with muscle. His biceps were the size of softballs. Justin had great legs, and the tightest little ass I'd ever seen. Maybe it was his face. . . . Justin's features were sensual, intense, and masculine. He could be both arousing and intimidating at the same time. His gray eyes only added to that effect. Maybe it was his hair. . . . A lot of guys go ape-shit over blond hair, but they wouldn't if they got a look at Justin. His hair was a light, sandy brown, a little curly, and it suited him beautifully. Maybe it was his attitude. . . . Justin was kind of a punk. I don't know exactly what it was that made me so crazy over him, but I was on the verge of being obsessed with him. I'd never wanted anything so much in all my life.

At eighteen, I was still a virgin. That was a situation I intended to change as quickly as possible. Finding another boy who shared my attraction to males was hard enough, but I'd set my sights on Justin. I knew it was probably a mistake. Hell, it was probably suicidal, but I always went after what I wanted, and I was desperate to get my hands on Justin's hot, hard body.

I watched and waited for my chance. I was like a vulture circling, just waiting until I could swoop in. One afternoon, just after last-period gym class, I got my chance. All the guys were dressing in the locker room and bullshitting about all the babes they'd plowed. It was the usual stuff.

"Fuck, I'm so horny I bet I could ram my dick through a brick wall!" said Justin.

"You're always horny!" shouted someone.

I grabbed an eyeful of Justin's crotch and sure enough, his dick was tenting his shorts. It was a real big tent too. Along with everything else he had going for him, Justin was hung. Justin caught me checking him out, so I tried to keep my eyes off him. It wasn't easy. I was always stealing glances at him, and Justin was always noticing. I lingered as the guys started clearing out. Justin started to go too, but I held him back.

"Could you stay a minute, Justin? There's something I want to talk to you about."

"Um, sure."

Justin had a questioning look on his face, probably because I didn't talk to him all that much. We weren't exactly friends. Maybe he detected the unevenness of my voice; I was so nervous my stomach was tying itself in knots. Justin didn't know it, but I was about to make him an offer that I was sure he'd never had from another guy before. I couldn't believe I was really going to do it. In fact, I was almost sure I'd chicken out. I had to give it a try, though—I was in agony. At last, all the others cleared out and we were alone. I'd never been so anxious or frightened in all my life. I was silent for several long moments.

"So, Brandon, you wanted . . . ," he said questioningly.

I swallowed hard. I was having second thoughts. I was scared shitless, but I was also horny as hell. Justin would probably kick the shit out of me, but I wanted him so bad I had to try. I had to put an end to my self-torture.

"You said you were so horny you could stick your dick through a brick wall. I, uh, I could help you with that."

"Help me stick my dick through a wall?"

"No, uh. I, uh. I know I'm a guy, but I . . ." I could barely speak. My eyes drifted down to the bulge in Justin's shorts. I involuntarily licked my lips. Before I completely lost courage, I just blurted it out. "I want to give you a blow job!"

Justin looked a little shocked. I think it was more from my asking him than it was from the knowledge that I wanted him. I think he had a pretty good idea I had the hots for him, but having that confirmed was probably a bit unnerving.

"I'm not into guys," he said.

My hopes went crashing down. I was about to be dumped on. Quite likely, I was also about to get my ass kicked. Justin could read the disappointment in my face.

"Just how bad do you want to do it?" he asked.

I looked at him. He had a mischievous, wicked look in his eyes that both aroused and frightened me.

"Well?" he said. "How bad? Answer me." The tone of his voice was dominating. I swallowed the lump in my throat.

"More than anything." It was the truth, and probably also the wrong thing to say. I was just digging myself in deeper, giving him more of a reason to beat me senseless. Justin smiled. It was a sinister smile that made the hairs on the back of my neck stand on end.

"If I let you—and mind you, it's a big if—but, if I let you, are you willing to do whatever I want? Sucking my dick comes with a price. You willing to pay?"

I was sure it was some sick joke, some kind of trick, but I couldn't pass up the chance, no matter how slim.

"Yes," I answered. "I'll do anything." I meant it, too. I was that desperate for Justin's dick. I was that desperate for Justin.

"No one's at my house right now. Come on."

I got dressed and followed him. My cock was so hard I could barely walk, and I was so nervous and frightened I could barely think. I'd put my life in his hands. I'd given him the power to destroy me, if he chose to.

We entered his bedroom, and he closed and locked the door.

"Take off your shirt," he ordered. I did as I was told. I had a real nice build myself and wasn't the least bit ashamed to let Justin see me shirtless. Hell, he'd seen me naked plenty of times in the locker room. Embarrassment wasn't my problem; wondering if I was about to get my ass kicked was.

"Turn around."

I faced away from him. Justin pulled my hands behind my back and quickly slapped a pair of handcuffs on them.

"Hey!"

"You said you'd do anything. We can stop whenever you want, but until you do everything I want, you don't get my dick between your lips."

I shut up with that and turned back around. Being handcuffed aroused me more than ever—but I was more frightened than ever too. Letting him handcuff me was not a good idea at all. Of course, I hadn't exactly let him—I hadn't seen it coming. I was in a bad spot, however. Now he'd have an even easier time beating me if he wanted.

I was almost certain that Justin was just fucking with me, but I had to see it through. I lacked the willpower to walk away. Justin was my weakness.

Justin started slowly undressing right in front of me. As soon as he pulled off his shirt and revealed his firm, muscular torso, my dick tented my shorts—I mean *really* tented them. Justin looked at my bulge and smiled.

He pulled off his shoes, socks, shorts, and boxers. In no time at all he was completely naked. His cock was rock-hard. I was drooling over it. I wanted it so bad I could practically taste it.

"You know," said Justin, "the only thing I need better than a good suck is a good fuck." He stood there eyeing me, slowly stroking his pole. I grew fearful. I knew what he had in mind. Part of me was turned on by it, but most of me was just plain terrified.

Justin pulled a rubber from his desk drawer, ripped open the foil, and unrolled the condom over his long, thick dick. His cock looked so huge.

"Just remember, Brandon, you can tell me to stop anytime you want, but if you do, you'll never get your lips on this." He stroked his pole once more as he lubed it up.

Justin grabbed me and pushed me over the edge of his bed. He jerked down my shorts and boxers. My virgin ass was exposed, my wrists handcuffed behind my back. I was his to use and abuse. I'd let him do it, too, because I wanted him. I wanted him more than anything.

I swallowed hard for what seemed like the hundredth time that day and braced myself. I tried to relax. I felt the tip of Justin's cock against my hole. I felt him pressing against it. I was both terrified and aroused. The head of his cock slipped in. I tensed and grunted. The initial entry hurt, but not nearly like I'd imagined it would. I expected blinding pain, but what I got was more like a little discomfort. I closed my eyes and tried to relax. Justin pushed more of his cock up my ass.

"Yeah, that's it, baby. Just relax. This is gonna feel good for both of us."

Justin kept pushing more and more of his dick up my virgin ass. I lay there as he took my cherry, a virgin no more. I gave myself to him. All the pain disappeared. I concentrated on the sensation of his pole sliding deeper and deeper into me. My mind reeled: Justin was actually fucking me!

Justin moaned and groaned as he probed me ever deeper. I could feel his cock throb within me. Fuck, it felt good! Justin pushed his whole dick right up my ass. His pubes crushed against my butt cheeks and he gave one last shove to get his meat as deeply into me as possible.

"Fuck, Brandon, you are tight! Maybe I should have tried this with a guy before!"

Justin withdrew his dick. I felt the head pop from my ass, only to have Justin slide it in once more. He went a lot faster the second time. He shoved his entire pole right up my ass. I was ready for it. I wanted it. If this was the price I had to pay to suck Justin's dick then I was willing to pay and pay and pay. My fear was gone. Justin wasn't just jerking me around. He wasn't going to beat me, he was just going to fuck my ass good and hard!

Justin bottomed out again, his cock probing parts of me I didn't even know existed. He pulled free, then rammed it in again, his nuts slapping hard against me. I lay over the edge of the bed as Justin fucked my brains out. I reveled in the joy of being used by the stud of my dreams. It was *my* ass he was fucking. It was *my* body that was creating the pleasure of the fuck for him. The way Justin moaned, groaned, and whimpered, I knew just how good it felt for him. He was getting the fuck of his life. So was I.

Justin grabbed my hips and pounded me as hard as he could manage—and that was hard! He didn't just use his hips to sink his dick deep into me, he used his whole body. His biceps and pecs strained as he pulled himself against me. He used every muscle to probe me deeper and deeper. What a fuck!

Justin kept fucking me and fucking me. Five minutes turned into ten, then fifteen. Finally, he howled at the top of his lungs and blasted his load up my ass. I could feel him cumming. I could feel his cock throb, and I could even feel his hot jizz as it fired from his rod. Justin spewed spurt after spurt of his jock jizz deep into my ass. He planted his seed, claiming me as his own.

Justin fucked me hard as he shot his load up my ass. That hot jock just kept cumming more and more. I usually shot a big load, but nothing like that. Speaking of my load, my cock was throbbing like crazy. My nuts had been churning ever since we were in the locker room, and I was about to pop. The sensation of Justin's cumming up my ass sent me over the top. My eyes rolled back into my head, I moaned, and I blew a huge fucking load against the side of Justin's bed. Every time Justin drove his cock into me, I spewed a big shot of hot jizz. I'd never felt anything so awesome in all my life!

We came together, blowing our loads at the same time. Fuck, it was good! At last our balls were drained, and Justin pulled his cock from my ass.

"You are one good fuck, Brandon," Justin said as he uncuffed me.

"Thanks," I said, smiling. "My ass is yours anytime you want it."

"Good," answered Justin, "because I'm going to want it a lot."

Justin lay back on his bed, looking magnificent. His hard, muscular body was so beautiful. I ran my hands over his chest. Justin didn't stop me, so I felt every inch of his torso. I leaned over and licked his chest. He didn't object, so I lathered his pecs with my tongue. Justin even pressed my head hard against his chest as I licked and sucked on his nipples. They grew hard, and he moaned.

I licked lower and lower, exploring each row of hard abdominal muscle. Justin had such a fantastic body. I was mere inches away from his impressive manhood. It was so close I could feel the heat emanating from it. Justin was hard again, his cock a towering piece of throbbing meat. I actually trembled at the thought of sucking it. I looked up at Justin with pleading eyes.

"Go ahead, suck it."

I smiled and dove for his dick. I wrapped my lips around the head and pulled it into my mouth. I swirled my tongue around it once, then pulled the whole cock in. I wanted to take it slow and make it last, but I couldn't. I greedily sucked down Justin's cock, each inch pure pleasure for my lips. His pole throbbed and flexed in response to the blow job I was giving him. I had Justin moaning and groaning in no time at all. I went nuts on him.

Justin's dickhead banged against the back of my throat. I relaxed my throat muscles and let it slide down. I took in more and more until I had taken it all.

"Fuck, dude!" said Justin. "No girl can do that!"

I would have smiled, but my mouth was full of manmeat. I held Justin's dick in my mouth and nuzzled my nose in his pubes. I loved every second of it.

I ran my lips back up to the tip of his tool, only to swallow him once more. Up and down, up and down, my lips rode his pole. I was starved for cock. I was a cocksucking maniac and oh, was it good!

I sucked him frantically, wildly. It was too much for Justin. He threw his head back, howled with pure pleasure, and blew his load. Jet after thick jet of his stud cream spewed between my lips. It was far better than when he'd blown up my ass. When he blew in my mouth, I could taste it. His spunk was creamy and sweet. I sucked it down and worked on his tool for more. Justin shot jet after jet of his sweet jizz between my lips, filling my mouth nearly to overflowing. I let none escape, however; I took it all. With one last huge spurt of punk spunk, he emptied his nuts and pulled his cock from my mouth.

"You are one good cocksucker, Brandon."

"I'm glad you think so, because I want to suck your cock again and again."

"Do you?"

"Yeah, and I'm willing to do anything for it."

Justin smiled at me wickedly. I knew he was thinking up something that would drive both of us wild. I could hardly wait.

The Inquisition

Dave MacMillan

We faced each other, both naked and tied to separate sawhorses on either side of the bonfire. Our blond hair was cropped short to CSC specifications, our bodies were still teenaged slim but rippled with muscles built up from months of work at St. Ignatius Loyola Camp for the Christian Soldiers Corps. Now our bodies glistened with sweat from the bonfire that lit the inquisition our fellow Corpsmen had been called together to watch as twilight became night on the Montana flatlands.

I'd made the mistake earlier in the afternoon of confessing to Preacher that Jimmy had gotten off while relieving me. Jimmy'd been hard and drooling a lot lately when I fucked him; but seeing my identical twin shooting a load under me scared me enough that I'd finally confessed it.

It didn't take Preacher long to bring in Brother Ralph and let Corps discipline take over. It'd taken even less time for the two men to tie me up, gag me, put me in the barn, and send a search party to look for Jimmy. In less than half an hour, my brother was in the barn with me, bound up as I was, awaiting the full, public inquisition Preacher had ordered.

Brother Ralph was behind Jimmy and a Corps underleader behind me, and a fully clothed Preacher stood between the two of us, holding an open Bible in one hand and a riding crop in the other as night completely claimed our Montana camp.

Brother Ralph's shirt was pulled behind his head as he repeatedly rammed his cock into Jimmy's ass. The completely naked Corps underleader had his cock buried deep in me, grinding his pubes against the tender sides of the cleft between my globes with his every downstroke. The faces of both men were masks covering the pleasure they felt at their impending orgasms. Preacher watched our cocks—mine and Jimmy's—intently for signs of tumescence as the Corpsmaster and the underleader fucked us.

Corpsmen sat nude in a circle around us and the bonfire, witness to our spiritual reclamation. Senior Corpsmen sat in the first row of spectators and several of Brother Ralph's underleaders patrolled the sidelines, watching for signs of prurient interest from our witnesses. Ten other sawhorses in addition to the ones we were tied to awaited any sinners who got aroused at our reclamation.

"Sodomy is a sin against God!" Preacher shouted into the growing darkness, making himself heard. "Hear me now, soldiers—sodomy is abomination. Abomination is possession by Satan; it's taking pleasure in relieving others; it's submitting to the animal in us and denying our duty to be godlike—"

He stopped and smiled when his sharp eyes caught Jimmy's cock beginning to thicken between his legs. Preacher raised the crop over his head and brought it down hard on my twin's shoulders. The report of leather slamming into skin and Jimmy's scream touched each Corpsman, and there was a ripple of movement through the assembly as every witness flinched.

Brother Ralph's pummeling of my brother's ass was becoming short and fast. Sweat beaded across the Corpsmaster's face. Beneath him, Jimmy's ass grabbed instinctively at his cock. Jimmy's fuck-meat drooled and grew as his love gland continued to be savagely massaged. I saw he was losing his concentration on keeping pleasure at bay with Brother Ralph closing in on an orgasm inside him. That was my twin, all right—he'd come to really love having his butt plugged since we'd joined the Corps six months ago, right out of high school.

The pain of the crop hitting his shoulder shattered his concentration. His cock jumped immediately into full erection before Preacher and all the assembled Corpsmen. Brother Ralph grabbed Jimmy's hips and pulled himself deep into his ass as his balls churned and pushed jizz into his dick.

"I expel you, Satan, in the name of the one God," Preacher yelled, and rushed around the sawhorse as the Corpsmaster pulled out of Jimmy, his cock still pulsing. Preacher stopped before my twin's upturned ass, pushed Brother Ralph away, and raised his crop.

The assembled Corpsmen listened in silence as the crop whistled through the night toward Jimmy's ass. "Out, I say! Leave him in the hands of the Father who loves him!" Preacher yelled, and Jimmy screamed as the crop slammed against his cheeks. Moments later the crop was whistling through the air again to crash against his backside. I watched helplessly as his balls churned, his cock riding his tight belly. Jimmy lost the last vestige of control and his first rope of spunk erupted as Preacher's crop found his ass again.

I watched drops of blood erupt from the repeated thrashing and flash in the light of the bonfire as the crop fell on Jimmy's ass over and over again. His cock lost its size and his chest collapsed against the sawhorse; he stared dazedly at me as the Corps underleader's hands gripped my hips and his strokes in my ass became short and fast.

I concentrated everything I had on not getting hard. It was difficult, because I had one of the few men I'd ever fantasized about in my ass and getting ready to shoot his load in me; but I held on, forcing myself to think of anything but the cock in my ass and the man it was attached to. I latched onto the whipping Jimmy had got, replaying it in my mind and hoping it and its pain would keep Satan away from me.

Preacher moved to stand between us again and looked at the Corps around us. "It is right we help our comrades, men," he proclaimed to them. "We're animals and we have animal needs. Relieving each other is our Christian duty." His gaze fell to Jimmy and then to me as the man behind me wedged his cock as deep in me as it would go and unloaded himself.

"But . . ." The word hung for long moments in the air over us all. "Even as we give ourselves to our duty and help relieve our comrades' needs, we must be vigilant. We must guard against Satan slipping into us during that most intimate moment. We must guard against the pleasure of succumbing to animal lust. Helping one another out is Christian; enjoying it is sodomy. It's satanic. It's abomination."

He glanced at Jimmy beside him, then raised his head and looked again at the assembled Corpsmen. "You!" He pointed to a noncommissioned Corpsman in the first row. "Come up here and relieve yourself with your comrade."

The man pushed himself off the ground and started toward us, pulling on his meat as he moved. Randy Homell! He was the biggest buck rabbit in camp—ready to fuck anything, anytime. He'd lucked out in getting Jimmy, even if my twin's ass was bloodied and already abused and he was half-unconscious from his beating. I noticed Randy was doing a damned good job of keeping a grin off his face as he approached downwind from Jimmy.

"Relieve yourself, soldier. Your comrade gives himself to you," Preacher told him. That was all the invitation Randy needed; he walked right up to my brother's ass, pulled it up to groin level, and sank his putter in.

The Corps underleader pushed off me, patting my butt affectionately with one hand while wiping sweat from his face with the other. Preacher glared at me like he was unhappy his crop hadn't tasted my ass yet. He pointed to a Corpsman in the third row and called: "Come up here, man. Relieve yourself in your comrade."

I watched the man approach. He was new to the Corps,

and I'd never seen him naked before. Now, I was happy the Corps underleader had stretched me some and left me lubricated with his slime. This boy was huge! He'd gotten his cock hard by the time he reached the bonfire and started toward me.

One of the noncommissioned officers yelped and grabbed another new Corpsman from the circle. Two more men joined him and they pulled the poor boy up to a vacant sawhorse and tied him to it. The boy's eyes were round as he stared at me, then at Jimmy, and finally at Preacher with his crop and Bible.

Preacher hurried around the bonfire to him, a knowing smile on his face. "Satan has hardened you in order to defile these boys' purification," he purred, loud enough for everybody to hear. I saw that the Corpsman was still hard despite his fear. So did Preacher.

As big-cock situated himself behind me and placed his meat at my already spunk-coated ass lips, Preacher circled behind the new man and raised his crop.

As big-cock began to ease into me, the kid screamed as the crop crashed against his ass.

I groaned softly. This boy knew how to fuck a man. He wanted his partner to feel him in his bum and enjoy it. He was pushing inch after inch of thick, hard meat into my ass—in front of the entire Corps, and with Preacher ready to use his crop at the first sign of carnal interest.

I was in trouble and knew it. My cock twitched between my legs and sweat beaded on my forehead as I concentrated on the flailing the boy down from us was getting. Anything—just so I didn't get hard with big-cock in my ass.

Only, it wasn't working. My meat welcomed the man inside me the only way it knew how. It oozed ball-juice and grew as those inches massaged my love gland. I forgot the men circled around me. I forgot the beating my brother had just taken and the one the new man was now getting. I forgot the months of control I'd perfected. My cock was eight inches of throbbing, hard man-meat by the time big-cock's pubes pressed against my cheeks. All I wanted now was him fucking me forever.

Big-cock's hands splayed out over my back as he continued to press against my butt. "You're tight," he mumbled as his hips withdrew most of him, leaving me feeling empty.

"Fuck me!" I hissed under my breath.

His hand went around my hip and found I was hard and drooling. "You're getting off on this," he whispered without missing a stroke. "I like that—a tight bottom that knows what it wants. Yeah."

I gave in to him, surrendering to the pleasure shooting out of my ass and covering all parts of me simultaneously.

"I'm going to want this more than just this once," I told him.

"Not like tonight, though, baby." He ground his meat as he pushed himself back into my love chute, touching it all and claiming it as his own. "I don't turn on too much to spectators."

Preacher was through expelling Satan from the newly tied Corpsman and turned him over to another senior Corpsman to pummel. I knew I had to somehow establish control of my cock before he could reach me.

I knew it, but my cock and balls rejected the knowledge. Instead, my nuts climbed up on either side of my cock, trying to strangle it. I was close. My pole rode my tight abdomen. I wanted to shoot my load with big-cock in my ass.

He quickened his tempo inside me, and his massage of my love gland became rough, short jabs punching at it. I moaned and knew I was finding heaven here on earth. Its name was big-cock. Randy Homell was already through in Jimmy, pulling out of him and stepping back to leave my twin's bum hole to leak his spunk. Through the haze of my pleasure, I saw him leer at my brother's ass. The horse's ass had finally scored one of us after six months of trying.

I didn't see Preacher's approach. The first warning I had that he'd found me out was when I heard the crop's whistle as it came down against my shoulder.

I screamed as pain spread out over me, pushing the pleasure big-cock was giving me before it. I jumped, the aftereffects of the pain quivering through me and spasming my ass all along the meat buried in me.

It was enough. He unloaded deep inside me, giving me one last moment of the heaven he'd brought me to with his fuck.

"Get out of him!" Preacher growled, his hand and Bible pushing big-cock from me. "This is abomination!" he screamed to the assembly, his crop pulling my hard meat from my belly and showing it to any who were in a position to see it. He pulled the crop away, and my cock splatted against my belly, still hard and demanding relief.

I was somewhere between heaven and realization of

where I was when I heard the whistle of the riding crop diving through the air toward me. I braced myself just before it hit my ass.

Pleasure and pain stood together, holding me in the limbo between the two of them as I bucked. My cock was hard, my balls tight, my sweat ran into my eyes, my ass leaked jizz. The next time the crop splayed across my ass, I shot my load. My balls emptied themselves and I cried out.

"There are others," Preacher told me and the rest of the Corps. "I want their names!" he demanded as the crop landed across my bottom. "Help your brothers. Help me rid them of Satan." The crop landed again.

I lost count of how many times he hit me. My throat was sore from screaming my pain. My cock shriveled. Parts of my brain were turning off.

Others? Who?

"Randy Homell!" I screamed with what was left of my throat as the crop landed against my ass again. Then I blacked out, my head hanging over, the sawhorse pressing into my chest.

I passed in and out of consciousness. Hoarse screaming from the ring of spectators pulled me back into awareness, and I realized that, mercifully, Preacher had decided he'd bested Satan in me. I heard another scream and turned my head in its direction. Two of Brother Ralph's burliest noncoms had Randy Homell firmly by the arms and were leading him into the circle lighted by the bonfire. I saw the fear in his face as one of the noncoms tied him to a nearby sawhorse. I also saw that most of the sawhorses now had men tied to them. More of Brother Ralph's boys were slipping into the lighted circle, carrying their own crops. Preacher had a full-fledged inquisition going now.

I passed out again, but a groan pulled me back to the circle. I watched a Corpsman sink his meat into Randy's bum. Across the flames from me, Jimmy's chest rode the sawhorse as yet another Corpsman relieved himself in him. His cock wasn't getting hard this time, though, and I knew Preacher had expelled Satan from him.

It took me several more moments of consciousness to realize I had another groin grinding itself against my own bum. Slowly, I raised my head enough to look over my shoulder, and saw a man pile-driving me—and I wasn't even feeling it.

I smiled. Satan was out of me too. I'd been right to confess to Preacher after all.

It was only then I remembered big-cock, and what he'd been doing for me. No matter what Preacher said, that'd felt too much like heaven to be the work of Satan. I supposed it was sort of like how Jimmy felt when I was working his ass.

I sank back toward unconsciousness, telling myself I was just going to have to be careful when I was getting it on with big-cock or Jimmy. Very, very careful, because I didn't want to be an intimate member of another inquisition anytime soon.

Metro Heat

Cuauhtémoc Q. Kish

Morning classes had dragged on interminably. I grabbed my brown, weathered briefcase, anchored the leather straps on my shoulder, and headed toward the exit door, still ingesting the nauseating chalkboard smell that permeated the salon.

Yesterday I had been chastised for being too "friendly" with my students. I was ordered to follow the strict policy set by the executive board or face the consequences of expulsion. "There must be a professional distance between faculty and student," they kept reciting, ad nauseam. I was counseled privately by the huge woman who called herself president of this organization, Ms. Langworthy. They called her Titanic, and we prayed that like her namesake, she would meet with catastrophe. "Die, bitch" were the words most often recited by visitors exiting her office, usually invited in for a scolding for some infraction of the golden rules.

I needed to prep for my afternoon classes and work on "professional distance." I made a beeline for the metro, which would take me home in six quick stops. My thigh guided the entry turnstile to the left as my ticket to ride was accepted.

The subway doors whooshed open with a heavy sigh and passengers exited quickly as others anxiously waited to board. An annoying bell chimed its announcement that the doors were closing as frantic individuals lunged forward and squeezed themselves on before the doors managed to close.

I was trapped between several guys, warmed by their muscled heat. I seldom minded the crowding, and always kept a blue eye open wide for the more pleasing souls that lined the metro cars like cattle.

As the train jerked to a halt at the next stop, I felt my ass being caressed by a fellow passenger directly behind me. His hardened member seemed to insinuate its way into my ass crack through the tight cotton jeans I was wearing and throbbed between my cheeks as we waited for the doors to close once again. Few passengers exited, but more pushed onboard, allowing me to feel the outline of the cock resting comfortably between my cheeks.

I felt the heat in the car rise, and it assisted my own frontal swelling, which found housing in the ass of the young man in front of me. He seemed to maneuver his butt cheeks backward, with the intention of discovering the weight and size of my organ. His hand assisted the process as he outlined my member, then pulled at my thighs, closing the gap between our bodies.

As the metro car rattled forward in its journey, making a slight curve to reach its next destination, I felt pressure from both behind and in front. My cock was bulging with excited new blood at the simultaneous motion, front and back; I was being taken to nirvana.

Suddenly the car jerked to a dead stop. Some passengers screamed, and darkness followed.

I wasn't about to complain. I would much rather make the best of the situation. But predicting the duration of the temporary power outage and resulting darkness was difficult. The lights could go back up immediately, or they could be out for quite a few minutes. At any rate, I had to think fast.

My traveling companions obviously felt the same way. The one in front quickly maneuvered his right hand to my zipper and proceeded to yank it down, allowing for easier access to the monster within. It flew out and was guided into his butthole while he moved back and forth as my member grew in size. Breathing in the car had increased, and I could barely catch my breath when my pants were inched down by the passenger behind me, who quickly discovered my pink buns. He thrust two saliva-covered fingers into my hole and spread my cheeks outward. Once my opening was lubricated his cock entered with gusto, and I felt his ball sac against my exposed white thighs, pushing slowly back and forth so as not to disturb other passengers and alert them to our movement in the darkness.

With the urgency of our situation, our passion was

intense and short-lived. Within moments I let loose a string of jism into the tightening ass in front of me, while I felt hands pulling my ass cheeks backward against a gigantic mass of hardened flesh. I felt the stranger behind me shudder spasmodically as his load fired deep inside my hungry cavern.

All breathing seemed to intensify, and oxygen became scarce.

Pants were pulled back into place and zippers were drawn up and mumbled "Thanks" were heard throughout the metro car.

As the lights came back on and eyes found comfort once again with the bright lighting inside the car, I noticed the bulges of the passengers on my right and left. They were obviously also stimulated by the momentary darkness in our crowded metro car.

I heard the bell, called out "Excuse me," and pushed my way to the door. I looked back and saw a sea of smiles. For the first time, I noticed the faces of the passengers who had stood in front and in back of me in the momentary darkness. I recognized them both from my morning class at the Institute.

As I headed toward my apartment, I chastised myself for being too friendly with my students and vowed to work on my professional distance. But not today; perhaps tomorrow.

Pantsed

L. B. Fox

When I went to a porn-star pool party fund-raiser, the last thing I expected was to be part of the entertainment—but that's exactly what happened. It all started when I came up behind this one porn star I know while he was standing with a friend of his and talking to a group of admirers. He was wearing a Hawaiian print shirt and a pair of long shorts. Feeling a little mischievous—and wanting to surprise him—I snuck up behind my porn friend and tugged down on the legs of his shorts. I was sure he had them tied and they wouldn't come down, but it would still be a funny gesture. Imagine my surprise when, two seconds later, my friend was standing in front of me—facing his crowd of admirers—with his shorts down around his ankles!

I fell to the ground, shocked, and laughing uncontrollably.

“Oh, my God!” I exclaimed between breaths. “That wasn’t supposed to happen! I thought you’d have them tied! That SO wasn’t supposed to happen! Oh, my God!”

My friend just stood there for several long seconds, looking down at himself and then at me, incredulously. It wasn’t the first time he’d been naked in public—the day we met he tried to get me to go swimming naked with him and a bunch of other porn stars—so I knew he wasn’t embarrassed about having his body seen. And his small crowd of admirers certainly wasn’t bothered by the impromptu unveiling. They responded instantly with their cameras and camcorders, recording the moment for posterity.

After a minute my friend pulled up his shorts—then he focused his attention on me, still lying on the ground laughing.

“Oh, you think that’s funny?” he said, looming over me. “You really think that’s funny, huh? Well, let’s see how funny you think it is when it’s you with your pants down and your dick hanging out for everyone to see!”

He dropped on top of me, pinning my arms to my chest with one hand and going for my shorts with the other.

“No!” I screamed, still laughing nervously and struggling to escape from his grip. “No, please! I didn’t mean it! It was an accident! That wasn’t supposed to happen! Please! No-o-o!”

But my cries fell on deaf ears. This guy was determined to get my pants off, and I was powerless to stop him. We struggled for maybe a minute before he sat on my chest, pinned my arms with his legs, and reached behind himself to work my shorts down and off. I kept kicking my legs, trying to make it as difficult for him as possible, but soon I was lying there on the grass, naked from the waist down.

"So," my friend said, looking down into my eyes, "how do you like it? How do you like having your pants pulled down and all these guys looking at your dick?"

I turned to the side and saw that the crowd of admirers was still there watching. In fact, our struggle had drawn the attention of quite a few more onlookers. There were cameras flashing and camcorders going, and I saw growing bulges in more than one pair of trunks. I had to admit, the forced exposure and all the attention was starting to get me excited. And I wasn't the only one who noticed.

"Looks like he likes it a lot!" a voice called out. "He's starting to spring a major boner!"

"Is that so?" my friend said with a grin on his face. "Hmm, let's see." Then he reached behind himself, between my legs, and found my hard cock. Wrapping his fingers around it, he gave it a few good squeezes. "Well now, what have we here?"

"Come on, man," I said nervously. "Please don't do this. Please?"

"I dunno, buddy," he replied. "Your mouth is saying 'Don't,' but your body's saying 'Please do!' " He looked up at his friend and said, "Come and hold his hands for me."

"Aw, no, man, no!" I said in protest. I tried to get up when my friend shifted his weight, but he held me fast and seconds later his friend had my arms pinned above my head. With me held securely, my friend scooted down between my legs and held them open. Taking my hard dick in his hand, he gave me a devilish look just before he went down on me and enveloped my cock with his mouth.

"Oh, shi-i-it!" I hissed as I started squirming again, more from pleasure this time than from trying to escape. My friend put his big hands on my inner thighs and pressed them down, spreading them wide apart as he continued to devour me in front of the crowd's watching eyes.

My friend may have been used to having sex with people watching, but this was a whole new experience for me—and not an altogether unpleasant one, I had to admit. The thought of all these guys watching this hunky porn star suck my cock was kind of hot. I was getting so excited I thought I would blow my load any second. But my friend had other plans.

"You like that, huh?" he said, coming up off my dick. I just looked at him, stunned, unable to speak. "Well, there's more."

He stood up and took off his shirt, then dropped his shorts again. His dick sprang up from his pubes, hard and thick. Stepping over me again, he knelt and squatted over my chest so that his cock hovered inches away from my face. Putting a hand behind my head, he lifted my face toward his dick and said, "Suck it."

Without even the slightest protest, I parted my lips and let him slide his cock between them.

"Mmm," he hummed as he entered my mouth. "Yeah, that's it. Suck it good. Man, your mouth feels incredible! Oh yeah, work my dick with your tongue. Oh yeah!"

I wasn't sure if he was performing for the crowd or if

he was really enjoying the blow job I was giving him, but I didn't care. Either way worked for me.

As he humped my face he reached around and kept stroking my cock. "Somebody get me a condom and some lube," I heard him say. *Oh God,* I thought. *What's he going to do now?*

"Here ya go," someone said from the crowd, and my friend said, "Suit him up for me." It was like we were on a porn set and my friend had become a performer-turned-director. I jumped a little as I felt an unknown hand take hold of my dick and roll a rubber along the shaft and then slick it up with lube. When my unseen attendant was done, my friend pulled his cock out of my mouth and scooted down my body until he was straddling my groin. He gave me a lewd look as he applied some lube to his hole. Then, without a word, he positioned the head of my cock at his asshole and lowered himself, and I slid inside him.

I couldn't say anything. I just sucked in my breath sharply and held it, momentarily forgetting how to breathe. My friend's mouth, however, was working just fine.

"Aw yeah, man, that dick feels good!" he said as he settled down on top of me. "How's that feel to you?" he asked as he wiggled his hips and squeezed his ass muscles around my dick.

"O-o-oh, good," I moaned in response.

"Yeah, man! Ride that dick!" the guy holding my arms said.

And ride it he did. Getting his feet under him, he rose to a squat over my cock, and lifted his balls so I could see my hardness sliding in and out of his soft hole. I looked up at my friend and took in the sight of his strong chest heaving and his hard cock bouncing. Even though it was *my* dick in *him*, it was more like *he* was fucking *me* with his ass. He moved up and down, back and forth, and side to side. He worked my dick so well I thought he was going to break it off and keep it inside him. Soon my hips took over and I was humping involuntarily, bucking up into him and fucking like a wild man. This went on for a while—how long, I couldn't say; I was too lost in the sensations to keep track of time. I did notice, though, when I felt fingers probing between my cheeks and two slippery digits poking into my asshole. At first I thought he was just massaging my prostate to add to my pleasure, but when he stuck a third finger in me I realized he was preparing me for entry.

"Somebody suit me up," he said, and an eager onlooker stepped forward to comply. Once he was covered, he disengaged himself from my dick and positioned himself between my thighs. Taking my ankles in his hands, he pushed my legs up and spread them wide, exposing my now-open asshole for all to see. I had never felt so vulnerable—or so excited.

"You ready for this?" he asked rhetorically, not really expecting or planning to wait for an answer as he scooted forward and nudged his knob against my opening. Again, I caught my breath sharply, this time as *he* entered *me.* I froze as his bulbous head broke my rim, and I begged him to hold still for a minute to let me get used to the intrusion. He did, then he slowly worked in the next two inches—which were followed quickly by the last six as he suddenly slammed them into me.

"Oh, shit!" I cried out at the sudden invasion. "Fuck!"

"That's exactly what I had in mind!" my friend said with a wicked grin on his face. He spread my legs, turned my ass up, stretched out over me, and went to work. I'd seen him do this to guys before in videos, but now he was doing it to me—and people were watching. Through my sex-induced haze I was vaguely aware of guys standing around stroking their cocks, and I could hear some of their grunts and groans over my own. The guy above me had shifted to pin my arms under his knees and was now stroking his cock along with the rest of the crowd. It was all such a frenzy, so intense as everybody watched my friend pounding my ass, I knew it couldn't last long. And from the way he was moaning and groaning above me, I knew he wouldn't last long either. Finally he lowered my legs and said to me, "All right, baby. Time for your money shot." Then he took my dick in his hand, stripped off the rubber, and started stroking it. With him still giving my prostate a persistent pounding, it didn't take long. My breathing quickened and I started squirming uncontrollably. "Unh . . . unh . . . unh" was all I could manage to get out, then seconds later I was shooting my load all over my stomach.

"Yeah, baby, that's it! Shoot that load!" my friend exclaimed. "Yeah! Now it's my turn."

Then he pulled out of me, whipped the condom off, and fisted his dick roughly until it blasted a load all over my stomach and chest. "Yeah! Yeah! YEAH!!!" he cried.

After my friend blew his load, everyone watching followed suit amid a chorus of moans, groans, "Oh, fucks," and "Oh, yeahs." Once the action had subsided, the onlookers dispersed and made their way back to the rest of the party.

I just lay on the ground, exhausted and not moving, even after the guy above me released my arms.

"Dude," he said, "that shit was hot! You should consider getting into the business."

Looking up at him, then at my friend, I said, "Right now, the only thing I want to get into . . . is my pants."

The Rag

Jonathan Asche

At midnight we all drew small, folded squares of paper from a fishbowl. All but one of those pieces of paper read "cum." Mine read "rag."

Minutes later I was at the front of the room, naked, climbing onto a chair designed for fucking, not sitting. My stomach rested on the seat, as it were, tilting upward slightly so my ass was in the air. Rests for my knees were positioned so that my legs remained spread. My hands were strapped to my sides—not to prevent escape so much as to prevent me from grabbing my own cock, which was already hard with anticipation.

The rest of the men in the room converged.

The first dick thrust in my face belonged to a short, stocky man with thick arms and pecs and minimal body hair. His sizable cock was only semihard when he batted me in the face with it. It was my job to get it completely hard. I opened my mouth, and in it went. His cock seemed to stiffen the moment it touched my tongue, swelling and rising to scrape across the roof of my mouth. He thrust his hips forward, pushing his rod deeper into my mouth, down my throat.

Behind me mystery hands played with my bare ass, squeezing my buttocks, then prying them apart. Thick fingers slid between my cheeks, rubbing my butthole. I twitched a little, moving my ass against the strokes of those fingers. My cock throbbed out of my reach.

The short, stocky guy was gently fucking my mouth, whispering so softly I couldn't understand what he said. The man behind him—taller, with a Roman nose and a three-day stubble covering the lower half of his face—was more vocal. "Oh, yeah, man," he grunted while playing with the stocky guy's butt. "Shove that dick down his throat." They weren't much quieter behind me—lots of "Oh, yeahs," peppered with the occasional "Hot ass!"

I felt warm breath against my hole, then the wetness of a tongue. I had no idea who it was, but I knew he had facial hair—I could feel it scraping against my butt crack. His tongue lightly swabbed my ass lips. "Yeah, find out if it tastes as good as it looks," someone muttered. The tongue became more forceful, pushing against my tightly closed sphincter. When it pushed its way inside, my body shuddered involuntarily. The tongue wiggled and jabbed inside my chute. I gyrated my ass against the unseen face, rubbing against the tip of the man's nose, feeling the planes of his face. "Eat that ass," someone cheered.

The stocky guy began gulping in air, and his movements became jerky. "Shoot in his mouth," said the guy behind him, and I braced myself for the oncoming flood. At the last second, though, the stocky guy pulled out. I licked his balls, all drawn up tight in their fuzzy nut sac, while he frantically jerked off. A second later, his body froze and his breath seemed to catch in his throat. I felt his load, warm and thick, splash down onto my shaved head. Apparently it was quite impressive, because several guys behind the stocky guy oohed and aahhed when he came, like he'd just hit a home run.

Once the stocky guy stepped away, the taller guy with stubble immediately took his place. He had a narrower frame, with cleanly defined muscles girding his torso like armor. His cock and balls were encircled by a silver band. His dick was not much longer than average, but it was thick and veiny. He roughly ran his hands over my head and face, rubbing in the stocky guy's cum. He poked a thumb in my mouth. "That taste good, slut?" he snarled. I licked his thumb clean. Then he shoved his cock into my mouth, almost making me gag. "Swallow that cock," he grunted, clasping his hands on my head and stabbing his dick down my throat.

A different mouth was at my asshole now. I could tell because this new man was clean-shaven. He was being helped by someone else who held my butt cheeks apart. The man eating my ass alternated between gently lapping at my ass lips and violently pushing his tongue inside my hole. I squirmed against the restraints. The pleasure became agony. "Let me at that ass," someone said gruffly, pushing away the man already eating my hole. This new, third mouth tore into my butthole brutally, gnawing at my sphincter, pulling at my ass hairs. When his tongue speared my hole, an electric tingle crackled beneath my skin.

The tall man with stubble continued to fuck my mouth, shoving his dick so far down my throat I could feel the metal of his cock ring with the tip of my nose. I was not surprised that it didn't take him long to cum. "Stick out your tongue, boy," he hissed, cupping my chin with one hand and stroking his rod with the other. I did as I was told, then waited. He cried out fiercely as he fired his jizz. The first spurt missed my tongue and hit my nose. The second shot caught me right above my upper lip, sticking to my mustache. The third and final shot finally made its intended target. It wasn't a very copious load—I barely felt the small splat that landed on my tongue. The tall man pushed the head of his dick against my extended tongue, managing to squeeze out one more watery drop. "Like to eat cum?" I said nothing, bringing my tongue inside my mouth to savor the mild saltiness of his jism.

Fingers started to probe my ass. I could feel two, and suspected they belonged to different hands. They worked in tandem, one sliding in as the other retreated and vice versa. My sphincter fought the invasion, pressing against the fingers as if trying to squeeze them out. All my asshole got for its resistance was a third finger. Someone felt compelled to state the obvious: "Tight ass," he muttered.

After the tall guy with the cock ring staggered off, I was presented with two cocks. One was average-size but uncut, attached to a swarthy Italian whose rippled torso was carpeted with black, curly hairs. The other dick was at least eight inches long, with a fat, mushroom-shaped crown. Its owner was a smooth-skinned, athletic younger man with a tattoo of a sun surrounding his navel. Both men smacked me in the face with their cocks, leaving sticky deposits of precum on my cheeks and lips.

My *other* cheeks and lips were getting a thorough working over. I had four fingers inside me now, stretching my ass muscles and massaging my prostate. I felt the wetness of lube trickling over my butthole. "That's right, get 'im all slick," someone growled.

The Italian and the tattooed guy were taking turns stuffing my mouth with their drooling dicks. At one point, I sucked on them simultaneously, my lips stretched to an uncomfortable degree. The men twisted their hips, getting off on rubbing their cocks together inside my mouth. One of them—the Italian—pulled out, giving me some momentary relief. The tattooed man thrust his large tool into my gullet while the Italian stood by and watched, stroking his cock all the while.

I heard the tearing of condom wrappers. My asshole twitched.

"I'm going to cum," the tattooed guy said in a pinched whisper, still thrusting his dick into my mouth. "I'm going to shoot!" When he came, his juice coursed over my tongue and drained down my throat. He pulled his cock out, getting off another healthy squirt that caught in my goatee. Seeing this apparently pushed the Italian over the edge, because he started groaning and trembling, frenetically pulling his rod. His load erupted all over his tattooed friend's cock, icing the shaft like it was strudel.

When he'd squeezed out the last creamy white drop, the Italian man looked down at me. "Lick 'im clean," he snarled. The tattooed guy pushed his sticky cockhead against my parted lips. Obediently, I licked the Italian's tangy sauce off his friend's sausage.

Suddenly, my body went rigid and my breath froze in my lungs. The blunt head of a dick was being forced past my sphincter, but not without protest from my tight hole. There was a moment of unbearable tension, when I felt as if I was about to be ripped open, then a sharp burst of pain that immediately dulled to a mild soreness. The anonymous cock was inside me now. Thankfully, he didn't start pumping immediately, the way a lot of guys do at these things. He let me get over the initial shock before fucking me senseless. He started out with a slow grind, his cock moving in and out of me in short, slow strokes. But the other guys egged him on, urging him to fuck me harder.

He gradually picked up speed. A smoldering pleasure spread through me as this unseen cock pushed against the walls of my rectum. His hands rested on the small of my back, and I could feel his weight as he plowed into me. Little whimpers and gasps escaped from my throat each time the anonymous dick sank into my chute.

There to stifle my moans was another cock. It was an older guy—in his forties, maybe. In the brief moment I got to look at him before my face was buried in his crotch, I could see he was handsome. His hairline was receding, but he'd augmented that by growing a beard, which was turning gray. And, by all appearances, he'd been frequenting the gym. His body was solid—and so was his dick, which was now hitting me in the nose. He didn't say anything. There was no need to: I just opened my mouth, and he guided his cock inside.

The guy fucking me was really pounding me now. My body and the chair were shaking as he slammed his cock into me. The older guy I was sucking caressed my bald head. I could hear him mumbling as I gobbled his prick. I couldn't decipher what he was saying, but I caught the words "fucking," "good," and "God."

My cock had siphoned so much of my blood that I was beginning to feel light-headed. This was agony, to be so horny and not able to even jack off. I'm sure my dick was purple by now. I was sure that when I could finally get off—when everyone else had had his turn with me—I'd shoot within three seconds. As it was, the slightest breeze against my swollen rod could've made me cum.

The older guy's grip tightened around my head, and he started thrusting his dick into my mouth in frantic, jerky movements. He made a harsh, gasping sound before flooding my mouth with his tangy jizz. I could feel his cock pumping against my lower lip. When his balls were empty, he pulled out, his cockhead still connected to my mouth by one silvery string of cum and saliva.

From behind, I heard the telltale gasps and grunts that accompanied a cock erupting. The guy fucking me squeezed my ass cheeks as he came. He stayed inside me for just a moment before pulling out. My butthole barely had a chance to close before another guy was pushing into me. I don't know if it was because my ass lips had already been stretched, but this guy seemed smaller than the other one.

He slid in easily and a lot more comfortably. Immediately, he started humping my ass like it was the last ass he'd ever fuck.

Another dick was in front of me, this one curved like a rhino horn. The guy attached to it had the thick, brawny build of a football player, and the goofy smile of a kid being given candy. He was a redhead, and his pubes were a light strawberry-blond. The head of his cock grazed my lips a few times before he did an about-face and bent over. He reached back and pulled his full, round buttocks apart (he had a real nice ass) to show me his pink, almost hairless asshole. I was allowed only a moment to admire his little pucker before he leaned back against me, sandwiching my face in the crack of his ass.

My nose was filled with his musk. My lips were against his ass lips. I pressed my tongue against his hole, getting it all nice and wet before pressing inside. If I could've used my hands, I would've forced those tightly shut lips apart with my fingers. Instead, I had to force my tongue against his wrinkled opening, getting just past his pucker, but no deeper. He helped, again reaching back to stretch his hole open with his fingers. When his asshole was widened to a nickel-size opening, I plunged inside. My tongue wiggled and quivered inside his moist cavern. His body wiggled and quivered as well.

The man fucking me like a jackrabbit stopped abruptly. After a pause, he withdrew. I guess he came, though he wasn't very vocal about it. I heard a lot more "Oh, yeahs" behind me, plus a few utterances of "Give it to him good." That these phrases were spoken with such relish should have been a tip-off, but I wasn't too concerned. More lube was drizzled onto my asshole, and another condom wrapper was torn open. Someone said, "Sure that'll fit you?" There was laughter. Still, I wasn't worried—until the guy started pushing his cock up my ass.

At least I *think* it was his cock. As wide as it was stretching my sphincter, I started to have my doubts. I've been with guys who had some pretty healthy-size dicks, but this one didn't even seem human. It felt like I was being fucked with a scuba tank! I shrieked as this monster eased into my butthole, my cries dying between the cheeks of the ass I was eating. My aching, swollen cock found temporary relief—though not the kind I wanted—wilting as the endurance of my asshole was challenged. As this behemoth cock filled my insides, I thought I might actually pass out.

But I didn't. To this giant's credit, he was gentle. My ass muscles grudgingly accepted his huge tool. My legs shook as he inched into me. I made a whimpering sound. "That's OK," said the man splitting me in two. "I'll go slow."

I tried to focus past the pain by concentrating on the asshole at my lips. I'd been so busy sniveling that I'd all but forgotten the rim job I'd been giving. I resumed with forced gusto, driving my tongue deep into the redhead's chute. He moaned and bounced his ass against my face. "Eat it," he grunted.

The weight of another body fell across my back. Coarse hairs grated against my smooth skin. Hot breath hit the nape of my neck. "You got a hot ass," said a deep, gravelly voice. It was the man fucking me. Gently, he pumped my tortured hole. "Not many guys can take it," he said, like I had a choice. He made a quick stab deep into my rectum as if to test my resilience. By this point I was numb to the girth and length of his cock, though his sudden, sharp movement coaxed a sob from my lips.

He began to fuck me a bit harder, his beer can–size schlong working against my trembling sphincter. I continued to lick the redhead's ass, my face getting shoved against his pucker every time the man fucking me buried his dick in my butt. The din around us was growing in volume as the men in the room cheered the plundering of my anus. The man with the gargantuan prick snarled in my ear, sounding like a wolf about to tear its prey apart.

"Got a nice, tight hole," he growled in my ear. Considering his freakish endowment, I'd doubt he'd encounter anything *but* tight holes.

The redhead did an about-face. His cock was now much redder than his hair, and the plump crown was taking on a purplish color. I licked the precum oozing out of his piss slit while he gripped the shaft. "I'm so close," he panted, stroking his purple-headed dick with greater and greater speed. "So . . . fuckin' . . . *close.*"

His cock exploded in my face, his viscous white jism hitting me in my forehead, landing on my nose, and stinging my left eye. The stranger fucking me grunted his approval. When the redhead was finally drained, the man atop me ran one of his broad, meaty hands over my cum-soaked face. His palm smelled faintly of cigars. He raked up the redhead's juice with his fingers, then stuffed those fingers in my mouth. "Eat it, rag," he whispered in my ear as I sucked the sperm off his fat fingers.

Once I'd eaten the jizz off his fingers, the man with

the mammoth dick moved both hands to my shoulders and pushed himself up. His weight resting on my shoulders, he began plowing my ass in quick, fierce thrusts. The parade of dicks approaching my mouth paused, the men stopping to watch this man slam his fantastically proportioned cock into my ass. By this time I was past the point of crying out and could only gulp for air like a fish on dry land. Yet, to my surprise, my dick was once again rock-hard.

All of a sudden the man froze. His savage howls filled the room, and other men roared along with him as he came. Then a silence fell, and all that could be heard was the man on top of me breathing heavy and me gasping. Some chuckles rippled through the room. A couple of people even clapped.

The man pulled out of me. My asshole snapped shut—though with less snap than before—the moment his cock popped out. I cannot recall a time recently when I've been more relieved. My gut relaxed, and I could actually feel lube and sweat ooze out of my sore hole and drip between my legs.

The next cock I saw belonged to . . . the man who'd just fucked me cross-eyed. It was like being confronted by my attacker. I stared, awestruck. I'm not sure I could ever describe it properly. The man's cock was of a length and diameter that I did not think existed outside the imagination of Tom of Finland. Yet here it was, wrapped in a glistening rubber, the tip of which drooped from the weight of his load. It seemed impossible to believe that I'd had this fence post of a dick buried inside me, though I had the lingering feeling in my ass to testify it had been so. I turned my head so I could look up at my recent top man. He was older, maybe in his mid-forties. He wore the extra years well. His woolly body was sturdy and corded with muscle. An intricate tattoo covered his right arm like a sleeve, and both nipples were pierced. His steel-gray hair was buzzed back close to his scalp, and his upper lip was shaded by a thick, black mustache.

He looked down at me, smiling, and pulled the condom off his still-hard cock. Once the rubber was removed, he upended it over my head, squeezing his thick, lumpy man-cream onto my shiny pate. I twisted my head from side to side, like I'd just put my head under the hot spray of a shower. Globs of his jizz streamed over the dome of my skull, running down my face and the back of my neck. He dipped two fingers in his cooling spooge, placed those sticky fingers to my lips, and made a wet kissing noise.

Then, chuckling, he dropped his emptied condom to the floor and walked away.

Other men stepped forward. At my mouth stood a beautiful African-American guy, his body the color and hardness of mahogany. I took his big, uncut chocolate rod between my lips. I'd never had black cock before and was glad to experience one now. I gulped it down, my tongue prodding his thick foreskin. He purred, his voice deep and rich. Behind me another man was mounting my tender ass. His cock—thankfully, of human measurement—slid in effortlessly. I was grateful that he moved in slow, methodical strokes. Though my ass lips were still a bit sensitive, this new cock felt good inside me.

It didn't take long for either the guy I was sucking or the guy topping me to cum. The African-American's load seemed to bubble out of his dick, like soup boiling over, and onto my tongue. Like the cum rag I was, I drank his sharp-tasting juice. Or tried to—he pulled out the moment he started to cum. His cock burped out another blast of cream just as the head was clearing my lower lip. Then two more spurts spilled out of his piss slit. I stared, fascinated by the contrast of the white jism dripping off his black dick. He suddenly pressed his cock back between my lips. My tongue caught the last heavy drop he managed to squeeze out of his balls.

The man now fucking my ass kept up a steady pace, his cock moving easily within my moist chute. He kneaded my butt cheeks as his dick slid in and out of me. Only when he neared climax did he increase his speed, pushing into me in short, rapid thrusts. When he came, he made a sound like he'd just been punched in the kidneys. And then he was done. He gave me an affectionate slap on my ass after pulling out.

He was replaced with another, as was the African-American man who'd just left my mouth. These men, the ones at the end of the line who'd been watching all this time and getting thoroughly turned on, came very quickly when it was their turn to participate. In less than fifteen minutes I had five men—three fore, two aft. They shoved their cocks in my mouth and in my ass, pumped, and came. I, however, had to wait before my rigid, aching, *untouched* prick could get release.

When the last two men pulled out of me, my hands were unbound and I was helped to my feet. I had difficulty standing. My arms were numb, my legs were gelatin, and my ass muscles felt loose and rubbery. Lube trickled down the inside of my thighs. My face was slimy with cum and spit. My entire body was wet with sweat, and my dick looked as if it were about to rupture, it was so swollen and purple. A long, thick, silvery thread of precum hung from the end of my cock.

The crowd formed a semicircle. One man stood apart from them, and I was led to him. He had an average face—neither ugly nor attractive, just the kind of face you forget a minute after looking at it. His body was much more memorable: hard muscles bulging beneath tan skin; a diamond of silky dark hair between his hard pecs; and a trail of hair leading to his crotch. His cock was hard, with a bell-shaped head. His balls were being strangled by a black leather strap that encircled his ball sac.

I recognized this man. This was last month's rag.

I was led to this man. Through my cum-blurred vision I saw him smile. Someone handed him a cloth, and he began to clean my face. The cloth was warm and damp and felt good against my skin as he wiped away the spooge that covered me. Then he kissed me, deeply, before getting to his knees and taking my turgid dick into his sweet mouth.

I shot my load in seconds. A dry, rasping moan clawed its way out of my throat. The man—last month's rag—jerked his head back away from my cock. I came so forcefully my load rocketed three feet into the air, landing on the ex-rag's broad shoulders and firm pecs. My legs began to buckle. I caught myself on his broad shoulders, then, slowly, I too sank to my knees. The room filled with cheers and applause; even though the noise was deafening, it sounded far away.

The former rag embraced me, the present rag, in his big arms. He kissed me again. I savored his taste and the moment, knowing that next month, I'd be having this same moment with the new rag. And then, like all rags, I'd be discarded.

The Sex Scene

Dave MacMillan

There wasn't a name in the English language that I'd not called Iain Campbell, Earl of Inverness, in the four hours it had taken the bleeding train to reach Edinburgh from London. I'd gone through my limited knowledge of American, German, and French nasty names as I was being chauffeured deeper and deeper into the bloody Highlands. The burly Scotsman behind the wheel of the Land Rover hadn't said more than two words to me since I got in the car.

Me, a bloody rentboy? Again? I still couldn't believe it. I was well past that year of my life when I turned my bum up for any bloke with a tenner. I'd pulled myself up—and right out of that life. Now, I had the most desired arse on two continents—and a face and body that went with it. No more King's Cross for Max Molloy. I'd starred in American, French, and German videos. I'd won Best Actor at last year's Berlin Erotic Film Festival. I was well paid—handsomely. Just to shag for the bloody camera. And, now, this!

I sighed again. What my agent wouldn't do if there was money involved. I was nearly as bad. Five thousand pounds, minus the agent's 15 percent, of course. For a Highlands weekend with this Iain Campbell on his bloody estate. No kink. All vanilla.

I had decided that this Campbell had to be old and ugly. It was the only explanation for his paying that kind of money to have me. I didn't do old and ugly. I couldn't even get erect for it. This weekend was going to be a disaster; I bloody well knew it in my bones.

The house was big enough to remind me of St. James's Palace, but considerably more ancient. The large wooden doors of the entrance opened and I saw a tall lad in a kilt walk toward me.

He was striking. Taller than my 6 feet—slim, with flaming red hair, pale translucent skin, and freckles everywhere. And he was young.

He grinned as he opened the car door for me. Immediately, I wondered why Earl Inverness wanted me. He had an absolutely beautiful boy in this lad. His Lordship obviously ignored Britain's age of consent; this lad was a bit too young. That, however, was Iain Campbell's problem, not mine.

"Max Molloy?" the lad asked, and then blushed. "But of course you are. I would recognize you anywhere."

"You would?" I couldn't hide my surprise. In King's Cross a lad of this one's age might well have seen my vids, but here on top of a mountain in Scotland?

He laughed. "I would—with or without your clothes."

"His Lordship allows you to watch them?"

"His Lordship?" He studied me strangely for a moment before smiling again.

"What's he like, old and fat?" I asked without thinking. "And ugly as sin?"

The lad blinked, and I heard the driver guffaw as he opened up the back of the Land Rover to get my overnighter.

"Max, I'm Iain Campbell, Laird of Inverness," the ginger-haired cutie told me, his blue eyes twinkling.

"You?" I shuddered, mentally kissing 5,000 pounds good-bye. "My Lord, I'll need to be driven back to Edinburgh, if you don't mind."

Surprise covered the lad's face, making it even whiter. "Is something wrong?" he managed to ask.

"I'm not going to get into something with someone your age. I'm sorry, My Lord, but if the police found out—I can't. I'm not going to jail, no matter what the pay is."

He started to chuckle then, joining the driver. I didn't see the joke. "Max," he said, "I graduated Oxford this year. I'm only a year younger than you are."

I stared at the lad—no, the man—before me. I tried to swallow but, somehow, my heart had found its way into my throat. I knew I had put myself in a pickle.

"Won't you come in?" he asked finally, and stood back from the car door.

"Are you angry at me then, sir?" I asked as I stepped onto the gravel.

He grinned. "How could I be? Everyone makes the

same mistake." He shrugged. "It's genetic—my father looked to be in his mid-twenties the day he died."

"I'm sorry, sir," I said, not remembering my father appearing even once in my life over the past twenty-three years. I carried my mother's maiden name, and it no longer bothered me. "He didn't suffer, did he?"

His Lordship's body stiffened and his face became blank. "A car accident, Max. It was fast." I watched him force himself to relax. "Thanks for asking," he said. "That was two years ago. I'm over it now." He glanced at the entranceway, then turned back to face me. "Let's go in, have a drink, and get acquainted."

I thought I knew what that last part meant. I watched this laird's kilt swirl half up his thighs as he turned. I really was interested now that I knew I wasn't getting involved with jailbait. Most definitely. I was looking forward to knowing Earl Inverness better. Intimately.

Iain Campbell led me into his study. There was an austerity to the room—though the young Celtic god had softened it somewhat with the addition of a sofa and a TV and VCR. "Please, be seated. Drink?" he asked as he stepped to the sideboard.

"Yes."

"There's whisky or gin—"

"I can make do with a good malt, Your Lordship."

A moment later, he returned to me carrying two glasses filled with several jiggers of Scotland's greatest treasure. "You may call me Iain, Max. Even the estate's retainers do. I don't stand on formalities; and I do want us to become friends."

He offered me my drink and moved easily to the other end of the sofa. Adjusting his kilt as he sat down, His Lordship turned to face me. "Are you wondering why I invited you here and paid such an exorbitant sum to make it happen?"

I smiled knowingly and settled comfortably into my end of the sofa. He was certainly straightforward enough. "I suspect I can guess, sir," I told him.

He blushed. "Well, there is that, of course. But what I wanted to do was get to know you a bit. The real Max Molloy, as it were." I noticed his accent now that we were alone and I wasn't suffering one shock after another. There was no burr to his speech at all. It was pure Oxfordian—something one would expect from Buck House or the highest levels of the civil service.

"Get to know me, sir?"

"Iain please, Max."

"In what way do you want to get to know me . . . Iain?" I asked, sitting back up and placing my drink on the end table. King's Cross was far behind me—four years and a million miles away. I'd even forced myself to learn to speak English so a bloke didn't have to listen hard to understand me. Max Molloy was not one to take strolls down memory lane—especially his own.

His Lordship took a long draught of his whisky and set it down before facing me fully. He took a deep breath and tried to smile. He didn't succeed; the tension that had sprung up between us was thick enough to cut with a knife.

"First off, I became infatuated with you my first year at uni. Your first video, I think." He blushed. "Your body, Max." He chuckled to himself. "I was a horny young lad then. It kept me buying each new video you made. I bought the foreign-made ones in Holland or France during school holidays."

He pushed himself off the sofa and began to pace slowly. "After Father died, something changed. I became obsessed with you then," he mumbled barely loud enough for me to hear him. "You were the new constant in my life once he was gone." He stopped his pacing and faced me, a guilty smile on his lips. "It had become more than just a sexual attraction for me. I wanted you as a friend, as someone I could turn to, someone I could hold and be held by. I wanted you as a lover."

I wasn't sure how I felt about what this young nobleman was saying. I liked his being such a fan, of course—my contract had called for a percentage of sales the last two years. But I wasn't naive: I'd made two movies in America, and I knew all about stalkers. Earl Inverness had resumed his pacing, and I wasn't watching him as he circled behind his desk and stopped.

That Hinckley bloke had stalked that actress before he shot Ronald Reagan. And some madman had killed another actress outside her flat. Another had killed John Lennon. My countrymen had a tendency to take on the worst American habits, as well. And here I was in the wilds of Scotland—alone with a bloke who admitted to being obsessed with me. Part of me was beginning to wonder if I would be alive when the time came to return to London.

"You want me to be your lover, Your Lordship?" I asked slowly, unable to completely believe the possible mess my agent and I had got me into. I looked up then and saw him standing behind the desk, studying me.

His hand darted into an open drawer, and I was quickly staring down the barrel of a pistol, pointed at me. My eyes crossed.

Iain Campbell smiled angelically. "I'm going to have you as my lover, Max. You're never going to leave me." His smile widened as he rounded the desk and approached me, becoming beatific. "On your knees, lad. We're going to seal our love forever with your swallowing my cum."

"Don't do this, My Lord," I mumbled, even as I was slipping my arse off the sofa and getting to my knees before him.

"Open my kilt. Take it out. I want you to get to know my prick well."

My fingers fumbled nervously at the front of his kilt, but I could feel what was under it. It was hard and demanding. And long and thick. I almost forgot that Earl Inverness was holding a pistol to my head.

Shagging with a beautiful man the likes of Iain Campbell would be a real pleasure—he was as lovely as any lad I'd invited into my bed in the past three years—as long as I wasn't seeing that pistol aimed at me. I unbuckled his belt and quickly pulled the tartan down. Anticipating what they would find, my fingers made short work of that job.

I sat back on my haunches, and as the wool slid down over his buttocks, my gaze was momentarily glued to the thick tube that jutted out from his pubes.

My fingers touched the smooth translucent skin of the flanks, pushing his loose shirt up onto his chest as my tongue found his deep-set belly button and began to rim it properly. My hands moved slowly onto his back and followed his spine down to his arse as he pulled his shirt over his head. My lips followed his treasure trail down the front. They traced the width and length of the piece of Scotland that now thrust past my cheek so proudly. My hands still gripped his ass cheeks.

His ginger pubes tickled my nose, but I couldn't get enough of the smell of him. My tongue guided his cock-head past my lips. "Take it, Max. Show me you want it. Swallow it!" he whispered from above me.

Wide and thick, his helmet pushed deep into my mouth, entering my throat. My hands gripped his ass cheeks as I pulled him into me. I wanted all of him. I wanted to taste him. He moaned above me and began to pump my throat with his knob. I took him past my tonsils, letting him possess me as I fumbled to loosen my jeans.

Iain Campbell was beautiful. He was a work of the finest Celtic art. His cock was more manly than most men could hope theirs to be, and at this moment it was mine. My lips finally reached his pubes; all of him was inside me. My lips retreated until I could wash his cockhead with my tongue, then went down again until my nose pressed against his smooth belly. His ball sac began to tighten, his bollocks closing in on his rod, threatening to ride it.

He pulled away, his hand holding my head so my lips couldn't follow him. "I want your arse, Max," he said hoarsely as his dick left my mouth with a plop. "Get naked." I looked up, following his smooth, wide chest to his eyes and hoping mine showed my longing for more of him. "I want to see this bum of yours." He chuckled. "I've paid enough for it."

I stood up and pulled off my shirt as my jeans hung open at my hips. Iain stepped behind his desk and opened a drawer. I sat down and shoved my jeans and white briefs to my knees; my prick was drooling precum. It was now so hard, the loose skin had pulled back and was snuggled hopefully behind the flare of its helmet. I lay back on the floor. "Take them off, Iain," I told him as I lifted both legs toward him and reached for my dick.

He smiled down at me and pulled off one of my shoes, then the other. A moment later he had my jeans and underpants puddled on the floor behind him. He tore open the condom packet he'd brought over from the desk. I watched him unfurl the latex across his bell-end and roll it down the shaft, pushing his foreskin before it. We were both filled with lust. Nothing else mattered now. I wanted him inside me. I wanted to feel him making love to me. I smiled wantonly and spread my legs wide in invitation. I began to wank slowly and cupped my bollocks as he got to his knees beneath me. I was a bitch in heat and Iain Campbell had the goods to raise me out of my need.

I felt the cold metal of the pistol in his hand as he lifted my left leg onto his shoulder and turned my head so I wouldn't see it. "Put it away," I groaned up at him. "You don't need it. I'm yours," I told him, and emphasized my words by putting my free leg on his other shoulder.

He started to lean into me, his hands on each of my thighs and his wide helmet beginning to press at my back entrance. I smiled at my little victory.

I gasped as his cockhead entered me, and my eyes flew open. I watched him watching me as his hips pushed his dick ever deeper into my bowel. I reached between us and found my prick pressed against his belly. I began to pull on it as his face moved slowly down toward mine. I allowed myself a smile; Max Molloy was learning about Iain Campbell. He was the best lover a man could have.

I raised my head off the floor and our lips met just as his pubes began to scratch the underside of my ball sac. His tongue slid between my parted lips and dueled mine as I ground my bottom against his crotch and felt his dick touch all those spots deep inside me that make me whimper and want to melt.

"You're a good one, Max Molloy," he whispered as he pulled away from the kiss, his lips tracing my jaw back to my ear.

"Shag me good," I growled. "I want to feel you in me. All of you. Make me yours, My Lord."

I felt his pole begin to retreat through my bowel, leaving an uncomfortable emptiness. The nerves at my entrance longed to hold him in me. Instinctively, my sphincter tightened around his latex-covered width. I grunted and began to wank in earnest.

He began to slide in and out of me, tickling my sphincter and massaging my prostate. I began to fly. Mindless pleasure coursed through me in waves. I thrust up to meet each new stroke, and I groaned my pleasure up to him. Iain chewed at my earlobes and nibbled at my lips. His tongue slithered down my neck onto my shoulders. His hips flexed as he moved in me. I moaned, floating on the sea of pleasure building throughout my body, and bucked up to meet his red-thatched crotch each time it neared.

He bit one nipple hard, sending me over the edge.

Orgasm erupted within me, cum splashing onto his chest and neck as he teased my nipples, and still his prick moved steadily in and out of my arse.

Pressure began to build inside me, whipping up the pleasure and excitement and need that was sex into a storm. I grabbed his flexing hips between my legs, forcing him even closer as I surrendered to the eruption from my bollocks. My cock stayed hard as it bounded across my cum-coated belly. His lips found mine and we kissed with my pole caught between us, riding our bellies as he continued to fuck me. He pummeled my arse, and I knew I would never get enough of this.

His tempo changed and he pulled away from our kiss, his breathing labored. His thrusts quickly became short and fast. He was pounding himself into me. I could feel my bollocks again riding the shaft of my prick. I smiled as he moved against me, his body covering mine; we were going to cum together.

He pulled out of me hurriedly, sitting up on his haunches even as he pulled the condom off. My cock erupted as I watched him wank once . . . twice. . . . His muscles tightened, his mouth opened in a soundless scream. A rope of jizz hit my shoulder, another the center of my chest.

He took a breath, then another, then collapsed on me. My arms went around his shoulders and I held him close as our breathing began to return to normal and the hottest sex scene I'd ever done came to an end.

The Interrogation

Jordan Baker

I suppose this should begin with something like "It was a dark and stormy night"—but it wasn't.

It was a glaringly bright New Orleans afternoon. The heat index was somewhere above 110 degrees, and the humidity was so high I felt as if I were breathing steam. My briefs were soaked in sweat, and I could feel them clenching my balls tighter with each step.

That's the problem with New Orleans in the summer: Everyone has terminal jock itch and a bad attitude. You can find yourself punched in the jaw because your facial expression slipped at a crucial moment in a discussion.

I was in no mood to be around people, so instead of sitting quietly in my air-conditioned office, I was out wandering amid the masses on Decatur Street.

The hustler I was shadowing was mildly amusing. He was too young and inexperienced to realize I was following him. To be honest, I don't think he'd have noticed a marching band trailing along behind him over the din from his Walkman. Twice he almost stepped into traffic before his peripheral vision kicked in and he pulled back.

He was, as my old mentor might have pointed out, a type: young, blond, pretty in a feminine way, and totally self-absorbed. Slithering in and out of the crowd with practiced grace, he never seemed to notice the people he jostled his way by.

When I first spotted him, the kid was dancing at an intersection. He wasn't performing for tips. He wasn't doing street theater. He quite simply wasn't aware that he was on a public street and began moving to the music.

If someone were to tell him there are people in the world, the kid would be amazed.

He made me when we walked into the pet shop. The fact that I'd followed him into four different stores finally got through the mist of his consciousness.

Grinning, I tipped a friendly salute and scooped a large studded dog collar and chain leash from a Peg-Board by the register.

"What kind of animal do you have?" the clerk asked.

"A chicken," I said, allowing my voice to carry the proper distance.

"Sir?" she asked.

"It's a rather large chicken," I said, leering openly at my mark. "About a hundred fifty pounds, I'd say. I fancy chicken from time to time."

The towhead pulled a face and slipped by me as I pocketed my change. He wasn't sure yet whether he should be worried or complimented by my interest.

Frankly, neither was I.

He was walking faster now, no longer window-shopping or pausing to dance at intersections. In fact, he'd lost the Walkman altogether by the first intersection. Instead of dancing, he was bouncing from one foot to the next, mentally willing the "Don't Walk" sign to fade.

The adrenaline would be flowing now. There was no doubt I was following him; all that was unclear was my motive. I was big enough and scary enough that he didn't want to risk finding out. I knew what I looked like to him: 220 pounds on a 6-3 frame, nearing forty, enough of a beard to look older. I had the potential to be dangerous.

To give him a nudge, I smiled warmly and reached out my hand as I caught up to him on the corner. He recoiled from the handshake as if I'd offered him a cobra, then turned on his heels to race down the street.

I caught up with him a few moments later in a blind alley. In a way, he was almost cute, pressing his back to the wall, shifting his eyes about frantically in a pantomime of the trapped animal.

"Well," I said, sauntering toward him. "Since we both know why I'm here, I suppose we can skip the exposition."

He had no clue what I meant.

"You do understand why I've been tailing you?" I suggested helpfully. "Randall McCullough?"

Again, no hint of recognition. He was either truly stupid or truly innocent.

"You really don't know Randall?" I asked in what I hoped was a friendly tone.

The kid bolted. Well, he *tried* to bolt. As he raced by, I managed to whip the dog collar out of my pocket and around his throat. The impact almost pulled me off my feet as I drew it tight. The youth's feet actually did leave the ground.

I shoved him against the brick wall of the alley and pinned him with my weight as I fastened the collar and snapped the end of the leash to it. When I stepped back, I had the young man effectively tethered on a four-foot piece of chain.

Wrapping the chain around my left forearm, I kept tension on the line as I flipped my wallet open to show my ID.

"Robert Madigan, private investigator," I said. "You can go as soon as you've told me everything you know about Randall."

The kid was pulling hard against the chain. Keeping him steady was like boating a marlin. Finally I tired of the game and jerked sharply on the chain, bringing him neatly to his knees on the pavement.

"Do we really have to do this the hard way?" I asked.

He levered up from the ground, his shoulder catching me neatly in the midsection. I backpedaled furiously across the alley until my back hit the opposite wall. The breath left my body on impact, and he might have gotten away then if the chain hadn't still been wrapped around my wrist. Instead, I was able to jerk him back down to the ground.

When wrestling a twenty-something suspect to the ground, most middle-aged detectives learn, a certain amount of ruthless efficiency is necessary. I grabbed a fistful of balls through the kid's chinos. To my surprise, he was sporting a hard-on.

I laughed in spite of myself. The struggle was turning the little slut on.

"You like this, don't you?" I grinned, chuckling at the furious expression flashing over the kid's face. "You want the big, bad detective to rape you?"

He began bucking harder. For a moment, I thought he might actually get out from under me. Pressing my forearm across his windpipe, I shoved him down forcefully against the pavement and began unbuckling his belt. The kid really went nuts when I flipped him on his stomach and lashed his wrists behind his back with the belt.

"By the way," I said, tugging the slacks over his slim hips, "do you have a name or should I just call you shithead? Or fucktoy?"

His only response was an inarticulate howl of rage as I ripped his Jockeys. His cock sprang free and spanked the gravel.

"That's gotta hurt, fucktoy," I chuckled.

"My name is Alan," he hissed.

I spread his cheeks and spat on his asshole, then ran my thumb over the newly lubed opening.

"Do you like taking it up the ass, Alan?" I said obligingly. "Because if you don't, you really should tell me what you know about Randall."

"Fuck you," Alan hissed.

I pressed my cock against his asshole through my slacks and amiably suggested, "Maybe later."

"No," he whined. "Please . . . I'm not ready for this. . . ."

Lurching to my feet, I jerked the chain, bringing Alan's face level with my crotch.

"What are you ready for, Alan?" I said.

He began gnawing at my slacks, chewing my cock through the fabric. I couldn't tell if he was trying to hurt me or just provide foreplay. Either way, I enjoyed the sensation and let him go for a few moments.

Since Alan's hands were tied, I unbuckled my belt and opened my pants for him, letting my cock bounce against his face a few times before thrusting against his lips. The kid didn't even struggle. Instead, he swallowed it, taking my length deep into his mouth with a quick, almost bird-like motion.

He had the kind of short, spiky blond hair that always put me in mind of petting a hedgehog. I laced my fingers through it and drew him down deeper on my cock. His throat convulsed against my glans as I stabbed my dick into his mouth. I could feel him choking, but I held the embrace a bit longer before pulling away.

Alan recovered slightly before I rammed my cock home again. This time, I let him gag as I fucked his mouth with all my might. He was sucking air through his nose in deep, hoarse gasps as I pumped. I came straight down his throat, tugging his hair hard as I thrust one final time.

He was coughing uncontrollably when I hauled him back to his feet. Roughly, I grabbed his balls, intending to twist them as I asked my question again.

Instead, I gasped in surprise. Alan still had a hard-on.

"You're enjoying this, aren't you?" I chuckled. "Tell me you like it, you little slut."

The blond was glassy-eyed and still gasping. He shook

his head violently and I jerked it back until he was looking me in the eye.

"Say it," I said, favoring him with a wolfish grin.

"Fine," he whispered. "I like it."

I pushed him back to his knees. He actually flicked out his tongue to lick at my cock as I rubbed precum over his lips with it. I pulled away, leaving it just out of reach of his mouth.

"What do you know about Randall?" I teased.

Groaning, Alan shook his head. I slapped him hard across the face with my cock. It was already getting stiff again.

"You're a little bitch," I remarked.

He nodded, and stroked my cock with his tongue.

"Tell me what you want. . . ."

"You already know," he said.

"I want to hear you say it," I smirked. "It's not a proper investigation if you keep your mouth shut."

"Fuck me," he said.

Shoving him against the wall, I jerked Alan's jeans down over his hips. I took a moment to admire the line of his back. The kid had a good body, with broad shoulders and a back that tapered nicely to his hips. He was shivering as I spread his ass cheeks again and spit between them.

The kid whimpered as I worked a finger into his ass. With my other hand, I roughly pumped his cock. If anything, it had gotten harder.

"You really are a sick little bitch, aren't you?" I said.

He started to answer but my cock pierced his ass before he could form the words, so instead he howled. I think it was probably from pain at first, but almost instantly, Alan was humping his ass back against me, trying to impale himself more completely.

I loved the sensation of his ass squeezing my cock. It was like being caught in a rubber vise. I kept one hand in his hair and the other on the chain as I jerked his body back against mine. Alan was lost. He cried out with each thrust, a high-pitched, keening plea for me to stop.

I didn't stop, of course. I was too far gone myself. I wanted more of him. I wanted to punch through him, to become one with the moment. I could feel the orgasm building in the pit of my stomach, but Alan wasn't quite there yet. I leaned forward and sank my teeth into his shoulder.

With a final cry, he began shooting his cum against the brick wall in front of him. I thrust one more time, holding his cheek against the wall as my cock spasmed inside him.

"That's better," I said, stepping away from Alan to zip up.

I untied his hands and he fell to his knees, not bothering to pull his pants up. Leaning over, I pulled his head back by the hair and kissed him hard on the lips.

"Get dressed and get out of here," I said. "I'm done with you."

Then I walked away. The whole thing had taken less than fifteen minutes. I was almost back to the street before the young man had recovered enough to call out.

"I really don't know anyone named Randall McCullough," he said.

For a moment, I considered walking away without telling him. The idea of letting him wonder had a certain appeal. Instead, I let him in on the joke.

Grinning, I turned back to Alan, cocked my head, and said, “Who?”

The Plan

Charles Alexander

The club is pretty packed tonight, the heavy, voluptuous beat driving the crowd onto the dance floor.

I spot Nick at a table in the corner, stirring his straw listlessly in his tequila sunrise. I snag the chair in front of him and turn it around, sitting in it with my forearms resting on the back. "What's up, baby?"

Nick sighs. "Hey, BJ."

"Why aren't you bustin' a move out there with everyone else? Something wrong?"

He peers up at me with big blue eyes. "It's Devin." A lock of blond hair falls into his eyes and he pushes it back angrily. "He gave me another lecture today. He acts like he's my dad or something."

"Kinky." I smirk. "So what was the lecture on this time? Did you leave the lights on again?"

"I forgot to change the toilet paper when it ran out,"

he mumbles. "He just kept going on and on about how he was stranded and blah-blah-blah."

I bite my lip to keep from laughing. "Being stranded like that is quite demoralizing, you know."

"I know, I know. But that's not the point. He doesn't respect me. It's like I'm just his dumb blond plaything."

"Aren't you?"

He glares at me. "Funny."

I shrug and toss him a shit-eating grin.

He slumps back in his chair. "I just wanna do something, you know, something to show him I'm not just another dumb blond. I want him to see me differently, like, I dunno, an authority figure or a hero or something."

I don't suppress my snort. "What are you gonna do? Dress up in tights and save his life?"

He makes a face. "I don't think I could pull off the tights with my ass."

"But I like your ass. It's so round and smackable." I take a sip of his drink and smack my lips loudly.

"Shut up." He grabs the drink out of my hand and stirs his straw around some more. "But that saving-his-life thing ain't such a bad idea."

I choke on the drink and finally manage to swallow, tequila burning down the back of my throat. "What do you have in mind?" I croak.

He shrugs. "Dunno."

My finger taps my chin. "You could always hire someone to try and run him over and then push him out of the way."

"Nah. It's been done."

I tug on the small hoop in my right ear. "Really now?"

Nick nods. "Yeah, you know Josh and Ryan? That's how they met."

"Didn't Ryan go psycho and chase Josh with a broken plate?"

"Oh, right." Nick chews his bottom lip thoughtfully. He has really nice lips. Red and lush. I bet they feel like expensive silk.

"That could work," he says.

I tear my gaze away from his lips. "You're going to chase Devin with a broken plate?"

"What?" His forehead wrinkles. "No, I'm going to get a psycho to try and rape him."

"Uh . . . OK." I'm not even going to try and decipher the workings of Blondie's mind. "So where are you gonna find a psycho?"

Sitting back in his chair, he scratches his head as his eyes survey the room, finally returning to me. His mouth breaks into a big smile. "You could do it."

"Whoa, me? Since when am I a psycho?"

Nick shrugs. "You could be a psycho. All those tattoos and piercings." He raises an eyebrow at me. "You can't be completely normal."

"Devin would never believe I'm a psycho."

"Don't give me that shit, BJ. You're a great actor. I mean, you had me convinced you were straight when I first met you."

"Yeah, well, you're blond. It's not hard."

His eyes narrow at me. "Ha. Ha."

"Anyway, Devin's twice my size," I continue.

"Size doesn't matter when you have a gun."

I cough. "Since when doesn't size matter to you?"

Nick takes a hasty sip of his drink. "Well, you do have a gun, right?"

I waggle my eyebrows at him. "Baby, I got a rifle."

Nick smiles. "So you'll do it?"

"Hmm. Depends." I stroke my goatee. Devin *does* need someone to pull that high-and-mighty stick out of his ass—and maybe stuff something else *in* it. This could be a really fun way to do it. "What do I get in return?"

"What do you want?"

I purse my lips. "You have to clean my house."

Nick's mouth drops open. "But your house is disgusting! If I slipped and fell, it would take days to find me in all the trash! Nuh-uh, man, I wouldn't go within a hundred feet of your house!"

"Fine. Then I won't rape your boyfriend."

"But—" He tugs on a lock of hair and gives me his best set of puppy-dog eyes, lower lip stuck out and everything.

I cross my arms and stare right back him.

He sighs, sitting back in his chair. "All right, I'll do it."

I stick out my hand. "Deal."

Nick owes me for this. Big time. Like, I better be able to eat off my floor when he's done cleaning.

I really went all out: black leather pants, black leather boots, black leather gloves, and a long black leather trench coat.

Psychos like black leather, right?

Hmm, if they do, that doesn't bode particularly well

for my sanity, considering I just happened to have all this stuff lying around.

And then there's the fact that I'm actually going through with this ridiculous little plan.

Add to that the knife tucked in my boot, the handcuffs in my back pocket, and a fake handgun tucked into my belt, and maybe acting like a psycho isn't such a stretch for me after all.

I run my thumb over the key Nick gave me and look at the door in front of me. The last time I was here, we all ate takeout and watched *Attack of the 50 Ft. Woman.*

I hope Nick knows what he's doing. Oh hell, Nick doesn't even know how to dress himself properly. What the fuck possessed me to agree to this? That's right. I thought it would be fun. Maybe I'll make Nick put that pretty mouth to some good use and lick my floor clean.

I slip the key into the lock and turn it, opening the door slowly and quietly. Peeking inside, I spot Devin lounging on the sofa, bathed in the blue light from the TV. His long legs are stretched out in front of him and he's wearing black sweatpants and a white wifebeater that bares his nicely shaped arms and hints at the hard build of his chest. His dark hair brushes the tops of his shoulders, framing his classically chiseled profile.

Showtime.

I slink inside, pulling the gun out of my belt. Devin's fixated on some news story about a rabid deer attacking local cats. I walk up behind him and press the muzzle of the gun into the back of his skull.

Leaning over, I whisper in his ear, "Hello, Devin."

He stiffens. I slide the gun down the back of his neck, draping my arm across his shoulders, brushing the barrel along his strong jaw.

"What are you doing?" His voice is soft and low.

I chuckle, letting my tongue dart against his earlobe. "Just having a little fun." I push the muzzle into the pulse point at the back of his jaw. "You never have any fun, do you, Devin?" I blow lightly in his ear. "We'll have to fix that, won't we?"

He tries to pull away but I grab his shoulder and keep him anchored to the sofa, gun digging into his neck.

He swallows. "This isn't funny, BJ."

"Oh, I'm finding it quite amusing." My leather-clad fingers slip through his soft, feathery hair. "You don't think I notice, do you?"

"Notice what?"

I jab the gun deeper into his neck and he grunts softly.

"The way you look at me. Those mocking stares when you're shoving your tongue down Nick's throat right in front of me." I rest my cheek on the top of his head, breathing in the clean pine-and-musk scent of him. "You know I want you." I let the flat of the gun rest over his rapidly beating heart. "And you like it. Having that power to make me hard with just a look, a touch." I wrap my hand around his jaw and turn his face to me. "Well not anymore, Devin. You're mine now." I capture his wide, sensual mouth in a fierce kiss.

He jerks away, scrambling backward to the other side of the sofa, panting hard. "What the fuck is wrong with you?"

"Nothing you can't fix." I slip off my coat and drape it over the back of the couch. His wide green eyes watch me intently.

"Like what you see?" I grin and do a little pirouette, bringing the gun back up to his pale face. Stalking around to the other side of the sofa, I grab his arm and yank him up, jabbing the gun into the small of his back as he regains his footing. Smoothing my palm up the back of his thigh and over his tight, round ass, I draw my tongue up the nape of his neck. My arms wrap around his waist, my hips pressing into his ass. I am actually getting hard now.

What can I say? Devin's hot.

"Feel what you do to me? You drive me *crazy.*" My sick grin turns into a laugh, all raspy and low. Very psycho, if I do say so myself.

My hands dance down the hard ripples of muscle in his stomach, dipping into the waistband of his sweat-pants. My fingertips draw little circles around his hipbone as I rub my crotch against his ass. Shit, that feels good. Grasping his hips, I thrust myself harder against him, moaning loudly.

Nick better get his ass here soon or I really *am* going to rape his boyfriend.

"You don't have to do this, BJ." His voice is thick and deep, and trembles just a bit. It hits my skin like a warm drizzle.

I shudder and step back, jabbing the gun into his spine again. "Shut up, bitch." I shove him in the direction of the bedroom. He stumbles forward and then turns around, eyes bright and lips parted.

"If you wanted me, you could've just asked." He reaches a long-fingered hand out and brushes my cheek.

I back up quickly.

Whoa, this is not supposed to happen.

Devin advances on me. "I didn't know you felt like this, BJ." He raises his arms helplessly. "I mean, if you felt you had to go through all this to have me . . ." He grabs my wrist and eases the gun from my hand.

Shit shit shit. Nick, where the fuck are you?

Still holding my wrist, he sets the gun down on the coffee table and brings my hand down to his crotch, and damn, he's fucking hung—and quite happy to see me. He steps in and kisses me shallowly, teasing, leaving my lips tingling.

He rests his forehead against mine and my eyes flutter shut. Oh fuck.

This is bad.

Devin pushes me up against the wall, his long, hard body pressing into mine as he plants warm kisses along my jaw.

Very bad.

I groan as his hands grip my ass.

Very, *very* good. No, wait—bad.

He lifts his head and cocks an eyebrow at me. "What have we got here?" His hand slips into my back pocket and closes around the handcuffs. He pulls them out and dangles them in front of me. "Kinky little bitch, aren't you?"

I try to grab the handcuffs, but he lifts them above his head and grabs my hands, locking the cuffs on me.

OK, to say this isn't going as planned is quite the understatement.

He grinds his hips into mine and kisses me again, hard and deep this time. His hand slips under my shirt, and he tugs on my nipple ring, making me groan into his mouth and thrust my aching crotch against his.

His voice is a husky whisper next to my ear, vibrating deep into my spine. "That's it, baby. This is what you wanted, isn't it?" His tongue dances over the crease of my lips until my mouth opens for him and it slips inside, his teeth tugging at my lower lip.

He strips off his wifebeater, and then begins to nibble on the sensitive flesh of my throat. The handcuffs are biting into my wrists even through the gloves, and my hands are trapped against the warm, hard surface of his chest, fingertips brushing his collarbone as he bites my nipple, sucking on the ring through the cloth of my shirt.

He lets it slip out of his mouth and shakes his head. "This has got to go." Reaching down, he slides the knife out of my boot.

Trailing the flat of the blade down my cheek, he licks his lips, and then begins to cut my shirt off.

Damn, and I really liked this shirt too.

Oh, but damn, I think I like his tongue better, making tiny circles over my heart, sliding down my chest and tracing the sun tattoo that circles my navel. His fingers are busy unfastening my pants, tugging my throbbing cock free. I groan and arch against his hand as he draws a finger up its length, lightly pinching the swollen head.

"Like that?"

I nod, and then he's on his knees, his warm, wet

mouth surrounding me, lips sliding up and down my shaft, tongue caressing the ridge on the underside.

"Oh fuck." I moan as his teeth scrape lightly over my balls. I grasp the top of his head with my handcuffed hands, loving the soft, electric feel of his hair even through my gloves.

His tongue runs over the slit in the head of my dick, licking away a bead of precum, swirling around the base before taking me in his mouth again. Pleasure rolls hot and rich in my belly.

Devin's green eyes burn into mine as I watch myself disappear past his pink lips. My head lolls back and my eyes close as the churning-hot pleasure spills into my limbs, and I pull Devin's hair hard, thrusting up into his wet, hot mouth, feeling the head of my cock hit the back of his throat.

"Don't worry, Devin! I'll save you!"

I pry open my eyes to see Nick charging in the door, face flushed and golden hair falling in his eyes, wearing a big blue Superman T-shirt.

Devin stands up and smiles. "Nick, you're just in time to join the fun."

Nick's golden brows knit together and he pushes his hair out of his eyes, looking suddenly lost. "Uh . . . what's going on?"

Devin walks over and closes the door, then clasps Nick's hand and kisses him softly, leading him to the sofa. Nick shoots me a "What the fuck?" look, and I just shrug, holding up my handcuffed wrists.

Devin settles on the couch, pulling Nick into his lap and kissing him thoroughly.

He tugs off Nick's Superman shirt. "Thought you were gonna save me, huh, baby?"

Nick looks down sheepishly. "Maybe."

Devin laughs and nips at Nick's ear. "You're so cute."

I clear my throat.

Devin glances at me, then turns back to Nick. "Want to help BJ out with his little problem, baby?"

"It's not little," I grumble.

Nick tilts his head to the side and chews thoughtfully on his bottom lip. A slow grin spreads across his face as he crooks a finger at me.

I head over and Nick grabs my handcuffs, pulling me down onto the couch. He crawls into my lap and presses his rosy-soft lips to mine, the velvet scrap of his tongue invading my mouth. His hand wraps around my dick and begins to pump it slowly. Devin appears behind him, long fingers massaging Nick's back, starting at his shoulders and slowly working their way down to his tailbone, sliding around his hips and disappearing down the front of his jeans. Nick moans into my mouth and begins to pump me faster. Devin is licking up the back of Nick's neck, grinding his hips into Nick's ass. He tugs on Nick's golden hair. "I want to watch you suck him."

Nick takes his hand off my cock and I groan in disappointment. As he yanks down my leather pants, I obligingly lift my hips so he can peel them down my legs. He crawls between my thighs and takes me in his mouth, instantly swallowing my dick. The plush satin muscles of his throat work around my cock, his fingertip tracing my sun tattoo.

A hot, wet tongue darts over my shoulder and I look over at Devin's dark head, sliding down my arm, mouth twisting across the dragon tattooed there.

Nick lets my cock slide out of his mouth and Devin leans down to capture his mouth in a kiss. Their tongues tangle with each other, sliding past red, glistening lips. They turn to look at me, their devious smiles mirroring each other.

Devin climbs up my body and Nick climbs down, Devin's fingers stroking my face and Nick pulling off my boots and sliding my pants off the rest of the way. Devin pushes me back so I'm stretched out on the sofa, and he straddles my chest. Hooking his thumbs in the waistband of his sweatpants, he pulls them down his hips, revealing his large, uncircumcised cock.

Nick parts my legs and reaches beneath my balls, fingering my hole. The pulsing head of Devin's cock brushes my lips and my tongue snakes out, circling the tip, gently sucking it into my mouth, as I feel Nick's tongue rimming me.

I steady Devin's cock with my hand as I nurse the head, slowly jacking his shaft, the foreskin sliding through my glove-enclosed palm like satin. He groans and Nick appears over his shoulder, nuzzling his neck, as Nick's hard cock slides up against mine. Desire knots low in my belly. Nick's arms wrap around Devin's waist as they begin to kiss again, and Nick's hips begin to move in a slow circle. He begins to play with Devin's nipples and Devin moans, thrusting hard against my lips. I start to work him faster, tonguing his slit, thumbing the seam in the underside of his cock. Straining against the handcuffs, my other hand cups his balls, my leather-clad fingers trickling over them.

Nick disappears, returning after a moment. He slides a pillow under my hips and I feel a lube-slicked finger pressing inside me, working back and forth, loosening me up. He slides out the finger and lifts up my legs, pushing at my entrance, sticky and blunt. Then he's sliding inside me, with a slow, exquisite burn that eats its way through my stomach and up into my chest. My eyes squeeze shut, head falling back as a jolt of pleasure shoots through the pulsing burn. Nick grasps my cock and begins to stroke it, slowly easing himself out and back into me, rocking his hips gently.

I continue to jack Devin, arching up to meet Nick's thrusts, a warm tingling crawling all over my flesh. Nick begins to thrust faster and harder, really fucking me good now, and I match his pace on Devin's cock, panting hard as sweat trickles down my neck.

Devin's hard, sculpted body quivers with tension as he struggles to maintain control. His head is thrown back, dark tendrils of hair clinging to his face, lips slightly parted. He moans and grips my shoulders hard, starting to thrust into my hand, his control cracking.

A hot buzz builds under my skin as Nick starts short, hard thrusts, punching my prostate, hand squeezing my dick, rolling it against the warm flesh of his hand.

Suddenly Devin groans loudly and milky cum hits my face in thick, musky spurts. He slumps on top of me, grip loosening on my shoulders. His eyes flutter open and he gives me a satisfied smile, leaning over to kiss me. With long strokes of his suede-soft tongue, he licks my face and neck clean.

Nick's hand speeds up on my cock and I can feel the barely leashed tension wracking his body before he cries out, and I feel his load hit the walls of my rectum, slick and searing. He squeezes my cock and my orgasm rolls over me in a rushing wave, hot and powerful, bathing me in sultry release.

I slowly open my eyes. Nick is resting his head on Devin's shoulder, harsh breaths whispering over his sweaty skin. Nipping at the flesh of Devin's neck, he mutters, "You changed the plan."

Devin strokes Nick's hair. "Sorry, baby. I just couldn't help myself with BJ's sexy ass rubbing all over me."

Nick sits up and pouts. "But I was supposed to save you. I wanted you to see me in action."

Devin's hand slides around the back of Nick's neck and he pulls him in for a kiss. "I don't know about you, but I saw plenty of action. I think my little plan was quite a success."

I blink at Devin as his words sink in. "This was all *your* plan?"

Devin laughs. "You think Nicky could've come up with something like this all by himself?" He ruffles Nick's hair, and Nick shoves his hand away.

"I could too."

Devin presses a kiss to Nick's forehead. "Of course you could, baby."

I sit up. "So what the fuck was the point of me dressing up like a psycho and trying to rape you?"

Devin lifts his hands. "How else were we gonna get a piece of your nice little ass?"

"Um . . . you could've just asked?"

"Oh, but this was *so* much more fun." Nick giggles.

Devin's eyes twinkle. They fucking twinkle. "Yeah, the look on your face when I handcuffed you was priceless."

I climb off the couch, grab my mangled shirt, and wipe the cum off my stomach. Then I begin searching through my discarded clothes, trying to hide my burning face. I find the key to the handcuffs and unlock them, tossing them to the ground. "Hey, Nick?"

His arms wrap around me from behind, pulling me up against his warm, soft body. "Hmm?"

"I'll expect you early tomorrow."

He lets go of me. "For what?"

"We made a deal, remember? It's gonna take you all day and probably half the night to get my house clean."

Nick's eyes widen. "But . . . I . . . It was just to get you to agree to the plan!"

I grin and pat his ass. "See you around eight then?"

"But . . . Devin!" he whines. "Help!"

Devin laughs from the sofa. "Don't worry, Nick."

Nick tosses me a cheeky grin and Devin continues.

"I'll be sure to wake you up early."

Backyard Brawl

T. Hitman

The warm, wet tickle of a tongue against the sensitive flesh of his asshole woke Adam Valico from sleep. Drew was back from his morning jog.

He'd had a sense of the other man's presence in the room: the sound of footsteps, a burp, the rough fumble of a hand spreading his butt cheeks open enough to bare the prize. The scrape of an unshaved chin along the inside of his crack and several more hungry laps along his most private spot snapped Adam fully awake. It also toughened the half-hard cock he'd been pumping into the mattress up to all of its hooded seven inches.

"You awake?" growled a deep voice that was muffled by his ass.

Adam answered, "I am now." He moaned out a yawn and spread his legs to allow the invader easier access.

A probing finger joined Drew's tongue. Adam's guts

caught fire. *"Sweet,"* he sighed between gasps for breath. He pounded his uncut cock into the mattress and knew from the slippery feel of the sheets beneath him that Drew's attention was already making him leak.

"Speaking of which, I bumped into that new guy this morning," Drew said.

Adam raised his head off the pillow and whipped around. Drew's finger slipped free of his hole with a muted popping sound. "Huh?"

"That young stud who moved in a few houses down," Drew answered. Adam focused his gaze on the other man's handsome, unshaved face. Drew's short, dark brown hair and his old gray T-shirt were wet from his morning jog. His pale blue eyes and glistening mouth had a predatory quality in the early light. Drew shuffled off the bed and stood to remove his clothes. As he stood, the tent in Drew's jogging shorts showed his stiffness.

"I invited him to our football game," Drew said. He squeezed his chubby before kicking off his sneakers. Drew's T-shirt and track pants followed, leaving him only in sweat socks and compression shorts.

Adam pushed a pillow behind his head and watched his buddy strip. "You think the other dudes will mind?"

"Shit," huffed Drew, "every one of them's been stroking their dicks over that walking wet dream since he moved in. I met up with him jogging through the Common. Said he'd love to play some touch football with the guys, make some friends in the neighborhood." He peeled down his socks and freed his decent-sized cock and beefy sac of nuts from their prison before crawling back into bed. The pungent, raw smell of his fresh sweat reignited

Adam's hunger. "His name's Brady. Brady Thompson. Said he'll be here Sunday morning."

"Hot fuck," Adam sighed. He reached between Drew's solid, hairy legs and fondled his cock. The other man's size-13 feet rubbed against Adam's size 12s. Their legs rubbed together as Adam moved on top of Drew's toned body. Their lips met briefly. Adam tasted himself on his buddy's tongue.

"Seems like a cool dude," Drew said as he pulled away from the kiss, his eyes locking on some peripheral target in the room. "He's gotta be six-four or five. I'm six-three and the fucker's a hair taller than me. And the hot little fuck's only twenty-four."

Adam took a whiff off the moist, clean bush of Drew's nearest pit. "Just a pup," he said. "Why does he want to hang out and play football with a bunch of old bucks?"

"Fuck that," Drew chuckled. "I'm thirty, you're twenty-eight. He ain't that much younger than us!"

"Yeah, but dude—did you tell him about us and the rest of the guys?" Adam countered.

Drew's eyes narrowed. "Fuck no. Not yet. I don't know about him. Can't tell yet if he's cool enough to let him know that all of our neighborhood buddies like sucking dick. But he sure as fuck is hot, and we could use another guy to play."

Adam sighed his agreement while running a hand over Drew's hairy, muscled chest. He looked into his housemate's eyes to find them distant and trained elsewhere.

"Suck my dick," Drew eventually said.

He cupped the back of Adam's jet black buzz cut and

forced him down toward his straining seven-incher. Adam slid down the other man's flat, furry belly toward the musty-smelling patch of hair that lined Drew's abdomen. Drew's nuts were wet with a sheen of sweaty slime—too hot to resist getting a taste of. Adam lapped at the loose, hairy skin before giving each stone a gentle suck. From there, it was up to former New Jersey quarterback Drew Harridge's rock-solid cock.

The familiar, salty-sweet taste of Drew's precum hit Adam's tongue instantly. He swirled the goo along the underside of his buddy's dickhead and found the sensitive spot. Drew tensed beneath him.

"Keep sucking," the other man huffed, begged.

Adam glanced up to see his housemate smiling widely, his eyes half-shut. Adam knew the score: in Drew's mind, it was the new guy going down on him, the twenty-four-year-old hot fuck who'd moved in two doors away. He also knew by the amount of fluid leaking out of Drew's pee-hole and the steely state of his tool that he was pretty close to blowing his load.

At the last minute, Adam spit out Drew's cock. "Roll over," he ordered.

Drew's half-closed eyes shot open. "Huh?"

Adam licked his lips and shot Drew a mean look. "On your stomach—*now.*"

Slowly, reluctantly, Drew obeyed the order and turned over, revealing his hard, square beaut of an ass. Adam placed a hand on each of the muscled cheeks and stroked them, spreading the halves apart to bare Drew's tight, furry pucker. Before Drew could argue, Adam slid his tongue into the crack. The steamy knot was moist from Drew's jog. Adam moaned as he swabbed at Drew's hairy pucker. The sweaty taste drove his cock back up to its full girth. He lapped and sucked, loosening Drew for what he planned next. Once he'd gotten him plenty wet, Adam scurried into position on top of Drew.

"Don't get too comfortable up there," Drew warned lightly.

"Shut the fuck up," Adam said. He closed his eyes and pushed forward with his cock. The tight, moist knot of Drew's asshole denied him at first, but eventually, his fleshy cock knob found entrance. Adam eased in. The incredible tightness sucked on his shaft like a man's skilled mouth.

Adam fucked Drew in this position, with his eyes clamped shut. In his fantasy, it wasn't Drew beneath him, but Brady Thompson. Two could play at this game.

Drew set the cooler on the back porch and loaded it up with ice and beer, then went back inside. Adam stayed on the porch, absently lacing up his sneakers, adjusting the length of his OTC whites, and fumbling with his package while waiting for the guys to arrive. To his surprise, the first to show was Brady, the new guy.

Adam turned to the sound of the back gate swinging open, and there the handsome fucking jock stood, slightly taller than Drew, with a neat crop of dark blond hair and a goofy smile that showed off the dimple in his chin. Their new neighbor had pale blue eyes, a blue that was nearly gray. Adam quickly sized him up while extending a hand.

"Hey," he growled.

Brady shook back. " 'Sup, dude?"

"Nada—yet," said Adam.

Brady was wearing a white T-shirt, a pair of loose-fitting navy-colored cotton shorts, and sneakers with no socks. His legs were muscled and not overly hairy, just enough to match his arms. Adam squeezed down on the other man's rough fingers. Brady returned the gesture with a vicelike pump. Along with their hands, their eyes soon met. Adam realized how handsome the newcomer was—and how resentful he was of his presence because of that. This was Adam's game, Adam's home, Adam's territory, and somehow, Brady threatened all of it.

Brady's eyes deflected to the tall fence of box elders and arborvitae that divided the spacious backyard on two sides, running to the garage on the third. "Decent setup you got, dude. Nice and private. My place is wide open."

"That sucks," Adam said coldly. He folded his arms and sucked in a breath of the warm September air.

Drew's appearance at the sliding glass door saved Adam from having to make further small talk.

"Hey, dude," Drew exclaimed, his face lighting up at seeing Brady. The two men high-fived, and as much as it secretly pissed Adam off, it also excited him in ways he couldn't deny. The thought of seeing Brady and Drew together sent an image flashing through Adam's mind. Their new neighbor exuded raw sexuality, a mix of his boyish good looks, his soft-spoken baritone, and that goofy, dimpled smile. Adam felt his cock begin to stir and turned away.

Their forty-year-old buddy Russ opened the gate. Jackson, an ex-Marine, and Alex followed. After introducing them all to Brady, Drew brought out the football.

"A game of shirts versus skins," he said. Then he hooted, "You losers ready to get thrashed?"

Brady planted his feet and reached down, gripping the tails of his T-shirt.

Time seemed to slip out of focus for Adam as he lifted the shirt over his head, slowly baring his flat, tanned six-pack and the treasure trail of hair that split it down the middle. Trying not to appear obvious, Adam couldn't help but stare. He knew the others were looking, too.

Brady's belly button appeared, and then the sculpture of his chest, the tiny copper points of his nipples, and the crossbar of thin fur that divided his pecs. Brady stood dressed from the waist up in nothing but a gold chain and a grin. Adam blinked when Drew clapped a hand against Brady's bare shoulder. Time came rushing sharply back into focus.

Drew yanked his T-shirt over his head. His chest matched Brady's—muscled, with a dusting of hair. Not to be outdone, Adam followed suit. His chest was naturally smooth except for the bristle of black hairs that cut in a line down his stomach.

"Why do you knobs get the new guy?" groused Russ.

Adam snapped his T-shirt like a towel at the other

man. "Lose that beer gut and you can play with the skins," he joked.

Russ flipped his middle finger. Alex, their handsome Latino friend, said, "What a bunch of studs."

Drew clapped his hands together and both sides assumed position at the line of scrimmage. Adam huddled down beside Brady and tipped his gaze toward the younger man to find that Brady's blue-gray eyes were already on him. This close, he could smell the clean, masculine scent of deodorant and soap on Brady's naked skin.

"Seventeen!" Drew shouted at their backs. "Blue eleven . . ." Adam waited for the signal. *"Blue ten!"*

That was it! He pushed up and into Russ, then spun around him as the two sides collided. Shaking free of Alex's pawing hand, he dug in and faced Drew, showing that he was open. Drew dodged Jackson's tackle, snapped back, and fired. But the ball sailed over Adam's head and past him, and safely into Brady's waiting arms.

Brady lay on his back on the grass, his hair and shorts soaked in sweat, his bare chest and legs glistening.

"Phew, dudes, this is fun," he chuckled. "I haven't had a workout like this in months."

Alex tossed Brady a can of beer. Brady caught it effortlessly. "You call it fun," Alex said. "To me, it's an excuse to take a sick day tomorrow to recover."

"Yeah, we ain't all as young as you," Jackson added.

Drew emerged from the house, his discarded T-shirt wrapped around his waist. He carried an empty plastic bag, which he filled with ice from the cooler. He walked it over to Brady and knelt down to set it on his skinned knee.

"You OK?" Drew asked.

Brady nodded. "Just tripped over my line buddy over there." He indicated Adam, who figured his look of guilt must have betrayed him. He'd tripped Brady, and—he admitted in silence—it hadn't been an accident.

"Sorry," he grumbled.

Brady flashed that sexy, dumb grin again and waved a hand. "Naw, don't be. With a skinned knee, I feel like part of the skins team now."

Adam shook his head. "Do you?"

Brady nodded. "You, me, Drew—even bleeding, we're killing these dudes." A round of swears and huffs erupted from the shirts team, all of it good-natured. As the other guys bitched, Adam noticed that Drew's and Brady's eyes were locked. He also saw that Drew's hand was lingering on the younger man's grass-stained knee.

"So you like playing on our team?" Adam asked. Brady nodded. Adam felt the eyes of the other men on him, but kept his own trained on Brady. "Drew tell you everything about us?"

Drew rose from his crouch beside the younger man. "Adam—"

Adam cut him off. "Well, if he's gonna be part of the party, he should know the rules."

"Adam," Drew reprimanded.

Adam faced Drew's look of disapproval. "Whatever you say," he sighed, rising from the deck. "I gotta piss."

He stormed into the house and went to the bathroom. But instead of draining his bladder, Adam splashed cold water on his face. The sweat coating his hair, pits, crotch, and toes quickly cooled and turned clammy. He couldn't pinpoint exactly what he was feeling: jealousy, anger, attraction—or a combination of the three.

Adam wiped his face and toweled his armpits before exiting the bathroom. He opened the door, and waiting on the other side stood Drew. The former football jock looked mad.

"Dude, what's up with you today?"

"Nothing," Adam huffed.

"Nothing? You nearly attacked Brady out there. What's got you so pissed off?"

"I figured if you wanted your new best friend to feel at home with us, he should at least know the score."

A shuffle of footsteps sounded at Drew's back. "I pretty much figured it out on my own," said a voice from the kitchen. They turned to see Brady limp into the house. He shook out his leg and approached them, clapping a hand onto Drew's bare shoulder. "Wasn't too hard. None of you dudes are married, and you two live together," Brady said. "You guys a couple?"

Drew chuckled and said, "Not exactly. More like buddies who live together."

Adam's eyes locked with the younger man's. "Fuck buddies, if you need to know," he said. "You got a problem with that?"

"Nope," said Brady. "I came here to play some touch football, not get in the middle of a lovers' fight."

Adam shook his head. "You got balls, so let's play. Let's do it," he said. He brushed past them both, but gave Brady a bump with his shoulder on his way out of the house.

Adam held on to the ball as the pile of sweaty bodies pulled him down. He felt the press of bare skin and muscles against his own and looked up to see Brady among the tangle of shirts. Since the revelation twenty minutes earlier, Brady had gotten more aggressive, especially with Adam. Their friendly pickup game of touch football was becoming more physical.

Brady pulled free of the others and moved to stand, but the hand that had taken him down remained in place. As Adam watched, Brady's shorts slid far enough down his perfect, muscled ass to expose the straps of the jock he wore underneath, the halves of his butt cheeks, and the furry hole at the center of his crack.

Brady whipped around in response, and when he did, the twisting of his shorts bared his dense patch of crotch hair and the pouch of his jockstrap, which hung heavy and full for all to see. Brady didn't recognize Alex's hand as the culprit. His eyes locked with Adam.

"You did that on purpose, dude," Brady huffed, the accusation flying as Adam tried to stand. Before he could respond, Brady lashed out. His tackle knocked them both back to the ground.

"It wasn't me!" Adam protested.

"Yeah, right!" spat Brady, ignoring him. "See how *you* like it!"

As Adam struggled beneath the young stud's weight, Brady forced down his shorts and underwear, baring his manhood. A wave of air swept over Adam's sweating nuts and the sensitive ridges of foreskin that lined his uncut knob. To his shock—and the unexpected delight of the others—Brady slid a hand down into the warmth between his legs and felt him up.

"What the fuck!" Adam shouted. He resisted, pushing Brady off him. But the other man quickly reassumed the position, pinning Adam down. Sitting on Adam's chest, Brady's hairy butthole was inches from Adam's face, and was now in clear view.

With Adam's next angry gasp for breath, the heady smell of Brady's perspiration-soaked crotch filled his nostrils. He tried to fight back, but couldn't stop his dick from stiffening in the young jock's hand. With Brady jerking him off and the hot fuck's beaut of an ass so close, Adam huffed out an expletive and leaned in, burying his face in the swampy crack of Brady's ass. Anger quickly turned to hunger.

Adam tongued and slurped out the other jock's sweaty hole like a starving dog. At one point, he reached between Brady's spread legs and felt up the moist pouch of his jockstrap.

"Do it, dude," he heard Drew urge.

Lying flat on his back beneath the other man's legs, Adam glanced up to see that Drew had whipped out his cock. He was fully hard, and stood stroking it openly in front of the others. The sound of a zipper being lowered drew his eyes to Alex, who fished out his thick, dark-skinned cock with its moist pink head. From his position, Adam couldn't tell if Jackson and Russ were doing the same, but he figured they were. The air filled with muffled grunts and groans.

The hand stroking Adam's cock eased down to grip his

boner by the root. Adam felt a gust of warm breath over the crimped ridges of his foreskin, and then the glide of a wet tongue tickling his dickhead. Finally, Brady's mouth encircled his tool, sucking it in fully. Adam moaned and seized in place beneath him.

"Suck the dude's dick!" huffed Drew.

Shaking off the last of his anger, Adam pulled aside the sweaty cotton pouch of Brady's jockstrap. Two bloated, hairy nuts that were ripe with the smell of man-sweat spilled out and into his face.

"Fuck, yeah," one of the guys grunted.

Adam jabbed his nose into Brady's balls and sniffed them while hauling back his curved dick. Brady was rock-hard, a good thick seven inches of hot, pulsing meat. Adam gave the young stud's sac a couple of licks before sucking the head of his cock between his lips, then gobbled a few more inches until he was halfway down the length of Brady's shaft. Brady moaned and responded by taking Adam's tool all the way to the pubes.

After another minute or so on his back, with Brady's cock lodged in his face, Adam again heard Drew moan. He looked up to see his roommate masturbating at full speed. Drew's cockhead glistened in the light of the afternoon sun, its peehole gummed with precum.

Adam eased Brady off him. The younger man didn't resist this time, and slid onto his naked back, a wide, wet smile on his handsome face. Adam gave Brady's cock a firm shake and readied to go back down on him, but before he did, he looked around and saw that all of the guys had their dicks out and were stroking them, all due to the show he and the new guy were putting on.

The energy in the air, the sweat and roughness, and the juice dripping from Drew's dick all worked to spur Adam into action. He opened wide and plunged down on Brady's hard cock, sucking it as deep and fast as he could. Adam spread his legs for Brady's benefit, and welcomed the amazing feel of the other man's lips around his tool as they continued to sixty-nine. The fact that they were being watched by the rest of their football buddies added a whole new level to Adam's excitement.

Eyes half-closed, Adam was savoring the taste of Brady's syrup when he heard Alex grunt, then felt something wet spray the side of his face. Adam looked down to see thick drops of cum splatter on Brady's outer thigh.

He passed a hand through the warm juice and massaged it into Brady's muscled quads. Brady moaned something unintelligible around Adam's cock as another of the guys started to shoot. Russ howled out a string of swears and blew his wad. A ribbon of spunk struck Adam's bare shoulder.

Jackson blasted next, but it was the promise of Drew's load that launched Adam over the edge. He tipped his eyes up to see his best pal and fuck buddy milk out a wad of pure white jizz. The second squirt flew far enough to hit Adam's face. He closed his eyes fully and pumped his tool deep into Brady's face, and as he pulled back, he felt the itchy-hot burn in the head of his cock that signaled he was about to cum.

He sucked harder on Brady's dick. A shudder tore through his body. Adam grunted, and then so did Brady, and just as Adam's load began to fly, a ribbon of salty, young-jock ball snot hit the roof of his mouth.

Brady sat up. Cum dripped off his chest, face, and torso.

"Welcome to the neighborhood," said Russ. He ogled Brady's spent cock before zipping up his pants.

"Yeah," said Adam. He extended a hand. Brady accepted the offer, and Adam pulled the handsome fucker to his feet. "Welcome, dude. Sorry about that misunderstanding."

"You mean that?" Brady asked, a glint of skepticism in his eyes.

Adam nodded. "I do." He turned as Drew exited the house with some clean towels under one arm. When Drew was close enough, Adam took hold of his best pal and crushed their lips together, sharing Brady's taste with him. The kiss was brief and harsh, just enough to reestablish boundaries.

"Thanks, dude," Drew said, a wicked smile on his face.

Adam broke the embrace and pulled up his shorts, and in a loud voice shouted, "Enough of this shit. Are you pussies planning to quit or are we going to play some football?"

Fucked by the Foreman

Colt Spencer

I work in customer service for a mortgage company. It's not a very exciting job, but it pays the bills. Sometimes you have to match wits on the phone with an angry customer who didn't mail his payment on time, but that's about it. However, something happened at work this summer that made the job a lot more bearable.

It was a typical miserable Monday at work when I looked out the window and saw four men spilling out of a battered red pickup truck. Talk about a pleasant surprise. I immediately lost track of whatever I was doing and watched as they began to unload their equipment. I wondered where these Adonises had come from, until I remembered my supervisor mentioning something about the company hiring some contractors to put in a sprinkler system on the front lawn.

The muscles in their arms rippled as they hauled pipes

and whatnot across the lawn. Once they put it all down on the ground, they stripped their T-shirts off, revealing smooth, tanned skin over classically muscular frames. It was obvious in how they moved that they were very aware of the power of their presence. They swaggered about, swinging pipes and other tools around as if they were baseball bats. As I watched them, my loins stirred with that familiar feeling of primal lust.

I was particularly attracted to the guy who seemed to be the foreman. Like the others, he was dressed in a T-shirt, jeans, and work boots when they arrived, but he acted more mature than his coworkers. He was tall, about 6-2, with brown hair that was cut very short. I like facial hair, so it didn't hurt that he had a perfectly trimmed goatee that accentuated his features handsomely. Furthermore, his eyes danced when he smiled, which was often. In short, the guy turned me on.

The guys were there all week, working on the lawn and, by default, getting *me* all worked up. Every day at one-thirty, when it was time for my lunch break, I would take the long way down to my car, going out the front of the building and walking all the way around the side just so I could walk by them and ogle those beautiful examples of manhood. And each time I did, one or two of them would look my way and they'd kind of snicker to each other before turning back to their work. Sometimes my coworker Tonya would come along to check them out as well, grabbing my arm as she drooled over their primal masculinity.

That Friday, I took a quick lunch alone in the cafeteria, because the call volume was so heavy. As I made my way to a table to eat, I saw the four workers sharing another table close by. I tried not to stare at them, but I'm sure that I caught them looking over my way a few times. Eventually, three of the guys finished their lunches and got up from their table, leaving the foreman behind. I couldn't help but watch as they passed by my table. I could smell the musky scent of their rich, masculine sweat, which sent me close to the edge of arousal. When I turned to see what the other guy was up to, I was quite embarrassed to find him looking right at me. I'd been caught staring at his hot buddies! I turned back to my food and didn't look back at him once.

I returned to the phones, but I couldn't get those shirtless men out of my mind. After lunch I kept looking out the window as they continued to sweat under the sun. Whenever women walked by, the guys would turn and look. I couldn't help wishing I had breasts and a perky butt.

By the time my mid-afternoon break came I really needed to take a piss. I raced for the bathroom and breathed a heavy sigh as I relieved myself at the urinal.

At that moment the door opened. I turned, and damned if Mr. Foreman himself wasn't walking into the bathroom. He was using his faded blue T-shirt to wipe the sweat from his chest and armpits. He looked up and saw me staring at him. I turned quickly back to the urinal, my heart beating a mile a minute. What if he said something about me checking him out all week? There was nothing to say that he wouldn't beat me up for. I was trying to figure out how to stuff my suddenly stiff cock back in my pants without being too obvious when I heard a husky voice behind me.

"You like working here?"

I turned my head. He was leaning against the sink, arms folded across his naked chest, his sweat-soaked shirt slung casually over one shoulder.

"Uh," I stuttered, "I work in customer service. I don't really like it, but it's OK."

"Must be boring." His eyes fixed on me with a level stare. "So . . . my buddies tell me you've been watching us."

He moved toward me. *Shit, here it comes.* How could I explain a black eye to my coworkers when all I'd done was go to the rest room?

"Uh—I was probably just looking because my girlfriend kept gawking at you," I lied.

"You mean that girl who was walkin' with you the other day?" he said, then paused to consider. "She's pretty hot. The fellas like her."

"Yeah, well . . ."

"You're taking an awfully long time to piss there, buddy."

I couldn't think of an answer to that one. Then, he stepped right up behind me; his breath was hot on my neck.

"I bet she gives good head," he said, close to a whisper.

My face was flaming red, I was sweating, and my heart was racing. I couldn't take much more of this. What did this guy want from me?

I gulped and said, "Well, that's kind of personal, don't you think?"

"Shit," he said, "don't matter anyway." There was a pause. My pulse thudded in my ears. Then: "I bet *you* give good head too."

I gulped. I wanted to get the hell out of there, but something forced me to stay put. I had managed to get my erection back inside my pants, but it now stood at full attention. I turned around. He had a broad grin on his face. It was obvious that he noticed my . . . er, uh, physical state.

"Why do you say that?" I asked, with more toughness than I necessarily felt.

"Oh, I don't know," he said, licking his lips and scratching his chest. "You just look like the type."

I had never expected this, least of all from this butch number standing before me. I drew in a quick breath.

"What do you say? I've been watching you all week, and it looks like you could use a break from work."

"What—what did you have in mind?" I stuttered, my legs shaking.

"Whatever," he said, his gaze falling to my crotch again. "Looks like you wouldn't mind at all."

His hand reached for me. An electric current jolted through my body when I felt his rough workman's fingers through my khakis. His thumb massaged the underside of my shaft, behind the head. I felt a drop of precum staining the front of my briefs.

"I got an idea," he said, looking past me to the rear of the bathroom. "How 'bout we go in that stall back there and you show me just how good you are at giving head? Do a good job and I may even fuck your ass. Think you could handle that?"

"Um, well . . ." I nodded, not trusting myself to speak.

"Yeah, I think you'll be able to handle that," he whispered menacingly. "Now get your ass in there."

I tried to protest, but he pushed me into the stall and shut the door behind us. The seconds seemed to go by so slowly as I stood there, the anticipation of what was to come making my stomach turn somersaults. After what seemed like an eternity, he moved close to me, grabbed my hand, and placed it on his crotch. "All right, get to work," he said.

I was nervous, but I could see that there was no sense arguing with him. Sensing my hesitation, he raised one of his arms, grabbed the back of my neck with his other hand, and shoved my nose into his moist armpit, forcing me to take a deep whiff. You'd have thought that he would have stunk after being out in the sun all day long, but he smelled of sweat—the good clean sweat of a man who's been working hard.

"Yeah," he growled in my ear. "Eat those sweaty pits, boy. You like that, huh? Do you, boy?"

"Mmmmmmph" was all I could say.

From his pits I kissed my way down his bare chest, paying attention to his rock-hard nipples, licking the salty-sweet droplets of man-sweat from his body. He moaned loudly as I clenched his nipples between my teeth, flicking my tongue back and forth over the tips as I gently bit down on them. I was afraid someone would hear us, but I didn't stop.

Soon he was pushing on my head, and I knew what he wanted. I unbuttoned the top button of his jeans and slid my hand into his hot and sweaty crotch. I wrapped my fingers around the hardness inside the pouch of his damp jockstrap.

I parted his jeans so I could see the outline of his cockhead appear through the pouch of the jock. He looked so damn fine in that thing I almost busted my nut right then.

"Eat my dick through my jock," he ordered. And I did, nibbling on his increasingly hard dick through the slightly yellowed and sweat-dampened material.

"You're gonna love having that in your throat," he told me. I slowly began peeling his jock down over his cock, tasting each bit of his flesh as I did so, moving my tongue all over his shaft, pressing against it with my mouth. Finally, I yanked the jock down to his knees with his jeans and slid my mouth over the head of his salty-tasting pecker.

Again he moaned. That was all I needed. I swallowed his cock in one swift motion, relaxing my throat and taking it deep.

"Fuuuuuuck," he cried.

I groaned, loving his reaction. I sucked him long and slow, taking his cock as deep as I could each time. The sweat of his workday and the natural scent of his body were really turning me on. Every time my nose nestled into his pubes, my cock gave a little leap inside my pants. I spit on my hand, wrapped it around his hot cock, and then began to tongue his sac. I sucked his balls into my mouth, rolling them around on my tongue.

Suddenly, he grabbed my head from above and held it firmly in place, tilting it upward just slightly so that I was looking directly into his eyes.

"Open your mouth," he said, then leaned down and spit into it. He tilted my head back, then held it tight as he pushed his cock into my mouth again and proceeded to face-fuck me like I'd never been face-fucked before. He grabbed the back of my head and forced me to take his cock deep into my throat, my gag reflex kicking in as his dick assaulted my tonsils.

"Fuck yeah," he purred from above. "Gag on it, bitch."

Then he turned around and bent over, revealing a perfectly puckered asshole. I didn't even wait for him to tell me what to do. I knew what he wanted. I went in for the kill, pressing the tip of my tongue to his anus.

"Yeah," he barked. "Tongue my sweaty butthole. Eat it."

I parted his cheeks, darting my tongue in and out of his anus, pressing my lips up against it and rubbing them back and forth. I tongue-fucked his salty-tasting hole hungrily, spurred on by the way he was writhing above me. He grabbed his cheeks and spread them even farther with one hand, while the other clamped onto the back of my head and forced my face deeper into his crack.

"Munch that fuckin' hole, pig!" he commanded. "You love it, don't you? Yeah, you do. My hot little butt-muncher."

Suddenly he spun around, took hold of my arm, pulled me roughly up to his face, and said, "My turn."

He began to undo my belt with his big hands. After he'd unzipped me, he pushed my Calvins down past my balls. Then, with brute force, he turned me around to face away from him. He parted my cheeks and spit into them, then began lapping at my hole the way I had his. I bent over, resting my hands on my knees as he feverishly devoured my hole.

"Look at that," he cooed from behind me. "That hot, tight little hole." He spit into it again, then began to slide his fingers back and forth along the entrance. "It's so perfect. Damn."

He munched on it just a little longer before I suddenly felt his mouth on the back of my neck, his arm circling around my chest. He gripped me tightly from behind, then clamped his teeth down on my earlobe.

"I want to fuck you," he whispered. "I want to be inside your tight hole."

By this point, I had completely forgotten about my break coming to an end. I just hoped no one came into the bathroom.

"Get ready, boy," he growled in my ear. I could still hear a trace of the menace he'd revealed before.

I bent over farther and put my hands against the wall behind the toilet, pushing my exposed ass back toward him as he slid a finger inside me. It hurt at first, as there was no lube in sight and I hadn't been prepared for it. I felt his cock sliding back and forth against my ass cheek as he roughly fingered my hole, sliding a second finger into me as he continued to ooh and aaah.

"Such a tight ass," he said, just as I felt the tip of his cock pushing at the opening of my hole. I heard him spit behind me, then felt his cock roughly sliding inside my hole. I gasped at the invasion, biting down on my bottom lip as he forcefully took me as his own.

"Fuck yeah," he groaned, pumping his cock in and out of my chute. "Love that tight ass. That tight ass just for me. All for me."

The rawness of his words seeped into my consciousness, bringing out the primal animal lust that had been hidden for so long. My senses were tingling like crazy. Everything was amplified. I was riding the wave of a high such as I'd never been on before, and I never wanted it to stop.

"Poke my hole," I said, a whisper that soon grew into a full-fledged cry. "Poke that fuckin' hole, stud. Rip me apart."

"Yeah, take that cock, boy. Take my fuckin' cock up your tight hole!"

He slammed into me, his balls slapping against mine as he continued to dominate me. The air smelled of pungent sweat and raw sex. The scent of it filled my head and made me even dizzier than before. I gripped my cock and tugged on it as his cock continued to slide in and out of my chute.

Suddenly, he pulled out of my ass. He lifted my shirt, pushing it up my back, then cried out. "Yeah!" he said, that single syllable followed by the sudden warm splash of his cum landing on my back, followed by another, and another, the last few spurts falling on my ass in thick jets of man-juice.

"That's it," I cried. "I'm coming!"

"Yeah," he said. "Lemme see that load I just fucked out of you." He grabbed me roughly and pulled me to a standing position, just in time to see the first blast of cum from my nuts. He grabbed my dick and jerked me off as my load spewed forth in thick spurts and landed on the rim of the toilet. Jet after jet of hot jizz painted the porcelain bowl as he moaned his approval.

"Yeah! What a load!"

Then, suddenly, it was over. I stood there panting as he shook my cum off his fingers and the head of my cock.

"Holy fuck," I said. "That was hot as hell."

I wished we could go another round, but I knew I had to get back to work. As it was, I was going to have quite a time trying to explain why I had taken so long for a ten-minute break, not to mention the fact that I was all scruffed up. Then I realized that he was going to have some explaining to do too.

"So," I said, "what are you going to tell your buddies about catching me looking at you?"

Wiping himself with his sweaty and now cum-stained T-shirt, he turned me around to face him.

"I'm just going to tell them that I took care of it," he said. "Yeah, I'm going to tell them that I gave it to you real good."

And the truth was, he had done just that.

Diamonds in the Rough

Barry Alexander

Why in the hell did I ever take this fucking job? I wondered as I stopped to wipe the sweat off my face before continuing my patrol. Three months of walking up and down the deserted corridors of this mall after hours were about to drive me nuts. I'd thought listing "security guard" on my resume would look good when I finished my police science courses, and give me a little experience besides. Hell, all it ever gave me was calluses.

Nothing ever happened. Nothing ever changed. "What do you want," Hank had asked, "break-ins and bomb threats?" Well, yeah, I did. I didn't want anyone to get hurt or anything, but catching a burglar or putting out a fire would break up the monotony and give a little oomph to my resume. The daytime guards at least got to chase shoplifters once in a while.

Tonight was really the pits. The air-conditioning broke down about five o'clock. I'll bet it took the mall manager all of two seconds to rule out overtime repairs before he drove home to his air-conditioned house in his air-conditioned Lincoln. When the mall doors locked, all the heat from a blazing summer day quickly built to sauna level.

I wondered how Hank was making out. When I'd passed him on the last round, it didn't look like the bastard was even breaking a sweat. Hank Jackson was a big bull of a man who looked like a cross between a Marine drill sergeant and the Incredible Hulk. Broad shoulders and a massive chest filled his uniform shirt to khaki perfection, then tapered to football-player thighs and a ridiculously tiny ass. The first day I met him, I went home and jerked off. But the severe buzz cut of his chestnut hair and the scowl on his handsome face told me I'd better keep those fantasies to myself.

I still didn't know much about him. Hank didn't talk much. He just didn't seem like the kind of guy you could get chummy with. He'd never yelled at me, but I got the impression that he was just watching for that first mistake.

My footsteps echoed as I walked down the darkened corridor. The carnival smell of greasy donuts, popcorn, and pizza still lingered in the motionless air as I passed the food court.

I watched my reflection pacing me in the store windows. I'd never felt small until I stood next to Hank. Four years of hard work at my dad's lumberyard had packed a lot of solid muscle onto my 6-foot frame. I didn't turn heads, but no one turned away either. I liked my body, except for the freckles spattered across my smooth chest. I used to bleach them, until I discovered that some men actually liked freckles. Go figure. To me, nothing is sexier than a man with a thick pelt of chest hair.

At the end of the mall, I unlocked the access panel and punched my code into the alarm system. Hank was probably doing the same thing at the opposite end of the mall. We each had a fifty-minute window to reach the other alarm and punch in—long enough to check every window or stop in the john, but not long enough to nap, read, or have a really hot jerk-off. If we were more than ten minutes late, the alarm would sound, the cops would come, and we'd be out on our tails if we didn't have a damn good excuse.

I stopped in front of the western store to peer through the steel portcullis at the new display. A young cowstud was standing next to the twin of the Marlboro Man, one boot planted on a hay bale and a lariat in his hand. The older one looked great: tight jeans molded over his hips, flannel shirt, Stetson pushed back over his thick dark hair, even beard stubble on his chin.

I liked to make up stories about the mannequins; it helped to pass the time. This one was clearly showing the younger one the ropes.. I gave my cock a couple of half-hearted strokes, but it was just too damned hot.

I walked past the exercise equipment display in the middle of the hall and the Tower of Power sports drink display. Some idiot had actually spent hours building the huge tower of Orange Octane and Indy Grape sports drink cans. Give me a break. Like drinking that crap and spending a few minutes on the Slope Master could give you a great body like Hank's.

I snagged an abandoned shopping cart for a quick ride. The wheels rumbled as it careened down the hallway, creating the first breeze I'd felt all night. I thought I saw something move as I whizzed past a window. It had to be my reflection, but as I turned to look, the cart turned, too. I hopped off just in time to keep from smashing into the pink marble pillars flanking the new Diamond Exchange Outlet. I put the cart away.

Under a big skylight near the center of the mall was a small indoor park. Miniature trees, shrubs, and drifts of white flowers surrounded a two-level pond. Baskets of ivy hung overhead, dripping green tendrils over their sides. I looked longingly at the water flowing from the upper pond over the wide spillway of deep blue ceramic tiles.

I checked my watch. I had a good twenty minutes to hit the other alarm. I kicked off my shoes, peeled off my sweaty socks, and plunged my burning feet into the cool water. Heaven! The goldfish fled to the far corner of the pond, giving me fishy stares as they French-kissed the water.

Sweat trickled down my spine and into the crevice between my buttocks. That tumbling water sure would feel great washing over my naked body. Why not? The hell with Hank Jackson and the hell with this job. I unbuckled my gun belt and set it aside carefully so it wouldn't get wet, then ripped my uniform off and tossed it over the bushes.

Since the water was only waist-deep, I did a shallow surface dive. In two strokes, I reached the other side of the pond. Goldfish flashed out of my way as I twisted around and returned. But the pool was too small for swimming, so I leaned back against the tiles and just let the rippled waterfall spill over me.

Through the skylight above me, stars as bright as diamonds glinted against the night sky. I closed my eyes and sighed. I stretched my arms out to make a water angel. Cool water bubbled over my bare shoulders, coursed down my arms, and filled my open hands. *Just a few minutes,* I told myself, but I could have stayed there forever.

I don't know how long I'd been there when I heard the click of shoes on tile. Damn! I'd waited too long. I thought about grabbing my clothes and ducking under the bushes, but there wasn't time. Besides, it would be more embarrassing (and bare-assing!) to have Hank spot my white butt poking up out of the bushes. And part of me was dying to see the expression on old poker face's puss.

The footsteps stopped. I heard the sharp intake of his breath. I kept my eyes shut and waited for him to swear or yell or clear his throat or something. The total silence was unnerving. What was he doing? Taking pictures? I had to open my eyes.

I couldn't believe the look on his face. I'd been prepared for shock, or anger, or outraged morality, but not this. It was pure envy, and a kind of shy hunger. One hand rested beside his crotch. He jerked it away and flushed as he stepped behind the bushes. It was too late; there was no mistaking what I'd seen. Hank had a hard-on. And from the way that bulge snaked down his pants leg, I knew it must be a big mother.

I was going to say something smart and give him a hard time about springing a rod, but I stopped when I saw the naked longing in his eyes. And something more—a nervous uncertainty. He wanted me, and he was afraid to do anything about it. He started to back away, his mouth opening and closing like a fish, with no words coming out. Hell, from the way he was acting, you'd think he'd never seen a naked man before.

"Don't," I said softly. "Why don't you come in and join me?"

He stood frozen under my gaze like a deer trapped in the headlights. He shook his head. "I can't," he whispered.

"Yes you can." I stood up and waded through the thigh-deep water, scattering fish and light reflections. I could imagine how I looked: cool water dripping off my golden skin, beading on my naked flesh, and trickling between my pecs and over the ridges of my stomach. My cock arched full and heavy, a cascade of flesh over my low-hanging balls. He couldn't take his eyes off me. Mesmerized, he watched as I climbed out of the pool and stood close to him, dripping water over his perfectly polished shoes.

"No," he whispered. He started to back away.

I stopped him with a touch. His heart hammered beneath my palm. He could have broken me in two, but he just stood there, frozen by the light touch. I cupped my hand around the thick column of his neck and stood on my toes to kiss him, pressing my naked flesh against the stiff fabric of his uniform. I brushed my lips over his. Heat radiated from the stonelike rigidity of his body.

I unbuttoned his shirt and slipped my hand inside, where I found a dense mat of moist fur. *Oh, yeah.* I slid my fingers through the thick shag, combing the silky curls with my fingertips. He trembled as I rimmed his mouth with my tongue and slid it along the tightly closed crevice.

Suddenly, all the stiffness went out of him. Well, not *all* the stiffness. One part of him was *very* stiff. He moaned and crushed me against him, savaging my mouth like a man starved for the taste and touch of another man. The hard ridge of his cock pressed against mine. We ground our pelvises against each other frantically. I yanked his shirt free and slid my hands up his sculptured back as he sucked hungrily on my tongue.

We broke apart for air and stood panting at each other. He looked like he was in shock. "I've never done anything like that before," he said with his eyes down, too embarrassed to look at me.

"Then it's about time you did. Come here, Hank. I want you."

For a moment, I thought he was going to bolt and run, but his desire was stronger than his rigid upbringing. His hands shook as he fumbled with the rest of his buttons. I brushed his fingers aside and peeled the shirt off his massive shoulders. Dense coils of moist russet fur covered his chest and belly, disappearing below his belt. He looked like a huge cinnamon bear. I couldn't resist. Running both hands through the luxuriant pelt, I leaned in to nuzzle him, drinking in his warm, musky scent. Almost hidden by the dense growth, his big copper nipples begged for attention. Hank moaned as I sucked one into a hard point, then lapped the silky strands into a gilded sunburst around the deep red peak.

Hank stroked my back and shoulders cautiously, as if he were afraid to explore my body. "It's OK," I said. "You can touch me anywhere you want." I put his hand on my belly.

His big warm palm covered my whole pubic area. His fingers trembled as they started to inch down. When his thumb brushed the base of my cock, he pulled back.

"Anywhere," I repeated as I worked on his belt.

His hand wrapped around me, dwarfing my six-inch rod. He watched with fascination as my cock, cradled in his palm, filled and stiffened with little jerks. I tried to slip my hand down the front of his slacks, but his cock was so large there was no room. When I unfastened his slacks, the huge urgent mass forced the zipper down. I peeled his slacks and briefs off his sweat-damp thighs. His cock sprang up like a battering ram. It was magnificent: eight inches of proud man-meat, straight, thick-veined, and crowned with a fat, dusky red glans. Two plump balls weighted the furry sac swaying between his muscular thighs. My mouth watered just looking at it.

I tugged on his cock playfully, then did a cannonball into the pool, splashing water all over him. "Come and get me."

He tried to kick out of his pants without taking off his shoes first and almost fell on his butt. I looked up at him and laughed as he hopped around on one foot, trying to untie his tangled laces. Finally, he freed himself. With a roar, he launched himself into the pool and tried to grab me. We played in the cool water, cavorting like dolphins.

"Now I have you," he said, smiling triumphantly as he trapped me in the corner.

I dove between his widespread legs to escape and grabbed his ankle, pulling him down. He toppled into the water with a huge splash, but even as he fell, his arm snaked out to grab me. He pulled me to him for a long underwater kiss. Even when I started to run out of air, I didn't want to break the hungry passion of that kiss. We struggled to our feet and stared at each other. "Wow!" I said.

He looked at me uncertainly. "Now what?"

I had a few ideas. I guided him over to the waterfall and pushed him back against the spillway. Water rippled over him while I explored his beautiful body, finding all the sensitive spots—the places that made him sigh with pleasure, the ones that made him groan, and those that made him quiver with delight.

There was so much of him I wanted to explore: the furry hollows under his arms, the dimple of his belly button, the deep crevice between the full moons that concealed the unplumbed crater. But I couldn't wait. I had to have his cock now.

As my warm breath washed over it, his cock jumped. I planted my tongue at the base and slowly licked all the way up. His back arched as my lips engulfed his warm prick. It was so thick I couldn't take all of it, but his nonstop litany of gasps and sighs told me he was more than happy with the blow job. His balls had ridden so far up the cords that they were clamped around his cock like bookends. It was hot watching him get so aroused, but my cock was aching to nestle into a warm hollow.

"Turn around."

He looked scared. "I've never done that," he protested. "Won't it hurt? You're awfully big."

I grinned up at him. "Not as big as you, buddy. Don't worry—I'm not planning on fucking you." *Not tonight, anyway,* I thought. If we didn't finish in time to punch in, we were both going to be in enough trouble without breaking into the drugstore for a pack of condoms. "Trust me. This'll be just as hot, but safe."

When he rolled over, I stepped up behind him and pressed my body against his. The water flowing over us did nothing to cool the fiery heat of my cock as it rested against his tightly clenched buttocks. I moved down, kissing and tonguing the hard marbles of his spine. Gradually, he relaxed as I gently stroked his sides and hips.

The water rippled over his broad shoulders, sluiced down his back, and converged in the deep chasm between the snowy mounds of his tiny ass. He shuddered as my tongue scouted the edge of the musky crevice.

"Oh, God, you can't do that! Not there!"

"Shh, it's OK." I wriggled my tongue between the tightly clamped muscles. My hands cupped his ass, kneading the solid spheres.

He groaned, spreading his legs to give me the access I desired. My tongue rolled over the quivering ring, then slid down to lap his furry balls. Teasing him with my fingers, I circled the throbbing pink whorl. He moaned when I worked a finger inside, and his sphincter grabbed me and held tight when I tried to slip it out. By the time I had two fingers inside him, he was clawing the tiles and humping furiously.

Dropping my bloated cock between his cheeks, I drove it up the tight trench. He pushed back against me. "You like that, huh?" I asked.

"Oh, yeah!"

Eager for more, he wriggled his butt, sliding it up and down my rigid shaft. It must have looked obscene—the way his hot butt was waggling and pumping my dick—but it felt wonderful. I grabbed his hips and started some serious humping.

He squeezed his cheeks together, creating an exquisite friction. I was lost in the sensations and the sounds of hot man-sex: the wet slap of flesh against flesh as my thighs thudded against his, the gentle gurgle of cool water over our hot bodies, the excited panting of two men in heat, the zing of a man's zipper opening—

What the fuck? Neither of us was wearing anything with a zipper. I froze, listening, but all I could hear was Hank's heart thudding against my ear. Then I heard it: the unmistakable sound of a man beating his meat.

"Someone's watching us," I whispered in Hank's ear.

"Huh? Oh, OK. I read about that. Whatever makes you hot."

"No, you idiot. He's really there." I was ready to hit him.

"Sure. What's he wearing?" Hank asked in a sexy voice.

"I'm wearing an Armani shirt in shades of cream and cinnamon, winter-wheat linen slacks, and a pair of Mauri loafers."

Hank moved so fast, I slid off his back and fell in the water. He came to an abrupt halt two steps away from the intruder. Standing at the edge of the pool was a tall, elegantly dressed man with a very big cock protruding from his open slacks and a very big gun protruding from his fist.

"But enough about me," he said. "Please go back to what you were doing. I insist."

"That gun pointed at my gut doesn't exactly put me in the mood."

"I'm sure your friend can rectify the situation." He waved his gun at me. "Get down on your knees and give your giant companion a hand—or a mouth."

I glanced up at the pile of our clothes. Our guns were concealed underneath, but we'd never reach them in time. "Who the fuck are you?" He was a good-looking guy, whoever he was. Curly black hair, handsome face, slim build.

"Please," he said with a gracious smile when he saw my hesitation. "I must insist."

There's no arguing when a big dick or a big gun is aimed straight at you. My mind raced as I slowly obeyed. The guy was so relaxed and sure of himself, he had to be some kind of a pro. An amateur burglar would have been nervous and certainly wouldn't have been so damned polite. Unless the guy was a total nutcase. What kind of thief stops to jerk off? *A damned horny one,* I thought as I watched his dark red cock jump. The guy himself didn't move an inch.

I knelt before Hank. His cock hung limply over his balls, but it was still swollen and a fat pearl of precum clung to the gaping slit. I gave his cock a few halfhearted licks while I tried to formulate a plan. The warm musk rising from his balls was inviting, and I licked the sweat off the long strands of silky hair. In spite of myself, I started to get aroused again.

"Yeah, that's it. Lick those big rocks," the man said.

It was exciting, in a perverse sort of way, knowing that

someone was watching. He was really getting into this. If we could distract him enough, we could jump him when he was ready to cum. If we didn't do something fast, those alarms were going to go off in fifteen minutes, and I sure as hell didn't want to try explaining this.

I tried to signal Hank, rolling my eyes and jerking my thumb at the guy behind us. Hank nodded and winked at me. I sure hoped he understood.

I bobbed my head up and down with exaggerated vigor and made lots of loud, slurpy noises like I was really getting into it. Trouble is, I was.

Hank grabbed my head, crammed his prick down my throat, and started pumping with so many "Oh yeah's," "Oh shit's," and "Suck my big fucking cock's" that I knew he must have watched at least one porn video—he had the raunchy talk down pat.

I don't know about the thief, but he had me convinced. I pistoned up and down his huge rod eagerly. I loved the slippery heat and bulk of it as it glided over my tongue, thumped against my palate, and coasted right down my open throat. I liked it so much, I forgot about our audience.

When Hank pulled back, I wrapped my hands around his ass and gulped his cock back down. He had to hit his fist against my shoulder before I remembered. Out of the corner of my eye, I could see the burglar choking his dick with both hands. His knees were quivering and his head was thrown back as he came.

Hank and I tackled him. We wrestled around in the bushes for a few minutes; he must have known how to fight because he got in a couple of good ones. He toppled

Hank with some kind of karate chop, knocking him right on top of me and pinning me beneath his weight. I tried to wriggle free. Something hard was jabbing me in the back and it was hard to breathe with all of Hank on top of me. He groaned and rolled off me.

"Are you OK?"

"Yeah, let's get the bastard!"

As I started to get up, my hand touched the object that had poked me in the back—the guy's gun. By the time we got to our feet, the thief was already fleeing down the corridor, his limp cock bouncing up and down with each step.

"Stop or I'll shoot," I yelled. When he kept running, I pulled the trigger to fire a warning shot. Nothing happened. Shit, the damned thing wasn't even loaded.

Hank and I streaked down the hall after him, arms pumping, dicks bobbing, feet slapping the floor. I pulled ahead and bore down on the thief just as he was passing the display of exercise equipment. Suddenly, there was a crash like thunder and I was trying to keep on my feet beneath an avalanche of sports drink cans from the Tower of Power.

My feet went out from under me. I landed flat on my ass. By the time Hank helped me up, the bastard was out of sight.

"Come on, let's go get him!" I said. "He has to still be here. The door alarm didn't go off."

"He didn't trip it when he came in; he probably left the same way."

"Maybe he was hiding when the mall closed."

"I don't think so. He wouldn't have stayed in hiding that long after the place was locked up."

"*Now* what the fuck are we going to do? We have to report this in case he stole something."

"The first thing we have to do is get to those alarms before—"

"INTRUDER ALERT! INTRUDER ALERT! SECURITY HAS BEEN COMPROMISED! POLICE ARE ON THE WAY!"

"Before *that,*" Hank finished. "Come on, we've got six minutes to get our clothes on and come up with some kind of story."

We were really up to our asses in it, but as I watched the play of muscles in Hank's backside, the only thing I regretted was the interruption. We threw on our clothes as fast as we'd taken them off. When I bent over to pick up my gun belt, I spotted a dark bag under the bushes.

"Holy shit, Hank! Look at this!"

Hank whistled as I poured the sparkling contents of the bag into my hand. Diamonds! Lots and lots of glittering diamonds.

"He robbed the Diamond Exchange Outlet. Nothing really big, but uncut stones are easy to fence, and there's enough here to pay both our salaries for several years."

We looked at each other for a moment. I'm not sure what we would have done, but the cops came running in at that moment and it was too late. I like to think we would have given them back anyway.

We were heroes for two weeks. And almost every night we had sex somewhere in the mall: in the pool, over the benches, on top of the display cars. Hank had really loosened up.

A month later, we were out on our butts. The bastard came back and hit the Diamond Outlet again. But it wasn't the second robbery that got us fired. It was the damned video cameras they'd secretly installed that showed us fucking our brains out.

We were just grateful they didn't find the note our thief had left:

"Damn, you two are hot! Keep it up!"

Attached to the note was a tiny package. Inside were two perfect diamonds. I don't think they would have let us keep them.

About the Author

AUSTIN FOXXE is the former editor in chief of *Men* and *Freshmen,* the two bestselling gay male erotic magazines in America. He has co-edited four books in the acclaimed Friction series of gay erotica and also edited the anthologies *Slow Grind* and *Three the Hard Way.* To find out about future projects or to enlist his help with a project of your own, contact Austin at foxxe_fiction@yahoo.com.

Look for the Manhandled companion video series, bringing the hottest stories to life right before your eyes! Coming soon from Erotic Fox Entertainment. For more information contact eroticfox@yahoo.com.